Rapid Descent

Rapid Descent

Disaster in Boston Harbor

J. P. Polidoro

Longtail Publishing

Manufactured in the United States of America
Library of Congress Control Number: 00-90044
ISBN: 0-9677619-0-5
Book design and production by Tabby House
Cover design: Pearl and Associates
Photo of author used by permission of photographer Pam Berry

Any resemblance to any person, either living or dead,
in the novel, *Rapid Descent,* is purely coincidental.

Longtail Publishing
1391 Old North Main St.
Laconia, NH 03246
(603) 524-1102

For Brenda and my children, Michael, Christopher, Kimberly, Stephanie and John Perri.

Acknowledgements

First, to my wife Brenda and children, I thank you for the love, support and freedom to pursue a dream outside of science and music. The lost mornings, evenings and weekends of family times while writing this novel will be paid back to you.

I am indebted to my brother Tony, and also to a commercial pilot from Annapolis for sharing their knowledge and experience of aviation with me. Thanks is also extended to George Sanborn at the Transportation Library in Boston.

I am grateful to noted New Hampshire authors, Tom Coughlin and Don Wolfe for their helpful suggestions and kind words on the back cover. I am flattered that they took the time to review the manuscript.

Finally, my deep appreciation is extended to Don Black, Ph.D., my graduate school advisor and mentor at the University of Massachusetts. He nurtured my career in science, influenced my writing style and taught me how to write succinctly.

Prologue

Rush-hour congestion and traffic snarls have not yet cleared the tunnels under Boston Harbor on this hot late summer evening when a threefold-disaster begins to unfold. As commuters fume about the traffic jam, the pilot of a small commuter airline is delayed enough that he is unable to personally do his detailed flight check, leaving that task to his copilot. Meanwhile, a boat filled with party-goers heads out for a booze cruise under the stars with a special birthday surprise for one of the guests. The lives of ordinary people are about to be changed and a city's emergency response capability tested to the limit.

1

United Air America Flight 1074 arrived five minutes early, a feat unheard of at Boston's Logan International Airport. As the plane touched down, a burst of blue smoke followed each wheel, quickly dissipating into the exhaust from the engines. The 757's nose gear dropped slowly and, once the wheel assembly was in contact with the runway, the pilots reversed engines creating a vibration of the contents in the overhead bin.

The headset for Jack Danton's seat eased out of the seat pocket and dropped to the floor. Seat 1A was a First Class bulkhead seat, and Jack placed his feet casually on the rug wall in front of him as if to assist the pilots in their braking process. He was home, he thought, finally home. He sighed as the plane turned left and waited for permission to cross another north/south active runway. Closing his eyes, he imagined his beautiful lady waiting for him. Touching ground and taxiing made him feel like he was already in Boston, not just at the airport.

His face was refreshed from the lemon oil towelette that the flight attendant had passed out to the First Class passengers just before landing. He ached from sitting in one position for hours. His knees were stiff from the edge of the seat that cut off the circulation to his legs.

The flight attendant, a young blonde of twenty-two or twenty-three, was quick to remind the passengers to remain seated until they reached the gate. This was her third flight segment today and by mistake she welcomed everyone to "Hartford." Most passengers laughed at the *faux pas*. She corrected herself and apologized. She was tired as well; she had picked up the continuing flight in Pittsburgh. Once again, like a recording, she welcomed everyone on the plane to Logan and correctly recited the "local time" as 7:04 P.M.

"Thank you for flying United Air America, and have a pleasant evening in Boston or wherever your travels may take you," she said.

Jack was eager to get off the flight, which had originated in San Francisco. His day was already long enough. His back hurt from the seat that was broken and couldn't recline. Sleeping on the long flight had been difficult for him in the vertical seat position, and Jack had to deal with a crying child in First Class, as well as his arrogant parents. Sharing the flight with the "gifted child" was tempestuous at best.

The boy, about two years old, was not far from Jack's seat and the constant conversation between parents and boy was annoying. They read books to the child during the entire flight across the United States. Books like *Winnie the Pooh* and other Golden Books could be heard above the roar of the massive GE engines on the 757. The parents made sure everyone was aware of their child's abilities, yet they babied him the entire flight. At one point, after the boy spilled his drink on himself and on his mother, he was scolded loudly by the father. Patience as parents was not one of their redeeming qualities. Add those episodes to the lousy food and extended six-hour-and-thirty-six-minute flight and Jack was ready to get off that plane.

The stopover in Pittsburgh had been brief; the only time the child was silent. Jack considered First Class the quiet area of the plane, but some Frequent Flyer passengers traveled so much that they were awarded upgrades for the whole family, rug rats and all. Even with his stereo headset on during the flight, Jack could hear the child singing and banging his feet on the seat diagonal from him. Jack had finished a new novel by John Grisham during the flight, and occupied the remainder of the last hour of flight listening to the country music channel on the audio system. He had the volume pumped up to "9" to override the child's voice and his questionable "singing" of Barney tunes.

Taxiing to Terminal C was a welcome relief after the long ordeal. Soon he would be rid of the arrogant couple and their troublesome little bastard.

As with most trips, Jack Danton yanked his carry-on bag from the overhead compartment and took his suit coat, which the flight attendant had just handed to him. She had hung it up front when he had boarded in San Francisco. He no longer checked bags in the abyss below. Too many previous trips had resulted in lost baggage and embarrassing moments at sales appointments on the road. Showing up for a meeting in jeans because his luggage had been diverted to some other city by mistake was not appreciated. He now traveled in a suit with daily changes of shirts, ties and underwear neatly compacted in his carry-on luggage. Between the carry-on and his briefcase, he had learned how to travel light. He laughed at the "neophytes" who dragged garment bags, "pull-alongs," overcoats and gifts all at one time.

Now that he was nearly home, Jack had to remember where he had parked in the Terminal C garage. Was it Level 2 or Level 3, he wondered? Section 15 or Section 16? Row A or Row B? You were supposed to write that information down before you left on a trip but he had forgotten to, or had left it to his failing short-term memory.

With the jet-way in place and the front door of the plane open, he proceeded to exit the plane and bid the flight attendant, "good-bye." She was sweet, he thought. But he had something better waiting for him at home. He would see her soon he thought, as soon as he could get his butt out of this congested, impersonal terminal. As he crossed the main floor of Terminal C, he remembered that he needed to get some cash from the ATM to the right of the exit. He would need that to get his vehicle out of hock. Highway robbery. Twenty dollars a day or fifty dollars a week to park your car only to come home and have jet exhaust all over the exterior finish. What a deal! It just sat there and you paid MASSPORT all that money to have it get all crapped up.

Finally remembering his parking location, Jack took the elevator to Level 3 and found his BMW 525i sitting patiently. Noting a new scratch and bent side mirror on the driver's side of the jet-black car, he mumbled some obscenities at the unknown person who had dragged a bag along the side of his car while he was away. He threw his luggage in the trunk of his "'B'mer" and headed the car down the ramp to pay the parking toll. They would "scalp" him once again, but it didn't really matter since his company would reimburse him. Once he emerged from the parking garage, he headed past an airport hotel and veered left off to the airport exit road to eventually go through the Sumner Tunnel toward Boston.

2

Captain William Bullock, a forty-nine-year-old commuter pilot for North East Air, rushed through security, flashing his credentials for the guards standing near the conveyor and X-ray machine. Captain Bill, a nineteen-year veteran, had just returned from a vacation in the Bahamas and was not ready to return to work—he was still OTB—"on the beach." He had enjoyed a great week at a tropical paradise and had just kissed his still-tanned wife good-bye outside International and Commuter Terminal E, at Logan.

Tonight he would fly the short hop to Manchester, New Hampshire. He was scheduled to go back and forth two times this evening. His flight, NEAir Flight 2158, was due to leave at 7:35 P.M. The twin-engine Dressler 205 STOL was a reliable aircraft for short commuter hops. The "short takeoff and landing" aircraft was a flexible bird. He had flown the route to New Hampshire for years and often interspersed the flights with commuter runs to Rutland, Vermont; Providence, Rhode Island; and Portland, Maine. Tonight it was back to Manchester. North East Air flew eight flights daily on small Beechcraft, SAAB, De Havillands, and the new Dressler 205s.

Flights to those cities and the aircraft of choice varied with the number of passengers and the total seats needed to remain profitable. It was not cost effective to fly a fifty-passenger plane when there were only twelve passengers. Smaller commuter flights were generally "connectors" used to access the longer nonstop flights from Logan across country. The commuter flights varied from seventeen to thirty-four minutes between the commuter airports in New England. Passenger numbers might vary from twelve to forty-seven depending on the flight destination or hour of the day.

NEAir had recently added three Dressler 205s to its fleet. Made in two locations in Great Britain and on the European continent, the twin-engine, top-winged aircraft was a workhorse for the commuter industry. It was designed for multi-weather flying and was a frequent shuttle between the U.K. and France. Accustomed to being utilized in foul-weather conditions of rain, sleet and snow, the Dressler was powered by two British Barrington turboprop engines of 1,800-shaft horsepower. The four-bladed reversible pitch props and the extended flap wingspan could pull the 205 into the air in a short distance of 3,000 feet of runway. Due to the extensive wingspan square footage, liftoff was rapid for the Dressler, even when fully loaded.

NEAir had acquired each of the newer aircraft with some 6,000–8,000 flying hours on them. A commuter line in England had gone belly-up and the twin-engine craft were available for a song. The 205's primary feature, besides reliability, was the modern avionics on board. They had the latest digital AFCS, digital air data systems and a state-of-the-art weather system. The NAV/COMM systems were recently upgraded and surpassed all FAA standards for commuter aircraft. The eighty-foot wingspan was ten feet longer than the fuselage but the overall design accommodated the passengers' need for leg room, baggage and overhead storage. It was basically the "wide body" of commuters, some ten feet wide at midsection. The seating included two rows of two seats, each separated by a common center aisle. The Dressler 205 could hold twenty-eight to thirty-two passengers depending on the model. A row of seats could be added in the extreme rear of the airplane when needed. Dresslers could fly as high as 20,000 feet although this was not a common commuter altitude over New England. They rarely exceeded 12,000 feet on most of the short flights to and from Boston. Flights from Logan to area airports rarely exceeded 300 nautical miles either, so the Dressler's maximum flight range of 1,100 miles was not utilized very often. With a capacity of 800 U.S. gallons of fuel at a weight of 7,000 pounds, it could take off at a loaded weight of 35,000 pounds.

The twin Barringtons were stock engines from former military aircraft design and could handle wingspans and commercial load weights in excess of the Dressler's needs. The engines had a flawless record for performance. They had aviation safety records that would match the renowned and reliable U.S. mail planes known as the DC 3 (C-47 military) aircraft. Since most runways are longer than one mile at U.S. airports, the normal, extended-length runways at Logan, were longer than the Dressler 205 required. There was a huge measure of safety built in. The 205 would use less than one third of those runways to lift off, and only 2,500 feet for landing. With flaps extended, it could land in less length. Its popularity and versatility in the industry made the Dressler 205 an excellent candidate for commuter travel to ski resorts where local runways were usually short and weather conditions were often variable and difficult.

This night's passenger and cargo weight would not even approach the maximum for takeoff. With all passengers and crew aboard, baggage and some routine U.S. mail cargo, it would probably end up with 33,500 pounds.

Captain Bullock knew that he was late for the flight check, but most commuters never left on time anyway. Passengers regarded the planes as claustrophobic tuna cans and found them a necessary inconvenience. Most commuter connections were from Terminal E to Terminals A, B or C. Although international flights went out of Terminal E, major domestic carriers were at the other terminals. If one connected to an international flight, passengers could stay in Terminal E for the connection.

Bullock thanked the security guard for his carry-on and headed rapidly toward the commuter gates. There, one of the guards recognized him as a "frequent pilot" and teased him with a "late again, eh?" Bullock smiled and said, "Traffic was bad." He was still OTB in his own mind. His shoe heels hit the tiles like a crack on stone as he rushed toward his gate. Generally Logan's buses circled the terminals and aided pilots and passengers who needed to go to other terminals in the complex. Since Bullock's wife had dropped him off in front of E, he didn't have to wait for public transportation, or put up with passenger attitudes and derogatory comments from late flights. When he was on their bus, they talked louder about their problems so that he could hear them.

Small buses in the commuter terminal area brought passengers to planes parked at a distance from the door and boarding area. Captain Bullock did not wait for a bus and ran to the plane waiting on the tarmac. The distance was short and he knew he was late. Often-tardy baggage transfers delayed flights so he still had time to get acquainted with tonight's flying partner.

First Officer John Bell patiently awaited his pilot. He was unsure of who would be in the left seat tonight. Realizing the delay that might be caused by waiting for his partner, John had initiated his instrument flight check and his walk around the plane. That way they could leave relatively on time—if there were no mechanical or controller problems to be resolved. As Bob Connolly, a baggage crew member, threw the last of the luggage into the hold toward the rear of the plane, a shuttle bus stopped to the left of the plane to drop off one or two stragglers from Gate 23A, the gate for 2158.

Bob Connolly lived north of Boston, and although he had a family, he often spent his weekends with friends at the local sports bar to watch the Red Sox, Bruins or Celtics play, depending on the season. They were all avid sports fans and often got into loud discussions about which team or player was best. Red Auerbach's 1986 Boston Celtics was a favorite of his. Their wives despised their disregard for the family times, but they knew their men wouldn't change. Some of the guys had been pals in high school and played ball together. Drinking beer, they'd reminisce about the old days and the girls that they collected as trophies back then. They exaggerated a bit and took credit for more conquests than they really had accomplished. No one cared; they were friends.

Connolly drank too much many weekends. He often had a hangover on Monday mornings and he kept large bottles of generic aspirin and antacid handy in his locker. As social as he was with his drinking buddies, at work he seemed to be a loner and appeared standoffish at times—especially on Monday mornings. He still managed to do his work, which sometimes required refueling, baggage and general light maintenance on the smaller aircraft, including the twin-engine Dressler 205.

He was a lady's man—or so he thought. He was often heard bragging about his sexual prowess and how women "hit" on him at the local pubs. They were probably "barflies" he was talking about. Most of his coworkers thought that he fabricated a lot of stories. Maybe some stories were true, but the women were nothing to write home about—regulars at the bar or seasoned female bartenders who shared their own war stories. The local barflies were there to drown their sorrows. He figured his wife wasn't aware of them because she hadn't confronted him about anything—or about his evenings away from home "with the boys."

To his friends, over a few beers at his favorite pub, Big Irish Jim's, he bragged that a new beautiful chick was hot for him. Connolly said she was deprived because her husband wasn't "servicing the account." Unlike his wife, this woman was game for anything, even some kinky stuff. Most of his friends just tolerated Connolly and gave him the "yeh, sure, stud" on the escapades that he related, especially this one.

19

But his relationship with this woman was different than the others. At first it seemed that she was lonely and seeking attention, which he was most happy to provide while her husband was frequently out of town, like many yuppies in suburbia. He had fallen hard for her. Not only was she stunning, she was dynamite in bed and seemed to crave his raw desires. Excited by the fact that someone still found him desirable, he began wondering about making the arrangement with her permanent. Imagine having someone to come home to who was beautiful and sexy. Her husband, the bastard, didn't deserve her. Connolly began thinking. They could both dump their spouses and move in together. But she had grown silent when he floated that idea after a passionate love-making session a few months earlier. She said she felt bound to her marriage vows to stay with her husband "till death do us part." She said that she still hoped that perhaps things would be better some day. "This has been fun, Bob, and I want us to continue our relationship. But don't get the idea that it can be more than it is today. You have your wife and kids, and I have my husband. And that's the way it will be," she said as she touched his cheek. Stunned at her rejection, he rolled over angrily and stared at the wall.

Connolly greeted the late passengers with a friendly hello, followed by his usual, "Have a nice flight!" or "I'll take that bag for you, ma'am." or "Thanks for flying North East Air." They were relieved to have made the flight after being detained in heavy rush hour traffic.

Connolly had learned to be friendly to passengers during previous training classes at flight school. Desperately wanting to become a commercial pilot, he had failed to pass the original screening for flight instruction; medical reasons were his primary shortcomings during early training. A slight heart murmur was detected by doctors when he was young, and failing eyesight with severe astigmatism squashed his future as a North East Air pilot. Leaving flight school training, he was comfortable just to be around planes and sought training as a mechanic on smaller engines which were standard prop or turboprops. With NEAir, even helping with baggage was a plus for Bob. He had taken some classes in instrumentation and avionics and was able to service minor cockpit problems, usually with the help of a certified mechanic. The sound of aircraft engines and the smell of Jet A excited him. He loved aircraft and everything about them.

3

First Officer Bell proceeded with the internal flight check of gauges, flight plan and weather information. He had grabbed the latest weather data from the computer at Gate 23A. Bob Connolly had given him the "fuel slip" for the refueling of the Manchester flight.

Bell was younger than Captain Bullock. He had just rounded forty a month earlier. Marisa, his wife of seven years, had thrown a wonderful but small party for him; a few close friends from work had been invited.

Marisa, herself, had once been employed in the airline industry. She had met John when she was a flight attendant for an international airline carrier. She was beautiful, a classy dresser on and off duty and had European facial features. Five feet six inches tall, she was curvaceous, had long brown hair and blue eyes. They met when John had "comped" a flight to Europe for a vacation some years back. Marisa was a flight attendant on that flight and they felt the chemistry immediately. It was love at first sight. Love on a 747—in mind and soul.

Her shining hair had a glow of cleanliness and purity. She appeared hygienically perfect, with immaculate skin tone and a perfectly pressed airline uniform. Everything that she wore was fitted by a tailor. Marisa was the most beautiful thing he had ever seen and he had seen many flight attendants over the years. He had noticed there was no ring on her finger, but thought that she had to be "with" someone. No one like her could be floating around "free."

The timing was good. Marisa had just ended a long-distance relationship. She was ready to settle down and start a family if she found the right man. Too many years on the job and too many repetitive flights had finally taken their toll on her. She was aware that flight attendants usually last about seven or eight years, then move on to something else. "Lifers" as attendants were a rare breed in the airline industry.

John and Marisa courted for a year—he pursued her rapidly in Europe. In her off hours they hung out together and true love grew in Italy. They were married the next year and now, seven years later, they were contemplating having a baby. At first John had convinced her to wait a while on the baby "thing." He also had just started a new job with the airline when they first met and he was on a fast track for a career with NEAir. Now that they were hoping to conceive a baby, there were minor fertility problems.

Marisa had been to a gynecologist and nothing anatomical was wrong with her reproductive system. An occasional irregular menstrual cycle length ran in the family. It had taken her mother many years to conceive Marisa and her brother. Trying to start a family was further complicated by the fact that Bell was often away at mid-cycle for optimum fertility. *Will he be around to participate in a family,* she wondered? John, on the other hand, felt that their biological time-clocks were ticking and they needed to do something, now. He did not want to be a father of young children when he was too old. But John was away more than he was home, and her life seemed empty without either a husband around or a baby to care for.

Marisa had left the airline business after eight years. As a homemaker, she had a nice life and was financially secure, but she was an attractive, young, and bored housewife. Her prior profession had been exciting. Her beauty was radiating and her personality matched the outward beauty. She was always meeting new people and enjoyed many friendships in the industry. She missed that interaction desperately. There were no longer male passengers "hitting" on her or paying attention to her perfume or clothes. She lived for the attention and loved teasing the businessmen—a flirtation of sorts. She was popular as an attendant and often was assigned First Class duty.

In their neighborhood she could see the children playing and often she wept, wondering if she would have that laughter in her own back yard. She read romance novels; she had gone through dozens in the last year. She was a sensual, romantic person by nature and loved to make love. Marisa never denied John's wishes but sometimes felt like she was going through the motions. He was so busy that often he did not take the time to focus on her needs. She had even contemplated getting herself a "sex toy" while he was away. Fantasy was not all bad. When they first met, she and John were all over one another. Now they had all they could do to spend some serious time in bed. She needed the love and comfort of a warm body next to her, but he was away far too often for that. Daytime soap operas and romance novels or a house pet would not cut it for her. The vacation John had planned so secretly needed to be shared with her soon. It just might get things back on track and reset the priorities for both of them.

She enjoyed talking to the neighborhood kids and had more of a bond to the men because of her experiences during her prior employment, where her interaction had been greater with men than women. Most neighborhood women were jealous of her. They knew she worked out and jogged regularly, and had no children. Some women had the middle-aged spread after a child or two and never took the time to regain their figures. Others were more conscientious and had aged gracefully. Marisa had always found the male neighbors to be more intelligent, interesting and entertaining, but few met her standards for sexiness. It was like having airline passenger interaction all over again—with occasional, casual sexual encounters to satisfy the "itch." Nothing serious. John would never know. She did, however, have one female friend and confidant, Belinda.

Some Friday nights, when John was out of town, Belinda and Marisa had a few drinks together and shared their innermost secrets—boredom, a desire to have children and lack of male companionship. And one night, when Marisa had consumed too much wine, she hinted that she was having an affair. Belinda figured that, in time, her friend would discuss the specifics of her breach of fidelity.

Belinda's brother and his family also lived in the small suburban community where neighbors seemed to have at least a speaking relationship with each other. Belinda would often stop to say hello to her brother's family when she was visiting her friend.

John loved Marisa beyond compare and didn't want to believe that she could be sad and bored when he was away. He had been faithful since meeting her and he certainly had many opportunities to meet and have other women, who found him just as desirable as Marisa did. He chose to avoid those opportunities by staying in his hotel room at night on longer flights. He avoided the boring hotel bars and clubs where the pilots and flight attendants might pass the evening away. He wasn't much of a drinker anyway. The FAA rules of aviation prevented much of that and flying so often he would violate the eight-hour rule of no alcohol before flying. Why bother? He didn't want to lose his job or be labeled a "womanizer" or an "alcoholic" out of boredom. Most nights away he watched a movie—thrillers or soft porn—in his room. Why not? The movies were there for the offering. Besides they were training films, he thought. He would approach Marisa with some new exciting ways to please each other.

Realizing that it might be good to spend time together, John was planning a surprise trip to the islands and had even placed a deposit on a trip with the local travel agency. A trip to the Caribbean in a month or so would be perfect, just as cooler and often rainy fall weather came to New England.

As he did his preflight check, John thought that perhaps after the next week of flying assignments, he could share his Caribbean vacation secret with her. She would surely look forward to that getaway, and he didn't want to take his marriage to her for granted.

4

The last passenger to board NEAir Flight 2158 was Mary Hutton, a teacher from Manchester High School in New Hampshire. She was connecting from a Pittsburgh flight that had just landed at Terminal C. The flight was the same one that Jack Danton had arrived on as well. She joined the flight in the "Pitts" as they say. They had sat together on the second leg of the west coast flight to Boston. So she was used to First Class upgrades.

Flight 2158 had no First Class cabin service; it actually had no "class" at all. It was simply a commuter to bring her home to New Hampshire, the "Live Free or Die" state!" The motto for her state always bothered her, but she taught her kids that Gen. John Stark was the person who "coined" the phrase. She would kid the children into believing that what he really said way back when was "Live, Freeze or Die!"

"I'll take that, ma'am," Connolly said, as Mary Hutton left her bag at the base of the short stairs into the Dressler 205. The bright-orange gate check tag on the oversized bag flipped in the breeze as he took it to the baggage compartment at the rear of the plane.

"Thanks," she hollered above the other noises of the night, and Bob acknowledged her with a hand wave.

"Here, take this—you'll need it in New Hampshire to claim your bag."

"Thank you, my good man," Mary said.

"My pleasure."

The orange stub was her record of the bag going to Manchester. Since she saw him load it onto the plane out the corner of her eye, there was little chance the bag would disappear in flight. *Stranger things have happened,* she thought. Lost baggage was common these days. They still had to take it "off " the plane upon arrival, she joked to herself.

Mary was impressed with Connolly, judging him to be a polite middle-aged man.

Was he attached? She hadn't seen a ring on his hand, but it was there.

Captain Bullock arrived winded, shortly after Mary had boarded. He greeted passengers as he crouched in the doorway and looked back at the rear of the cabin. Dim green lights on the cockpit display faced him as he joined his first officer. He took off his hat and hung it behind the seat.

"Hello, Captain—you're here! Thought we were going without you. Traffic problems?"

"Yeh," Bullock said, "the name's Bill Bullock . . . yours?"

"John Bell."

"Thanks for starting the process, John . . . how's she look?"

"She's clean, Captain. Fuel's aboard; they fueled her before they hauled her to the gate. Here's the fuel slip. Ground crew person just left as I boarded. He replaced a light in the console. 'Burned out,' he said."

"I'm almost done with the flight check. She'll weigh in light since some cargo didn't transfer. Postal service didn't make it in time, but passenger luggage from connecting flights appears to have made it, even from the late connections. We may be three- to-four K pounds light at takeoff; no strain tonight for the Barringtons!"

"That's good, mate," Bullock replied.

John smiled and continued, "Traffic in the tunnel, or access road?"

He is a chatterbox, Bullock thought.

"Both," he replied. "Getting to this friggin' place is awful after five P.M. Rush hour must start at three."

Captain Bullock buckled himself into the seat and grabbed his head gear. Still mumbling about the traffic, Bill commented, "How do they expect pilots and passengers to get here from downtown Boston when you have four lanes entering two lanes in the Callahan Tunnel. Damn thing is always congested."

John understood his comment since he had been in that traffic a half hour earlier. The entrance to the Callahan Tunnel borders on the Italian North End, Faneuil Hall and Route 93 South, better known as the Southeast Expressway. On or about five o'clock in the evening, the area approaching the Callahan is at a standstill.

"I was there myself a few minutes before you so I know the feeling. I left home after four-thirty."

"How's the weather pattern shaping up?" Bullock asked. "Any changes in the low ceiling?"

"Not really, Captain. It's supposed to stay like this for the evening." He cast his eyes skyward through the windshield and into the night.

"Basically, it should be a relatively fast one to 'Cow Hampshire,'" Bullock joked. "Looks like last night's weather—winds at twenty."

"Yeh," Bell replied, "there were earlier reports of some moderate chop from other aircraft. They reported light winds from the northwest as well."

Bullock felt secure with Bell in the right-hand seat. He remembered now that they had flown some flight segments together in the past. He was trying to recollect where they might had flown on those occasions.

Back on the ground outside the plane, Connolly had secured the luggage compartment. He removed the belt which prevented the left propeller from turning as people boarded. Normal procedure was to leave the propeller stationary so that no one was in danger if the wind caught it free-floating while boarding. He grabbed the wheel chocks with a yank and stood below Bullock's left cockpit window. The right engine was idling and now the left-side engine could be fired up. Connolly motioned to the captain to crank the left side over, then gave Bullock a thumbs up and a friendly salute. With the right-side engine started and idling, Bullock checked the RPMs on the left, and then the right engines. The brakes were on and the "bird" wanted to move forward. He idled the engines again. The props slowly turned, and as they gained rotation, the painted tips blended into a beautiful circle. The taxi and takeoff lights shone brightly through the mesmerizing spinning props. Bullock contacted ground control at Tower Central and requested permission to proceed to preassigned Runway 33L.

High above Terminal C, and to the southeast of Terminal E stood twin towers connected in the middle. A glassed-in area with numerous air traffic controllers bustling about sat atop the cement structures and provided a 360-degree view of Logan International Airport. Directly underneath the secured control tower were various levels of offices and an observation tower restaurant and bar with the finest view of the airport and runways. Open to the public, the bar, restaurant and enclosed observation deck offered views of the city of Boston and Boston Harbor in one direction, and the airport runways on the opposite side.

"Big Lou," a large black bartender in the Skyline Bar adjacent to the restaurant, was mixing a pitcher of margaritas for four young businessmen who had just arrived on a flight to Boston. They were among the few people who were aware of the bar at the top of the tower. They sat in large simulated-leather chairs that swiveled and that looked like Fisher Price children's miniature table and chair sets. The chairs were black and surrounded a round, white table with a candle in the middle. The bartender had just stopped to check on their drink requirements and saw that they were still nursing their current round of drinks. They were settled in pretty good.

"More snacks?" he asked.

"You mean, more kibbles and bits, nuts and twigs?" one of the men retorted. "This stuff's stale, Lou."

"Got any more fresh stuff?" another man said.

"Sure, I'll get a new bag for you guys right away. I'll be right back."

The businessmen were still in suits but their ties were loosened and collars were unbuttoned. They had been there a while and were "feelin' no pain." They were having a third pitcher and still had not confirmed their hotel rooms for that evening. They didn't care. Their rooms were guaranteed by their AMEX cards. Occasionally a woman would pass by their table and they would ogle her. *Just a bunch of horny men on the road,* Big Lou thought.

Big Lou weighed some 350 pounds and had a distended midriff from sampling beers behind the bar over the years. He loved his Budweiser after hours. A congenial fellow with a big smile and heart of gold, he was a good listener so being a bartender was a nice job for him. Lou's crew-cut hair style was reminiscent of a Marine cut or that of an old boxer. His stubby nose inferred the latter. This was a second job for him and late nights killed him physically. Returning to the table of four, Lou cut into their conversation.

"Here's some fresh munchies for ya," he said. "They should be better tastin'."

"Thanks Lou," one of the four men said as he lit up another cigarette.

"Hey, do you guys remember the plane that went in the drink at Logan one winter's night?" one of the men asked the others.

"A few years back?"

"Sure—it was ten years or so, right?"

"Think so!" another guy said.

"She buried her nose in the harbor. Right?" asked another.

They proceeded to revisit the fate of a famous Logan Airport crash from a decade earlier. It would be a long story and few facts were remembered correctly. The men were going nowhere soon tonight and were telling stories and enjoying each other's company.

Big Lou listened intently. He had worked the bar that night and had seen the plane slide off the iced runway into the north end of Boston Harbor. At least two male passengers were lost in the water that night and their bodies were never recovered. His thoughts of revisiting that night were not pleasant and he returned to his station behind the bar. *Besides*, he thought, *their facts are all wrong.* So he merely flipped the TV channels to the evening news and pretended to not know a thing about the ill-fated crash. One thing was certain, Big Lou had always thought that Logan's response to the crash was poor and that innocent lives were lost for no reason. Logan Airport emergency crews were not prepared back then to handle a wide-body plane going into the drink.

Since that time, safety and emergency teams were specially trained to react to emergencies on runways or in water. The response team "ALERT" was now established at the airport. ALERT stood for "A Logan Emergency Response Team." The name was not novel, but reflected the nature of their duties. The emergency response team was prepared to handle any problems that might occur. It took a disaster to establish adequate training and sophisticated equipment for future airport tragedies. The budget to establish ALERT was in the millions. *Thank God they now existed*, Big Lou thought. His mind wandered back to the episode ten years earlier. He wiped some glasses dry as he stared aimlessly at the TV above him.

5

Eight toll takers were busily grabbing dollar bills as taxis, buses and cars converged en masse at the mouth of the Sumner Tunnel. A fee of two dollars was collected at the eastern end, heading into Boston. Traffic entering the Callahan Tunnel from the Boston side did not have to pay. The toll attendants got them on the return to "Beantown." The twin, parallel tunnels carry thousands of people traveling to and from the airport each day. Completed respectively in 1934 and 1961, the Sumner and the Callahan tunnels appear antiquated even after occasional renovations.

They provide the most direct route to the airport. Alternate routes such as Route 1 or Route 16 do not save much time getting to Logan Airport. The highways are out of the way for the Boston-based traffic and cannot be easily reached from Boston proper, especially during peak hours. The most direct route to the airport was the Callahan, except for travelers from the north or from Maine and New Hampshire.

Tom Harper, a veteran toll taker and approaching forty-two years old, yelled to his colleague in the next tollbooth. His voice was nearly drowned out by the engines of the passing cars.

"Hey, Jeff, I could use some change. Got any ones?"

Jeff Clark nodded as he gave someone change.

"Yeh, hang on, Harper. Gotta dig it out of the drawer."

Tom ran over to Jeff's booth, almost getting hit by a Volvo that was rushing through the gate. The nerd in the Volvo tapped his horn as if to hurry Tom up. The driver popped "the bird" to Tom as he drove away.

"Screw you, too, Bud," Tom said, as he returned the favor.

The exhaust of the Volvo hit him in the face. He coughed in the blue smoke. The guy peeled out leaving a strip of rubber. Tom came close to being hit again as he grabbed a wad of ones and fives from Jeff, then scooted back to his own booth. Toll takers were constantly subjected to abuse, and over time they became more distant and less tolerant toward the drivers. After all, the job was boring as hell and very tedious at peak times. Standing in a tiny booth all night, trying to be nice to people who have been backed up for any length of time, was difficult. They hardly had time even to go to the restroom.

Once he was back in the booth, Tom "fanned" the piles of one and five dollar bills and stashed them in the cash drawer. He was tired, and part of his shirt was outside his pants. The job was getting old.

"Shit!" he mumbled to himself. "Basta'd almost got me."

He had come very close to banging his kneecaps on the Volvo bumper and the driver really didn't care. Tom could have reported the license plate to the state police but opted not to waste his time. The guy in the Volvo was just another "Masshole," he smirked to himself. There are a million of them that pass through the tolls. Nobody likes to pay tolls or wait in line to do it. Verbal abuse was common at the Sumner.

Jeff hooted over to him and laughed at the Volvo episode.

"Close one, eh? You're slowin' down, Harper. You're gettin' old!"

"Eat shit!" Tom said. "Next time bring me the bills. I've got seniority over you!"

"Fat chance," came the reply from the other booth. "You just came close to losin' your seniority, Señor!"

"Eat me!" Tom retorted with a smile.

Too many years of this crap, Tom thought. Jeff was a neophyte with only four and a half years under his belt. Just then another guy in a minivan handed him a twenty dollar bill.

"Hey, man," he said, "anything smaller?"

"Nope. Sorry."

"Don't you folks ever have smaller bills?" he said as he gave the change. "I mean like fives and tens?"

The guy in the van looked perplexed after Tom's comment and drove away. The driver said to himself, "That guy needs a nap!" Twenties tended to show up because people coming from the airport would stop and get cash from the ATMs in the terminals. The ATMs always spit out twenties.

Therefore, an easy way for the drivers to break the large bills was to do it at the tollbooths. They didn't care. They figured that the toll takers had endless amounts of change.

"Someday, I'll get out of this job," Tom mumbled to himself. "Need more money anyway!"

During slow times at the booth he would daydream of vacations on islands or of going back to school to learn another trade—one that paid well and had less hassle. Tom Harper hadn't vacationed in two years and his wife, Becky, wanted them to get away someplace warm with a beach— something other than Crane's Beach north of Boston.

Tom took eight quarters from the next guy. Nice that he had exact change. Then he thought to himself. *Why wouldn't the guy use the "automatic," or "exact change" lanes? Go figure*, he thought. *The idiot drove a Ford Escort . . . what a dunce . . . a friggin' Escort . . . Car of the Year!" car magazines said. Some car! . . . Some award! Piece of shit!*

Tom was about as negative as he could be at this point. The Volvo driver really had gotten to him. He was still pissed and taking it out on other people. He really didn't mean to. He was just upset that he almost lost his kneecaps.

Tom was due to get off work at 9:00 P.M. and he was anxious to get home. Becky had cooked his favorite meal of spaghetti and meatballs—a simple meal, but good. He had called her earlier and she was preparing the sauce. After the last car, he really needed to chill out. The job was getting to him and he was losing his patience with Boston drivers.

Tom and Becky had a home on Hanover Street adjacent to many fine restaurants and Italian bakeries. Life was good and the food was fantastic. They had acquired many recipes from friends in the North End—for tomato sauce, breads, pasta and desserts. He grabbed another five dollar bill from a driver and thought to himself, *I'll be home soon— pasta and sauce.*

Becky had befriended Mrs. Girardi next door who had shared with her a great red spaghetti sauce recipe. Other neighbors were aware of this secret sauce but the "secret" ingredients were just that, a secret. Any time Anna Girardi gave away the sauce recipe, she left out a critical spice—bay leaves. No one ever had the whole recipe. Even Becky would have to figure that out herself. Mrs. Girardi, now eighty-four, would take that to her grave. She wore traditional black dresses—older Italian women always looked like they were going to a wake—and she smelled of garlic. Everything Mrs.

Girardi made had garlic in it. She also ate one garlic clove a week for health reasons. "Garlica, gooda fa you!" she would say.

Tom couldn't wait to get home and taste the pasta, especially if it involved the Girardi recipe. On a good windy day, the culinary odors of Little Italy in the North End or East Boston would drift toward the eastern tollbooths. That always made him hungry. It tended to show up around his midriff, since he and Becky had moved to the North End. They were both wearing clothes two or three sizes larger.

He knew he had to lose weight but never got to exercise and he loved the food too much. After dinner, he thought that they might hit Joe's Pastries for a cannoli and coffee. That was a fun family treat. There was nothing like Italian pastries with ricotta cheese, sprinkles or chocolate dipped. A nice bottle of Chianti with dinner. *Now that was a meal*, he thought! *Every Friday night—this is becoming our tradition.*

Despite his age and weight, Tom daydreamed a lot in the tollbooth. In anticipation of someday leaving this job, he had been taking evening classes for EMT training. The Emergency Medical Technician course was taught locally and Tom aspired to becoming an EMT full time. *It is a thrilling occupation*, he thought. He was proud that he was nearing final exam time and he felt that he was ready for the test. His wife would ask him questions as a practice test. *This*, he thought, *might be a job where I can gain some self-respect, pride and advancement with time. Advancement means more money down the line. Then I could bag this tollbooth job.* After today's Volvo experience, he was even more determined to move on.

The only excitement he had experienced on his current job was an occasional problem in Sumner Tunnel, which required him to help out. This could be a breakdown, a medical emergency in slow traffic or a car fire. Car fires were the most exciting. Vehicular accidents, where people crossed the double yellow lines in the tunnel, were frequent occurrences. People liked to move lane to lane to advance in traffic. Even though it was prohibited, some "Massholes" did it anyway. Major accidents and tie-ups were created on those occasions. Although previously untrained in medical emergencies, Tom had always enjoyed helping people in need. The close proximity of the tollbooths to the tunnel entrance afforded him the opportunity to be one of the first on the scene when trouble occurred.

With sixteen weeks of EMT classes, he felt more prepared for those emergencies. He had learned to assist in the delivery of children, how to stop bleeding and how to stabilize blood pressure. In each of the practice procedures, he had topped his classmates.

The last major incident had occurred two weeks earlier. A taxi cab had burst into flames for no apparent reason. Car fires were common and this one generated extensive smoke in the Sumner Tunnel, creating a backup of traffic, both leaving the airport and also westbound through the tunnel to Boston. People entering the Sumner Tunnel at the east Boston end believed it was routine traffic trying to access Route 93 North on the Boston side of the Sumner. The smoke from the burning cab ended up three-fourths of the way into the tunnel. The prevailing winds blew west to east and people were evacuating their cars and heading toward the east Boston end, the end from which they entered.

Some affected passengers joked about the cab being torched, but eventually saw the seriousness of the situation and left the tunnel on foot. Some people even left in an orderly fashion. "Orderly fashion" is not a normal procedure for Bostonians. Most of the people involved were surprised by the behavior of the people in the smoke-filled tunnel. They were being too damn nice for Boston.

Tom followed a state trooper as he walked briskly through the tunnel and tried to order people back to their cars. He felt that it was not a critical situation and staying in their cars would facilitate exiting from the tunnel when the mini-crisis was over.

"It won't help to have you leave your vehicles!" the state trooper, a former Marine sergeant, barked. "Get back to your cars! Do not leave your vehicles unattended!"

Tom noticed a well-dressed woman who made a passing comment as the trooper briskly strutted past her on his way to the western end of the tunnel.

"Eat shit—go screw yourself!" she murmured as he passed. "I'm not stayin' in here. You nuts?"

The trooper gave her a stern look but he was on a mission from hell and kept right on moving.

She could see the smoke fast approaching the area where she had left her car. The rapidly spreading smoke was noxious and made breathing difficult. With the wind entering from the Boston side, there was no way that she would return to her car until the episode was over. By now, the black, acrid cloud was overpowering and the trooper had no idea of what he was doing or getting himself into. Tom stopped briefly to acknowledge the woman's comment. He smiled and told her to remain calm. He then ran to catch up to the trooper who had managed to get some fifty feet ahead of him into the tunnel.

A charter bus with elderly people aboard was among the stranded vehicles and Tom stopped again to assure them of their safety. The bus driver sat leaning on his steering wheel with both arms, bored and impatient with frustration. The smoke had not reached them yet. The bus was still running to maintain the air conditioning for its passengers. Diesel exhaust from the bus permeated that area of the tunnel and people coughed as they passed by on their way out. Passersby heading for cleaner air at the eastern end were offended by the bus driver's disregard for their health. The air became more stagnant and oppressive. By the time Tom and the trooper returned to the eastern end of the tunnel, many of the people that had evacuated were experiencing headaches and nausea from the fumes. Carbon monoxide and carbon dioxide levels continued to rise. The twenty-eight exhaust fans in the tunnel, which were designed for normal ventilation and exhaust, were inadequate to handle the increased load of fumes from a taxi fire and idling vehicle engines.

The Boston Fire Department had responded to the fire alarm from their regional Hanover Street location. The department's quick response substantially reduced the danger of the situation and facilitated the evacuation necessary to prevent further injury for those trapped in the Sumner. Within three-quarters of an hour, people were able to return their vehicles. After a ramp truck removed the charred taxi, cars could be seen exiting the tunnel again and traffic flow through the tunnel was beginning to pick up.

Once the crisis was over Tom returned to his post in the tollbooth. He knew that it would be hours before the airport access and egress roads would flow smoothly again.

6

Long Wharf on the Boston side juts out into Boston Harbor. It and the other wharves resemble spokes extending from downtown and radiating toward Logan Airport. The waterfront's design is not dissimilar from that of San Francisco or New York City when viewed from the air. In the colonial days, sailing ships loaded and unloaded cargo at these ports and wharves, often after long journeys from Europe and the Orient.

Most of the warehouses on Boston's wharves, once used for shipping, were now converted into housing and condo units. Others became office space in the 1970s and 1980s. A few piers to the south of Lewis and Lincoln wharves were maintained for maritime shipment and deployment of modern cruise ships to the islands of the Caribbean.

Horses and carriages, which thrived at these ports of call, were replaced by cars and sidewalks along the harbor. Bostonians and visitors walk along the harbor's edge on a Sunday morning or bright summer day. Hotels, an aquarium and convention centers dot the harbor front. They cut in and out of the numerous piers from yesteryear. Seagulls perch on the tips of the pier supports, scattering noisily when approached by people. Their calls echo as they are temporarily scared from their perches. They return rapidly when people move past but their white excrement is a reminder of their constant presence in the harbor.

The *Queen of Shoals*, a harbor cruise ship, made four journeys daily out of the harbor, in and out of the islands. The boat, which could accommodate 225 passengers, was a steel, single-hull design and had an upper and lower deck for passenger sightseeing. Powered by twin diesels, the

Queen departed every evening in the summer and early fall for the renowned "booze cruise"—a Boston tradition. Many boat lines operating in the harbor offered these party cruises. Tonight the *Queen* was under the watchful eye of Captain Warren Holland, who was for many years a captain in the Merchant Marine. He had prior experience as well on the great paddle wheelers on the Mississippi before deciding to try his hand at the open ocean. He could navigate tortuous freshwater rivers and saltwater harbors as well.

Captain Holland greeted passengers with, "Welcome to Boston and the *Queen of Shoals*." His crew of eight was experienced and versatile at multiple responsibilities during the course of the evening. Aside from general duties, they also helped with the cocktail bars and food service. Once out of port, the drinks could flow and the party would begin.

Some years ago the lower deck had been enclosed to offer refuge to the passengers traveling in rough New England weather. The lower deck would occasionally bear the brunt of sea spray heading out of the harbor. Winds from the southeast could do it all the time. Those people who were adventurous or had too much to drink often stood by the bow and faced the wind like a dog with its head out the car window. After all, it was Boston and the weather could change every ten minutes.

The enclosed deck also offered a dance floor and small stage for the entertainment. "Booze cruise" passengers could then dance the night away and still view Beantown from afar. During most cruises of three-hour duration, local rock bands were hired to perform. The bands added to the evening of fun and frivolity. Many people got into the music. Those who wanted to could drink and listen, or drink and dance. The passengers who wished to avoid the loud noise of the band could migrate to the upper deck. Two stairways allowed the passengers to access an upper level where a moonlit sky often bathed the night-lit office buildings. This view was a serene departure from the hustle and bustle of the wharf and downtown Boston.

Captain Holland directed the first mate and crew to retract the gangway and prepare for departure. The harbor directly behind him appeared serene, with the lights from Logan Airport reflected on the water. They were still docked with the *Queen*'s bow facing towards the city of Boston.

The half-moon to the southeast meant a clear night for now. The night sky would change as the clouds rolled in from the west. The captain enjoyed nights like this. When the weather was OK, he could hand the boat over to his first mate and enjoy the crowd of passengers during an occasional break from the wheelhouse and bridge. Boston weather was subject to change every few minutes it seemed and overcast skies were predicted at departure time. For now it looked more promising. The harbor had little boat traffic at this time and the sound of rushing water along the bow became more apparent as the *Queen* was backed from her moorings. At the stern of the boat, the mighty diesels blew smoke that mixed with the water in the aft section. The noise level of the exhausts increased as she left the dock. At times it was deafening for those passengers standing near the stern. The helmsman spun her bow around and she motored slowly into the harbor.

Kristin, Julie and Karen were young summer-crew staff from Boston area colleges. They had prepped the bars and food stands on the *Queen*'s decks between trips. However, they would not serve drinks for a few minutes and Kristin still had to slice a few more lemons and limes for the popular summertime drinks, especially the ones with gin or vodka. She knew that Bostonians on these tours really enjoyed their "Cape Codders" and their gin and tonics.

"More ice please," she called to Scott, another mate.

"Be right there, babe," he responded as he passed by her bar.

"Gonna need a five-gallon pail, too, hon."

"AOK . . . consider it done."

"You always take care of me, Scottie boy."

"Certainly do," he said. "Certainly do!"

It was well known that Scott had "a thing" for Kristin and had even coaxed her into one of the heads on the lower level on a previous cruise. He had managed to get her pretty aroused with that little impromptu maneuver. He felt pretty proud of his accomplishment since Kristin was not one to give herself freely to just anyone. He had long admired her attractive, young body, blonde hair and pristine appearance. Notwithstanding, she had been voted by the male crew as the girl with the finest ass.

Kristin was aware of her accolade and often accentuated her body lines by wearing her shorts just a bit tighter than the other ladies on board did. *Why not,* she thought. *If you got it, flaunt it!* White shorts on her tanned body were truly a sight to behold and tonight was no exception. She looked pretty awesome, having just returned from a few days off in the sun on Cape Cod.

Scott returned shortly with two five-gallon pails of ice for the bar wells. "Here, babe. Here's your frozen water," he said. "Got you two pails of the stuff—might be a heavy night." He also checked her supply of napkins and beer cups.

Kristin winked affectionately at him and thanked him with a quick tap on the butt. He quickly responded by commenting on her own butt and joked, "You know, Kristin, touching a guy between the waist and his knees is a no-no! Could get you a citation for sexual misconduct."

Kristin laughed and continued to cut the citrus for the drinks.

"Who's gonna turn me in? You?" she laughed. "And, besides, I know you like it."

"Ah, Kristin, you know me too well. You can do that anytime—as long as I have equal time."

He smiled as he walked away, almost bumping into a cabin support pole as he turned toward the storage room to get more napkins for her setup.

Overhead, the ship's horn sounded as Captain Holland signaled his impending departure. The green and red buoys in the harbor glistened on the water as their lights guided the *Queen* on its usual path out of the wharf area and into the harbor proper. He had to quickly navigate his boat around a sailboat which had crossed his path—almost in defiance. It was not unusual to have harbor abuse since many sailors with boats moored in marinas around the wharves considered the local cruise lines a nuisance.

They tended to take chances around the cruise boats knowing that they were slow and awkward. In actuality, the *Queen* could be their demise if they weren't careful. Hitting her side would surely break the fiberglass hulls of the day sailers. They didn't care. Some of the nighttime sailors were known to moon the passengers on the cruise boats. They were less likely to be caught by the harbor patrol performing this ritual at night. It was really fun when some of the braver male passengers on the *Queen* returned the favor. Two or more imbibed men would sometimes give the sailboats a "multi-moon" in return. The captain had little objection to the friendly gestures.

Captain Holland was quick to call out to his first mate, "Any other Christopher Columbus's out there?"

It was usually the part-time local sailors who presented the problem to the cruise boats. Sailboats had the right of way in general, since their speed and path of sail was not always predictable.

The mate responded, "None in sight, Captain."

"Good, we'll head south of Georges Island once we clear that power boat on the port side," Captain Holland responded.

Some yuppies had expensive water craft. It was not unusual to see Cigarette boats or large cruisers out there at night. Many had parties of their own going on board.

Once the smaller boat was behind them, they proceeded southeasterly toward the outer island. The Chris Columbus of the day was behind them and they could relax a bit before the partying began.

On board the *Queen*, members of the rock band EXZILLERATION had completed the setup of their sound equipment on the small stage across from Kristin's bar. They had played the night before and the three previous nights as well. The Peavey sound system was the workhorse of the sound equipment and very compact. The band had two, six-channel amplifiers that were sufficient to handle all the mikes, guitars, bass, keyboard and a "kick-ass drummer's" drum roll.

Robie Brooks, the lead singer and lead guitarist, was their non-appointed band leader of sorts. He had spent two years touring with "The Rotten Maggots," a cult band, prior to joining EXZILLERATION. He was pleased to be part of the regular Boston music scene again where people might actually listen to the words and music. He was now happy with playing conventional "cover tunes" and old time rock and roll. Occasionally, he would perform songs which he had written over the years. Many were ballads—acoustical music.

The Fender Stratocaster, which Robie had purchased years ago, showed its wear and tear from being on the road. Pulling the "Strat" out of its beat-up case, it was clear to see where he and the guitar had been. The case had numerous stickers on it obtained from New Jersey gigs to California bars, clubs and radio stations. The stickers served another purpose as well. They held the corners of the case together. Many of the stickers were interspersed with duct tape, the universal bandage for anything broken.

Robie had been lucky when one radio station in L.A. played one of his originals, "I'll Be Back," on its Saturday night jam for new artists. He was proud of that, but the tune went nowhere. He never got much air time after that. Robie would play it tonight if the mood was right. He was teased about the song title since everyone equated it with Schwarzenegger.

He casually ran his hand across the strings of the unplugged Strat as if to see if it were still in tune after the ride in the trunk of his car—it didn't sound too bad. He used an electronic guitar tuner to get one string back in tune. The intonation was now perfect.

"Are we wired yet?" he asked Joey, the bass player.

"Yeh," he responded, "we're 'hot' and ready to rock and roll, man."

"All right . . . give me a little gain on the monitor, will ya?"

"Sure . . . how's that!"

"Fine . . . no feedback . . . she's cool."

Joey had just returned from the starboard head where he urinated and also did some "blow." He always did some recreational drugs before playing to a middle-aged crowd of after-work geeks. It put him in a mood where nothing mattered except the music. Everyone in the band, including Robie, was aware of Joey's need for "nose candy" but they overlooked the situation. Confronting him with his frequent use of mood elevators might cause him to leave the band. His bass was critical to their sound and he was reliable and on time for gigs and practice sessions. He played the hottest bass licks in town and they figured that how he spent his paycheck from the gigs was none of their business. Much of his money was wasted on weed as well. Joey no longer sang harmony primarily due to the fact that his nasal septum was gone from the years of snorting coke. As it was, he needed surgery to repair the damage to the inside of his nose and Joey had no money for that kind of medical treatment to correct the years of abuse.

Vocal harmony with Robie was covered by Jeff, the drummer, and that was sufficient for the cover tunes on cruise nights. After all, they would be doing covers by bands like "The Eagles," "America," "Jackson Browne" and other Top Forty artists. Their harmonies only suffered on their Crosby, Stills & Nash tunes. Three voices were needed for those songs. Crosby's and Nash's harmonies were unique and tough to learn.

They would sometimes invite boat guests up on stage for the third harmony, the one for Stills. Major mistakes by the guests could be hidden by the strong band voices. In the end, the guests would have fun and the songs would sound OK.

Cover tunes performed by the band were polished to the alert ears of the guests on board. Guests who knew the band often requested original tunes from Robie and Jeff. They always obliged. That was a chance to shine and possibly be heard by someone in the music industry who might be on board. Celebrities were known to show up on some cruises.

Although Robie loved playing electric guitar, he really preferred playing his acoustic 1937 Martin D28 guitar for the slower, more tender ballads. Many of his own songs had been written for that instrument. His father had passed it down to him many years earlier and the tradition of song writing was inbred within the Brooks family. The Martin D28 was a honey of an instrument, with rosewood sides and back and a solid mahogany neck. Bobby loved the guitar because it had once belonged to the "Nashville Cat," Clinton B. Cline, a distant relative of Patsy's. Robie had modified the guitar with an electronic pickup under the bridge of the guitar's German silver spruce sound board. That way he could use it electrified in the band, or unplugged when he was being creative or just "pickin'" around the house. The sound of the Martin far surpassed the "beater" Ovation that he usually used in the band.

The Ovation guitar was a workhorse for playing at gigs but it always sounded like shit to Robie. The tinny sound and sibilance of the strings, an "after ring," he found annoying. The Ovation was great for the road since nothing could kill it during hard travel. The airlines couldn't even kill it! His Ovation was an older model and the company that made them had problems with the tops of guitars delaminating from the parabolic back of the guitar. The problem had to do with the bowl-shaped preformed guitar body—a synthetic fiberglass-type composite. The bonding of the wooden guitar top to the synthetic back was a problem. Often the top would become unglued due to severe weather changes while on the road. He kept a bottle of Duco cement with him when traveling in case the guitar had problems. It kept the guitar intact. When he wasn't playing the "Strat," he had the Ovation in his hands. It worked well for the band.

EXZILLERATION was about to play but Jeff, who was a fanatic about sound, wanted to do one more sound check. He spoke into each mike, "Testes 1,2,3…. testes 1,2,3."

He must have done this every night that they played. He would make a popping noise as well. That way he was covering all ranges of their voices.

Few people noticed the humor of the "testes 1,2,3." Some people laughed when they caught on. Nightly sound checks were necessary since the sound system was torn down and stashed for the night when they were done. Jeff wanted to be sure that everything was "balanced for sound" for the show.

A faint electrical "AC hum" could be heard through the speakers when they were first turned on. Often wires between the amp and speakers became brittle with age or broken from being stepped on, thus the unwanted hum was created. Once the band began playing, any background noise in the system would not be heard.

7

Jack Danton had just celebrated his fortieth birthday. Jack was well-educated and was successful in his current job. He had attended a small New England college for four years. He then earned a master's and a Ph.D. from U. Mass. in Amherst, Massachusetts. His field of study in graduate school was veterinary and animal sciences, with a strong emphasis in physiology and endocrinology. The research for his doctorate involved the role of natural steroids in ovarian function of cattle, so his knowledge of reproductive biology was extensive as well. He had credible scientific publications in many peer-reviewed journals and some of his research was cited in major review articles on veterinary reproductive biology. Over the years, however, he had become bored with the basic research government granting programs. He saw the National Institutes of Health (NIH) funding drying up in Washington. The Ronald Reagan years were not kind to scientific research funding to universities.

With Danton's knowledge of the pharmaceutical and biotechnology industries, he decide to pursue a career that might be more "people oriented" as opposed to research oriented. The marketing and sales of pharmaceutical products was an option; however, he wanted to remain close to his science as well. Aware of Danton's scientific skills and extroverted personality, Kendall Square BioMedical Company in Cambridge caught wind of his desires to change careers by way of a headhunter. KSB, as the company was called, offered him a job marketing and selling its contract laboratory services in toxicology and endocrinology to the general pharmaceutical industry. His career and life changed in a very positive manner with the new employment opportunity. He would still have his hands in the "science," but could exercise his creative mind and have far more day to day interaction with potential clientele. It also gave him the opportunity to see much of the United States. His sales trips took him from the east to the west coasts. Many of his clients were in California and across the center of the nation. The predominant pharmaceutical territories also included New Jersey, Philadelphia, Chicago and the West Coast in general. San Diego, San Francisco and Seattle were priorities due to their concentrated biotechnology community. His current trip was his fifth and a return from the "left coast."

The access road from Logan Airport to the Sumner Tunnel was once again congested. Jack had time to reflect on his year-old career change. His father had great communication skills and people admired his dad over the years. His father was a one-company man and had spent forty-eight years with GE in Pittsfield, Massachusetts. When he retired, the CEO of GE attended his party. Jack's dad's overall philosophy in business was simple: "Treat people like you would like to be treated." Jack would use that approach in his day-to-day work ethic. Jack's train of thought was broken by the traffic jam around him.

"What the hell is the delay here?" he mumbled. "Why aren't we moving?"

He looked about him. Everyone else was frustrated as well. His hands were ready for the horn on the steering wheel. He could see a distant blue light flashing. As traffic once again inched forward, he finally could see that a Massachusetts state trooper had strategically placed his vehicle across the ramp leading to the Sumner Tunnel direct access road. Jack knew that he would have to divert to Route 1, and head north toward Revere. The detour was a common alternate route at rush hour. The state police created this diversion to prevent the airport traffic from backing up all the way to the terminals at Logan. The detour would take Jack north when he needed to go south. At the next exit, he could reverse direction and head south again toward the tunnel. The state trooper standing next to his patrol car had his arms crossed and his legs were spread-eagled as he leaned against the car door. The Massachusetts State Police have an intimidating look about them. Perhaps it's the uniform, but one avoids arguing with them when they instruct you to go in a certain direction. The aviation-style sunglasses (at this hour unneeded) hid the trooper's eyes, preventing Jack from sensing what the man was thinking. Jack headed north toward Route 1, while mumbling obscenities as he passed the flashing blue lights of the trooper's vehicle. "Dickweed!" he mumbled to himself. "I've just traveled 3,000 miles and now it's another ten out of my way." The trooper just stared back knowing that every driver was probably pissed at him. What did he care?

Who planned this airport access anyway, Jack thought. *What the hell were they thinking back then? It's always a nightmare anyway.* Road construction or traffic always affects accessibility to the airport or to the tunnels. He loved flying, but not in and out of Logan. The traffic reminded him of that.

The alternating, flashing headlights and huge flashing yellow arrow behind the police car were a reminder that he was being routed north. He would be late getting home. He was not alone tonight. Weary travelers, including Boston visitors and commuters, all had to heed the trooper's directions. The only consolation for Jack was that he knew his lady—Fawn— was waiting for him in Cambridge.

Jack and Fawn's rented apartment/condo overlooked the Charles River towards central Boston. *I could have avoided all this traffic*, he thought, *by having a drink or two at the airport until it cleared out, but I can't wait to see Fawn.* They had a fine relationship, and had recently decided to live together. Their new scenario and shared apartment was exciting to both of them. Their love was obviously growing stronger. Their desire for each other increased each time he returned from business travel. She really missed him, and was eager to have him close to her again.

Fawn DiNardi was a beauty to behold. Her figure was slight, but elegant, and she was polished and classy at twenty-nine years of age. She would be thirty in a month or so and was dreading that fact. She and Jack had met in a club near Boston Harbor when both were fresh out of recent relationships that had lacked commitment and communication. They were tired of the week-to-week dating scene between serious relationships. Every weekend was the "same ol', same ol' " bars, clubs, parties and reinventing their past history to complete strangers. It had gotten repetitive and stagnant—smoky bars and loud, obnoxious drunks. Neither of them smoked and they were tired of coming home from bars with their clothes smelling like they had smoked a pack that night.

Fawn was mostly of Italian descent with a little French tossed in. She had grown up in Boston's North End. Her father, Nick DiNardi, owned a small bakery and restaurant near the Paul Revere House. The historic area drew many people to his bakery. Not born of wealth, he had managed to save enough money to send Fawn to a well-known finishing school in New York City. He had hopes of his lovely daughter becoming a professional model. The potential was there and her facial features included a Sophia Loren-like jaw line. He felt that the jaw line was her ticket to her future modeling success. Her fashion career might serve two purposes: achieving her personal fame and saving her from a future in the family bakery business. That would be a waste of a beautiful woman, he thought. He wanted only the best for his daughter—a new way of life for her—where she would not be stifled by the restrictions of life in the North End. There was no future for her there. Bakery life for him began at four A.M.; it ended at six P.M. or later. It had taken its toll on other family members and he did not want it taking its toll on her. He saved his "bread money" to send her to school.

Fawn did well for a while at school where she was recognized for her potential in the business. Hassled by New York's lifestyle, Fawn returned to Boston in an attempt to model for catalog stores such as JC Penney and Sears. She had visions of modeling for large department stores in the Washington Street area of downtown Boston. Filene's, Macy's and other high-end department stores might provide her with increased exposure. *After all,* she thought, *the Boston newspapers are mostly advertisements anyway. Pages and pages of ads dominate the papers with intermittent news articles, especially on Sunday.*

Although their news sources were respectable and their stories generally well-written, the Boston papers were inundated with clothing ads and models in their latest fashions. Fawn might also get involved with the Newbury Street scene. The shops on Newbury Street had the finest leather, shoes and fabrics from around the world. She would be an excellent hometown model for any one of them. *Not a bad career,* she often thought. She would be close to her family. Perhaps she would be seen by Victoria's Secret and replace one of the five beauties that saturated their catalogs. Her dreams at almost thirty were possible but somewhat unlikely. Competing with the likes of Naomi Campbell and other fine models was only a goal at this point. Wonder Bras and nighttime apparel were not really what she wanted to be seen in. Her father, a devout Catholic Italian, would not be happy with that kind of modeling—of that she was sure.

Jack was now headed north on the Route 1 diversion. He was still only two miles away from Logan Airport. He signaled right to exit the highway and once again was bogged down by the traffic on the ramp. He would finally be heading southwest toward the Sumner Tunnel. His thoughts of Fawn were focused on how they first met near Lewis Wharf on Boston's historic harbor-front area. Now, after being on the road for four days, he was anxious to make love to her in their new abode. She would be equally as excited to see him. This could mean he would have a "hump till you drop" night of marathon sex—something to compete with the *real* Boston Marathon.

Fawn's genetics of French and Italian descent had naturally created a very sensitive and seductive woman. Just the thought of her sent a rush to his brain, and libido. The warm thoughts of her overcame his anger and frustration from all the traffic congestion that he was in. Just four days earlier, Jack and Fawn had made love on their new couch. One of their first purchases, they were anxious to christen it before he went away. Lechmere's, a department store in Cambridge, had just delivered it the day he was leaving for this trip. Fawn had wanted Jack to be sure that he knew he would be missed, and she had spent four hours that day depleting him of his bodily fluids before he left. He would like nothing better than to repeat that scene tonight.

At 6:00 P.M. Fawn arrived home from her Cambridge-based consulting job. She had bought some 1987 Grich Hills Chardonnay, and some imported cheese and crackers for appetizers. She stopped at a fish market on her way home and picked out two, one-and-one-half-pound lobsters for dinner. For dessert, she had purchased a new, peach-colored camisole with French-cut matching panties. *This is going to be a night to remember*, she thought.

Checking her Movado wristwatch, she knew that the "Jack man" would be home soon. She couldn't wait to see him and to finally not having to sleep alone. She missed Jack's body beside her at night. She had become used to having him around. All that she really wanted was more and more of him. He loved the attention. She was everything that he needed physically and emotionally.

Although modeling was her desire in life, Fawn had taken a job locally as an executive secretary/administrative assistant reporting to the vice president of research at Global Computer Consultants in Cambridge. It was located on Memorial Drive a short distance from where they lived. Her modest but adequate salary added another $42,000 to Jack's already stable income of $98,000, and she was due for a merit increase in a month or so.

She had left New York only a few months earlier. She could always practice her beauty and modeling in front of visitors to her company. Since she never knew who might be visiting Global, someone linked to that industry might walk in the lobby and discover her, right there. Global had a wide clientele from major industries passing through their offices every day; they dealt with advertising agencies as well. She daydreamed often at work of being discovered.

Jack's yearly bonus would bring him up to $110K by year end. Together their salaries made for very comfortable living. They dined out often and went to the theater. They began saving some money in hopes of owning their own place someday.

Fawn sat quietly on the couch absorbing the latest Martha Stewart magazine, *Living*, which had just arrived. She transposed many of Martha's ideas into her future home. Someday she would have a house that looked like the magazine pictures. Gardens, fences, flower pots and unique furniture would adorn her fantasy abode. For tonight, she would peruse the fancy dessert recipes and an article on antique tea strainers while she waited for Jack.

8

At 7:35 P.M., Captain Bullock was given permission by Tower Central to taxi NEAir 2158 to north-facing Runway 33 Left at Logan. Ground control had cleared the flight to hold in the number three position parallel to the active runway. All cockpit instruments had flight-checked normal for the twin-engine Dressler commuter. Awaiting additional tower instructions, First Officer Bell joked about the preseason exhibition game that the New England Patriots had played against the New York Jets that past Sunday. The Jets had creamed the "Pats" 35-7 at home in Foxboro Stadium—a depressing start for the Patriots. If this was an indicator of the forthcoming season, it was apparent that the stadium was a better venue for rock concerts than for football. Bob Kraft, the "Pats" owner, was not pleased. Adding to the embarrassment was the fact that the Jets now had the former "Pats" coach on board. They wanted to beat his ass bad.

"What's the problem with the 'Pats' this year, anyway?" Bullock asked. "Can't they get past the memory of Coach Parcells?"

Bell retorted, "Look at the defense! They have nobody who's healthy and the season hasn't even begun yet."

"They could use some new blood and better draft picks," said the captain, "too much money for the existing players!"

"There is no incentive to play when you're guaranteed three million per year for six years," Bell said.

"Baseball's not even over yet and here these guys are already doin' the 'exhibition' thing." Bullock said. "Maybe they'll shape up in a month or so of practice."

The drone of the left engine near Bullock could be heard through their headgear. The prop pitch was set so that no vibration could be felt while they awaited their next instructions from the ground controller.

The tower had them hold when it became apparent that they were number two or three in line for takeoff. Planes fed the runway from both sides. Runway 33L was as busy as usual and often backed up due to weather changes. As they waited, they could see five to seven aircraft behind them. Some were blocked from view by the huge wings of the 737s and 727s directly behind them. One plane lifted off to their left; the bright white lights under the wings getting smaller as it disappeared down the runway, parallel to the taxiway. Already sensing a delay, Bell advised the passengers of the impending position for takeoff. There was a minor groan of voices that could be heard through the open doorway to the cockpit. It would not be long but some people still had connections to worry about in Manchester. Bullock offered some false consolation by saying that the flight was short and that they could make the quick hop even shorter if needed. In a commuter aircraft, little time could be made up. After all this wasn't a jet, but Manchester, New Hampshire, was only a twelve to fifteen minute flight anyway.

United Flight 100, a 727 shuttle to Chicago departed Runway 33L, veering left shortly after takeoff. In the night, the flashing wing lights could be seen fading into the night sky. She would have a two-hour flight northwest to O'Hare International. The pilot of United 100 leveled off at 10,000 feet as normal and awaited further clearance to proceed to 27,000. He radioed back to Logan of "mild chop" on takeoff. This had been experienced by earlier flights as well. Winds off the Massachusetts coastline, especially near the harbor, were not uncommon. Due to noise abatement regulations at Logan, planes climbed to 10,000 feet rapidly and at a steep angle. This new ruling appeased the local residents to the north of Boston, but made for bumpy liftoffs on occasion. Mayor McGarrity of Lynnfield had worked hard to get the ruling passed during a previous election year. He had petitioned both local and Commonwealth politicians for abatement. They were sympathetic to his town's needs.

Captain Bullock, still taxiing, was now approaching Runway 33L and was about 3,000 feet away from taking off. Bullock was aware of the "backwash" or "wake turbulence" often associated with following larger aircraft out of Boston. Through his headset he could hear the instructions and advisories for the pilots ahead of him and knew that initial takeoff might be a bit rough, but the Dressler 205 was a workhorse commuter and could easily handle mild chop. She floated easily through cross winds and had significant power on takeoff. Changing the prop pitch, Bullock proceeded forward. Flight 2158 would be next and number one for takeoff. Officer Bell asked the passengers to resecure their seat belts. These short flights to New Hampshire were so routine and frequent that more time was spent on taxiways and taxiing than on actual flying. They were basically an alternative to driving an hour and fifteen minutes. Travel on the highways from Logan to Manchester could vary from one to three hours in bad weather, so the commuter flights were timesaving and less stressful.

Ground control at Logan tower had assigned North East Air flight 2158 a transponder number of 0624, a preassigned I.D. for the radar monitoring of each departing flight. The aircraft would now appear as a blip on the green radar screen at tower control at Logan. Once Flight 2158 had reached the "hash line" and was number one for takeoff, their instructions for departure would be transferred over to "tower control" from "ground control." The hash line was the stopping point demarcation line before entering the active runway.

Bullock awaited the command to proceed onto "active 33L." After an approaching aircraft from Portland, Maine, had landed, they would be cleared for takeoff.

Positioned perpendicular to the runway, Bullock felt the mild crosswinds from the Portland flight rock the Dressler 205 gently. He and Bell patiently awaited further instructions from the boys in the tower. Blinking red, white and green lights from a multitude of aircraft around the airport were a bright contrast to the dim blue taxiway lights lining the pavement.

Tower controller Frank Wells had spent much of his career as an air traffic controller at the FAA Center in Nashua, New Hampshire. The FAA's Northeast Sector of the United States, situated four miles from the Massachusetts border, was controlled by the Nashua FAA Center.

Frank was fast approaching his twenty-fifth anniversary as a controller and a party was being planned on his behalf by his immediate supervisor for December. Frank, a private pilot and expert controller at the green boards, had provided guidance to pilots of all types of aircraft for years. After time at Nashua, he had transferred to Logan, where he would complete his career. It was Frank who had gotten Captain Bullock to the hash line. With two converging taxi approaches to the "line," Frank had instructed Bullock to bear left and follow the 727 to his left. A brief burst of the three engines from a 727 had rocked the wings of the small commuter as it passed in front of the flight to New Hampshire. The 727 had been waiting at an opposing taxiway hash line and was already delayed for takeoff. Bullock, who aspired to fly jets one day, wished he was in that 727's seat.

"NEAir 2158, you're now number one," Frank said.

Bullock responded, "Roger, Tower, 2158— Number one for departure."

In the back of the Dressler 205 an assortment of businessmen and women patiently stared out their windows. The plane was often full at this hour of the night. Many commuters grabbed the last few flights in the early evening.

Those sitting by the engines could see the propellers cut through the night air and distant lights of the airport. The blurred vision through the props became surreal as the pilots changed pitch to move forward with each tower command.

Mary Hutton in seat 3A had that exact view out her window. Reacting to the jet wash from the 727, she whispered sarcastically to a passenger across the aisle, "That was cute! I wonder if these little planes can really fly?"

The passenger gently smiled and acknowledged the comment, then bowed her head down toward the new novel that she was reading. The dim light of the overhead panel reflected off the page of the book and onto her face. She wasn't paying much attention to anything but the book.

Mary Hutton, a teacher for many years, had prior flying experience, but most had been on larger aircraft. She had accompanied her students on many charter flights to Florida during school breaks.

In an effort to conserve fuel, Captain Bullock had reduced the left engine's RPMs thereby advancing the plane with only the right engine. He brought both of them up to matching RPMs before leaving the hash line. He was asked by Frank Wells to proceed onto the active runway. Adjusting the pitch of the propellers on both engines, there was a reverberating flutter that rocked the cabin back and forth as Bullock continued to move and brake near the active runway. Mary's eyes focused on a particular rivet on the wing. It danced to the vibration like a circling top, rotating feverishly to the engines' vibration. Each time the engines were "juiced" it would dance counterclockwise. *With thousands of rivets on the plane, one loose one is not an issue,* she thought. She focused on it as the brakes occasionally groaned from the stop-and-go motion below her feet. These were the noises of the night that she probably wouldn't notice if the flight was during the day. The cabin lights flickered off and on and Mary adjusted her seat belt—low and across her lap—one more time. This was force of habit for her, even though it was secured some three minutes earlier at the first officer's request. Each tightening of the belt made her feel safer. After one or two deep sighs, she closed her eyes and relaxed against the headrest.

With the sound of a muted bell, the NO SMOKING sign illuminated above her head. *The red slash across the facsimile of a cigarette seems frivolous and unnecessary,* she thought, *since the FAA had banned smoking ages ago on all flights.* The plane must have been an older model if the NO SMOKING sign was part of the overhead compartment. It lit up in conjunction with the FASTEN SEAT BELT sign. *A reminder to fasten one's seat belt also seems redundant. One would have had to grow up in a closet not to know when or how to do that! More bureaucratic rules of the FAA,* she thought, as she smiled to herself.

The passenger on Mary's right, across the aisle, was now fast asleep. The novel resting in her hands, was still perched under the beam of the overhead light.

The safety information card, read by almost no one, poked out of the seat pocket in front of Mary. Written in four languages, the tri-folded instruction card highlighted the emergency exits. Mary's closest functional exit was the one marked "C" on the card. It would be directly in front of her if needed. "A" and "B" exits were in the rear of the aircraft. She scanned the card and found the schematics of the people and their fashions obsolete. *When was this plane made anyway?* she wondered. *It looked newer than the card!* She replaced the card in front of the little paper bag in the seat pouch. Even the bag had instructions on how to fold it after "motion discomfort." Cute little phrase for vomiting, she thought. Basically, the airline expected you to read the instructions before, or shortly after filling the bag. Behind the bag was a copy of the airline's award-winning *High Flyer* magazine. *An odd name,* she thought, *for a magazine on low-flying commuters.* After all they wouldn't be flying all that high and the magazine title was more applicable to the larger, higher-flying aircraft. Sitting there all sweaty, and pale with a green glow, they expected you to read something! No instructions needed for her. She could fold it if needed. As a frequent user of the dermal patch for motion sickness, she convinced herself that she had no need for the little bag. During these thoughts, the plane was close to being positioned for takeoff. Turning on the plane's landing lights, 2158 would await the ground controller's instructions.

Meanwhile, Jack had made it to Airport Boulevard West and reached for the cellular phone in his briefcase. He would call Fawn and hope that dinner was not already on the stove. He had made little progress in the last few minutes. A call to her would make him feel better. In this kind of situation, just the sound of her voice would relax him.

9

Captain Pete Thompson had been a crusty lobster fisherman for more than thirty-two years. He had been seeking the crustacean *Homarus americanus,* otherwise known as the common Maine lobster for more than three decades. His boat, the *Ellie May*, was almost his age, and was kept at a fishing wharf near Chelsea, Massachusetts. The *Ellie May* was a fixture around the harbor, and while in port, frequently served as a seagull perch. The red paint had been christened with many a white gull dropping over the years. The mast and other high perches received the greatest abuse; gulls prefer to crap from high places. The vessel was a diesel-powered, low-draft boat with a white stripe along both sides. The gunwales were typical and enabled lobster fishermen to haul in the heavy traps each day without killing themselves or straining their backs. Captain Thompson's lobster trap markers were hand-painted buoys that matched the boat's color and stripes. Everyone knew "Capt'n Pete" and the color sequence of his traps. He moored his *Ellie* just off shore in Chelsea at Bud Travis's Boat Yard.

Old Bud was about the same age as Pete but had long ago given up the fishing business to run the boatyard. He no longer cared for the winters at sea or the danger in foul weather; he figured he had enough "salt in his veins." Bud was comfortable just running the boatyard and being around other fishermen. He was a storyteller as well. Over the years he had told a lot of them, mostly exaggerations of his trips at sea.

Except for an occasional run, when Atlantic bluefish were in season, Pete Thompson was generally out each day checking his thirty to forty lobster pots, which were most often strewn in the outer harbor northeast of

Logan Airport. No one ever questioned Pete's skills or credentials as a captain since he had always been known as "Capt'n Pete." It didn't matter if his "title" was self-appointed or if he had certification of the accolade; he had been out there far too many years for anyone to question his credentials as a seaman. A Xerox copy of a pseudocertificate of his "credentials" was framed in the wheelhouse of the *Ellie May*. It was so faded that it could hardly be read. No one really cared anyway. Even the harbor patrol knew him as captain. With the facial profile of an Old Salt typified in an Winslow Homer painting, or described in Ernest Hemingway's *Old Man and the Sea*, Captain Pete's weathered face and white beard brought him all the credibility that he needed.

For years many of the lobstermen in the area had relied on Captain Pete's lobster charts that predicted the best spots for traps to be laid out. He shared his knowledge with friends since he felt there were plenty of the beasts to go around. These cold-water delicacies liked the deep, frigid water and often sought out holes in rocky areas to hide. Pete knew by memory where they were most likely to be. *I don't need any sophisticated, fancy-dandy equipment to find 'em*, he thought. Many years of fishing off the Boston harbor entrance had taught him the best spots to lower the traps.

A native of Maine near Casco Bay, Thompson had lived near Portland for many years and married his high school sweetheart, Ellie May Browning. A widower now, Pete's entire life was the sea. Ellie May had succumbed to uterine cancer after a period of prolonged agony and pain. He had no reason to remain in Portland—there were many painful reminders of their life together. He returned to her grave on occasion, always on Memorial Day, Christmas Day, their anniversary and her birthday. That was reminder enough. Even on the coldest anniversary dates, he would bring flowers to her grave. She had many gardens in their yard and this was a token memory of her love for their beauty and fragrance. Pete was a crusty old salt, but a sentimental one.

Only a few friends saw that side of him. The remainder of the time he was busy at sea. His memories of his devoted wife were perpetually maintained on the stern of his boat, as well as the sides of the wheelhouse. Two circular life buoys also were emblazoned with the name *Ellie May*. Every day he checked to make sure some son-of-a bitch'n gull hadn't tainted the letters of her name. If they had, he cleaned it up immediately. A bottle of Windex on board always guaranteed that her name would be bright and clean. A small photo of them together graced the clipboard over the boat's wheel. He and Ellie May were much younger in the picture—he could not remember the date when it was taken. He just liked the pose and her smile. At sea, she was always with him, in spirit. He felt her luck every day that the catch was good. He never blamed her when the catch was short.

The previous week Pete had won a quick fifty bucks at bingo at a nearby church. On Tuesdays he had nothing to do so months earlier he started socializing with friends every other Tuesday night. With his winnings, he bought a new yellow slicker—some called it foul-weather gear—to wear on the boat. He was wearing it this night.

He would be unloading his catch shortly as dusk came over the harbor. The now overcast sky made it darker earlier that night. He cast his cigarette to the sea and negotiated the *Ellie* to a fishing pier at Commercial Wharf. His exhaled smoke from the last drag was followed by a hacking cough typical of longtime smokers.

Pete had long dealt his catch to Bay Harbor Lobster Company, which for years had provided local fish markets and smaller restaurants with the finest of the crustaceans. Once considered a garbage fish unfit to eat, the two-clawed, high-protein creature soon became the favorite meal for tourists who spent time in New England. From Maine to Cape Cod, the delicacy of the lobster was renowned.

A man who worked at the lobster company spotted him coming in and met him at the pier.

"How'd ya do, Pete?" he asked.

"I've got a couple hundred for you," he shouted back.

Captain Pete had eased the *Ellie May* against the pier while the dockhand tied her up. A squeak here and there could be heard as the bow touched the rubber pier bumpers of the dock.

"I even had a blue one for you," he continued. "But the chick was too small. Had to throw her back."

"Too bad," the dockhand said. "Haven't seen one in awhile."

"Me neither . . . cute little bugger," Pete added.

A rare find indeed. When a lobsterman was lucky enough to catch a "blue" lobster it often ended up in the New England Aquarium for all to see. A genetic anomaly, the shell of some lobsters was blue, instead of dark green. *I might catch her again someday*, he thought, *when she's of legal size*. The largest blue Capt'n Pete had ever seen was fourteen to sixteen pounds. Fishermen had respect for the blues. The "old codgers" who had fished these parts for years thought the blues brought them good luck, sort of like a lucky penny or four-leaf clover.

Thompson grasped the mooring line with his wrinkled hands that were chapped from weather and age. Finally secured to the fish pier, the *Ellie May* rocked quietly against the old wooden structure. The weight of the lobsters in the hold kept her stable. Three fluorescent orange flotation balls with tethers helped buffer her from dock damage. Just before docking, he tossed them over the side.

"Only been out a day or two," he shouted, "but not a bad catch."

"Any large ones in the bunch?" asked the dockhand.

"Yeh, a sixteen-pounder, I think," he answered.

"Really? Got a buyer for that one!" came the reply.

"Sure," Pete said. "You get eighty bucks and I get twenty-five of it! Where's the fairness?"

That one lobster will command a good price for the Lobster Company, he thought. People often bought them for larger parties or to impress friends. The claws would be five to six inches across. The captain was tired. He had checked the pots every other day, in good weather, to prevent cannibalization by the lobsters if the traps became too full. With nothing left to eat after the bait was gone, they start looking at one another as food—victims of Darwin's theory.

This trip Pete had been lucky since only one buoy was adrift. Lines were often accidentally cut by the propellers of other fishing boats. If they weren't recovered, they ended up on the shoreline and became souvenirs for beachcombers.

Pete was from the old school of lobstering. He used the traditional traps made of wood and netting. He weighed them down with cement squares placed strategically in the trap compartments. His lobster license registration number, a required permit, was embossed in the cement blocks and on his lobster buoys. Lobsters are bottom feeders, so the traps must rest on the bottom of the ocean in order to catch them. The floating buoy is attached by a rope to each pot to mark the location of the trap. The color code on each buoy is unique and establishes ownership of the traps.

Pete brought in some traps that needed repair. They were stacked tall in the back of his boat. Once the lobsters were removed from the traps while at sea, he would examine each trap for rips and tears in the netting and broken wooden slats. On shore in the off hours, he would repair them by sewing the netting and replacing the broken wood. After all, a trap out of water was no trap at all. Lost revenue was incurred when they were on land for repair instead of under the deep blue. Nothing seemed to bother the old man since his age almost matched that of the boat, winches, traps and lines. These tools were his life. *Don't fix nothin' that don't need fixin'*, he thought.

Beside the *Ellie May* life preserver stood the American flag. It moved gently in the light evening wind as Pete jumped from the side of the boat to the dock. The dock lights illuminated the boat and cast a yellow hue over the white boat stripes. He would need help unloading the catch. For him, the day was not over yet and some of the hardest work still needed to be done. They would need to transfer the lobsters from the boat to the chilled seawater holding tanks inside the Bay Harbor Lobster Company building.

Across the harbor, a 747 bound for Europe lifted off at Logan. The bright light on the rudder illuminated the logo for Air Europe. Departing initially to the northwest, she passed over the *Ellie May* on her ascent into the night sky. Her nighttime journey would get her to Switzerland at day-break, European time. She banked right and headed east into the cloud cover over the open ocean.

The Bay Harbor Lobster Company had been in business for over fifty years and Ted Price, the owner, came out to personally greet his old friend, the captain. Price was working late that evening and had stuck around to see Pete before he headed home himself.

"You goin' out again tomorrow?" he asked. "Hope not," he continued. "Supposed to be rough seas."

"Hey, Ted, sorry . . . didn't see ya," Pete replied. "Is theya any day that I'm not theya?" barked the old sea dog. "How else can I keep you and the boys in business? You'd be broke without me! Since ya heah, why not help me unload? That way I can get home earlier! Plus, you probably have nothin' to do," Pete said, as he lit up a cigarette.

Ted Price laughed and just stood there with his hands on his hips and said, "Ya know . . . I was goin' ta help ya but you was so busy griping—maybe I'll just go home!"

"Wad eva!" Pete replied. "Ya need ya sleep!"

The first drag from Pete's cigarette made him cough, but that didn't bother him. He had been smoking for thirty-six years and nothing would make him stop now.

"Ya dang fool, give me a hand. I ain't got all night, ya know! After unloadin', I'll need to head north and touch base back home. The *Ellie May*'s been runnin' rough and I may need to mess with the engines tonight if I'm to get out again t'morra."

"OK. OK!" Ted responded. "You're damn lucky ya got me—as a friend. No one else would put up with an ol' fart like you!"

"Ol' fart? Who ya callin' ol' fart? You're older than me!"

"Don't think so—you've just forgotten your age!" Ted quipped.

"Got any dockhands back there?" Captain Pete asked Ted. "Sure would speed up the process. Ya know me, I hate runnin' the *Ellie* at night between them red and green buoys. These old eyes don't work so good at night."

"I'll see who's still back theya," mimicked Price as he headed back to the lobster shack.

Pete could hear him calling for one or two dockhands who might be available to help unload the catch. Dusk had fast become darkness. Stars were masked by the clouds that had rolled in.

As he waited for help, the dock lights cast an eerie shadow on the captain's face. His eyes, with bags under them, were tired from the night's journey. The lines below his eyes were a testimony to the long days at sea. His "baby blues" normally matched the color of the ocean on a sunny day. Cataracts had reduced his night vision substantially. He knew that at some point he would need surgery to correct the problem, but taking time off for that would mean the loss of income. He couldn't do that at this time without being financially strapped. The boat maintenance was expensive in Boston Harbor.

Recent repairs to the *Ellie May* had yet to be paid off and lobster prices were down from the wholesalers this year. The loan on the boat had a few years to go. Pete once thought a decent wage could be earned lobstering, but with the overfishing of the harbor and the influx of Canadian lobster imports, competition was strong. Retailers were only getting $3.25 to $5.00 a pound so wholesale prices were one-half of that. *It's hardly worth the effort*, he thought. He flicked his cigarette into the water.

Two of Price's employees came out to help unload the lobsters and Captain Pete grabbed a hose to wash down the deck. Seaweed and extraneous marine life from the traps made for a slimy and slippery deck. He would need to remove the mess as soon as possible to maintain the *Ellie May* deck in good condition. Ted Price provided the free hose and water to his friend.

They basically relied on each other to survive. It was a symbiotic relationship of friendship and perseverance over the good and bad seasons.

"Come on you guys! Shake a leg . . . we ain't got all night!" Price ordered his men.

"We're comin', we're comin' . . . why you so late?" a dockhand asked Pete.

"Never you mind, just unload," said the foreman. "You guys want a check this week? If so, start unloadin'!"

It took no time at all to transfer the lobsters. Everyone pitched in and the boat was emptied and cleaned quickly. Thirty-five minutes later, with the lobsters unloaded and their claws banded, Captain Thompson fired up the *Ellie May* and proceeded north toward Chelsea. It would be well after nine before he would see home port. He hoped the rough-running engines would get him there.

"Catch ya layda," he called back to Price. "Many thanks, guys!"

"See ya t'morra, Pete," was the response from the dock. "Safe travel!"

"Ayut. Bye fur nah." His voice faded in the sound of the boat motors.

The stern lights on the *Ellie May* glowed in the night as he departed from the dock. The journey home never seemed to get any shorter for Pete and this night's was to be longer than he would ever imagine. He normally could time the trip home down to the minute but halfway home his plans would be altered.

He lit another cigarette and headed into the windy harbor. There was a slight chill in the evening air. Pete looked at his watch. It was 7:30 P.M. A half-moon broke through a ragged spot in the clouds.

10

Fawn peered out of her bedroom window high above the Charles River and stood motionless looking at the Boston skyline to the south. Tall buildings, across the river behind the outdoor Hatch Shell performance center, became illuminated as the office lights on each floor contrasted with the night sky. All was quiet at the Hatch Shell tonight where on the night before Maestro Ozawa and the Boston Pops Orchestra had performed. Many nights, with the right wind, she and Jack could sip wine and enjoy the music from across the river. The small balcony of their apartment faced the Hatch Shell and a lone lounge chair was shared by both of them on soft summer nights. More than once they had made love during a Pops performance.

Tonight, the only music playing was in their living room. The Gordon Lightfoot "Don Quixote" album from his early days had just been re-released on CD and she would surprise Jack with its soft, acoustic tunes. Candlelight created a romantic effect for the dinner table.

She cast her eyes right to the top of the old John Hancock Insurance Company building. A landmark of its own, it stood adjacent to the new John Hancock, dwarfed by the newer "Tower of Glass." The top of the older building had a three-color light tower that for decades predicted Boston weather. Tonight the lights atop the tower were "blue," which indicated foul weather approaching. If the lights were "red," it meant severe weather. To the east and west there was cloud cover moving in from two fronts. There would be no "green light" at the tower to indicate clear weather.

The city is real pretty at night, Fawn thought. Between the cloud cover, a half-moon and city lights reflected on the water below their rented apartment. Shadows of sailboats dotted the other side of the Charles River. She had taken sailing lessons from the University Club there when she was younger. The Museum of Science was a shadow to the left and the domed Omni Theatre was reminiscent of a miniature United States Capitol building. The condo might hopefully be theirs someday. They had an option to buy it and she knew that if her relationship with Jack grew, they would eventually keep the unit. She decorated it as if it would be theirs for the future. She was in love and maintained a nice home for both of them. If they never had the larger dream house, that was OK. She could be perfectly happy right there on the water.

The softness of the night was startled by the ring of the telephone. Fawn lowered the Gordon Lightfoot tunes on the stereo and picked up the phone in the living room.

Jack's voice was bright and clear after she said hello. He was OK and that's all she cared about.

"Sorry, honey," he said. "Guess where I am? The first two guesses don't count," he said.

"East Boston?" she asked.

"Yes, hon . . . East Boston . . . it's gonna be a while. You wouldn't believe the traffic. I've been on the ground for some time and nothing is moving west. I have no idea when this will clear out. It could be a long, long while!"

"OK, hon, I'll read a magazine or somethin'. At least you're back in town. Did you have a decent trip?"

"Yeh . . . it was fine . . . just long . . . you know the routine."

"If it's any consolation, I really miss you!" Fawn added.

"Me, too. I'll be there as quick as I can. I'll keep you posted, hon. Bye for now."

He clicked off the cell phone and stared out the car windshield. *Damn. It will be a long night*, he thought. His headlights were shining on the trunk in front of him. A bumper sticker said ONE DAY AT A TIME. *Shit*, he thought, *another reformed alcoholic*. The platitude, however, did mimic the current traffic conditions, so he smiled.

After she hung up, Fawn gazed into the adjoining room where the dining room table was set. Their temporary set of used furniture looked beautiful. She had covered it with a lace tablecloth, new cloth napkins and her grandmother's silverware. Two candleholders were centered around a fresh bouquet of flowers. The romantic place settings and table arrangements were perfect. It was a "Martha Stewart" table setting, just like the one shown in a recent issue of her magazine. She gently blew out the candles for now. It would be a while before Jack would be there and she didn't want to waste them. The smoke from each candle ascended and curled about the flower arrangement.

Fawn plopped herself down in the enormous easy chair near the couch and draped her long legs across one of its arms. Her petite frame was dwarfed by the huge chair. After hearing from Jack and convinced that he was home safe, she relaxed and felt much better. At least now he could keep her posted on his progress and be in touch as needed.

She turned off the stereo and flipped on the local Channel 3 news. "Skycam," the station's traffic monitoring helicopter camera, showed the north and south expressways. Traffic was not moving. She switched from a "breaking" story to a talk show about celebrities. The lobsters Fawn had purchased sat in the sink and would shortly end up back in the refrigerator. They would need to be chilled since dinner would not be for a while.

The lights of a Fenway Park night baseball game and the illuminated CITGO sign caught her eye. She knew that the "BoSox" were in town but couldn't remember who they were playing. It didn't really matter since she and Jack wouldn't be going tonight anyway. As she rechecked the stove and the lobster pot, she could hear a distant roar at Fenway. A home run perhaps? Who cared? She was there and he was elsewhere. Depressed that Jack was going to be late, she clicked the TV remote aimlessly through channels until she found the Red Sox game. Sipping a glass of wine, she gazed out the balcony doorway and windows in hopes that Jack would call back with some good news about his progress in the traffic. It would be the first of three glasses of wine for her and she longed for the man that she loved. When he got home, dinner might have to wait. She would want to make love first, since the wine had just taken her to a new psychological level. Her body was warmed throughout and Jack was going to benefit from the chardonnay. He might even be glad that he had been stuck in traffic for a while.

11

Fred and Dave, two Metropolitan District Commission (MDC) tow truck operators for the Sumner Tunnel, sat in the yellow booth next to the west-side exit. Their MDC wrecker adjacent to the booth was affectionately named "Ms. Sumner." On this night, traffic flow to the tunnels was heavy in both the Callahan east, and Sumner west. Earlier in the evening, a flat tire on a Saab 900 had delayed the traffic flow until Fred and Dave could get to the car and tow her out. The female driver was more concerned about how people would feel about her than the flat. *After all*, she thought to herself, *I've really screwed up the tunnel with this damn tire*. She was stranded in the tunnel at midpoint, about one-half mile from either end. This forced the two lanes in the tunnel down to one until help could arrive. In Boston, that amount of time can be an eternity and was a serious problem for the tunnel during peak traffic flow. Bostonians, having no patience at all, would not find the situation amusing. Although her local Saab dealership had a free tow policy as an incentive to buy their cars, they would not be reachable by cellular phone from inside the tunnel.

It didn't matter because the MDC provided free tow service. That was exactly why Fred and Dave sat there waiting. "Free Tow from Tunnel" was even written on the side of the truck. An emergency phone, a direct line to MDC help, was just outside her car window on the tiled wall of the tunnel. The exhaust residue on the tiles also coated the phone and receiver. She found it repulsive. Picking it up, she had immediate contact with the crew at the end of the Sumner. Amid the car horns and cat calls from passing drivers, she was able to describe her problem to the tow crew.

The crew entered the tunnel cautiously with "Ms. Sumner." They were backing in against the flow of traffic but had to wait until the congestion decreased to get to her. Yellow lights from the truck showed brightly against the tile and flashed for some distance down into the Sumner. Other drivers behind her could see the lights in the distance. For them it was a welcome sight because that meant that the problem would be corrected soon and normal traffic flow could resume.

The embarrassed woman returned to the car after making the call; she did not want to be outside her car while awaiting help. It was safer in the vehicle and she wanted to avoid being stared at by irate drivers behind her. Of course, no one would get out and help. Instead they just gawked at her situation. Gentlemen don't seem to exist in this situation. She could see the yellow lights getting closer. She chewed nervously on some antacid tablets in anticipation. She held her AAA card in her shaking hand.

It seemed like an eternity to her before Fred and Dave arrived to assist her but it was really just a short time before they backed up in front of her car. Dave jumped out and stopped traffic in the other lane. They knew exactly what to do.

The MDC was discouraged from changing flats in the Sumner or Callahan Tunnel and they decided to tow her out of the tunnel as quickly as possible. This would expedite a return to traffic flow and give the boys a chance to change her tire safely on the outside. Lighting would be better under the sodium lamps. The tunnel's lighting was dingy and had low footcandles. More modern tubular lighting was definitely needed.

Fred and Dave were quick to get the car rigged for towing. A specialized dolly was used to elevate the side with the flat. It would get the car out without ruining the wheel and tire. Not much was said since they were busy and occasionally staring at her when she wasn't looking. The woman had the choice of riding in the car or up front in "Ms. Sumner." She chose the latter for safety.

Because Fred would be driving, Dave helped her get up into the cab of the truck. The woman was attractive and Dave raised his eyebrows twice to Fred as they finally got into the truck cab. They were not used to having someone as pretty as her up front with them. She was all class and they were glad they could be of service. Her perfume was "Oscar" as in Oscar de la Renta. That fragrance would linger in the cab after she left. Outside the tunnel, Dave helped her down from the cab. She felt a sigh of relief seeing both lanes of the tunnel now moving. She knew people were aggravated but there was nothing she could have done differently.

"Thanks for the tow, guys."

"No problem ma'am, that's what we're he-ah fa." Fred smiled.

"We'll get ya on the road soon," Dave piped in, "you'll be good as new."

Under the high intensity lights outside the tunnel, the two men worked fast to lower the Saab and repair the flat. They would need to get back to the tow area soon since there was no other backup crew. The spare tire that Dave took out of the trunk was not much better than the tire they had removed. It looked bad but was holding air; that made the tow crew happy.

"Now, ma'am, don't drive too long on this one," Fred said. "It's not all that good and you could be in trouble all over again."

"I know," she said. "Been meanin' to get a new tire. That one doesn't look too good, does it?" she commented.

"Right on, ma'am. Probably want to take care of this one right away."

Dave reminded her, "Remember ma'am, you have no spare now."

She nodded to them in the affirmative as they tightened the lug nuts on the rear wheel. The one that they removed and placed in the trunk would not be repairable. A piece of metal had cut through the side wall.

"Thank you gentlemen," she exclaimed. "You guys are lifesavers! May I offer you a twenty for your time?" They smiled and declined the offer saying that it was their pleasure, and their job, to help. She gave them each a brief hug and was on her way. That was reward enough. They should have that kind of gratitude from all female drivers with disabled vehicles.

"Geez, that never happens!" Dave said.

"Not a chance," Fred joked.

"Did you smell that perfume? Damn expensive stuff. . . . Damn she was hot!"

"She's 'bout as good as it gets, I'd say!" Dave was scratching his head and still staring as she drove off.

"Did you see that ass?"

"Yeh, are you kiddin'? 'Course!" Fred responded with a gasp. "She was a ten if anyone was."

"Did you see those legs?" Dave retorted. "She was some package!"

"Yeh, someone's doin' that and it ain't us—somewhere in Beantown, there's a lucky guy!" Dave said.

"Maybe not, man. Maybe she's a lesbo," Fred joked.

"Fat chance," laughed Dave in amazement. "There's just no way! If she were, I'd be the first one out there tryin' ta cure her!"

"You couldn't cure a ham . . . you idiot! Not a friggin' ham."

"Asshole!"

They both lit cigarettes. Fred turned on the yellow flashers on top of the truck's cab so that they could cross over three lanes to the MDC hut near the exit of the Sumner. They backed the truck up and could still smell the perfume's lingering fragrance as they jumped down out of the truck. Back in the little MDC office, they started telling jokes to each another. That occupied them until another crisis. Every once in a while they thought of their "lady in distress." It would be days before their conversation would change to something else.

Jack Danton, inching his way toward the Sumner Tunnel, could finally see the tollbooths on his left. A Delta Airline billboard on the right side of the roadway caught his eye. Next to that billboard he noticed a cigarette advertisement. The gorgeous woman in the ad was lounging in a white chair on pink sand in front of calm turquoise water. *That's Bermuda!* he thought. It sure looked like Warwick Long Bay, a beach on the island's south shore.

The serenity of the billboard ad reminded Jack of his only trip to Bermuda with Fawn. Falling in love there was easy. The island just set the mood for them. They had gotten along famously and the vacation had jelled their relationship. They could use another trip like that again—except that their financial priorities were now some furniture for the new abode.

Jack's mind wandered back and forth between Bermuda's Chaplin Bay and Jobson's Cove, two exquisite hideaways near Warwick's Long Bay. A couple could escape from reality there. The coves were within walking distance to Mermaid Beach Club or the Sonesta Beach Resort on South Road. From Mermaid Beach, it was a straight shot along a gorgeous half-mile beach. They had chosen the Mermaid Beach Club as part of a vacation package plan. Meals were included in the total price and there was a private beach directly off their room. This was their first trip alone to an exotic paradise. They treated it like a real honeymoon even though they were not married. As much time was spent in their room as was spent on the beach.

Just then, behind Jack there was a surprise horn blast—far louder than expected for the size of the truck it came from. The idiot behind him had grown impatient. With his mind off the traffic and lost in thoughts of Bermuda, Jack was not moving ahead fast enough for the driver of the truck. In fact, Jack's hesitation allowed some other car to cut in, and that really upset the guy behind him.

"Eat me!" he said out loud to himself, as if the guy could hear him. "Where the hell do you think we can go anyway?" he muttered to himself. They were at a standstill again and Jack returned his thoughts to Bermuda.

It had only been a couple months since they had been there last and Jack and Fawn had the good fortune of fine weather. Since Bermuda is located 600 miles off the coast of North Carolina, winters there are cool. Located north of the Caribbean, weather remains warm throughout September. Although high season is May to October, the best time to go to Bermuda is in the late spring and early fall. June and July are optimum months, but the island is often overrun by passengers from cruise ships and honeymooners. The island during the summer months is in bloom with hibiscus and oleander. He remembered that a lot of flowers were out when they were there and he would go back in a heartbeat; perhaps next year when finances permitted it.

Still stalled in traffic, he continued to drift to the memory of Bermuda. The one-and-one-half hour flight from Logan was exceptional, he recalled. He and Fawn had been assigned seats number 45A and B. In the back of the plane, they were near the rest rooms, food service and garment bag closets. Basically they were assigned seats in the tail of an L1011. They really didn't care what seats they had as long as the plane was going to Bermuda.

Jack had surprised Fawn with a stretch limousine to the airport complete with a bottle of "Dom" and a shrimp platter. Chilled glasses and a cheese and cracker plate were also in the back. A dozen roses awaited Fawn as well—not just roses but "Sterling" roses. These fragrant, lavender beauties were three times the cost of regular long stems and were hard to find. The Cambridge Limousine Service had helped Jack order the flowers and appetizers and Fawn was in ecstasy when she first smelled the Sterling fragrance. For the short ride to the airport from Cambridge, Fawn and Jack toasted their love and then became entwined in a loving embrace for the entire ride to Terminal C. Subtle "I love you's" were exchanged along the way.

They were dressed the part for Bermuda in their pastel-colored clothes and casual shoes. Fawn radiated a glow in the morning, perhaps because of her beautiful hair and complexion. Her hair hung down and approached her waistline—a "Crystal Gayle look-alike" of sorts, but the hair was not nine feet long. She had a shimmering henna that accented red highlights in the sun. Her facial skin was perfect, the result of the use of a mild cleansing agent, rather than soap, at night. She was her own commercial for beauty cream.

Once checked in at the gate, they would soon be boarding. One of the two passports had expired but a current driver's license got them by. After all, they weren't going to Eastern Europe, just Bermuda. This trip wasn't to the Middle East or FBI, FAA or CIA restricted.

He and Fawn were more than ready to begin their well-deserved vacation. Once they boarded Bermuda Air Flight 54, he envisioned enjoying some cocktails at cruising altitude. Climbing to 10,000 feet, the plane leveled off and headed slightly southeast, toward the rising sun. The weather was conducive to an on-time arrival at BDA, Bermuda's International Airport.

He flagged down a passing flight attendant as soon as they began to move about the aisle. Ordering some champagne, he had another motive for getting started with the bubbly wine. He had planned the seating assignment to be near the rear of the aircraft. Aside from being safe in the tail of a plane, the seats were strategically located near the bathrooms, which lined the back wall like a series of porta-potties. Fawn had no idea that she was about to join the "Mile High Club."

Jack had hoped to get a few cocktails in her and then sneak back to one of the bathrooms to pursue a little action. Soon most passengers had settled into the flight, the movie had started and the flight attendants were between service. Fawn was nestled against his shoulder and a bit giddy from the champagne.

"Are you a member?" he whispered into her left ear.

"Member? Member of what?" she responded.

"The Club," he smiled. "The 'Mile High Club'."

She looked at him and in a coy fashion said, "What might that be? Having sex in Denver?"

"No silly, the Mile High Club . . . in an airplane," he whispered. She chuckled a bit and pretended hard not to understand.

"Is this one of those Frequent Flyer deals you get for lots of travel?" she asked.

"No, no . . . it's when you have sex in an airplane, ya know when you're a mile high up," he slurred his words again. His eyes were glassy and he blinked a lot. They were dry from the champagne.

At this point they were both feeling no pain and the champagne was giving them a fine buzz. She pretended to act stupid.

"Are we higher than 5,280 feet?" she asked.

"Yes, yes, of course. Look out the window, we are above the clouds. We're cruisin' at 35,000 feet," he whispered. "That's almost seven miles up," he grinned.

The captain had just told them the altitude and speed of the plane over the intercom.

Jack said, "Come on, I'll show you somethin'."

He plans to show me something all right, she thought.

His hand gently in hers, he took her to the back of the plane. No one else had need for the bathrooms and they quietly slipped in front of stall number three. The flight attendants had moved to the center portion of the plane to begin stacking breakfast platters on the cart. It would be some time before the flight attendants reached Jack and Fawn's row.

"It says vacant," he said excitedly. Look, it says vacant!"

"I can't go in there with you!" she said timidly. "Someone will see us."

Looking left, then right, over his shoulder, he surveyed the situation. No one was in the back of the plane or in the aisles. They were alone in the back.

"Sure ya can . . . come on . . . just follow me." She did.

A few bumps at cruising altitude had kept the FASTEN SEAT BELT sign on and the captain was reluctant to turn it off for a while. Everyone but the love birds were in their seats. Jack gently closed the door behind Fawn. The space in the L1011's bathroom was large, compared with other planes, but it was not designed for two people. He quickly secured the latch as the internal light came on above them. Outside their door, a small "occupied" sign lit up. The remainder of the doors about them remained unlit with a "vacant" sign. Facing the back wall of the small room, Jack reached around her and lowered the seat cover on the toilet. He kissed her neck and lower ear tenderly and gently unsnapped her bra, all in one motion, a two-fingered technique he had perfected in high school.

"Are you sure about this?" she asked cautiously. "What will people think when we come out of here together?"

71

Thinking as a man "in heat" he retorted, "Not to worry—no one will even know. Everyone is waiting for the pancakes and sausage "deal," so they don't even know we're in here."

Fawn looked up into his eyes and, feeling reassured by his comments, gently sat down on the toilet seat. Her desires were now heightened as she felt the front of his jeans and saw how excited he was. He was facing her with his back to the door, his eyes closed and head tilted slightly back. She slowly unbuckled the belt on his pants and could hear him breathing deeply. Unzipping his fly she gently lowered his pants to knee level. The slow and gentle process was exhilarating for both of them. No one or time mattered at this moment. He was in ecstasy as her moistened lips encompassed him. She adored him and took her time to please him. She loved the moment as much as he did. Oral sex was very gratifying to her as well. Prior to him, she was not well versed in it but he was a good teacher and communicator during sex, and told her what was most pleasing to him. Not wanting to disappoint him, she listened to his lustful comments and became expert at knowing what he loved the most.

At first motionless, he was not to deny her. He gently fondled her nipples and touched her inner thighs. She had helped him unbutton her shorts as well, making it easy for him to excite her with foreplay. He was magical at making her feel as good as he felt at this moment. Neither of them could stand the heightened excitement any longer and she wanted him inside her.

Jack gently had Fawn stand and turn to face the back wall. Caressing both her breasts from behind, he moved his hands down to her waist. Her white jean shorts fell to her ankles as he touched the inside of her pelvic area. It was clear that she was aroused. Her head leaned back on his shoulder as she breathed a deep moan by his ear. Nothing would stop this moment now, not even a headfirst dive by the airplane. In the heat of passion, she leaned over the toilet seat, spreading her legs as best she could with her jeans stretched to maximum between her ankles. Bracing one hand on the toilet seat, she gently helped him inside of her. This was their favorite position in the whole world. *Dogs have the right idea,* she thought. Looking down with her head slightly tilted, she could see him enter her. *He is unusually enormous*, she thought. The uniqueness of the situation combined with the champagne was overpowering. This would obviously be the best moment to date for both of them. He was careful to keep the movements slow and methodical because he would climax well ahead of her if he was not careful. He wanted to have a simultaneous orgasm. Leaning forward, she looked back at him, her face and ears red from excitement. He was in total command of her body as they consummated their love in unison. Within two minutes, they had gotten a "piece of heaven." She was now a member of the Mile High Club.

During this moment, she accidentally hit the "flush" button on the wall. She giggled out loud as the toilet could be heard swirling under the cover. *How could a hotel room or beach ever match this event*, she thought. Little did she know Bermuda would be just as good.

As reality set in, they both scrambled to get dressed, bumping into one another. *How will we exit?* she worried. Who might be outside the door? Jack didn't care, as he smiled and tried to compose himself. He was still aroused as he gently opened the bathroom door. The light went dim as she exited. Standing patiently in front of their door was an elderly woman totally expressionless. She had been there for some of their vocalization and gave them a disdainful look as they left the rest room. Jack and Fawn looked at each other as if nothing had happened.

"Thanks, honey—for helping me with the broken zipper," she said.

"No problem, baby," he replied.

They giggled all the way back to their row. Still flushed from the moment, they sat in their seats, exhausted.

"Did you see her expression?" Fawn gasped.

"Was she mortified or what?" He laughed, "Bet it's been a while for her!"

"Stop, hon . . . that isn't nice . . . maybe she's a member, too!" They roared at that one.

Leaning into one another shoulders, they would shorten the trip to the island by falling asleep.

"I love you," he whispered quietly.

"Not as much as I love you," she whispered back. "I've never been so happy."

She continued, "You make me happy—very happy."

As they gazed up the aisle before dozing, a very attractive female flight attendant winked at them and gave them a "thumbs up." They had been noticed after all and didn't know it. The older woman passed by them on the way to her seat. She mumbled something under her breath as she passed. She would have something to tell her elderly friends at the Princess Hotel in downtown Hamilton once she was in Bermuda. It would make good gossip on the verandah during lunch.

Having missed breakfast, Jack and Fawn would awaken hungry to the screeching tires of the plane landing. The trip had just begun and it would be a spectacular week of perfect weather.

All of a sudden, Jack became startled as the guy behind him blew his horn again. The guy just about ruined his daydreaming. He was back to reality and not much closer to the Sumner. *Jesus*, he thought. *Will this ever end?*

Fawn, by now, had started to doze in the easy chair with the TV on. The TV newscast that she had bypassed on Channel 3 would mention the traffic on the tunnel's east side but she would not hear it. She was deep in sleep. The water in the lobster pot was now lukewarm and the night would be long and quiet.

12

Kevin O'Malley kissed his wife and two children good-bye as he left for work as a tunnel attendant and safety officer in the Sumner. His journey from their home, in Winchester, just north of Boston, was not that long on most days. In heavy traffic and rush hours, the trip could be longer due in part to the Storrow Drive merge near the tunnel entrance. On bad traffic days, he could cross over to Route 1 south and avoid the Storrow Drive exit. Route 16 through Malden was a good way to get to Route 1. Traffic lights were the main obstacle. It seemed to him there were a hundred lights on that road. Stop and go, stop and go traffic was hard on him and their car. But sometimes that was the best access route to work.

Kevin's 1976 Volkswagen bus made it to East Boston in a half hour from Winchester. Because of a traffic advisory on the radio, Kevin opted for Route 1 today. Parking on Delancy Street at the tunnel's eastern end, he managed to arrive at work early enough to chat with two state troopers who were on duty at the MDC building near the Sumner tunnel entrance. It would be a little while before he would take over the tunnel patrol duties from his partner. He could see that the traffic was already atrocious. While on duty, he'd have headlights coming at him all night, he thought. Glare after glare of headlight beams was annoying in the confined area where he sat.

Kevin had enjoyed a great morning and afternoon with the children. He had taken Annie and Kate to a local park where they played Wiffle ball for hours. Kevin's wife, Marcy, had worked that day at St. Francis Hospital in Medford, Massachusetts. As an licensed practical nurse (LPN) on the third floor, she often worked the 7:00 A.M. to 3:00 P.M. shift. Often, on weekends, Kevin traded shifts with other tunnel attendants in order to accommodate her schedule. Tonight Kevin was on duty from 7:00 P.M. to 4:00 A.M.

It will be a long night, he thought, as he started walking the catwalk into the Sumner Tunnel. He was tired from playing with the children but knew that they valued his time with them. Marcy had read articles at work that suggested more interaction with fathers was needed by children of two-working-parent families. Kevin was glad to oblige and it gave him a sense of well-being to watch the girls grow. Besides, he was a baseball nut and loved the fact that the kids enjoyed Wiffle ball.

The safety monitoring booth was located one-third of the way through the Sumner. The walk wasn't too bad, but the fumes from the automobiles were obnoxious and nauseating during the short journey to it. The small enclosed area would be his home for the next few hours. Primarily assigned as a safety monitor, he wore many other hats as well. He was also utilized as a maintenance man and security officer. Although not paid for such responsibilities, he performed those jobs as needed. Due to recent budget cuts at the MDC, he was lucky to have the job he had. Staff had been recently reduced, thereby resulting in multifaceted jobs for those who were not in the layoff. The combination of jobs was stressful. A large bottle of citrus-flavored antacid tablets adorned the lower shelf of the booth. Kevin would be the lone wolf tonight in the tunnel.

The tiny room was stuffy and dirty and had the stench of stale cigarette smoke. To avoid boredom, Kevin often brought along the *Boston Gazette*, plus a tabloid or a recent issue of *Playboy*. Marcy was not aware of his *Playboy* subscription but probably wouldn't have minded anyway. As a nurse she was used to seeing male organs, so what if he enjoyed the air-brushed photos of beautiful females. This month the cover and featured beauty was none other than "Candy Apel." Kevin couldn't wait to get a look inside the magazine, which was sealed in a plastic sleeve.

In addition to sitting in the booth and watching traffic flow, Kevin's duties often included patrolling the catwalk and checking the fire extinguishers and fire hose connections for malfunctions or damage. His territory, which varied with the shift, included either a portion of, or sometimes all of, the mile-long tunnel.

As part of their cross-training during the downsizing of the MDC, Kevin had attended lectures at a local fire station and felt comfortable with his fire apparatus training. After all, he was instructed by firemen and fire engineers for potential Sumner and Callahan Tunnel emergencies. CPR was part of that training as well. When no crisis loomed, he could be excited to find a burned out or flickering fluorescent bulb along the catwalk. He would change the bulbs as needed. It broke up the routine of a lonely job.

Until recently, the tiled ceilings and walls had been a problem. Pieces often dropped off the wall or ceiling spontaneously and smashed on the roadway or catwalk. The missing tiles left sporadic black blotches on the ceiling throughout the tunnel. The new, larger tile renovations were more secure and rarely had a problem. They were a perfect aesthetic "mask" for an antiquated tunnel structure. No one traveling through the tunnel would see what was behind the new tiles. With an environmental impact study still in progress, some tunnel renovations were delayed. Major structural anomalies would require an approach from the harbor bottom, and little was known by the EPA as to how the construction renovations would affect the breeding grounds of certain fish and mollusks that lived in the old boots, tires and other inanimate objects on the harbor floor. The EPA's evaluation would take years to complete and the repairs made.

Kevin's day in the tube was further complicated by the booth in which he had to sit. Supposedly it had a positive pressure HVAC system to prevent tunnel air from entering the glass-enclosed unit, but it was not working properly and tunnel air leaked in along some loose glass seams. Kevin often had slight headaches from breathing the air. Nobody had checked recently, but the carbon monoxide and hydrocarbon levels must have been elevated. Carbon monoxide was odorless but diesel hydrocarbons were foul. It was like smelling the ass end of a Volkswagen diesel Rabbit. When diesels idle for extended periods, clouds of black smoke come out. Heavy tunnel traffic moving slowly toward Boston would definitely cause increasing concentrations of toxic fumes in the confines of the Sumner.

Kevin had recently been to his family practitioner in an attempt to address the frequency of his headaches. The doctor had suggested a job change if they persisted. For his own health and the welfare of his family, he was considering a job alternative. The drawback was the fact that work in the tunnel gave him both hazardous-duty pay and potential overtime. He wanted the higher pay because although his and Marcy's salaries met their financial needs, there was seldom any extra money for their hoped-for Disney World vacation.

When vacation funds were low, as they usually were, New Hampshire's Hampton Beach was their getaway vacation—a poor substitute for Disney World, but fun for young kids. The crowded, tacky summertime activity at Hampton was mostly comprised of video arcades and cotton-candy stands, which, along with the McDonald's on the main drag, closed for the winter.

Kevin's current position was basically described by other MDC employees as a "tit job" since there was often little to do over an eight-hour shift. Sit and wait, sit and read, sit and listen to the drone of the traffic passing through the Sumner. There was no one looking over his shoulder, and he could sit there and read about the current details of Lady Di's former lovers and her tragic-death theories. If traffic got sparse and it was late, he could snooze for a while and no one would be the wiser.

With the exception of an occasional punk teenager honking at him and giving him the finger, no one bothered to notice his presence as they passed by. He didn't mind that, since it was a common gesture for motorists in Boston—sort of a hello to many people. If perturbed enough, he'd flash one back at them. On Friday or Saturday nights, he was often "mooned" as well. It came with the territory. He chalked it up to kids who had too much alcohol, somewhere up Route 1. Bars and strip joints were up in that area, and also near Revere Beach. Late-night returns to Boston were to be expected.

After an initial check of the tunnel by catwalk, Kevin settled into the swivel chair in the booth. Badly in need of some oil, any movement of the chair caused a screech of the bearings below his butt. Someday, he thought, he would remember the 3-in-1 Oil can stored somewhere in his basement at home.

The same Red Sox game that Fawn DiNardi could hear out her apartment window in Cambridge was also what Kevin would listen to that night on his portable radio. With the typically poor reception inside the tunnel, the small radio/cassette player Kevin had used for years barely picked up the calls of the game from Fenway Park. Had his little cubicle been further in the tunnel, he would hear nothing at all. The FM radio band faded in and out, but it was enough for Kevin to hear the Yankees get a home run. The Yankee left fielder had just popped one over the left field wall known as "the Green Monster." The pin-striped team was now ahead. When Kevin got tired of the static on the radio he would play some tapes in the cassette player. The BoSox had the lead in the second inning and were now down by one run, 3 to 2. Kevin leaned back in the swivel chair and placed his mind in neutral for a while. The headset wire draped off his shoulder down to his waist. He always clipped the radio on his belt. He was bone tired and he had no idea what kind of night it would be. All he knew was that he was lonesome and would rather be home with his wife and kids. The newspaper fell across his lap as he leaned back in the chair. An occasional headlight bounced off the glass booth and soon he drifted off to sleep. His earphone headset was louder than the fresh air sound entering his little booth. The play-by-play action filled the tiny chamber. The telephone, used for communication with the outside world, sat silent on the shelf.

13

The dimly lit Callahan and Sumner tunnels were depressing to motorists as well as to the workers of the MDC. Motorists often turned on their headlights to compensate for the low-level tunnel illumination. It was apparent to many Boston travelers that other major cities had upgraded their lighting and Beantown was behind in that area. The Massachusetts Turnpike Authority (MTA) was responsible for upgrades of both the Callahan and Sumner tunnels. Fort McHenry Tunnel in Baltimore, and the Lincoln and Holland tunnels in New York City were examples of modernized lighting, up to the recommended standards of illumination.

The length of these two Boston tunnels differed by 583 feet, the longer being the Sumner at 5,653 feet. The 1999 World Almanac still listed them as being two of the longest underwater vehicular tunnels in North America. However, that was considered by many to be the tunnels' only claim to fame. Their claim to notoriety was how congested they often got. That hadn't been entered as a world record, but probably should have been, many years ago. Nothing much had changed in that department. The tunnels still were a pain in the ass to traverse.

Traveling through them, they appeared to dip downward at a slight angle until traffic reached the midpoint, about one-half mile in. The central part of Boston Harbor flowed directly above them. Although becoming antiquated, both tunnels provided a conduit for Boston travelers who needed access to the North Shore, Logan Airport and downtown Boston. Aside from the MBTA subway system, there was no other convenient access to and from Logan Airport. There were water shuttles on the harbor, but they were too infrequent for most travelers. Thousands of taxi cabs and cars traversed both tunnels daily.

The need for additional access to the east side of Boston and Logan had recently resulted in the addition of a new tunnel located at the southern end of the city. Named after a local Red Sox hero, Ted Williams, the tunnel opened with great fanfare in mid-1990s. Unfortunately for travelers, this multimillion dollar project restricted travel access to buses, cabs and other large vehicles going to Logan Airport. The restricted travel for cars was often lifted in peak times or on weekends, holidays or special occasions. It was no help to the average weekly commuter, therefore, and the Callahan and Sumner tunnels remained as congested as ever. After a decade of planning and construction, the Ted Williams Tunnel added little value to the larger scope of the Boston traffic problem. It was meant to alleviate traffic from the south shore heading into the city and then going to Logan. It conveniently exited the traffic by Terminal A, hence the idea was a perfect solution for the average traveler to the airport.

Kevin O'Malley hoped to be transferred to the newer tunnel at some point in the future. It would mean a longer commute to work for him, but it would be a nicer, brighter and cleaner work environment.

Outside the entrance to the Sumner Tunnel, Tom Harper was about to take a break from collecting tolls when his supervisor approached his tollbooth between passing cars. This late in his shift, his presence usually meant "bad" news. He wanted to ask Tom to stay on duty for a while because a coworker hadn't yet arrived to relieve another attendant. Harper knew the work habits of this guy and surmised that he had called in sick. The supervisor was probably afraid to tell Tom the truth.

"Shit!" Tom said.

He figured the guy was somewhere in Boston playing hooky—probably at the Red Sox game.

"Bastard! Where is he?" Tom asked. "I could use the break. It's been hours ya know!"

"Sorry, Tom. He must be late or somethin'. We'll relieve you as soon as we can," he said, walking away.

Tom knew that his colleague had season's tickets to Fenway and tonight was a game against their historic arch-rival, the New York Yankees. This meant that Tom would not get the pasta dinner Becky had promised him before he had left for work. It was already dark outside and he was starving. After the supposed break he was entitled to, it would have been only another hour until he could head home. His supervisor had promised to call another worker, if he could find one. Otherwise Tom might have to do a double shift. This wasn't the first time his coworker had pulled a stunt like this. Tom was pissed. Three weeks earlier the guy was "sick" when the Baltimore Orioles were in town. Cal Ripken Jr. was facing Red Sox ace pitcher Pedro Martínez.

Tom agreed to stay there for a while. Maybe his supervisor would get him some relief soon. He might even remember Tom's dedication at his next performance review. He lit up a cigarette out of frustration and flicked the match out the tollbooth window. Against regulations, he still smoked on occasion in the tollbooth. He hid it well. His supervisor would not cite him on it. After all, he had just agreed to stay on during his break. He was a pack-a-day smoker and hoped to quit someday—but not today.

When there was an occasional break in the traffic, jets from Logan could be heard taking off above the tollbooth. They were heading in a northerly direction tonight. On clear, windless nights the sound repeated every minute or so. Loud echoes could be heard in the distance as some planes landed and reversed their engines after touching down. On some clear evenings Tom could see the internal cabin lights and people in the windows of some planes that climbed overhead. Tonight was overcast and the wind was picking up. There wasn't much to see.

With each two dollars that Tom received at the tollbooth, a bell would ring and a green light would illuminate on the display in front of him. At the automatic tollgates near Tom, the alarm occasionally went off. That meant that some fool had missed the toll bucket with his change. Some offenders would fake it and gesture with their arms as if they were tossing coins in the bin. The impression was that the coins had missed and had dropped. When the toll takers saw this, they would wave the vehicle through in order to keep things moving. The red lights would flash and bells would go off. The driver would yell over apologetically that the coin had fallen to the pavement. The toll takers affectionately called them "phantom quarters." The people who pulled off the sham were called a lot of other names, none of them complimentary.

A skinny Asian guy was selling single stem roses in front of the toll booth—a common sight in front of the nine booths. Tom's was the last in the row and was located to the far right as cars approached the tolls. The man with the roses was a Moonie, a follower of Reverend Moon, the controversial Korean religious zealot. *These flower-hawkers are a pain in the ass,* Tom thought. But the MDC could not have them removed. Free speech infringement, he thought. He might need a half-dozen roses himself once Becky found out that he was working overtime again. At two dollars apiece, he would gladly cough up twelve dollars for a half-dozen roses just to please her. A single rose would not get him out of this "jam" tonight.

14

Robie Brook's band, EXZILLERATION had already started their first set shortly after the *Queen of Shoals* had departed the wharf. They were well into satisfying the passengers on board with their choice of tunes. Robie had to refuse only one request; that was for a Sinatra tune. He apologized for not knowing "New York, New York" well enough to play it, but he was kind enough to offer "My Way." The older couple requesting Sinatra eagerly awaited Robie's rendition.

Hell, he thought, *I can fake it pretty good*. It wasn't even written by Sinatra. It was written by Paul Anka, basically for Sinatra, but even Anka supposedly had incorporated a portion of a tune or lyrics, presumably from a French songwriter, into the music.

At least twenty couples were rockin' and dancin' to the band's rendition of "Take it Easy." Joey's "licks" on bass guitar were hot tonight. He made it sound like it was fretless. People commented on his musical prowess and wondered why he was not on the road with a well-known performing artist. They thought he was *that* good.

About forty feet across from the band was Kristin's wet bar. People were ten deep waiting for drinks. Many in line faced the band and rocked to the tunes. The drinking crowd would settle down in time, but for now, Kristin was serving the people congregated in front of her.

Scottie replaced her "mixers" as needed and would change the kegs of "Bud" and "Lite" when they were empty. So far the night was young and the kegs were still full. Directly above the bar was a series of life jackets and an inflatable raft. The orange row of jackets was mandated by the U.S.

Coast Guard. They were strategically placed around the boat and in overheads above the primary passenger areas. Against the white superstructure of the boat, they were a colorful addition. A light coat of dust covered some of the life jackets above Kristin's head. Some straps attached to them dangled down above her blonde hair. She was serving drinks as fast as her arms would go. Someone else joined her to take the customers' money and run the register. It was that crowded. *Thirsty, thirsty, thirsty, they are!* she thought. Everyone was having about as much fun as they could have.

The captain knew it was a exuberant crop of party people. They would go home and tell their friends what a good time they had, and the word would spread that the *Queen* was the "booze cruise" to be on in Boston Harbor.

Off the front row of bow chairs was a distant dim view of the Georges Island lighthouse. Built in 1886, the lighthouse was one of the oldest in the harbor. Her crystal series of lenses was similar to the Gibbs Lighthouse in Bermuda. Both lighthouses were fashioned of cast iron, a rare form of construction. Most others were made of stone or cement.

The Georges Island lighthouse was meant to be around forever. Sections of her sides were bolted together like the inner structure of a ship's hull. The sheer weight of the cast iron made it difficult to work with and construct back then. A beacon in the night, she was a visual focal point for boats and passengers traveling around Boston Harbor. She would guide the *Queen of Shoals* out of the harbor and into the open waters that surrounded Boston. The music from the brightly lit *Queen* could be heard on shore as she headed out on her normal charted course across the harbor. The footprint of her wake remained as a calm line behind her. It broke the chop in the waters and became a vivid reminder of her path of travel. Passengers standing at her stern would look at the wake and view Boston behind them. It was a beautiful sight despite the overcast skies.

15

Logan Airport was a hub of frenzied activity that particular evening. The volume of planes going in and out necessitated use of all runways. Corresponding to the normal volume of air traffic, Logan has supportive services and emergency centers throughout the entire complex. As is true for many major airports, each terminal is prepared for potential crises. Medical problems—childbirth, passenger and traveler accidents in the various terminals and heart attacks—all are well covered. More serious disasters, such as plane crashes, fires and hazardous waste spills are handled by teams designed for rapid response around the complex. Since Logan has individual terminals for different airlines and international flights, each terminal, A through E, is independently prepared to deal with local emergency issues.

Even the Massachusetts State Police have barracks on site for emergencies, potential terrorist problems and routine surveillance. They also control traffic flow around the terminals and oversee parking violations, automobile breakdowns and other mundane problems with traffic flow. The state police have two subdivisions: highways and marine services. Often basic training of new officers covers both aspects. Water rescue teams, complete with small power boats for the recovery of people and watercraft, were often comprised of ex-military personnel like the Navy Seals. At Logan, they had facilities for dive support, medical support, body retrieval and a temporary morgue. Although a morbid thought for most officials, airline disasters were never predictable and readiness was paramount for the state-coordinated rescue efforts. Water rescue was emphasized because Logan was surrounded by water. The morgue at Logan was used on only one occasion and that was years ago. With a proven safety record, the room was more often a storage area for general files and office supplies. Space for equipment was at a premium in the state police offices, so every square foot of unused surplus area was grabbed, when possible. The coroner's "hot line" had never been used and the red phone hung on the wall covered with a light coat of dust. Anticipated for use when the passengers were missing from the wide-body jet that hit the water, there was never a use for the room as they were never retrieved. It was surmised that the poor passengers were basically lobster bait, never to be recovered. This was a scary thought since the water around Logan was very accessible. Most people thought that the recovery of the bodies should have been possible.

The MDC, on the other hand, handles parking garage activities including lost and stolen cars, dead batteries and flat tires. Many people forget where they were parked, so MDC officials drive them around the different levels in search of their vehicles. It is a frantic time for the travelers but often humorous for the parking attendants.

Pursuant to more serious airport problems or emergencies are dedicated Logan services that are immediate in response. Logan, like other large metropolitan airports, is prepared for the worst of events.

Logan's Emergency Response Team (ALERT), responsible for major emergencies, is located adjacent to Terminal A and just south of the central control tower. The central tower complex sits on two cement columns adjacent to Terminal C, the center point of all of Logan's complex. ALERT's facility is a medium-sized building that houses some fifteen emergency vehicles of various sizes and capabilities. Predominantly, they include a Fire Response Team with ambulances, HAZMAT (hazardous material) trucks and fire engines with anti-combustion "foam" capabilities.

HAZMAT staff and equipment respond to hazardous material spills, unknown chemical toxicants and radioactive material concerns. They work closely with the bomb squad crew and are there for all airline fuel spills. Virtually any airport catastrophe can be handled on site. Backup support for additional emergency vehicles is provided by the surrounding communities. They were all mutual aid respondents.

Some years back, ALERT had been requested and utilized for the wide-body jet that had landed in iced runway conditions. The airplane could not stop and slid off the runway into the north end of Boston Harbor. That fatal flight occurred on a winter night when runway conditions had deteriorated and the runway probably should have previously been shut down. It was the air traffic controller's call in the tower and they were reluctant to make that decision. Earlier aircraft had reported the runways to be marginal in condition, but functional. They were wrong about one runway. It was sheer ice at that hour. The jumbo-class jet overshot the runway. A portion of the nose and forward cabin ended up in the drink. Had the plane stayed intact, it would have resulted in no loss of lives. However, a large section of the front of the aircraft broke clean off the fuselage and temporarily immersed the pilots and a few of the crew in the harbor. The pilots escaped with their lives. Many passengers and attendants in the galley and First Class cabin were forced to swim in the near freezing harbor water and January air. But two men known as "the Metcalfs," who were in the front section of the plane, lost their lives on that flight and their bodies were never recovered from the icy waters. Evidently, they were paralyzed by the cold water or couldn't swim. One man was heard crying in the night for help but he disappeared under the water before he could be rescued.

Until Logan officials could figure out what to do with the disabled plane, it sat near the edge of the bay for the FAA personnel to investigate and determine the cause of the accident. It sat for weeks with its forward section near the water. Eventually, to avoid further embarrassment, the airline removed the company logo from the tail of the plane. It was an unwanted billboard for passengers to see on incoming flights.

The ALERT crew worked closely with the various fire fighting staff around the Logan complex. Ancillary fire departments and trucks were strategically located at the north and south ends of the airport.

Fire Captain Jerry Daley, a thirty-seven-year veteran of the Department, sat at his desk catching up on paperwork. In front of him was a large console with communication capability directly to Logan Tower, Massachusetts General Hospital (MGH), Boston fire departments and state and local police. The console was the heartbeat of disaster control at Logan.

Jerry Daley was often amused by the fact that the "State-ies" called themselves "state police" when in fact Massachusetts was a "Commonwealth," not a state. They should be called "Commonwealth Police" or "Commies," he thought. He often suggested that, and joked about it, with his friends on the force.

This night had been relatively quiet, with most crew members of ALERT performing their routine maintenance checks on vehicles and safety equipment. They prided themselves with early responses to potential flight problems. Their record was astonishing and they had received a multitude of awards over the years. The governor of the Commonwealth had even presented his annual "Governor's Award" to ALERT for emergency response excellence. A wall to the right of the console had numerous certificates and letters of commendation. The letters reflected the impeccable record for fast response and the lack of equipment failures in the preceding four-year period. Daley was "the man" who made it all happen and he was well respected by the entire fire crew and his ALERT colleagues.

Adjacent to the ALERT building was an annex of the state police. The Massachusetts State Police oversaw, among other things, the roadways at Logan, including the departure and arrival lanes in front of each terminal, where people were always parking illegally and fouling up traffic. Generally, they stood guard at passenger security points or had an austere presence near the passenger drop-off points. Well-trained and part of an elite force, they kept things moving in front of Terminals A through E. Known to ticket just about anything that sat in front of a terminal for longer than one minute, the "State-ies" were ever present when daily operations of the airport were extremely busy. The area in front of Terminal C, where many of the major carriers were located, was a case in point. Limousine, taxi and general passenger traffic was always busy there. Leaving a car unattended in front of a terminal would result in an immediate tow; there would be no discussion. Tow trucks were never very far away and their operators waited patiently for the summons to haul a violator away. Other major cities, like Newark, Baltimore and Philadelphia don't enforce this policy as often as Boston's Logan. At one of those other airports, one could actually wait directly out in front of the main terminal for arriving passengers, without being harassed. Warmth, tenderness and sensitivity to passengers was not part of the police training at Logan. All terminal security was implemented with an iron hand.

"Move along there!" the trooper sergeant barked. "Can't park there!"

The woman he had targeted responded with annoyance since she was dropping off her husband and he was already late for his flight. Unlike "friendly" Fenway Park, there was no equivalent "Friendly Logan."

"Damn those guys!" she muttered to her husband. "Can't they find somewhere else to go?" *Go chase somebody on Route 93,* she thought. Rolling down her window, she said sweetly, "Officer? I'll only be a minute, sir. My husband's late for his flight and needs to gate-check his luggage as soon as possible."

"Hurry!" the officer responded. "You are blocking a restricted area . . . but go ahead of that cab, ma'am. You've got thirty seconds to unload, so hurry! There is no parking here!"

"Thanks officer, we'll only be a minute," she responded nicely.

16

The water recovery team was headed by former Navy Seal Dick Smith. He and Captain Daley of the fire department were great friends. Smith, a 1970 Annapolis graduate, had been in the top fifty of his class. He had undergone Seal training in Coronado, California, not far from the famous Hotel Del Coronado. The Seals often used the Del's beach early in the morning to run laps. It was the beach where Marilyn Monroe and Tony Curtis filmed some sequences of "Some Like it Hot" in the 1960s. The ten-mile run was not pleasant, even though Coronado beach was a beautiful sight in the morning.

Smith was responsible for in-house water rescue training at Logan Airport. He drilled his "mates" with the authority of a Marine officer. Recently divorced from his second wife, he had no room for frivolity from his rescue unit personnel. His anger was really directed toward his ex-wife, Shelley. Ex-military men, especially Marines, are intensely trained. They often bring their troubles home at night and their frustration can carry over to their action with their spouses. Dick tried not to do this but Shelley became the object of his nastiness and arrogance. Finally the marriage was in trouble and she left him. "Irreconcilable differences" was the wording of the divorce suit. Dick obviously still loved Shelley and his demeanor had changed since she had walked out. His crew and students felt the effects of her departure. He considered trying get her back, but that would never occur. He just couldn't accept that as fact.

Dick and the fire captain, Jerry Daley, often played golf and Smith could hit the ball a country mile. This achievement of long-distance hitting was probably more the result of these frustrations ongoing in his life, than an artistic Sam Snead swing. Together at work they were an interactive team for a dedicated response to crises. This particular night, Dick stopped by to chat with Daley. They were planning a "cross-training" session for both departments and were in the formative stages of a training syllabus.

"How's it goin', Captain?" Dick said. "Ev'nin' slow for you?"

"Oh hi, Dick," Daley replied. "Sort of . . . we only had one issue tonight. Some Jet A fueling of a 727 spilled and we had to mop it up. Didn't bother with HAZMET, since the spill was small and easily contained. If I smell like Jet A, that's the residual from the spill."

"Relatively quiet for us as well," Dick continued. "I'm not sure all this training has a purpose. We never get the call for anything major."

"What?" Daley asked, "Are you lookin' for trouble? Are you hopin' for a disaster?"

"No," Smith said, after thinking about his comment. "Just a bit bored."

With Shelley gone, he had no excitement at work or at home. His life was golf and frequent nights at the Golden Banana, a strip club up Route 1, north of the airport. He was actually "seeing" one of the girls who worked there but hadn't told Daley. This chick did more than strip, after hours; she was a call girl on the side. The money was irresistible to her and the club didn't pay very well. Smith had actually seen "Chesty Morgan" there once, many years ago. She was a "Special Featured Performer" and wore a size 45 DD bra until she unleashed those puppies. Some people had said that she was Guinness World Record material. Those were the days when there were no silicone implants and jugs were natural. *None of this "Bay and Beach" stuff you see on TV*, he thought.

"Hey," he asked Daley, "What's up after work? Feel like havin' a couple of beers and seein' some T&A?"

"Possibly," replied Daley. "Where ya thinkin' of goin? The Banana again? Or is it the Golden Dildo?"

"Yeh," he replied, "the Banana! There's a new chick there—to die for. Her name is Crystal and she has moves on stage that would make even *you* blush. You have to see her," he said, not letting on that he was already doin' the chick.

"Let's see how the night goes," said Daley, "Sounds like a possible . . . possible."

Smith had spent most of the day checking out the new hovercraft, which they had purchased for rapid response in water emergencies and rescue.

The new vessel was the latest addition to the arsenal for the dive and rescue team and training for all members on the craft was already in progress. Many shakedown cruises would be needed in the harbor and open water. The staff of ALERT was excited to have a new toy to play with. Rapidly mobilized, it could hit 60–70 MPH without blinking an eye. It arrived on its own trailer from Dover, England. The craft was perfected in the United Kingdom where hovercraft were frequently used for commuter transportation between England and France. They could cross the twenty-seven-mile English Channel in minutes. This newer version was reduced in size and was a new market for the manufacturer. They were designed for the needs of rescue teams in Europe and the manufacturer thought the United States might be interested in those capabilities as well.

ALERT had a budget surplus from the past year and had lobbied hard for a state-of-the-art water-rescue craft. The mayor and governor agreed, since they were both lame ducks. What would they care? Spend the money! They thought that it would be a modern legacy to their terms in office. This model hovercraft could rescue eighty people maximum and was easily launched from its trailer.

The ALERT logo was imprinted on the sides of the hovercraft as well as on the four-wheel drive vehicle that pulled the trailer and boat. A new Mercedes truck from Germany was specially purchased to haul the hovercraft to disaster sites. Once in the water, the craft was like a monster. Rescue procedures would never be the same for ALERT. The inordinate expense of the craft would soon be justified. As yet unnamed, the crew of the hovercraft had toyed with a list of feminine attributes that might make a good logo to adorn her sides. A contest was in progress to name her. "Ms. Res-Q" had been suggested by Smith, but no one liked it. Affectionately she was temporarily referred to by the crew as "Ms. Blowjob," apparently because of the enormous twin-engine fans that propelled and lifted the craft off the water. It was unlikely that the disparaging name would be painted on her side. As a legacy to the governor and mayor, that would not be the name of choice. In a few days the contest would be over and a real name would be painted on her sides, hopefully with pride.

ALERT's role in water safety and rescue was intimately coordinated with the United States Coast Guard. The Guard had always had a major presence in the harbor area around Logan Airport. A local unit of the U.S. Coast Guard operated out of a building not far from Lincoln Wharf, located directly east of the Italian North End, abutting "Little Italy." With the numerous marinas north and south of Boston and within Boston Harbor proper, the Coast Guard has extensive responsibilities in the open waters. From the upper floors of the Lincoln Wharf condos, one could see Coast Guard vessels of varying sizes throughout the harbor. The traditional, diagonal red stripe on the bow of USCG vessels was a dead giveaway. During the recent Tall Ships festivities, the Coast Guard had an active presence in the monitoring of all boating during the Parade of Sails.

Their role was intensified on evenings when a fireworks display took place directly over the harbor. Fourth of July weekend was always an extremely busy time for the USCG. Boats moored to watch the explosions over the harbor created myriad potential problems for harbor traffic and increased the occurrence of accidents. At night, small blue flashing lights glittered on the water as Coast Guard vessels monitored the hundreds of power boats, sailboats and harbor cruise ships out to enjoy The Fourth. Combined with the daily boat traffic and increased number of vessels on holiday weekends or the arrival of the Tall Ships from around the World, one could imagine the difficulties that the USCG and marine patrol had to deal with.

On some occasions, a Cigarette-style boat, owned by some rich yuppie, was cited for speeding or driving to endanger in open waters. Recklessly, the driver would pass other craft as though they were "gates" in a slalom. Liquor was often involved in their behavior.

To the left of Lincoln Wharf was located the Charlestown Naval Yard, which served as the home of some retired U.S. Naval vessels, one of which is the grand lady of them all: "Old Ironsides"—the USS *Constitution*. The oldest commissioned ship in the Navy, the USS *Constitution*'s sister ship, the *Constellation* was permanently moored in Baltimore Harbor as a floating museum. The USS *Constitution* had resided in Charlestown for years. She was built some 200 years earlier and had last sailed on her own 116 years ago. On her forthcoming 200th Anniversary, she was to sail again under her own power.

Guided tours of her decks were provided daily to visitors for a small fee. During July and August, visitors stood in line for hours to tour her hull and living quarters. Nearby, enormous chains and anchors, reminders of the sailing of bygone days, surrounded the Maritime Museum adjacent to "Old Ironsides."

Each Fourth of July, the USS *Constitution* was towed out to sea to make its annual turnaround. The Navy and the Coast Guard worked together to turn the lady around. If she was facing into the harbor, she would be turned to face out the following year. Additionally, she left port under tow on occasion to serve as grand marshal of the parades or to greet the Tall Ships arriving from Europe. Completely restored, she was in the finest sailing condition ever seen. Her hull of black with white accents was characteristic of the tall ships of her day. Her masts, which had been replaced numerous times over the years, stood tall enough to be seen from Interstate 93. She remained under the tender loving care of the U.S. Navy and USCG.

The Coast Guard played an active role in the emergency response of the harbor. They often dealt with distress calls from sailors or the oil spills of commercial tankers coming into port. Their equipment for handling disasters was a testimony to the Coast Guard budget. They could surround oil spills with absorbent material or link long booms together for the containment of spills. Since the time that the *Exxon Valdez* spilled eleven million gallons of crude into the pristine Prince William Sound in Alaska, most ports in the United States had new procedures and materials in place to prevent a similar occurrence. Boston Harbor, already polluted, could not withstand an insult of that nature. The former governor had promised to clean Boston Harbor as part of his campaign rhetoric during his attempt at the presidential race. Harbor waters contained high levels of heavy metals and PCB's, the result of years of abuse. An EPA report compiled over a five-year period had confirmed the gravity of the situation. Extensive remediation would be required to restore the harbor's natural beauty and remove the toxins from her water.

In addition to their other duties, the U.S. Coast Guard maintained the red and green buoys that marked the shipping lanes. Without these floats for guidance, ships would find negotiation of the harbor impossible, especially at night. The occasional natural obstacles were serious threats to the variety of vessels attempting to traverse the harbor day to day. At night, the buoys served as beacons for safe harbor travel. Gently rocking from the wake of passing ships, the lighted buoys dotted the harbor like a runway on water. Some of the older buoys had bells on top providing a constant reminder of the harbor's frequent fog. If you couldn't see them, you could certainly hear them.

Captain Pete Thompson's *Ellie May* passed under the jumbo jet that departed overhead. The thunder of its engines reverberated as it climbed into the cloud cover of the night. The *Ellie May* was heading home to Chelsea, Massachusetts. The twin diesels were set at a slow rolling idle as she traversed the harbor. Pete knew the engines needed some work and didn't care to push his luck by going too fast. It would be some time before he got home and he had no desire to have an engine quit on him halfway. He puffed on his cigarette as he counted his money from the latest lobster haul. Ted Price always paid him in cash. That way Pete could claim what he wanted on income taxes. He did not always declare what he made. He needed a buffer to counteract the fact that his income was small. The monthly fluctuations in income corresponded to the high and low seasons for lobstering. Winter always meant less income. While checking the gauges on the console, he could estimate his time of arrival in Chelsea. Speed, engine RPMs and wind direction gauges would provide him with some indication of how long this journey would take. Heading north he saw no major problems. The harbor was quiet this evening and he pondered memories of his late wife, Ellie May. On quiet evenings when he had too much time on his hands, he often thought of her. He missed her terribly. His cigarette glowed with each draw of smoke. Another day was nearly over. He would be back at sea in a day or so, depending upon how much work the engines needed for maintenance. Down time of the engines meant no income for him and that's not what he wanted to think about. Passing to the west of Logan Airport, he watched as incoming planes made their final approach to Logan. They were almost exactly ninety seconds apart. At the lower levels of their approach, their landing lights looked like a straight line of pearls or beads in the night sky. Looking to his south off the stern of the *Ellie May* he saw how beautiful Boston could be in the night.

The Customs House building was beautifully lit and stood majestically above the other harborfront office buildings. The Customs House would soon be developed into an expensive hotel and condo complex. *They call that saving her*, he thought to himself. What else could you do with its unique structure? She no longer had a use in the Merchant Marine business. The tall ships of her day were long gone and there was no need for her services. She was just a landmark left from the days of old and that was fine for Capt'n Pete. *At least they aren't tearing her down*, he thought.

17

Ground control at Logan cleared Flight 2158 onto active Runway 33L at 7:38 P.M. Captain Bullock and First Officer Bell acknowledged the tower and watched as the jet they would follow rumbled down the runway at great speed. Lifting off at 180 knots, the jet left a trail of black smoke that could be seen in NEAir 2158's landing lights. The wing and tail lights blinked in the distance as the jet faded left toward the half-moon that was shining through the clouds.

The local weather report was right. Low cloud cover had arrived. Winds were out of the northwest at 20, and the ceiling was dropping.

Captain Bullock set his wing flaps at 20 degrees, enough for proper "lift" at about 80-90 knots. A small indicator light flickered on one of the fuel gauges, then became fully illuminated again. Neither pilot had noticed the light flickering. They were scanning the window views of the runways and taxiways to insure no other aircraft were near Runway 33L. Ground traffic was virtually absent in the area around them.

Following normal procedure, 2158's radio frequency was set for Tower Central at Logan. A frequency of 121.5 was the setting for emergencies. A sticker with that number was affixed on the cockpit console and served as a reminder for Bullock and Bell.

Pilots had confidence and avoided thinking that "that frequency" would be needed, but FAA regulations were stringent to insure that all safety measures were adhered to completely.

Having filed their flight plan in advance, Bullock and Bell knew the route north almost by heart. The preferred flight to Manchester was slightly northwest of Logan. The flight would take them on a known "vector highway," a virtual road map in the sky. They would fly at an altitude of 9,000 to 12,000 feet. Air traffic control would advise them of their final altitude after they had departed. Tonight's route would take them over Revere, Lynnfield and Lowell, Massachusetts, and then straight north to Manchester, New Hampshire. Once they were airborne, the FAA's Northeast Sector in Nashua, New Hampshire, would control the entire flight. Logan tower would ultimately release the flight to Nashua, once the plane leveled off shortly after takeoff.

The FAA Nashua Air Traffic Control Center is located just off Exit 4 on Route 3 in southern New Hampshire. The three hundred employees at the center control the Northeast corridor for all flights in New England, New York and even as far west as Chicago. The enormous FAA center is one of the largest air traffic control centers in the United States. International flights from Europe are picked up by Nashua FAA personnel somewhere over Newfoundland. They then are guided into the New York or New England area international airports including Bradley Field, LaGuardia, Kennedy, and Boston's Logan Airport. The Nashua FAA Center is responsible for hundreds of flights per week, including the commuters to Manchester.

Tonight, as usual, experienced controllers sat in pairs at the multitude of green radar screens in one large room of the FAA center. Two "buddy" controllers worked each screen to insure the accuracy of incoming and outgoing flight data. There was no room for error. Thousands of lives were at stake with each day's flights. On the computer screens, small or larger aircraft were equal in importance. FAA crew shift changes were performed with precision, making sure that current flight data for each sector was verbally transferred and graphically shown to the new controllers coming on duty. Each airplane appeared as a little green slash on the radar screen. A flight number beside the slash was all that represented the plane and passengers. Depending on the altitude range requested of the computer, there could be one or two green markings or forty. If a controller chose to show all aircraft from zero to 20,000 feet, all aircraft in that range appeared. Likewise if he requested altitudes of 10,000 to 12,000 feet there would be fewer planes displayed on the screen.

Controllers could access flights and pilots immediately, by microwave contact. Using the small ball on the console, like a joy stick on a video game, the controller positioned the arrow and highlighted a "green slash" on the computer screen. At that point, the controller was in immediate contact with the pilot of that specific aircraft.

In emergencies, a controller could divert the flight or advise a pilot of aircraft encroaching on their area. The controller could project the anticipated flight on the screen out to four, eight, twelve or sixteen minutes. This way the controller could know in advance if two aircraft might have collision potential and how many minutes or miles away that potential was in real time. Controllers could then advise one or both of the planes to change course or altitude to avoid an in-flight crash.

Telecommunications to any aircraft in the Northeast Sector were relayed to the pilots by microwave towers and instrumentation on the roof of the Nashua FAA center. In the nearby mountain ranges surrounding Jaffrey, Peterborough, New Boston and Temple, New Hampshire, were other microwave tower support. It included a nearby Air Force radar station for satellite tracking.

The importance of functional FAA centers around the United States was emphasized in the 1960s.

In 1964 when the New York blackout occurred and paralyzed the Northeast, it became obvious to officials that backup electrical systems were needed for FAA services countrywide. Winter storms and other catastrophes were unpredictable and could knock out power unexpectedly. The blizzard of '78 paralyzed the northeast United States as well.

To allow for continual operation in a disaster, backup electrical services were now maintained at FAA buildings. Adjacent to the FAA center in Nashua was a building constructed for the sole purpose of supplementary, auxiliary electrical power. It was basically a multitude of batteries that could maintain the FAA center, in case of a major electrical power outage. Without that backup, there could be no contact with aircraft in the Northeast Sector.

18

Captain Bullock positioned his Dressler 205 over the white center line on Runway 33L. He reminded the passengers to take the usual safety measures prior to the impending departure. He awaited clearance for takeoff from the controllers at Logan's Tower Central.

"2158, you are cleared for takeoff," a voice came over the intercom.

Bullock responded, "Roger Tower, 2158 cleared for takeoff."

"Ga-night, 2158," tower control replied.

"Roger, and goodnight to you too, sir."

Directly behind them, and next in line for takeoff was a Beechcraft twin-engine commuter. It would line up and follow 2158 north and then divert eastward for Portland, Maine. The Dressler 205's engines matched on the RPM and power gauges as Logan controllers awaited her taxi and takeoff.

"NEAir 2158, once airborne, ascend to 5,000, level off and advise," reminded the tower.

"Roger, Tower, NEAir 2158 to level off at 5-0-0-0," Bullock responded.

"We're rolling, Tower," he said.

"Roger, 2158."

With brakes released and both engines whining at full power, the plane began to accelerate down the runway. Both Bullock and Bell had one hand simultaneously on the throttle levers. Bell's hand covered Bullock's as a backup on takeoff. Inching the throttle forward in harmony, Flight 2158 was now passing the first of three one-thousand-foot markers on the runway. The rudder was positioned slightly left of center to compensate for the torque of the engines and propellers, and the plane followed the white center line precisely.

The luggage stowed in the overhead bin above Mary Hutton shifted slightly. Startled, she grasped the armrests of her seat. The plane shifted slightly left then right as Bullock worked the pedals and rudder to maintain his course down the runway. The cabin door was ajar due to carelessness. Some passengers could see out the front of the aircraft during the takeoff. The instrument panel was dimly illuminated in the cockpit and passengers could see the green instrument panel between the two pilots. A yellow flashing light for the VOR system was illuminated and blinking normally.

Firmly gripping the throttle with his right hand, Bullock gently pulled the yoke back with his left hand, precisely at the 3,000 foot runway markings. Bell had counted out 1,000, 2,000, then 3,000 feet as the markers appeared. The Dressler's nose wheel lifted off the tarmac. At 90 knots and 3,100 hundred feet down the runway, she was airborne and the runway disappeared rapidly below her landing gear. No longer touching the tarmac, the wheels under the wing gear continued to spin from the momentum of takeoff. As the nose of 2158 lifted off at a 30-degree angle, she felt momentarily weightless. Aerodynamically, physics had taken over. The leading edge of both wings, combined with the flaps extended for takeoff, created a natural vacuum over the top of the wings. With reduced pressure on top, the plane was lifted into the air from the positive pressure on the bottom of the wings. Climbing at 1,500 feet per minute, and air speed increasing, she was now more than a minute into her flight to Manchester. It was 7.41 P.M.

Bullock commanded Bell to retract the gear under the wings. The nose gear was already up. A loud "thunk" could be heard in the cabin as the landing gear elevated and the doors to the landing gear housing overlapped and closed. First Officer Bell was about to retract the wing flaps from their take off position when a "warning light" on the left fuel gauge turned "bright orange." An alarm began to sound in synchrony with the flashing light as the left engine sputtered in protest.

"Shit!" Bullock said, "What the hell?"

"What is it?" Bell added. "What's happened?"

"Don't know! Hit the left CO_2! NOW!"

"Roger, Captain, left extinguisher on."

As the plane entered the low clouds at an altitude of 3,100 feet and climbing, a puff of smoke exited the left engine and a small fire was apparent out the back of the exhaust cowling. A passenger seated on the left side behind Mary Hutton looked out the window and screamed. First Officer Bell, noticing the door open, abruptly reached back and slammed it.

"Fire!" she screamed as the rest of the terror-stricken passengers looked out their windows.

On the right side of the plane there was nothing to see in the night. As yet the captain had said nothing. He was too busy evaluating the situation. The plane veered slightly left as the right-side engine power dominated the plane. Bullock compensated by adding some right rudder to level off early, He tried to reduce the climb and strain on the aircraft.

"Kill the left engine," Bullock instructed Bell. "We'll run on one!"

"Engine killed, Captain," he replied frantically.

With the nose still angled up from takeoff, she was losing power. The flaps, only partially withdrawn, were now a "drag" on the airfoil. She was no longer flying. She was about to stall at that angle of ascent and an alarm sounded. Bullock knew the situation. Limited power, too much weight, wrong ascent angle equals stall!

The warning alarm for a stall continued as the dead left-engine propeller rotated gently from the forward motion of the plane. The propeller pitch on the left side had been changed to a position that reduced drag. The left engine was nonfunctional and smoke could still be seen exiting the back of the engine. As Bullock fought to maintain the yoke and try to level off, Bell called in on the emergency frequency of 121.5. He remained calm from years of training in simulators and took a deep breath.

"Mayday Logan! NEAir 2158. . . . Mayday! We have an engine fire! Do you read?"

"Roger NE 2158, we copy!" the Tower immediately responded. "Status please . . . how bad's the situation?"

"Need clearance to return immediately to Logan. Engine fire . . . left engine out . . . advise!" There was no immediate response from Logan.

He continued, "Advise immediately! Losin' power and forward ascent. Copy?"

"Roger 2158! We're assessing vector for you. . . . Hold, please!"

"Hold? . . .We can't hold! . . . Altitude now 3,200. . . . About to stall! Powering right engine, right side only. . . . Advise Tower! . . . Advise!"

"Roger 2158," responded the controller. "The airport is yours! Can you get back? Can you see any runway?"

"No! Cloud cover!" was the response from the air.

"Code Red in place," said the controller. "All aircraft are on hold, in the air and on ground. Can you power home?"

"No. . . . no power for that!" Bell yelled back.

"Estimate your distance please. You appear five miles out. Do you copy?"

"Roger, Logan! Five miles out." Bullock now jumped into the conversation. "We're dropping, rapidly! Losing lift! Post stall! . . . Advise!"

The red lights and alarms on the phones at the state police, fire department and the ALERT buildings simultaneously illuminated. Computer screens at all three sites immediately went to CODE RED. An advisory of the situation was appearing on the screen as Jerry Daley and Dick Smith were chatting.

"Holy shit!" Daley said, "Will you look at this! We have a Mayday!"

Both men focused on the monitor. It was 7:42 P.M.

Without a word, Dick departed Daley's office. The plans for tonight were abruptly changing—there would be no Golden Banana after work.

Back in his office, Dick was winded. He was out of shape and out of breath as a colleague sat looking intently at the emergency screen information. His headset was on and he was watching the updates from Tower Central.

ALERT central, the fire station and the police were in synch with the tower. They could now hear communications between the tower and NEAir 2158. It was also broadcast live into the offices and throughout the fire station and rescue units.

First to respond to the situation were the firemen who had already opened all the garage doors to the fire station. A number of the firemen were donning their silver-colored asbestos suits, while others were dressing in the black uniforms with iridescent yellow stripes. Some of the men were still in the process of yanking on clothing as they boarded the chartreuse-colored emergency vehicles. Doors slammed on the cabs as the last men entered the trucks. Red lights from each departed vehicle were flashing everywhere. Adrenaline was high and every emergency worker and rescue personnel knew this event was for real. They would be heading for an emergency runway; they just didn't know yet which one it would be. Three fire trucks with foam capabilities, an ambulance, a rescue vehicle with medical supplies and a HAZMAT truck departed the building. A total response was in progress. With the doors wide open in each rescue bay, and the lights on, empty vehicle parking spaces reflected the severity of the situation. A red light outside the building flashed in the night. No one was left to see it. It was 7:44 P.M.

The emergency vehicles formed a chain of flashing lights as they headed away from the building. No sirens were heard. This was a standard response since airport officials would not want to alarm other passengers who were boarding their flights. Traffic in the taxi area was light and there was no need at present for alarming sounds in the night. No one knew how serious this was yet.

Tower Central was advising incoming aircraft in the immediate air space to hold. Sequential holding patterns at various elevations were established. If there would be substantial delay during the impending emergency, tower controllers would begin diverting the planes to other airports. Bradley Field in Hartford, Connecticut, would be first to accommodate the larger jets. LaGuardia Airport on Long Island and T. F. Green Airport in Providence, Rhode Island, would be second, and third. Manchester Airport would be considered as well since their recent expansion allowed for the handling of 727s, 737s, Fokker 100s, MD 80s and ATR commuter aircraft. The FAA center at Nashua was already assisting Logan by holding or diverting flights headed to Boston from Chicago and other Midwest cities.

The 2158 situation north of Boston had priority. Pilots who were circling Boston's Logan did not want to interfere with the crisis and would divert to wherever they were told. They were professional, and proceeded to prepare their own passengers for the gravity of the situation.

With the exception of three incoming flights on final approach, all other flights remained on hold. All three were jumbo jets that were low on fuel and requested permission to land. None of the planes would interfere with the emergency procedures in place. They were vectored to a less active runway which would not be used for the emergency landing. The Nashua FAA center kept all regional airports in the loop as more information of 2158 became apparent. It was 7:45 P.M.

19

Bullock's passengers were white-knuckled. At this point it was obvious that there was trouble. The plane was becoming difficult to stabilize. Attempting to level her with the ailerons above 3,000 feet was to no avail. The nose of the Dressler 205 was still elevated and a stall was inevitable.

"Fuel pump problems on #2 now!" Bell screamed as the right side engines sputtered. "Dammit!" Bullock said. "Lines must be clogged or contaminated."

"No fuel to the engine!"

"Mayday! Mayday Tower! NEA 2158!" Bullock yelled into his headpiece. "Do you copy? Tower, do you copy?"

"Roger 2158, we're responding. Emergency vehicles have been deployed."

"Screw them," said Bullock. "Can you vector me home . . . we've stalled! . . .We've lost #2. . . . Repeat . . . #2 dead. . . . Fuel problems. . . no damn fuel. Get us home!"

"Copy 2158 . . . tryin'."

"Copy my ass! Help us! We goin' down unless . . . ."

Bullock was silent as he felt the plane initiate the stall.

By now the plane had stopped, with nose up and no forward movement. Crying and sobbing was heard in the back of the plane. The officers had no time to tell the passengers the nature of the problem. Suddenly the nose dropped and the air speed indicator went from zero to twenty knots. A dive was in progress and no "lift" existed. They were heading for a residential area below. Cloud cover prevented them from seeing the homes.

They had to regain lift. With no power, it would probably take a 2,000-foot drop to gain air under the wings and fly again. With a near vacuum under the wings she would need 90 to 120 knots of speed to regain lift. They were less than 2,500 feet up and that might not be enough altitude to pull her out of a dive.

"We've stalled, Tower," said Bullock, "We're goin' down! Repeat, Tower . . . we're goin' in!"

A tower controller shouted back, "Hold her! . . . Hold her! . . .You have time! . . . altitude OK . . . hold her!" He continued, "Let her get air! . . . repeat 2158! . . . let her get air!"

"Won't happen!" yelled Bullock. "There's no fuckin' lift!"

With the dark ground fast approaching and air speed indicator increasing from the free fall, they knew that every second was important. Bullock awaited Tower input. He knew damn well that the glide ratio would not permit them to reach Logan. The wingspan was too short and she could not glide that distance without power. His first priority was to regain lift before she bottomed out on some rooftop below them.

Mary Hutton and her fellow passengers were panicked and crying. The angle of the plane was down 45 degrees and dropping. They were pressed against their seats belts, some crying or screaming. Worried that the plane would crash, many recited prayers.

As the ALERT team took their positions near the runways, they still had no idea which runway would be attempted, or from which direction NEAir 2158 would make an approach. Strategically located everywhere, they could easily cover all runway possibilities from where they sat.

The airport activity was now quiet. No approaches and no departures were allowed. The critical jumbo jets were in and safe. Tail, body and wing lights of red and white flickered in the distance, and in every direction one could see. The grounded planes were scattered everywhere awaiting ground control to update them, move them out or send them back to their gates. Inside Terminal E, a multitude of faces were pressed against the glass windows. Everyone was wondering why none of the commuters were moving. They had seen the fire trucks, but no one had briefed them of the impending situation.

20

The *Queen of Shoals* had ventured out of the direct view of Boston and was returning to the harbor in the first of two legs of a three-hour cruise. Each leg of the cruise was about one and one-half hours, then the course would be repeated. Many of the people on board wouldn't even know the difference. Booze and loud conversation, along with the band's music, would mask the fact that they were going out and then into the harbor twice. The passengers didn't care. They were having fun and all the guys were hitting on any single woman they could find, and buying them drinks.

After the first set, the band would take a well-deserved break. As Robie Brooks stepped down from the stage, he was greeted by two groupies. They had been standing in front of him during the first set and thought he was pretty "hot." Impressed with his good looks and guitar playing, their eyes had been focusing on his cute face and guitar licks. Sally Desmond and her best friend, Donna Wright, were twenty-one-year-old students attending Northeastern University Coop classes on a trimester school plan. They had heard of the "booze cruises" and had selected The *Queen of Shoals* because friends at school felt that it was the best place to meet people—sort of a floating "meat factory" for singles. Of all the cruises, it was considered the most fun for their age group—certainly for the quality bands and entertainment. Only the best bands played on the *Queen*. This was a chance for the girls to meet guys from Boston College or Harvard. Summer school was in session and booze cruises were R&R activities for the students. Not much was happening on campus, since school attendance was light during the summer.

Sally and Donna had seen Bob Seger at the Centrum in Worcester two nights earlier and were on a rock-and-roll binge. They had met Seger at the Crown Plaza Hotel after the show. Someone in the Centrum Security Department had divulged the information on where the Seger band was staying. Waiting patiently after the show for two hours, they caught Seger as he returned from his gig. He was most responsive to their autograph requests, stayed for pictures, then hurried into the elevator and up to his room. Robie Brooks wasn't of Bob Seger's class, but his voice was similar in tone and voice range. They would request that Robie do "Someday Lady," a popular Seger tune.

Robie Brooks was not into groupies. He knew they tended to be promiscuous and he didn't like the side effects of their sexual habits. As much as he enjoyed meeting new women he was not about to get some venereal disease from some stranger. Besides he was the "star" of the band and women approached him all the time. If he were to get laid tonight, it would be with someone whom he knew well. He was not deprived.

But Sally was interesting to him as she coyly asked him for the Seger song request. She was a most attractive young lady with a very cute body. He placed his electric guitar in its stand at the edge of the stage and greeted the girls.

They responded with, "Hey, you're good. Know any Seger? 'Someday Lady'?"

"Sure, I can try that one after the break. Did you know he was recently in the area?" he asked.

"Yeh," Sally said with exuberance. "We just saw him in Worcester!"

"He was excellent!" Donna piped in.

"Really? Didn't know he was in Worcester. Where'd you see him?"

"Worcester Centrum!" Sally said, admiringly. "Ya know—you sound a lot like him at times."

"Really?" he responded.

He already knew that, since other people had told him that often. Acting flattered he said, "Thanks, that's a compliment! Do you guys come on these cruises often? I haven't seen you here before."

"Not really," Donna said. "We just found out about your boat recently. Do you play in Boston as well?"

"Yeh," he replied. "We often do a club in Somerville and also some places in Harvard Square. Check the *Boston Gazette*'s calendar section on

Thursdays and you'll see us listed under "Rock," somewhere in town. We play out five or six nights a week."

"Really?"

"Yup. We're a busy band," he boasted with a smile. "Not much time for fun!"

The conversation dropped off momentarily as he looked over towards Kristin's bar. He was thirsty for a shot of tequila, which he occasionally grabbed between sets. His voice got dry from singing and shots of the "nasty cactus" cured it. Since he was employed as an entertainer, he was actually "crew" on the ship and was not allowed to drink while working. The State Liquor Commission had hard rules on these cruises and often planted people to bust offenders. Tonight no one from the liquor commission was on board. Robie glanced back at the two girls as he walked over to Kristin. He caught them looking at him; they were probably talking about him as well. He was flattered by their comments and surmised that he could "have" one of them if he worked at it. Sally was really "fine," in his mind. At the very worst, he could give them his phone number and hook up at some other time.

Kristin was busy but saw him in the corner of her eye. She had a crush on him, too.

"Hey, babe," he said, "can you grab me a 'cactus'?"

"Sure, hon," she responded, as she poured him a shot. "You guys sound great tonight!"

"Much appreciated," he said, as he pounded down the drink.

He licked some salt he had sprinkled between his thumb and forefinger and then bit into a wedge of lime. He squinted his eyes and pursed his lips.

"Jeez Louise!" he said, "That was sour!" He would have another.

"Thanks, babe," he said as he stared at her body.

"What's the matter?" she asked, "They not interested in you? One of them is cute!"

"Who?"

"Them ," she said, pointing her finger. "The girls over there . . . they're hot for you!"

"Really," he said. "How did ya know that?"

"Easy. Can see it in their eyes and moves. They've been in front of you all night!"

"You been spyin' on them?"

"Ummm, not really. Was watchin' you, myself." Kristin said.

"Ooooh, now how did I miss that?"

He was aware that Scottie had been with Kristin once before. Scottie had spilled the beans one night in Cambridge where the two of them had shared some beers at the Zie Brew House, a restaurant and beer bar. It was not just a regular bar, but a bar with some four-hundred selections! Robie was very much interested in taking Kristin home, that is if Scottie had no prior arrangements. Besides he thought, Scottie only had one fling with her, and he was supposedly committed to someone else.

Kristin had been waiting for Robie to ask her out and preempted his thoughts by saying, "Hey, Robie, what's up for later, after the cruise? Do you have plans?"

"Nuttin' happenin' yet," he replied. "Any ideas?"

"Maybe we could hook up later!" she laughed, raising her eyebrows twice. "That is if you have no plans—no groupies chasin' after you!"

"Groupies, what groupies? Them? Not a chance. Sure you're not busy?"

"No—not too busy to hang with you," she replied.

"A-OK!" he said excitedly. "We're on for later. Gotta go. Gotta do some tunes now. Bye for now."

"Bye," Kristin said with a smile.

At that moment, he knew he was "in"—that she wanted to get together—tonight!

He winked and headed back over toward the stage. He was beside himself. Obviously Scottie was not in the picture tonight! Robie was fired up after that conversation. He was now on a mission. He would do his damnedest to get in the sack with Kristin. Now, sensing they were out of the picture, Sally and Donna were working on two guys from Boston University. They could see Robie and Kristin's connection and chemistry and knew they didn't have much of a chance with him. Robie's mind was elsewhere now as he pictured Kristin without her shorts. Scottie had told him of her preference for thong underwear and her appetite for "various sexual positions." She liked to keep her underwear on when making love and pull it to the side at critical moments, Scottie had said. Robie was getting aroused at the thought of her naked. It became noticeable to the band members. They teased the hell out of him. He would be thinking about her during the next set. It would be a long set, too.

The upper deck of the *Queen* was becoming chilly and most of the passengers had moved to the lower deck for protection from the wind. Overcast summer nights in the harbor could be cool especially when the cruise boats headed into the wind. An "ambassador" from a group of twenty or so passengers had requested the happy birthday song for a friend. During the second set Robie would oblige. After all they had paid $17.50 each for the cruise and appetizers. His job was to be as cordial as possible to the paying customers. The night before, he had to do that same song four times in three hours for four different birthday people. One of the men in the group tonight smiled and slipped him a twenty for the inconvenience. Robie just loved it when yuppies who worked in the financial district palmed him a twenty for such a simple gesture.

Tonight's cruise was a bit different in that it seemed to focus on a fortieth birthday bash for Mary Ellen Sawyer, a Boston travel agent. She worked for Charles River Travel Company at Kendall Square in Cambridge.

The delegation from her party asked the captain that the lights on the lower deck be lowered briefly when they were ready to bring out a huge birthday cake for Mary Ellen. Forty candles adorned the cake and it was slightly modified for her. It had been ordered from a bawdy pastry shop called Sweet Fantasy. The bakery was not far from the travel agency and the travel agents and staff often ordered specialty pastries from it. Tonight's creation was a reasonable facsimile of male genitalia complete with shredded cocoa-colored coconut for pubic hair and a cream filling. The coworkers figured that sweet old Mary Ellen, because she had never married, was an old maid and she probably had never seen the "wrinkled snake." After she was jilted at age twenty-eight, she had given up on men, other than casual dates, and concentrated on building a successful career. Not unattractive, she dressed matronly and acted as if she was older than her age. Her coworkers thought she would be more attractive if she wore youthful, more revealing, clothes. Although reserved about attention, she was secretly pleased that her coworkers had planned a birthday party in her honor.

However, she would flabbergasted by the cake they had ordered. Terri, another travel agent, had gone to great lengths to surprise Mary Ellen. To assist the baker, Jon Michel at Sweet Fantasy, with his creation, Terri provided him with a copy of *Playgirl*. Terri wanted the anatomy as long and as authentic as he could make on the sheet cake. Jon Michel smirked at the picture and said he could do better. He was no stranger to the anatomy he was about to create. He and his partner in life, Bruce, had moved from the "Castro" section of San Francisco to Boston. There was no doubt that any of his male bakery creations would look authentic. His shop was popular and it was not surprising that his business was booming. They made frequent deliveries to the Back Bay area of Boston. He and his successful business were recently featured in a low-profile *Newbury Street* magazine noted for, of all things, fashion.

Jon Michel laughed out loud at Terri's request for a facsimile of a black man's penis. Myth or folklore had swayed her decision for something very long and very dark. Milk chocolate would do for the skin tone. The tip would have a creamy white frosting accent. Mary Ellen was sure to be mortified. *The forty candles illuminating the exotic creation will certainly attract Mary Ellen's attention and will surely highlight her embarrassed face in the night,* Terri thought.

As the partying continued, Captain Warren Holland turned the *Queen of Shoals* northward and proceeded between the red and green buoys lining the Boston Harbor wharf area.

21

Martin Palmer stood at NEAir Gate 23A reviewing the departure screen suspended from a ceiling mount. It was just to the left of the North East Air gate check-in counter. He had missed Flight 2158 by minutes and he was pissed. There would be only one more flight to Manchester, New Hampshire, that evening and he would have to wait on standby. The later flight was full and, in fact, currently overbooked. Flights at Logan were generally overbooked by 30 percent to compensate for cancellations and this evening was no different. His luggage had probably been transferred to 2158. Martin had to come from Terminal A, some distance from the North East Air's departure gates in Terminal E. Each terminal at Logan was separate and it often took a long time to walk from one to the other. There were the standard buses and walkways between the terminals; however, the buses were unreliable and slow. Tonight they were virtually nonexistent.

Terminal A once had been the domain of the now-defunct Eastern Airlines. With Eastern's demise, Continental Airlines had taken over all gates at Terminal A. Martin's incoming flight from Phoenix was on time, but he had stopped for a beer and ended up talking to a gal sitting at a bar in Terminal A. Engrossed in conversation, he had lost track of time and missed the connection to Manchester. Little did he realize that the woman he had been talking to had probably saved him from disaster. As he looked at the screen, he had no idea that Flight NEAir 2158 was in peril. He knew that the flight had departed on time, but no one told him of the current situation.

Standing at the NEAir's check-in counter, he asked if he could get on the next flight to New Hampshire. He was panting like a dog from running all the way from Terminal A to Terminal E. Every flight on the monitor was delayed or on hold. The weather was not that bad. He wondered why the delays? The gate agent at 23A merely told him that the later flight was full, and he was number five on the standby list. She recommended that he check back with the desk in an hour or so. He was frustrated and thirsty.

On his way to the closest bar for a beer, he noticed people staring out of the terminal windows. They were all lined up side by side and the waiting area was dreadfully quiet. He peered out a north-facing window and saw aircraft congregated on the taxiways and parking areas. There was absolutely no movement out there. *Odd*, he thought. An occasional police car went by with blue lights flashing. It dawned on him that the whole airport appeared to be on hold.

"What's up?" he asked a woman at the window who seemed very distressed.

"We don't know," she said cautiously. "Apparently 2158 has a problem and the plane is returning to Logan. All they would tell us at the counter was that there has been a mechanical malfunction and that they need to come back. They have assured us that everything is OK. My husband is on that flight. I stayed long enough to watch the takeoff, and now this happens. We don't even know what the problem is," she sobbed.

He touched her shoulder in a reassuring way. "My God," he said. "I was to be on that flight, but I was late. What could have happened? I was just going for coffee. May I get you something?"

"Sure, that's nice of you. Coffee please, no cream or sugar," she added.

"My name is Martin. Be right back."

She thanked him and continued standing at the window, a well-used tissue tightly clasped in her hand.

Martin ordered two coffees to go at a nearby kiosk. The beer he had wanted could wait. He was not in the mood for it now. *Those last beers might have saved my life*, he thought. Until now he had never really contemplated crashes or "mechanicals" in the air. Martin returned to the woman and joined her standing and staring into the night.

In New Hampshire, Martin's friend Monica would be waiting for 2158. Perhaps, he thought, Monica would see that the flight was late and check her home answering machine once she arrived at Manchester Airport. He decided to leave her a message just in case. With all the commotion at Logan, it was sure to be magnified at Manchester's airport. Trying to reach her there might be difficult. Getting someone to answer the switchboard would be a greater challenge. Both airports would be bombarded with calls once the news broke.

Monica left Bow, New Hampshire, with time to spare. She anticipated that Marty might arrive early. If the plane was delayed, she could grab a drink at the Silver Wings lounge at the airport, find a table overlooking the runway and be able to see the plane touch down. Having him return home was always fun. Along the way in the car, she cranked up the local FM country music radio station. Martina McBride's "Independence Day" tune was playing, This was a "driving song," as well as an anthem for battered women. She loved that tune and knew every word by heart. As she drove on Interstate 89, she sang along. Continuing down Route 93 South, she merged onto Route 293, then peeled off onto Routes 101/114 east. Monica exited at Brown Avenue, a straight shot to the airport. She entered the short-term parking lot and headed for the terminal. As she walked across the parking lot humming the Martina song, she heard the engines reverse on a flight that had just come from Philadelphia. Marty's flight usually followed behind the 737 at that hour.

Stuffing her parking voucher in her purse as she walked, she entered the Manchester Airport terminal lobby and quickly checked the arrival monitor by baggage claim. NEAir 2158 was "delayed." No revised arrival time was displayed. She headed for the lounge and ordered a glass of merlot. This would be the first of many glasses of wine that night. She gazed out to the east and could see the green airport beacon on the hill. It danced in the fog and sent a cone of light from its beam. It flashed every ten seconds— mimicking that of a slow heart beat. The wine relaxed her. She waited for an updated arrival time on the monitor in the lounge to the right of where she sat. Monica did not think to check the NEAir ticket counter for an update.

22

Captain Pete's *Ellie May* had cleared the channel markers and was headed north toward Chelsea. He normally heard and saw the jets as they departed or landed at Logan, but tonight was different. There wasn't much activity for 7:45 P.M. *Odd*, he thought. He looked south toward the city and saw no airplane approach lights. There were usually strings of them, like Christmas lights, as the planes approached the runways. The lights of the incoming planes seemed larger in the front and smaller toward the back. He could see in the distance some red flashing lights at the north end of Logan, but he was too far away to discern what was going on there.

A lone sailor had just motored by his starboard side and tipped his hat as he passed. Looking back at Boston, Pete could see the beautifully illuminated spire of the Old North Church in the North End jutting upwards into the skyline. The white steeple is the same one that Paul Revere climbed and held his lantern out the window when the British were coming. Pete surmised that his view tonight was probably the view that the British had as they approached the harbor. Pete often went to dinner near the Old North Church. His favorite restaurant was Aqua Vita just off Hanover Street. Aqua Vita means water of life and he and Ellie May often would go there on Sunday nights. Since her passing, he found it difficult to return; however, he still requested their favorite table when he went alone. After dinner, he remembered, they would stroll the North End and stop by Café Angelico for cappuccino and a cannoli. At Aqua Vita, he normally ordered their veal special and tonight that thought made him hungry for something other than fish. He hadn't eaten yet and it was late.

23

Tony Tomasi, at twenty-three, was already considered an experienced ground crew member and baggage handler. He leaned over and touched a wet spot on the tarmac where 2158 had recently departed. Sniffing the tip of his right hand, he rolled the amber liquid between his thumb and third finger; he knew the smell and feel of Jet A fuel. *Flight 2158 had a minor spill*, he thought. He was well aware of the standing location of the plane prior to her departure since he was assigned to load another plane adjacent to where 2158 had sat. The fuel spot had trailed off from a larger center pool of fuel as if it were a snake with a large head. The pool of fuel was located directly under an area where the left engine and refueling port would have been located.

He remembered that 2158 had departed the Gate 23A area with only the right engine powered up. The left engine was idling to conserve fuel. This was a common practice by pilots when they anticipated a delay before take off. They did not want to waste fuel while waiting in line. Tony became concerned at the sight of the fuel leak. He knew that Bob Connolly was responsible for refueling 2158 that evening. Tony, who sometimes worked with Bob, did not want to be blamed for the fuel spill on the ground. There was no excuse for sloppy maintenance at Logan Airport. He also realized that 2158 may have had a fuel leak that went undetected before departure. *That would have been odd*, he thought, since the baggage handler or the pilot should have noticed it.

In addition, 2158 had departed the Gate 23A area before all paperwork confirming routine maintenance was provided to the captain. He knew this because he saw the paperwork still on the desk in the maintenance office. It was standard procedure to provide the paperwork to the pilot before departure. *Perhaps*, he thought, *this was a duplicate document.* After refueling, 2158 would have been relocated a short distance away to a parking area exclusively reserved for buses to shuttle passengers safely to each plane. Tony was perplexed.

He ran to the toolbox in the cab of the baggage truck and grabbed the large flashlight from the upper tray. He traced the flashlight beam across the fuel path on the asphalt where Flight 2158 had been parked. Occasionally, oil leaks in a turboprop were seen if they sat there for extended periods of time; but fuel leaks were not that common an occurrence. He grabbed his walkie-talkie to consult both his supervisor, and a crew chief.

As he was about to report his finding, Bob Connolly walked quickly from the service area to tell him of the emergency report concerning 2158. Bob had been notified by ALERT that 2158 was going to attempt an emergency landing, and that the FAA was immediately sending an inspection team to Gate 23A to await the plane and inspect the surrounding area. Anyone who had worked on the plane prior to departure was to remain in the gate area. Tony thought that Bob appeared indifferent when he told him of the impending 2158 crisis. There did not appear to be a sense of concern or emergency with Bob.

Tony had seen the emergency vehicles go by earlier and was somewhat aware that there was a problem. He didn't equate the emergency with an aircraft from a NEAir gate. As he thought of what he had just seen on the tarmac, the sweat rolled down his brow onto his temples. His armpits were soaked with perspiration. The denim blue uniform showed his nervousness. He would avoid being implicated in any problems since he did not work on the plane. He knew that both he and Bob should have noticed and reported the fuel spill before it had taken off. They were trained to notice those problems. If the plane went down there could be loss of life and negligence or incompetence was not something he wanted to be accused of.

Tony got an update on his walkie-talkie and said, "They're claiming engine problems! May have lost one and possibly two engines!"

"No, you're jokin', right?" Bob said.

"Hell no, it's no joke. Come on! They're hoping she can 'dead stick' it back to a runway. Everyone's on hold above us! Damn!" Tony yelled. "The fuel spot! There's a fuel spot!"

"What fuel spot? What are you talkin' about?" Bob asked.

"I just spotted a fuel spill! Right by where she was," Tony exclaimed as he ran. "Quick, come here! Quick, look here! Look at that!"

"Shit! When did you notice this?" Bob asked.

"Just a minute ago," Tony replied as his hand and flashlight shook.

"I never saw anything earlier," Bob said. "There's no way that it was here when she departed. Dresslers don't have fuel problems. They just don't lose fuel! I refueled her. There was no problem . . . no leaks!" He bent over and sniffed the liquid that he had touched with his finger.

Tony pointed the flashlight at the trail of fuel. Some fuel had evaporated but the residual stains of a spill could be seen. Bob followed the beam of light and looked at Tony in dismay. He knew that all ground crew were trained to observe engine problems and all areas around parked aircraft. They were trained to walk beneath the wings and along the fuselage prior to engine start-up and departure. The pilots check for those problems as well. They always do a "walkabout" before entering the cockpit.

Although the captain didn't have time to do that, the first officer had made the rounds but the plane had been moved after refueling.

"We're in deep shit!" Bob whispered to Tony. "Grab that bucket of surfactant and water over by the doorway. Bring some paper towels, too. Quick, grab it and bring it over here!" he said a little louder. He was now growing impatient with his young coworker.

"Hurry! Get the bucket! Bring it here!" he repeated with a sense of urgency.

Tony was confused. Bob Connolly certainly had seniority so Tony grabbed the bucket of detergent and began to splash it on the spot where the fuel had pooled. Slowly the rainbow lines of color from the fuel dissipated from the original spot. He poured the remainder of the bucket on the trail of fuel. Under Bob's flashlight beam, there was only a trace of the rainbow when the spilled fuel and water mixed. The towels mopped up most of the residue. Curious onlookers in the gate area looked down from above but could not see what the men were doing. A small child watched both men head back to the service area with an empty bucket in hand. Bob buried the wet paper towels in the bottom of the barrel outside the service bay door.

"They go there?" Tony asked.

"Nah, but it's the closest trash can. They'll be OK 'til I take the trash out later."

Tony was concerned since flammable liquids and rags were to go into a special vapor-proof container to prevent a fire or explosion, but he did not question Bob's directives.

Bob began scrubbing his hands with a fragrant soap, as if he had blood on them. Tony took some deep breaths and stood quietly nearby.

Bob turned and said, "Fuel spot? What fuel spot? Hey, Tony, you didn't see anything unusual prior to departure, did you?"

"No, ah, I guess not," Tony responded, shaking.

He was reluctant to be a part of this scheme and stared at Bob. It was beyond belief for him to imagine what was going on. Flight 2158 had not returned and Tony could see that Bob seemed unconcerned. Tony Tomasi looked at where they had cleaned up the fuel. There was nothing visible. Only a slight Jet A fuel odor radiated from the trash can. A lemony soap fragrance came from the mop sink in the maintenance area. A wet bar of Lava soap dripped on the side of the sink. Nothing more was said.

24

Kevin O'Malley sat in his booth in the Sumner and listened to the announcer at the Red Sox game yell, "That's six straight for Pedro! Pedro Martínez has just struck out his sixth consecutive batter! Holy cow! He might reach 20 K's tonight." The Yankees were still ahead 3-2 as the side was retired. Kevin planned to listen to most of the game because his duties as tunnel attendant were light tonight. Pedro Martínez was working on victory number fifteen and going for the Cy Young Award.

Kevin would love to be at the ballpark but perhaps he could catch a Martínez game when he was up again in the rotation. Maybe he would take the family this weekend. Pedro might be ready again by Sunday. With Fenway's ticket prices elevated again this year, ball games were fast approaching $150 a day for a family of four. Tickets, food, drinks, a program, a BoSox Team Yearbook and a facsimile-autographed baseball would easily add up to that.

His daydream of the weekend was shattered by the roar of the crowd on the radio. The game was now tied 3-3 as a home run was blasted over the left field wall, by John Valentin. Kevin shouted with glee inside his cubicle. No one could hear his exuberance, but he was ecstatic that the Sox had tied the game. *Awesome*, he thought. *They have a chance to win against the Yanks!*

25

Fire Captain Jerry Daley and Trooper Dick Smith were in constant communication with each other about ill-fated Flight 2158.

The safety of passengers, emergency crew and the public was a substantial portion of their responsibilities. Interacting with the professional controllers in the tower was key to overall success when disaster is impending. Emergency vehicles were now deployed and readied for response. With incoming planes on hold, as well as departure flights parked at gates and on taxiways, airport activity was at a standstill. Additional flights, which were low on fuel, had already been diverted to Bradley Field in Hartford.

Daley ordered the application of flame retardant foam on runways 33L and 33R. All emergency crews in the central Boston area were on call. There was yet no indication where 2158 might end up—on one of the prepared runways, in the water or on a house to the north of the city of Boston.

ALERT coordinated communications with municipal fire departments from the north to south shores of Boston. All local hospitals, including Massachusetts General Hospital were on "Code Red" as well. Medical trauma teams were alerted and on call, if needed. The new hovercraft from ALERT was mobilized to the north side of the airport.

If 2158 were "short," she would be in the water to the north of the runways. The crew of the hovercraft thought that this episode might be her christening. At 7:45 P.M. it was on the trailer at water's edge and the team, dressed and ready, awaited a command to deploy the new craft. The hovercraft was surrounded by the flashing blue lights of protective state police cars and officers. They had escorted her to the launch site at the northern portion of Logan's property. She weighed a ton but floated like a butterfly once launched. It was hard to believe that something that bulky and large could float, let alone elevate itself off the water's surface.

Jack Danton's car slowed to a stop a sixteenth of a mile in front of the Sumner Tunnel entrance. He fiddled with the radio in hopes of getting a news traffic update from some FM radio station. He hit the scan button and went around the dial a couple of times. *Fawn, if awake, would be concerned by now*, he thought. He was very late for her special dinner. He thought for a minute and concluded that all this delay was not normal. The tunnel got its share of traffic, but this was ridiculous.

Cabs, cars and two buses preceded him in his lane. When the buses moved ahead, he could finally see the green lights of the tollbooths. For the most part, the view had been partially blocked by the buses. He could smell the diesel exhaust as they idled. He had once been on a toxicology committee, which evaluated diesel emissions as they related to human inhalation exposure. Sitting in traffic, he felt like a test subject in a clinical trial. *It is toxicology at its finest, right here in line*, he thought. He was in a damn experiment. The odor from one of the commuter buses was making him light-headed. This was irritating to him in more ways than one since he had given up smoking years ago. Now he was faced with exposure to "second-hand bus!" He might have changed lanes at this point, but he already knew that staying to the right was a faster lane into the Sumner. He still had to contend with the jerk behind him who was blowing his horn in frustration.

"This isn't New York, ya ass!" he murmured to himself, "Why the horn? Can't be from Boston," he yelled out the window. "Cool your jets!"

Sitting there for what seemed to be forever, his attention was drawn out the left side window of his car. Across the Jersey barriers of cement, he could see two ambulances exiting the Callahan Tunnel. They were headed east and took the airport access road, moving at a high rate of speed with their lights flashing. No sirens were apparent. Moments later two more ambulances followed the route of the previous two. He noted that the logos on the side of each vehicle were the Town of Revere, Town of Charleston as well as two Boston ambulance companies. *Odd*, he thought. *Must be a situation at Logan. Something happened after I left the airport?*

Tom Harper, looked up from looking at his change drawer in the toll collection book and noticed the flashing lights as well. Soon two Massachusetts State Police cruisers emerged from the Callahan and headed in the same direction. *Something happened*, he thought. During his next coffee break, if he got one, Tom would call home or touch base with the troopers at the end of his tunnel. One way or another he would get the scoop from someone who had a scanner. The numerous police cars and ambulances indicated a major emergency.

Between tolls, Tom gazed at the sky. There was an eerie silence above. He had not seen or heard an aircraft for a few minutes and that, in and of itself, was odd. All he could hear were car engines running and the bells indicating a toll had been paid. Logan only shuts down in extremely foul weather. This was only an overcast sky. The weather was not that bad. The presence of ambulances and police cars and absence of flying planes had him baffled. At that point he knew there was something going on at Logan. This scenario had only occurred one time before, and that was ten years ago. He glanced at his watch. It was almost eight.

The state police had now positioned themselves on airport roadways entering and exiting the airport. Traffic from the eastbound Callahan was backed up from the airport access road to the tunnel exit. Traffic in both tunnels was now at a virtual standstill. *This has to be major,* Tom thought. In a few minutes on break he would find out. Taking another toll, he heard a low-flying helicopter overhead.

"Jesus!" he said as he saw the red cross on the side of the helicopter door. "That's LifeLine! What the hell are they doin' here?"

His voice could be heard by the other toll takers nearby. The emergency service medical helicopter LifeLine was usually used for transporting critically injured or burned patients from automobile accidents to a local trauma unit at Mass General. They most frequently were called to accidents on Interstate Routes 93, 495 and 95/128. Not tonight. The helicopter was heading to Logan. Distracted by the chopper, he shortchanged a driver at the tollbooth. He apologized and palmed him another dollar bill.

Tom shut down his booth by turning on the red light overhead and began counting his cash drawer prior to taking a break. His supervisor had just waved him into the main office. He would need a new cash drawer for the next shift. He could now go find out what the hell was going on at Logan.

26

Warren Holland, the *Queen*'s captain, decided that after 7:30, since the cruise was going well, he would turn the wheel over to his first mate while he mingled with the guests. He would probably join in with the birthday gang below. He only left the bridge when the water was fairly calm and the vessel, passengers and crew were not endangered by heavy boat traffic, or the occasional lone sailor in the night. His first mate, Pamela Belgard, was very capable and well trained. She was eager to take the wheel whenever possible. Pamela was almost manly in features, a big-boned and strong woman. She had trained with the Boston Harbor Shuttle Service—public transportation that provided passengers going to Logan with an alternative mode of transport other than the tunnel and MBTA subway. She knew the harbor lanes well and was an accomplished first mate.

Captain Holland knew and didn't care that Pamela preferred socializing with other women. She did her job well and her sexual preference was her own business. Even though she was not obvious with her homosexuality, most of the crew suspected that she leaned that way. She lived with her partner, Susan, in Central Square, Cambridge. She and Susan often took in the night life between Central and Harvard Square. Small clubs on Main Street favored the Indigo Girls' music or Indigo "wanna-bees."

Pamela filled out her uniform on the *Queen* in a masculine fashion. Although her facial features were attractive in many ways, she hid her breasts well underneath her boat attire. Her hair was always cut short and severe—typical of the crowd she hung out with during her off hours. She had no attraction to the men on deck but would eye Kristin, Julie or Karen just for fun. Her allegiance was to Susan, her partner, even though she had a wandering eye. On a couple of occasions she had screwed around with other women when Susan was away on business or had gone home to Connecticut for the holidays. After tonight's cruise she would hook up with Susan at a Middle Eastern bistro in Porter Square. A late dinner and drinks would be in order.

Captain Holland informed Pamela that he was going down below to mingle with the crowd. He would be available by walkie-talkie if needed. She gladly grabbed the wheel and told him to have a fun time.

"Keep her straight and true," he reminded her. "Take her out another twenty minutes and then we'll turn her back toward Boston."

She knew the routine and navigational landmarks well.

"Aye, aye, Captain," she replied dutifully, as he disappeared out of the wheelhouse.

The floor below Pamela's feet vibrated from the volume of the band's drums and bass. Straight ahead she saw lovers looking out over the bow. The flag flew above their heads and they giggled as they talked. The sky was overcast and only an occasional patch of stars could be seen. The boat was well lit and everyone was having a wonderful time and the crowd was interactive and jovial. With the wheelhouse doors closed to the left and right, Pamela stood by herself in the small room. She was "in command" and loved the power. She could see the captain joining in with the crowd and pointing up toward the bridge. She hoped that he was probably bragging about her prowess again. He was.

27

Flight 2158's Captain Bill Bullock was sweating profusely as he and First Officer Bell together held their yokes. They had attempted to restart the right engine to try to gain some airspeed and lift. The right-side engine sputtered and strained once in response to their efforts. As the plane was dropping from power loss, Bullock and Bell continued to feel the momentary weightlessness from the altitude loss and rapid descent. Their bodies separated from their seats as the plane started to dive from the stall. Only their seat belts would keep them secured. They could hear passengers crying and screaming behind them. They could only imagine what was going through the passengers' minds. They had no time to explain since they were in "crisis mode" and their attention was devoted to landing the plane in one piece if possible. Adrenaline had kicked in and they were as alert as one could be in a dangerous situation. All their knowledge of flight would come into play—all the training over the years.

One heavyset passenger, who had not been wearing his seat belt, bumped his head on the overhead compartment during the initial rapid descent. His flailing arm smashed his wristwatch into the armrest and the watch stopped at 7:42 P.M. His bald head was bleeding from hitting an overhead light. He was stunned by the jolt and was grasping for the loose ends of his seat belt. Able to finally buckle himself in, he leaned forward to rest his throbbing head on the food tray that had popped open. There was no one to help him since everyone was hanging onto their seat arms for support. His injuries were not life-threatening and he was too scared to worry about a laceration on his head. Blood dripped down his face. He took his handkerchief and pressed it down firmly on the wound. His life was at stake and he knew that everyone around him was as scared as he was.

With flaps extended, the wingspan of the Dressler 205 was adequate to gain air in an emergency. The problem was that the plane had only reached 3,400 feet before the fuel cutout had occurred with the engines. Under minimum engine power the flaps had a drag effect, not assisting in "lift." Compared to the length of the fuselage, the length of the wings had a decent glide ratio, even without power. To return to Logan, Bullock needed to figure how to get lift. A stalled plane needed to drop hundreds of feet to regain air and lift. He would need to do a 180-degree turn to return to a runway. *The U-turn will probably give us lift in a more rapid fashion*, he thought. He would deviate from normal procedure of dropping the nose to gain lift. If the plane failed to get lift, it might drop on the residences below. A hard left turn would get him back over the water and the sideslip would give him speed and lift. In anticipation of an emergency landing on a runway, First Officer Bell had dropped the gear under the wings and the nose. The right engine failed to respond and became silent. The pitch of both props was rotated to reduce drag on the plane's wings. The propellers were free flowing now and oscillated gently during the descent. The silence in the cockpit was broken by the tower asking them to give a status check.

"We're about to do a 180!" Bullock said.

"We have no lift!" Bell cried out. "We've gotta get wind. . . . We've gotta get wind."

"An over the wing 180 might do it. . . . I'm goin' for it!"

"Roger, Captain," said Bell reluctantly.

"Together. Do it now!" Bullock ordered, with confidence.

"Yes, sir!" Bell followed his moves.

The airspeed indicator was now moving from thirty to sixty knots. Bullock cranked the rudder pedal hard left and firmly held the yoke. The yoke mimicked the pedal action. Bell's movements were in concert with the captain's procedure. The plane responded by diving left as the nose was dropping rapidly in front of both pilots. The left wing sideslipped and tipped almost straight down. Left-side windows were looking at the ground, but cloud cover prevented the view. This was their only hope of gaining air and avoiding a crash over a residential area. Momentarily cutting the air with the left wing down, the passengers' heads jerked right from the movement. They felt the plane slip into an abrupt left turn. There was no warning of the move. This maneuver increased the speed of the plane faster than letting the nose drop straight from a stall. With a right rudder out of the turn, the plane might level off and gain some air. Once level, the wings would grab air faster and recreate the lift needed to "fly" again. With the dual runway system, Bullock was hopeful they would give them two chances to land at Logan. Parallel runways were vacant for him to hit terra firma. They would be his choice, if he in fact had the choice. Without engine power he would need to glide to whichever runway had the easiest approach. Logan Tower Central controllers requested continuous status reports if possible.

On auxiliary power, Bell retracted the gear tentatively to reduce the drag during flight. Every procedure was now in place to maximize their chances of reaching land. They would grab any runway that came in view. A mist of fuel vented from the left engine and behind the trailing edge of the wing. They could not see it from the cockpit. Three-quarters of the way through the hard left turn, Bullock had felt the plane gain lift. It had occurred at a 35-degree angle as he was leveling it off with the right pedal. He had pulled up the nose of the aircraft at the same time. Now leveled off at 1,200 feet, his elbows were cocked tight holding the yoke firmly at the ten and two o'clock position. For the first time he felt exhilaration that they had come out of the stall—a major accomplishment. He and Bell had to fight the left and right yokes to elevate the nose to the level of the plane. The altimeter now read 950 feet and was dropping rapidly. Less than a minute and a half had transpired during the emergency turn. Even with the wings level and no power she could only glide just so far. Beads of sweat poured off both of the pilots' foreheads and their white shirts were soaked under each armpit. They radioed Logan.

"Logan? . . . 2158, we're level at 950! Copy?"

"Roger, 2158!" Tower replied immediately. "Nice job!"

"Can you see the field 2158?" the tower controller asked.

"Affirmative!" Bullock responded frantically, "Looks too far! Definitely too far!" They were below the ceiling now.

"You've got one and one half miles, 2158. Closest runway is one and a half!" the controller responded. "At your rate of descent on our screen, you'll be short!"

"Roger, Tower, we copy!" Bullock hesitated, "Glide ratio no good for that distance. Looks like we'll have to swim!"

"Roger, 2158, we've got emergency coverage, land and sea!"

"Can you advise us? Speed and altitude?" another controller asked.

There was no response.

"Advise of preference, 2158. Water? Land? Can you advise?" the controller asked.

"Don't know yet! Hopin' for land. Fightin' the yoke!" was Bullock's response.

"Give us fifteen seconds! We need fifteen!"

"Ya got it." The tower was quiet for the moment. Fifteen seconds seemed like an eternity to them.

With "Code Red" in progress, the ALERT team was advised by Daley and Smith of the potential water landing, if 2158 was short. The hovercraft would be launched on demand. The team awaited orders from the command post.

As seconds became more precious, Captain Bullock informed the passengers of his intent to return to Logan. He had no time to explain anything except to reassure them that either a land or sea emergency landing was possible. Bell calmly reminded the passengers of their need to secure their seat belts and reach for their flotation gear underneath their seats.

He asked them to remember that the seat cushions they were sitting on were flotation as well. They might be used to save their lives. Although he had hoped for a runway, he wanted to cover all bases in advance of a potential water landing. With engines out, there was minimal emergency lighting in the cabin. The intercom worked but they strained to read their safety information cards in front of them. Some people wouldn't look at the cards. They were too scared to do anything. The hard left turn and rapid drop in altitude had left them in shock. Mary Hutton sat dazed and crying from the fear of dying in a potential crash.

Captain Bullock had told them in a reassuring voice that the aircraft could float long enough for them to escape. Of course he was trained to maintain calm, but he had no idea how long a Dressler 205 could float. If they chose to "pancake" it on the water with gear up, there would be minimal damage to the fuselage. If damage did occur, her belly would open and she'd sink like a rock.

Bullock rechecked the altimeter and snapped at Bell, "How high? How the hell high are we?"

"Six hundred fifty, Captain!" Bell responded under pressure. His stomach was rolling from fright.

"There's no way we'll make the runway with this rate of descent! Are gear retracted?" quizzed Bullock.

"Yes, sir!" replied Bell.

"The gear? . . . Are they retracted?" Bullock asked, as if he hadn't heard him.

"Yes, Captain, gear retracted!"

"Where are the flaps, in or out?" Bullock asked.

"Flaps deployed, sir!" said Bell firmly, but cautiously. He was now paranoid.

Bullock snapped again, "Pull them in five degrees! We need airspeed! Pull 'em in John! They're draggin' us down. Pull 'em in!"

"Flaps retracting!" Bell quickly retracted the flaps five degrees.

"Good job John! Good job!" Bullock said, positively.

John nodded thank you. He finally felt useful. The change in flaps maintained lift, but increased airspeed only slightly. *We should be able to go further in a shorter period of time,* he thought. Perhaps a runway could be reached.

The landing gear was still retracted since they had not decided on land or water.

"Take the flaps to zero!" Bullock ordered. "We need more speed and distance! We're dropping like lead. . . . Fuckin' plane! Fly, baby, fly!"

"Flaps to zero!"

"Dammit! She's like a truck. She's flyin' like a truck!" Bullock shouted.

Tower interjected, "Land or water? Advise please . . . land or water?"

"Water probable, Tower, but still tryin' for dirt!"

"Roger, 2158! Need a choice! Land, water, anything!"

Tower Control could hear mumbling over the radio transmission. Bullock and Bell were strategizing, as best they could.

It was "evaluate and implement . . . evaluate and implement," moment to moment for now. No one on the ground could assist other than to offer reassurance to the airborne crew.

The passengers in the front could hear the dialogue through the door. With engines out, the strain on the pilot's voices could be heard. The frightened, and now silent, passengers could foresee only doom.

Air traffic control at Logan watched the radar as Flight 2158 descended at a rapid rate in the direction of the northern-most runways. Of the two closest runways, they would have a chance at the one on the right side, if any at all. Five controllers huddled around one screen, fixated at the green glass monitor.

Sam Keating, a veteran controller, shook his head in dismay. He was seated directly in front of the monitor. His colleague and buddy to his right concurred.

"There's no way in hell that they can reach home field!" he gasped.

"Their descent is too rapid," another man added. "They're gonna hit the drink!"

"Look at the distance left and air speed. There's no way! No way to make it!"

"Advise them to keep their gear up and consider Boston Harbor," whispered a controller, who was looking over Sam's shoulder.

"They can lay her down in the harbor. Perhaps use the channel markers as a guide."

"What do you think, Sam?" a controller asked. "This should give them a corridor of safety, like landing lights!"

"Boats? What about boats?" a third controller asked.

"We don't know what's in the harbor? Call the Coast Guard!"

"No time. Doesn't matter," Sam replied firmly. "Boats or not, this may be their only chance to land!" Seeing the plane's rapid descent, Sam cried out, "Logan is out . . . not an option! Advise ALERT of a Boston Harbor approach!"

"Right! I'll do it!" someone responded nearby.

"I'm on the horn with them now!" the other controller shouted.

The hovercraft was launched immediately and rescuers awaited further orders.

From the intercom in the sky came a scream from Bullock to the tower, "Jesus! Has anyone figured somethin' out for us?"

"Roger, 2158. Decided for you! Go for water! I repeat, 2158, go for water!"

"Water?" he asked.

"Affirmative 2158, ANY water! No land available. Runways are a no-go! Confirm?"

"Roger, Tower, we confirm, 2158!"

Bullock and Bell had already resigned themselves to a harbor landing. They just wanted to hear the mandate from the Logan controllers.

Tower control advised Bullock of their angle of descent and confirmed their approach heading. Bullock was not surprised at their recommendation since he was struggling at the yoke and could see he was dropping short of the airport. In his mind he had prepared himself for a potential water landing. Bell had resigned himself to water as well. As a military man years ago, Bullock knew the basics of water landing and survival, and had undergone a Navy Seal training course. His mission now would be to insure the safety of Bell and the passengers aboard 2158.

Tower control had reminded Bullock that the instrumentation for landing at Logan's runways extended out into the harbor. They would surely hit the Instrument Landing System (ILS) piers in the harbor if they were too far left of their approach. Controllers would prevent that occurrence with feeding them proper vectors to land. Hitting the piers would mean certain death for all on board. The piers support the lighting system for final approach and were positioned well into the water in advance of every runway approach.

Landing away from the airport but in "the fat" of the harbor would allow ALERT rescue teams time to rapidly respond to their needs. The Dressler 205 would float long enough for help to safely disembark passengers from the aircraft. Damage to the plane would be minimal to the fuselage and wings. If ALERT was there fast enough, they might be able to secure flotation gear to the plane and save the Dressler; the priority however was the safe removal of all passengers and crew.

On a previous command, the hovercraft sat quietly in the harbor moored to an anchored auxiliary craft. The crew was aware that the decision had been made for 2158 to land on water. Divers were dressed in wet suits and tanks. They looked like something out of a James Bond rescue scene in the movies. They perched like cats on the sides of the boat as the four-wheel tow vehicle and trailer for the craft was being parked. Blue flashing lights from U.S. Coast Guard vessels began to saturate the harbor just north of the airport. This location of the harbor was a probable touchdown area for the plane and was becoming congested with rescue craft.

Fire Captain Jerry Daley and Trooper Dick Smith had informed all staff of an impending water landing for 2158, so all rescue units were mobilized. Local tugboats and Boston Fire Department fireboats were available south of the airport. They were to mobilize towards the north section of the harbor. Aside from on board firefighting equipment, they also had generators and high intensity lighting that could illuminate the harbor for facilitating the nighttime rescue. With the night rapidly cooling down and a mild chop in the harbor water, Daley knew that the increased winds would make the landing and rescue tricky. ALERT was best prepared for and experienced in runway emergencies, not water landings in the dark. The variable water conditions, wind and potential obstructions in the harbor could impact the landing and threaten the lives of the passengers and the rescuers. They were as prepared as they could be. For them, this was their first encounter with a water rescue of this magnitude. The "runway" was actually "the harbor" in its entirety. It could potentially be the most sophisticated rescue that ALERT would ever encounter.

28

Mary Ellen Sawyer stood near the bow of the *Queen of Shoals* and stared at the night sky above her head. It was cloud covered and getting chilly. Unaware of the special cake planned by her coworkers, she leaned over to her friend, Terri, and whispered, "It must be romantic to do this cruise with your boyfriend, huh, Ter?"

Terri acknowledged her with a nod and said that she and her boyfriend, Brad, had been on the cruises many times.

"Yeh," replied Terri, "wish he was here right now. We actually met here on the *Queen*. This boat means a lot to me. Wish he was here," she repeated.

"Sorry," Mary Ellen said.

"No problem. Tonight could be special, too," Terri said with a dirty laugh.

Mary Ellen was puzzled by the innuendo, but let it pass. Tonight, however, was girls' night out and no boyfriends would interfere with the plans for the party. Female coworkers and girlfriends of Mary Ellen's were the only ones invited.

The *Queen* moved smoothly through the harbor and had reached a turn-around point. First mate Pamela, still at the wheel, was about to head back on the return leg of the night's booze cruise. The captain was still down below and Pam could see him occasionally as he roamed the decks talking to passengers. Once she was turned around, the southern view from the ship became the skyline of Boston off to their right side. Beautifully lit, the Custom's Tower, financial buildings, and distant Prudential and John Hancock buildings stood out in the night. The State House at the top of

Beacon Hill could be seen as well. Closer to the water's edge were the lights of the Italian North End and the Lincoln Wharf buildings.

Robie Brooks reminded the band that they needed to sing happy birthday to Mary Ellen, but they still had a couple more cover tunes to do first.

Leaving Mary Ellen at the bow for a moment, Terri went back to the crowded deck to advise her friends and coworkers of the timing of the cake and candles. The huge phallic symbol of a cake was neatly hidden behind the bar. Kristin took delight in showing nonparty passengers the "monster" and joked that it once belonged to a boyfriend of hers. People were amazed at the realism of the cake and everyone got a good chuckle out of it. Scottie, who was nearby during one of her showings, bragged to Kristin that his was larger than that of the cake's.

"Sure," she said, "You wish! I've seen yours, you ass!" she joked, and poured a quick gin and tonic for a customer.

"This size is what men oughta have!" she quipped.

She then ran her finger over the tip of the creation and gently touched the frosting to her tongue.

"Too bad guys don't taste that sweet," she laughed.

Even the customer with the drink winced at that comment. He rolled his eyes and left.

The captain had just passed by and noticed the laughter. Everyone went silent and looked busy at work as he smiled and moved past the bar. He knew that Kristin and Scottie had dated on occasion and assumed what they were laughing at must have been sex-related.

After Kristin's last comment, Scottie went about his business as normal. He couldn't believe what she had just said. He joked to himself that he had a challenge ahead of him tonight if he was going to end up with Kristin. *If she's acting this way now, imagine what she will be like later tonight*, he thought. He figured that she was probably already sneakin' shots behind the bar. She was that giddy.

As the band neared the birthday song, couples danced slowly to The Eagle's tune "Desperado." Swaying back and forth, they embraced as if the words in the song were the story of their own lives. The only other person to ever do that song well was Linda Ronstadt and she had the voice for a sultry tune like that one.

The instrumental harmonies were complimentary to Robie's strong lead vocal. The passengers who were not dancing, stood in awe of the band's rendition of the tune. The boat seemed to pitch and yaw to the beat of the music. Mary Ellen stood at the bow of the *Queen,* mesmerized by the music. Her hair was swept back by the forward motion of the boat and the crosswinds. A U.S. flag flew high above her head and occasionally slapped the flagpole. The noise was reminiscent of a hand clap; it added a beat to the song. The rope supporting the flag rang out with a "ping" as the wind shifted the flag side to side.

The next song, "Happy Birthday," would begin the surprises for Mary Ellen.

29

Anticipating an emergency landing for 2158, Logan Airport was operationally on hold and had been shut down for the last three minutes. No flights could land except 2158; none could take off either. Ground traffic to and from Logan was further reduced to allow emergency vehicles to pass by. The heavy traffic jam was creating problems for rescue and fire crews. Passengers in automobiles and buses were stranded from services such as bathrooms, food and gasoline. No one would dare leave their car, yet they knew something was wrong. Many of them had seen the steady stream of police cars and ambulances heading for the airport. The police on duty wouldn't say much to people who asked about the situation. They didn't want to complicate matters by announcing flights being canceled or delayed.

Attempts to divert outgoing traffic from the airport up Route 1 toward Saugus were in vain. The frustrated passengers in cars fumed at the mess and lit cigarettes, which glowed like candles as puffs of smoke curled out of passenger windows. It would be hours before some would see Interstate Routes 93 or 95. Many people could be heard swearing and yelling comments in disgust. Comments like "What the hell, here!" "Friggin' Boston, friggin' tunnel." "What's this shit?" "What's the holdup, anybody know?"

The Quincy Market ramps north and south near Faneuil Hall were totally snarled and backed up on 93 South. Those ramps fed into the Callahan Tunnel from popular tourist areas on the Boston side. The Callahan received input from the west, the north and the south portions of Boston. From the eastern end, it was the airport traffic and western flow of Route 1 that headed toward the Sumner. To alleviate congestion, traffic from the Massachusetts Turnpike extension was routed south. State police were now strategically trying to reduce flow in and out of the area of the tunnels. Traffic to Boston from major arteries was diverted to Memorial Drive in Cambridge and Storrow Drive on the Boston side of the Charles River.

Tom Harper, back from a short break and tired from his first shift, gazed out of his tollbooth as cars became seemingly "parked" directly in front him. The mechanical toll arms that allow cars to pass were stuck in the open position. The last person to pay a toll to Tom had only moved ten feet. That meant that the cars supposedly exiting the Sumner one mile ahead were actually not exiting at all, he thought. He was right. The twin lanes of traffic of the westbound Sumner Tunnel were now full and at a standstill. Bright signs with flashing yellow lights illuminated the words STAY IN LANE at the Sumner entrance. The flashing lights reflected off shadows of people in cars and off the roofs of each vehicle. The flashing reminder for cars to stay in line was useless since no one was going anywhere.

One driver got out of his vehicle near the tollbooth and queried Tom about the delay.

"Don't know the problem," he replied. "Could be the 93 merger at the other end or an accident. This delay seems longer than most but it's not uncommon at this hour."

Annoyed at the limited feedback, the man returned to his car still mumbling. His hand hit the steering wheel in defiance. There was nothing Tom could do to appease anyone. No one would be moving for quite a while.

At the airport, the LifeLine helicopter had touched down on the marked helipad located adjacent to the ALERT building. The pilots emerged from the chopper only to be advised that they would be needed at the harbor. Communications had not updated them on their transit from Boston to Logan. At the control stick of the LifeLine's helicopter was Jim Keane, an ex-Army pilot with a track record of sixty or more missions in Vietnam. He had been shot down twice and knew what crashes were all about. Whether a plane or a helicopter, they often look the same on the ground after a crash. He was mentally ready for an emergency. He had seen most everything before this. His adrenaline was flowing. It was a chance to rescue someone just like in 'Nam. He was ready for action. He was a superb pilot with feather-like hands that flew the chopper like a surgeon operating on a brain.

Jim had carried out numerous rescues along the Mekong Delta in Vietnam and saved many lives.

LifeLine's aircraft was better equipped for emergencies than the Army versions for MASH. Each chopper was a "flying rescue unit" and miniature hospital, able to carry as many as six patients. A surgical suite was on board, which also contained instrumentation for resuscitation, defibrillation and a blood bank for transfusions. A copilot, a doctor and two nurses were aboard as well. For this flight a young intern joined the crew. As a "doc," this was his first mission in an actual emergency aboard LifeLine 1. It would be tight but they could accommodate that many for triage. What wasn't obvious was the one dozen black body bags hidden from view in storage. LifeLine was not a hearse but often had to act as one. Automobile crashes often had the worst outcomes and they had to be prepared. All in all, the crew was a precision "medical team." Combined with the emergency forces of ALERT, LifeLine's personnel and ALERT's medical staff often trained together for rapid response.

A state police helicopter was an integral part of the response teams. It was maintained and deployed at the ALERT building. It had just arrived from Boston and carried some state police officials from headquarters to monitor the Troop B at Logan. This chopper was normally used to transport the governor of the Commonwealth of Massachusetts, or to respond to automobile accidents on interstate highways, bank robberies, highway chases and boating and water rescues. Additionally, the state police chopper had stored within its emergency compartments limited scuba gear, oxygen, wet suits, and auxiliary searchlights for nighttime missions. State police dive units could be transported and dropped anywhere for water rescue. They were often called for missing boaters in lakes and ponds, for capsized vessels and for use in locating aircraft missing in woods or inaccessible mountain areas. Some flotation equipment was on board. The police were well trained to handle water and land emergencies.

Tonight, the two rescue helicopters would work in synchrony, coordinating their response to the situation. They might not be needed at all, but early indications from ALERT's staff were that Flight 2158 would be short of the runway. If there was a water emergency, the state police chopper had winches for personnel retrieval as well as rafts for deployment at the site of the crash. In less than one minute, both helicopters could be at a harbor site near Logan Airport. They would supplement the USCG efforts.

30

Robie Brooks and EXZILLERATION had just finished their last tune before the "Happy Birthday" request. He had signaled to Terri to get the cake and light the candles. On cue, Terri slipped quietly through the noisy crowd and headed to Kristin's bar.

"I'll help," Scottie said, as the two carried the large sheet cake to the side of the bandstand. Terri appreciated his assistance.

Mary Ellen was transfixed at the bow of the boat and was still unaware of the impending party in her honor. Captain Holland had made his way back downstairs after checking with Pamela. Aware of the birthday announcement, he would dim the lights on the lower deck when the lighted birthday cake emerged from the side of the stage. Scottie lit all forty candles and shielded it the best he could from the wind. Mary Ellen would need to be brought forward soon.

Robie Brooks stepped up to the center microphone and announced with enthusiasm that there was a special event about to happen. "Ladies and gentlemen, a special guest is here—one who is about to go over the hill!" he exclaimed.

The crowd nearest the bandstand went silent. Mary Ellen, realizing he was speaking about her, blushed as Terri escorted her to the stage. One hand covered her face as she was applauded by other passengers and friends. She was totally embarrassed. This was her first real birthday party in years and she hadn't anticipated so much public attention.

"Terri, you rat," she scolded as she shook her finger at her girlfriend. "How did you arrange this? I wasn't expecting all this."

Terri shrugged her shoulders and smiled with false innocence. Mary Ellen just shook her head while everyone clapped. Robie began the "Happy Birthday" song as the cake was brought from the side of the stage. People on the upper and lower decks joined singing the tune. The brightness of the forty candles illuminated her face; she was a very happy and blushing guest of honor. The captain even kissed her on the cheek.

"Here's to many, many more!" he said. "Happy birthday from the *Queen*!"

As Mary Ellen leaned forward to blow out the candles, the first mate at the helm, Pamela, blew the fog horn to celebrate the occasion. She would have done it forty times but the horn was loud and people would think it was an emergency. A couple of bursts of the horn was enough. As Mary Ellen looked down to blow out the candles she saw Jon Michel's creation and was mortified at what Terri had ordered.

"My God, what is this?" she croaked. "Terri! Get over here. Now!!"

Everyone laughed at the sight. The captain just rolled his eyes in amazement and walked casually away. He thought that the cake was novel.

The first mate continued to guide the *Queen* on a steady course between the buoys of the harbor. The *Queen* was nearing the southernmost wharves of Boston Harbor to her right. Positioned almost dead center in the harbor, the channel markers were almost equidistant from her port and starboard sides. She radioed home base of their location. The band and passengers were enjoying the party so much that the *Queen* might stay out in the harbor for one more go around.

31

Captain Bullock stared at the console in the cockpit. The altimeter was spinning in reverse. The plane had dropped 1,500 feet after the hard left turn and continued its rapid descent. At 650 feet, it had leveled off slightly.

Minimal lights were on in the cockpit and in the main cabin. The emergency power had kicked in when the engines finally cut out. Bullock looked at Bell and gazed below at the distant city, airport and water around Logan. Below the low ceiling, he could see more clearly out the cockpit window and visually judge the descent.

"Tower, 2158 requests vector for a water approach! Tower, do you read, 2158?"

"Roger, 2158," Tower responded. "Can you still see the harbor?"

"Roger, harbor in view! Vector us. Please!"

"Go right immediately! . . . 1-5-0 immediately! . . . You'll have your target . . . maximum opportunity for water. You'll be on final!"

"Roger, Tower 1-5-0, 2158!" said Bullock.

"Roger, 2158, you're cool! Hold her!" Tower responded. "Depending on your distance, you have the Chelsea and Mystic rivers, or Boston Harbor," the controller continued. "Take your pick!"

"Can we make the harbor?" Bullock asked. "It looks wider! . . . More latitude for the approach."

"Roger, 2158—radar shows it possible at your current descent!" replied the controller. "Bring nose up 5 degrees! Copy?" the controller continued.

"Roger, Tower, nose up 5 degrees, 2158."

143

"If you can reach the harbor, we can help you folks better," Tower suggested.

"Roger, Tower, we'll stretch her out . . . as best we can!" Bell said.

"Right now . . . ANY water looks good!" shouted Bullock.

"Copy, 2158 . . . do what you can. We're covering you for any water approach. 2158! Gear up?" continued the controller, nervously.

"Roger! . . . gear up, flaps retracted," replied Bell.

"Roll 'em out flaps to ten . . . if you can . . . less speed at impact!"

"Roger, Tower! Rollin' them to ten. Here goes . . . five . . . ten . . . we're there!"

Water approaches were not new to Bullock. He once had to "pancake" his plane in 'Nam. He knew what the feeling was like when the metal on the fuselage hit water. It was a sound that he had never forgotten in thirty years—much like the rest of the Vietnam conflict. He still had "jungle rot" after all those years. It manifested itself on hot summer days. His mind drifted . . . *Damn rot!* he thought. At that moment, in the confusion of descent, he flashed back to Vietnam. This "approach" was the same! His mind was now back in '65!

What's next? Position of the nose . . . they always said . . . flight leader always said watch the nose . . . the damn position of the nose! . . . puulll stick back! Trees! watch the trees! . . . "gooks" on right! . . . No! Not gunfire? . . . Shit! . . . "flame out" . . . no engines!

Bell yelled, "Bill, where are you? . . . Where the fuck are you? . . . Bill?"

"What? Wad 'ya say?"

"Where the hell were you? . . . You were MIA!"

"Sorry! Sorry man!"

"2158, Copy? 2158 . . . You OK?" yelled Keating in the tower. "Get back! 1-5-0 . . . 1-5-0!"

Bell yelled, "Copy, Tower . . . back on 1-5-0! . . . We're back . . . back on track."

"Good! Glad you're there!" retorted Keating.

If the approach was right, the nose would be slightly up and the plane would touch about midway back on the bottom of the fuselage. The propellers would not interfere; it was a top winged aircraft. They wouldn't touch the water. If the props did, it would be minimal unless she listed left or right upon impact. That was a serious complication because one or two blades could spin her about in a 180-degree turn if they grabbed hold of the water.

Bullock envisioned the landing in his mind. If she landed midsection, and the chop was light it would touch down like the *Blue Goose*—the Howard Hughes seaplane of notoriety—did years ago.

Bell finally hit the intercom button. This was his first announcement in minutes—very long minutes. To the passengers it felt like hours. He quickly and calmly told them that a decision had been made to land on water. There was a groan from the back of the cabin. There was no way to reach Logan without power he told them. Passengers scrambled to grab life vests under their seats. Some already had put them on. He reminded them of the exit rows and that the seats cushions could be used as backup. He assured them that the airplane would float for a period of time. There would be time to get out, and help was already on its way. Many hunched over as directed, with knees to chest.

"Stay calm. Stay calm," he repeated. "There are rescue craft waiting at this moment. Everyone will get out. You won't have to use your vests for long, if at all. I promise!"

He had a reassuring voice, which Mary Hutton found positive. Although scared, she had faith in what the two men up front were doing. *After all*, she thought, *they were trained for this, right?* She could see little to nothing out her window since the left side faced the ocean on the final approach. Any land was directly below them or behind them. In the darkness they would not see when they were going to touch down. If they reached Boston Harbor, the airport would be somewhere to the left and Boston to the right.

Bell reminded them that when he gave the command, they should put their heads between their knees and remain calm. The reason for the schematic drawings on the safety cards in front of each passenger were now becoming apparent. Having been reminded of safety features on hundreds of other normal flights, many people wondered if they would remember what had been told to them over and over again. Some passengers wished that they had paid more attention to the safety instructions. The time was almost 7:50 and the adrenaline was flowing. Survival was the thought—nothing but survival. Instinct would guide them.

Bullock and Bell conversed quietly as they struggled with the yoke. They were trying to decide the best landing location in the harbor. Occasional turbulence and bumps were felt during the descent. They were now at 620 feet and dropping rapidly. Winds were from the north. Since they were heading south, they could not take advantage of the wind to increase lift. They did gain speed from the tailwind. Bullock told the tower, "We're comin' in . . . 620 and dropping . . . wings level . . . holdin' her steady!" Bullock said nervously.

"Roger, 2158! . . . Good luck! . . . Coast Guard sees you! We've got you tracked," continued the Tower. "Your estimated water contact is 45 seconds! Airspeed 125 knots. . . . Confirm?"

"Roger. Airspeed 1-2-5 and descending, rapidly! Wish us luck!"

"You got luck!" the Tower replied confidently. "We've deployed ALERT rescue . . . we know where you'll be!"

"Five hundred fifty feet and lined up, Tower. Dead center!" Bell reported.

Bullock responded, "OK, John-Boy, count down every twenty till we're at sixty feet; then give me tens!"

"Roger Capt'n. . . . 500 . . . 480 . . . 460 . . . Elevating nose five more degrees . . . hold her, ho . . ld, . . . ho . . . ld her, ho . . . ld her, good, good, she's there! Steady. . . . Steady."

Bullock glanced both right and left. He was dead center between the red and green channel markers. The buoys were lit like a guided runway. He knew he was golden if he could maintain the midline of the harbor. *Like sewin' a needle in the night*, he thought. He was there!

"Four hundred . . . 380 . . . 360," Bell counted down.

"Altitude 360, Tower," responded Bullock.

Tower interjected "You're dead on . . . hold her . . . hold her!"

"Altitude 3-0-0."

They were crossing the Mystic Tobin Bridge and the Mystic River below. The river merged with the harbor ocean water; so did the Chelsea River to the left of the plane. They would be landing dead ahead on a wide, well-lit part of Boston Harbor that paralleled the wharves south of the Mystic River and by the Charlestown Naval Yard. Below the incoming Dressler 205 was "Old Ironsides," majestic and stationary with its dimly lit masts. The grand old lady of the harbor rocked quietly unaware of the impending danger above her. Two hundred years ago she sailed on her own; a battle horse that won all her battles and was still afloat. Like Flight 2158 above her, they would need luck as well to survive the punishing chop of the saline harbor.

If all went well, 2158 would fly over dry dock Number 1 and 2 by the USS *Constitution*. Flight 2158 was now on target. Bell called out at 220 feet. She was now over water slightly left of the U.S. Coast Guard base. At the current rate of descent, she would touch down adjacent to Constitution Wharf, then slide by Battery Wharf, then Union, Lewis and then stop somewhere between Commercial and Long wharves. It was uncanny that the Tall Ships that visit Boston end up at Commercial and Long wharves, as well. None were there at present but many had been there recently for Operation Sail, a worldwide event culminating in Boston Harbor. On shore, Christopher Columbus Park, across from the North End, looked out between the two wharves where 2158 might end up. This would be a wide area for rescue, an open area for emergency craft like ALERT, the U.S. Coast Guard and state police boats to congregate.

Bullock could see the blue lights of small rescue craft dotting the periphery of the harbor. Clearing the boats in this short amount of time would be impossible. No one knew where she would touch down, glide to, or even end up in the harbor. Would she stay afloat? No one had a clue. Fortunately for the USCG, there were few pleasure boats at that hour. People on the wharves were surprised by the sirens across the harbor and the number of blue flashing lights over the water. Some people at the Charlestown Naval Yard noticed the low altitude and the whirring sound of an engine-less plane. They could now see the shadow of 2158 in the distance. Her landing lights were now dim from the depletion of reserve power. They knew that she was off course for an approach to Logan. She wasn't even close.

Commercial and Northern avenues, along the line of wharves, were now congested by vehicles and spectators running across the street to view the excitement in the harbor. Many Bostonians had no idea what was going on. Not everyone had heard of the emergency at Logan. Some of the rescuers were in the dark until the last moment when the broadcast came over the "emergency frequency" that the plane would definitely touch down in the north part of Boston Harbor. The exact spot was not known.

They would be ready no matter where she landed; the hovercraft was released from its mooring and sat idling. In a few moments she would be under full power.

Flight 2158 was now at an altitude of 160 feet with an airspeed just under 100 knots. She would hit hard at that speed. She was barely flying now, and any further decrease in speed would "pancake" her on the water, like a flat stone dropping on a pond. Bullock wanted her to skim the water upon landing and had increased the angle of the nose to accomplish that approach. Relying on instruments with a limited view ahead, Bell knew from the readings that he was moments from touchdown.

Bell called out, "One hundred . . . eighty . . . sixty."

"Tower, sixty feet and goin' in!" Bullock informed them.

"Roger, 2158 . . . good luck!" was the immediate response from the controller at Logan approach. His jittery voice could be heard over the microphone.

"Say a Hail Mary for us," the cockpit pleaded.

"Roger, 2158, consider it done! We're with ya . . . all the way. You're lined up. Bring her home!" Tower said.

Bullock was too busy to respond. He was transfixed on the harbor.

Bell called out loudly, "Twenty feet, and eighty knots! Heads down!"

At eighty knots the water came up fast and the fuselage slammed onto the harbor surface. An enormous spray surrounded the plane on all sides and covered the windshield as water hit the side windows left and right. Both Bullock and Bell's views were temporarily obscured by the spray. A multitude of screams were heard in the back of the plane.

"We're gonna die, we're gonna die!" a passenger screamed.

"Ain't nobody dyin'," whispered Bell. "Nobody's dyin'."

"Not on this flight!" Bullock murmured, fighting the yoke.

They were down and skipping over the surface of the water like a stone. The windshield wipers cleared the cockpit window. The sound of the impact was deafening and the roar of the water resounded in the hollow hull of the fuselage. Flight 2158 was a boat now moving at sixty knots.

Neither Bullock or Bell could hear their passengers, since they were intent on stabilizing their course ahead. They now had to keep her afloat. The plane had hit water at 7:51 P.M.—earlier than they had anticipated. There was no way for them to judge the exact moment since the airspeed had dropped precipitously in the final moments.

The impact of the crash had jarred the overhead compartments and some luggage and bags fell to the floor. One small bag hit Mary on the head. She screamed but was not seriously injured. It wasn't that heavy a piece but the sudden landing and noise of the water underneath her feet vibrated the entire plane. It was frightening to her and to all on board.

Arms outstretched, straight and locked at the elbows, both Bell and Bullock pressed their backs against their seats and held the yoke firmly. Their mission now was to maintain a straight course no matter what. With the nose down and the plane level at fifty knots on the water, they had their first real view of the harbor. Bell flipped off the windshield wipers for a clearer view ahead. They were distracting at this point. The rippling of the harbor chop slapped the bottom of the fuselage like a boat and they skidded along the water not knowing when she would stop. They could not reverse engines; there were no engines, except dead ones and there were no brakes!

"Hold her, John," Bullock yelled, "She's fightin' me. Hold it!"

"Got it. I got it!"

"Steady. Straight and steady!"

At fifty feet of altitude, Tower had lost them on radar. They didn't know if the approach had worked. They just knew that 2158 was down—and in the harbor.

"2158, do you copy?"

"Roger, Tower! Down and surfin', 2158."

"Copy, 2158. Excellent!"

"Maintain radio! You're off our screen."

John Bell fought with the yoke as best he could. Between the two of them, she was level and stable and afloat. Bullock was busy—he could not respond to Tower. The sound of the water hitting the fuselage masked all other noise in the plane. It rumbled below their feet.

Midway in the harbor, the *Queen of Shoals* was just off a wharf by the North End. To her left, a small USCG craft was hurrying to catch her in the last remaining moments. The *Queen*'s crew had not been made aware of the impending problem and had no idea that the flashing blues behind them in the distance had anything to do with aircraft that was about to land on the water. People on the stern were startled by the appearance of lights that they thought were another rapidly approaching boat. The silent aircraft and dim lights had given them no clue that an airplane was approaching.

"What the hell is that?" Bullock screamed in a panic.

"It's a fuckin' boat! It's a ship! Jesus Christ! A boat! Dead ahead!"

"Go left! Hard left!" screamed Bullock again.

Bell responded with a hard left rudder pedal and yoke. "I thought the channel was clear!" he shouted. The tower could hear the intercom.

"Shit! Shit! We can't avoid her," Bullock cried out. "Shit! Right wing tip, right wing tip! She'll hit her!"

Just at that moment, a portion of the right wing tip hit the stern of the dimly-lit *Queen*. The jolt sent some passengers at the rear of the boat overboard. There was immediate confusion and screams from the boat. Those people who could not run forward in time hit the deck or jumped. A portion of 2158's right wing was severed and fuel was sprayed on deck and into the water. Sparks from the impact of the plane's metal hitting the metal of the boat ignited the rear end of the boat and right side of the aircraft. Absorbing the brunt of the crash, the plane's nose was forced right and inward. It veered toward the boat at mid-hull, pivoted around the right wing, severing some of the railings on the port side of the *Queen*, and as it slid down that side of the boat it tore everything in sight. Screams on the plane and on the deck were overpowering with gasps of horror emanating from the surrounding rescue craft personnel in the area. Those watching were horrified. The Queen mistakenly had been reported south of the landing area. The *Queen* quickly became illuminated by the impact and fire that ensued after the fuel spilled. There was pandemonium everywhere. The band and instruments on board were thrown off the stage and onto the deck in front of them. Flames spread as the thick black smoke shadowed the night. The harbor became illuminated as flames shot up from the water, the boat and the plane. The terrified and screaming passengers did not appear to listen to the announcements.

Both the captain and Pamela had been knocked to the floor of the wheelhouse and bridge. He knew he needed to get control of the situation immediately. He felt panicked, himself. No captain could have anticipated anything like this. The captain and first mate tried to instruct everyone to find a life jacket and abandon ship. "Grab a jacket, everyone grab a life jacket!" he screamed. "Go to the right side of the boat! Right side!"

He grabbed the wheel as Pamela reached for the microphone. Across the deck was heard, "Emergency! Everyone . . . Attention! Attention! Find a life vest! Orange vest!" But with all the panic and screaming, they weren't sure that anyone was listening.

When passengers at the bow saw the flames at the stern, they began jumping into the water. They had no time to get life jackets. One passenger, on fire, was shoved by a friend into the water. The fire was extinguished as his head was briefly submerged in the cold water of the harbor. He paddled in desperation and was confused by the events around him. Aviation fuel was on fire on the water's surface. Emergency craft and the hovercraft sped to the scene. Blue and red lights flashed in the night. The USCG, the ALERT team and state police were now en route and trying to evaluate how to handle the entire situation. No one expected a collision. This was supposed to be the rescue of passengers off a floating plane.

Fireboats were summoned; the plane was floating but barely able to sustain itself. The nose and much of the cockpit of 2158 were ripped off and the whereabouts of pilots Bullock and Bell unknown. No one had seen them after the impact. They probably never knew what hit them, rescuers surmised. Portions of their seats were there among the flames, but the seat belts were frayed from the impact. Twelve to fifteen feet to the left was all that they had needed to avoid the *Queen*. Now, there was a major catastrophe in progress.

The impact of the crash created a deep six-foot gash along the port side of the *Queen of Shoals*. The gash was underwater, partially below the draft line. The damage was not known and could not be seen in the fire and debris. Water poured into the hull at a rapid rate and she began to list to the left. The nose area of 2158 hung precariously off the left side of the boat, tied together in an appalling collage of twisted metal, wires and flames. The additional weight of the plane on the *Queen*'s side made the situation more grave. The boat listed left and deck chairs, tables and band equipment slid in that direction. Some white plastic chairs—many on fire—were floating nearby in the fuel soaked waves.

Pamela shut down the engines on the *Queen*. The back of her head was bleeding from her fall and blood covered the floor around her. She was dazed but coherent as she did her best to stop the boat's forward progress. She rushed below to join Captain Holland and fight the fire. On-board fire extinguishers and fire hoses were near the crash area. Pamela's strength came into play in this situation. She had a man's physique to start with, and her arm strength was greater than most men on the boat. She managed to get one pump started and a hose directed at some of the flames. The captain moved to the starboard side, assisting passengers with life vests and calmly instructing people on how to inflate one of the life boats. He remained vigilant in the turmoil and was dedicated to saving anyone he could. He knew that there would be help from rescuers, but some people couldn't wait.

Kristin's bar area was a mass of broken glass and spilled liquor. Every bottle on the shelf and every glass was broken. Some people were cut by the flying glass; blood could be seen on various portions of the wooden deck. Some women sat in alcoves and along the wheelhouse walls stunned and sobbing. Many of the unhurt male and female passengers came to the aid of people in distress. They became part of a community of lifesaving. The uninjured were applying first aid as best they could. Life jackets above the bar were now on the floor. Some people were selfish and hoarded what they could for their friends. The problem was that many of their friends had already jumped overboard in fear of the fire on the rear left of the *Queen*. Smoke billowed from the boat and plane tangle as rescue craft neared the sight of the confusion. They had to be careful since they knew that many boat passengers and potentially two pilots from the plane were in the water. They didn't need any propeller-induced deaths from rescue crafts that were supposed to be helping.

Massive search lights began to light up Boston Harbor as rescue craft surrounded the disaster and illuminated the entire area. Two helicopters were heard overhead as ALERT and state police rescue aircraft approached the scene from different angles. The harbor shoreline along Commercial and Atlantic avenues was jammed with cars and people standing on shore aghast at the scene in the water. The normally quiet harbor had never seen the likes of such an accident. There was fire, flashing blue and red lights, the sound of water craft, sirens and the rotors of the choppers that eerily contrasted the night sky that was lit by the reddish-orange flames at the crash scene. The shadows of people on deck scurrying around could be seen from shore and the twisted, mated sections of the plane and boat were horrifying to viewers on the shore. They knew there was death aboard the boat and in the water, but no one knew what amount of devastation and loss of life had occurred.

"Jesus! What the hell happened out there?" could be heard throughout the crowd on shore.

The scene became more morbid as people started describing what they had seen. Their imagination added fuel to the reality of the tragedy in the harbor. All of a sudden people were creating stories claiming that the plane was on fire before it landed or that the boat blew up with people flying through the air. These were fabrications that would become perfect head-lines in the tabloids around the country. None of those stories were true.

Minivans from area news TV stations converged along the wharf areas. Microwave towers were elevated from the news vehicles and people with cameras shoved their way through the throngs to get the best view and "scoop." They immediately interviewed anyone and everyone who may have witnessed the accident. They were on a mission to get the breaking news stories that they needed for 11 P.M. TV stations throughout the area cut into their normal programming with their news bulletins. They would have live coverage for hours to come. Newspaper headlines the following morning would show this to be the "first-time-ever" type of accident in the harbor. Nothing had ever come close to this in the history of the Boston harborfront.

A reporter from TV News 3 stood at the edge of North End Wharf. Microphone in hand and with camera and lights on him he solemnly stated: "This is News 3 . . . Breaking news at Boston Harbor! . . . Tonight, a commuter . . . "

As he continued his live-action report, other reporters found his strategic location perfect for viewing the crash and interviewing people. When out of facts, reporters would reiterate what was known. Conjecture and speculation would dominate the airwaves for hours. Interviews with local residents and witnesses would occupy their broadcast time. Most of the information would be sensationalism, not fact.

Two helicopters from area TV news organizations joined their ground support colleagues and hovered over the harbor from afar. They were instructed by Logan tower to keep their distance from the rescue operations. They were, however, kind enough to offer their assistance from the air, if needed. For the moment, they would grab what they could of the breaking news event and the impending "story of the decade." They were transmitting live pictures back to their parent TV stations north and west of Boston. All three local stations, Channels 3, 6 and 21, were now on the air with highlights of the evening. Only Channels 3 and 6 had live chopper coverage.

Massachusetts General Hospital and six other medical clinics were on full alert for potential trauma cases and were set to triage the incoming injured passengers. Backup personnel for all major hospitals were called in from home, if available. The Red Cross and blood banks were on alert. A local TV station gave out information of blood types currently in limited availability and types that would be needed for surgery. Type O, the universal donor, was requested. Type O was always needed. Type A was plentiful but B was needed.

Logan tower controllers, including Sam Keating, stood stunned in the dimmed lighting of the radar room. They could not have predicted this ending to 2158. A perfect landing had been in progress. Why did the harbor have the cruise ship in it? Why was the area not cleared out for the landing? Their confidence in the overall rescue system and operation was questioned. They had worked hard to bring her in. They had in fact brought her back. The ending was not supposed to be like this. Everyone was to survive and the tower personnel and pilots were to be heroes. They shook their heads in disbelief as they pondered their next step in reviewing the airport congestion in the air above and still on the ground. They would need to bring some planes in immediately, those with low amounts of fuel. Planes on the taxiways and at gates would need to be addressed as well. There was nothing they could do about the harbor crash. The FAA was notified, and the NTSB would be summoned as quickly as possible to investigate the crash.

Meanwhile in the Tower Restaurant and Skyline Lounge patrons clung to the glass windows facing Boston. In silence they stood there pondering the sight in the distance. No one was ordering drinks but some had their eyes cast on the TV and then back to the view of the harbor. Back and forth, their heads strained to decipher the situation. People could not believe what they were seeing.

32

Heading toward the mouth of the Chelsea Inlet north of Boston, Captain Pete Thompson tossed his cigarette butt over the side of the *Ellie May*. He was startled by the sight of an aircraft so low over the harbor. Turning his head rapidly over his shoulder, he remarked to himself, "That's odd—the plane's damn low. Too low!" Logan didn't have runway approaches from that angle anyway. *Not only that,* he thought, *I can usually hear planes taking off or landing over the rumbling engines of the* Ellie May. This airplane was silent. There was no sound from the plane as she passed by to the west of his boat. It was shortly thereafter that he saw the flames. He had just come from that area and nothing was wrong when he had unloaded his catch and left the fish pier.

Captain Thompson quickly turned the *Ellie May* around and throttled up her twins engines. He knew he had a couple of miles to go to get there and he could feel the old engines groan at his request for more power. They responded but occasionally one would backfire as he increased the throttles.

"Jesus!" he murmured. "What the hell has happened he-ah?"

He could not push the engines faster so he took the time to light another cigarette; it required three matches to get it lit. His weathered hands were shaking from the sight of the fireball in the distance.

The *Ellie May* had a dinghy, a life raft and flotation devices. Pete kept safety gear on board for the occasional rescue of a fellow lobsterman. He could now hear the sirens and saw numerous police and USCG boats with lights heading that way. A sight that took him by surprise was the giant alien-looking hovercraft that elevated itself from the surf. She was spraying water everywhere as she picked up speed over the water's surface. The sound of the air rushing beneath her scared the hell out of him. "What a contraption. What the hell is that?" he said at the sight of her austere presence. "What the. . . ."

His voice was deafened in the night air as the hovercraft captivated his mind. It was the most powerful contraption he had ever seen on water. "Well, I'll be," he said. "Must be that new thing they been talkin' 'bout."

The blue lights gave its ownership away and Pete finally realized that the harbor police or somebody had a new "toy"—a frightening new toy. The hovercraft was now under full power and heading in a southerly direction. She would be at the site of the crash in thirty seconds or less. She was fast because there was no resistance from the water on her hull. She glided above the surface and in the night resembled a Loch Ness demon of sorts. Below the white mist on the ventral side of her engines, he could now see the outline of her shape. At first, he thought that she looked like something out of a Batman movie—sort of an alien craft with flashing blues above her. Pete would follow in her wake, a smooth footprint from the massive air rush across the water. It was the widest wake he had ever seen.

Numerous scuba divers, fully suited with tanks on their backs, were shadows and silhouettes against the backdrop of the harbor fire. Captain Pete hit the throttle again but it was advanced to the maximum and the engines would go no faster. Behind him he could see other small craft heading toward the fire as well. It was a cardinal rule, sort of an eleventh commandment, that trouble on the water elicited a response from all able craft. Frequent calls to duty often include boat engine fires, dead engines, accidents, medical and nautical problems. The helicopters overhead were a sign of the magnitude of the situation. No other pleasure craft were in the harbor, perhaps at the direction of the USCG. They knew Pete's boat and no one would prevent him from assisting. He had an inexpensive, emergency red-flashing light which he had purchased at the hardware store, the kind that local snowplow operators placed on top of their pickup trucks. He placed it on the wheelhouse roof and plugged it in to the cigarette lighter on the console. The coiled wire unfolded out the windshield and followed the roof lines toward *Ellie May*'s centered flag mast. The mirror inside the dome of the emergency light spun slowly as the red flashes radiated across the bow of the *Ellie May*. He felt official now, as he finally neared the site of the disaster.

With one hand on the wheel, he deftly donned a bright orange life vest. It was new—neither the vest nor emergency light had been used. The back of the vest had been painted with the words "Stolen from the Ellie May"— something he thought was humorous if it ever disappeared or was stolen. Tonight there would be no humor. For the first time, he could really see fire and debris on the surface of the water. His floodlight on the bow was focused dead ahead. Fire was a concern to everyone in boats. He didn't need to have his boat go up in flames. Pockets of fuel on the water's surface formed aggregates of candles in the night. The scene was disconcerting. The severity of the situation became apparent when he saw the plane attached to the *Queen of Shoals*. He felt a lump in his throat since he knew the boat crew well, especially Captain Holland. They were contemporaries and old fishing buddies in the off hours. To see the *Queen* in distress was gut-wrenching to Captain Pete. He knew how many people she held and right now, in front of him, she was almost empty. With fire around her and the plane partially embedded in her port side, she was listing badly.

That was not a good sign to Pete. She would only do that if massive amounts of water were in her hull. *How will they keep her afloat?* he wondered. Who was dead? Was his friend dead too? Tears came to the salty dog's old eyes. He knew he had to help. Lives were in peril and if he saved only one person, he knew he would be of assistance. He throttled back and could hear the Coast Guard and the ALERT staff using megaphones to direct rescue and assist people both on deck and in the water. *How can I help*, he wondered? He was mesmerized by the flames in front of him and by the sight of the mangled plane and boat combination. The *Queen*'s anchors had never been deployed. She was adrift in the harbor.

He idled *Ellie*'s engines and the yellow-orange reflections of the flames flickered off the white portions of his *Ellie May. This isn't a movie*, he thought. This was real and he was part of it. He stood in silence, sort of praying in the dark. He had to snap out of it if he was to be of help. Could he do just that? Was he strong enough physically and emotionally? How would he handle death, or the *Queen* going under, if she was to go under? Where the hell was the help—the help to save the boat . . . the people who were aboard? Help was there, he just didn't realize it.

"Lord have mercy," he whispered to the sky. A flash from a scanning spotlight from another boat in the area illuminated a body directly in front of Pete's boat. He now knew where he was, it was "hell on earth."

33

At 7:52 P.M. Tom Harper gazed out from his tollbooth and could hear numerous sirens on the streets surrounding the entrance to the Sumner. Almost immediately, Kevin O'Malley emerged from the tunnel entrance and he was completely out of breath. He had just run from his traffic monitoring booth deep in the Sumner and was not in great physical shape. He was sweating and gasping for breath when he said to Tom, "There's been a crash at Logan. I mean not at Logan proper, but in Boston Harbor!"

"Are you shittin' me?" Kevin exclaimed. "What are you ramblin' about . . . a crash?"

"Yeh," replied Kevin, catching his breath.

By now other people, including drivers from nearby cars, were gathered around him.

Kevin continued, "The radio announcer interrupted the Sox game to say that a small commuter plane had just made an emergency landing on the water. Hit some cruise boat or somethin'."

"Jesus, Kevin, where was this? When did it happen?"

Kevin went on to explain that it happened above the Sumner and Callahan. He could hardly get his words out without stuttering.

"You mean above us, on the water?" Tom said.

"Yeh, sort of —they are rescuing people in the harbor above the midpoint of the tunnel . . . like right above the middle section . . . out across the harbor."

Kevin had been engrossed in the happenings at Fenway Park when the news bulletin came across describing a plane crash, the traffic jams in east

Boston, at Logan and on roadways leading to the Sumner and Callahan tunnels. The reports included alternate routes to avoid the traffic jam. Details were sketchy but one thing was for sure, many people were killed or injured on the boat and plane. They did not specify numbers of people lost, but they were substantial. The pilots were missing and presumed dead.

"There's fire in the harbor right now," Kevin exclaimed. "The friggin harbor is on fire from the airplane gas!"

"Who's got a radio on? Anybody here got the radio on?" Harper asked.

Tom Harper asked a driver parked near his booth to tune into any news station for updates. The man obliged and cranked up his speakers and opened his windows so that people could hear. Other drivers came running to the tollbooth to listen. One person was Jack Danton, who had just heard the news himself. The reports were still preliminary; little had changed since the first breaking news on the Red Sox station. At the moment, it didn't matter that the Red Sox were winning. They cared about the situation going on above the tunnels. What would have caused such a catastrophe? No wonder all the ambulances had been trying to get to Logan through the traffic snarl. Without realizing that a boat was involved, they speculated that the plane had been destined for Logan and fell short or aborted into the harbor.

In her apartment in Cambridge, Fawn was awakened by the sirens on the Cambridge side of the Charles River. Fire trucks and Cambridge Police cars were shooting across the Longfellow Bridge adjacent to the condo complex. She rubbed her eyes to clear some sleep out of them and pressed her thumb and third finger from one hand onto the sides of her eye sockets. It was almost eight and she realized that Jack was not home yet and the Red Sox game was still on, now with words printed across the bottom of the screen. The moving line of information stated that a plane had crash-landed in Boston Harbor and a local cruise boat was involved. The news did not elaborate except to say "film at 11 P.M." It was clear to her that the crisis would definitely affect Jack's travel home. He was likely to be right in the middle of it. She began to worry about him.

The pot filled with water for the lobsters was tepid now and there probably would be no dinner. She had no idea when he would call her again. She did not have his new cell phone number to try and reach him. She would wait for him to touch base and continued to stare transfixed at the TV. The pictures from the Channel 3 TV News helicopter were frightening. The pictures showed the latest live shots of the crash—telephoto shots of the fire in the harbor. The copy line at the bottom of the screen now said:

BULLETIN: COMMUTER PLANE-BOAT COLLISION—LIVE COVERAGE.

At the tollbooth, Tom, Kevin and others listened for radio news updates. The traffic was dead still. Radio and TV reporters were still setting up at the harbor. They switched radio stations to an AM station. One with twenty-four-hour news had continuous reporting from the scene. Some reporters, who would do anything for a scoop, had weaseled rides aboard small craft at some of the marinas in the area. They would get somewhat closer to the crash before being turned back by USCG harbor boats and the marine patrol.

The left side of the airplane had some movement as the tail section bobbed in the water. Mary Holland struggled to free herself of her seat belt. The crash had left the forward cabin somewhat elevated. She would have to try to exit the back of the plane because of the fire in the front. There was a window exit a few rows behind her but there were injured people in some of the seats next to the exit. Except for the firelight and light from the searchlights on the nearby rescue boats, there were no other functioning lights in the cabin. With major wiring cut in the crash, the automatic emergency lighting on the floor was dead. Wires and oxygen masks, deployed from the impact, hung like bats in the cabin. She batted one out of her face and prepared to look for the best escape route. Simultaneously appearing at her window was a mask peering into the plane. She screamed! It was a diver from the hovercraft. He had been sent to scout out the midsection of the plane which was partially submerged. He didn't expect to see anyone at the window and gasped at seeing Mary Hutton. He motioned with a single finger for her to wait a minute. She sat quietly as the plane rocked and creaked from the choppy water about her. Water was entering the aisle between the seats.

Passengers behind her heard her scream and started towards the midsection of the plane. All those people were congregating in one area and looking to escape from one exit. They were crying and sobbing and pushing their way to the window exits on both sides of the plane. Other divers appeared on the outside of the fuselage. Someone would have to open the window exits from the inside. Mary would not wait for the diver to reappear. She worked her way back toward the crowd. A businessman ripped off his suit jacket and shoes and released the hatch window. With a thrust of his arms he threw the window into the water. It splashed and floated away gently. Two divers appeared at the exit window to help people evacuate. Mary was quick to follow the men ahead of her. Some had flotation gear on and cushions. One fool had inflated his vest in advance of exiting. It would be difficult to exit the window with an inflated life vest. A diver at the opening was quick with a knife and punctured the man's vest, then handed him a seat cushion for flotation. He would be able to hang onto that for a while. He no longer was blocking the exit. One man ahead of her offered to help her exit.

She had no time to appreciate his thoughtfulness.

"Just go!" she screamed, "Just go! I'm right behind you! I can swim. Go! Go! Go!" she yelled. "We haven't much time."

He jumped to another waiting diver. The man couldn't swim but they got him safely into a raft. *How the hell is he going to help me*, Mary thought. *He can't do the dog paddle!*

The plane was taking on water and now the aft section was lower than before they had exited. The more the boat listed, the more the plane loosened from the hull it was attached to. The businessman and Mary had entered the water as fast as they could. She could swim even with clothes on but it was damn cold and that was something that she was not used to. After three paddles, she was grabbed by the diver who had appeared in her window. The man ahead of her had disappeared from view. She would not know if he made it. The diver had returned to her window and saw no one there. He then figured that she had moved to an exit a few rows back. With her vest inflated and his one arm under hers he could see that she was exhausted and traumatized. She literally passed out on his arm and he held her up as he sought assistance. Another diver soon came to their aid.

The *Queen of Shoals* was being sprayed with water from the fireboats. The port side fire was somewhat under control although not out. The remaining passengers moved to the starboard side as she listed to the left. They had trouble standing and they grabbed the rails while they awaited rescue. Some of the people could not swim and decided to wait for help. Passengers who were soaked had shed their clothing and were shivering in their underwear. They did not want to weigh themselves down in the water. Vanity and modesty were not issues at this point. After all, this was survival and if some people saw some breasts and ass, they didn't care. They probably would not see their rescuers again anyway, they thought. Besides, blankets and jackets were on rescue ships. They could cover up later . . . when they were safe.

As the band rushed to the high side, Robie watched in dismay as some speakers and his Fender "strat" guitar slid across the deck and into the water. His prized "axe" was gone—she was really gone. The acoustic Martin was gone as well. Awaiting rescue, Robie grabbed a nearby fire extinguisher and fought off flames that licked a portion of the starboard side. Foam flew everywhere—everywhere but on the fire. The wind blew it away from the flames. In frustration, Robie threw the fire extinguisher overboard. *Great help that was,* he thought. He would look for a life raft. As he passed Kristin's bar, he saw her sitting dazed, in broken glass. He quickly went behind and helped her up. No one had even seen her sitting there. Scottie, who was nearby, had been thrown in the other direction and was dazed.

Kristin's hands had been badly cut by a vodka bottle she had been holding when the two craft collided. Robie grabbed some paper towels and checked, but there appeared to be no glass in her wounds. He rinsed her hands with the water that she used as a mixer. She grimaced as he applied slight pressure to the cuts and wrapped the lacerations with paper towels. She had lost a considerable amount of blood. It was all over her white shorts. She was appreciative and he hugged her in a reassuring way. There was definite chemistry between them at that moment.

"You OK?" he asked.

"Yeh. Thanks Robie! What the hell happened?" She began to cry from the pain.

"We were hit—a plane hit the boat!" he said.

"A plane?" she said bewildered, "What plane?"

"Can't explain. We need to get off here!" he said encouragingly.

She would need some stitches or butterfly clips to close a couple of the wounds. For now the paper towels would serve as a bandage. No one could reach the emergency first aid kit hanging on the wall nearby. Fire was adjacent to the first aid box.

"I'll tell you later. Let's go! Let's get out of here!" he said as some rescue boats approached the starboard side of the *Queen.*

"We need to move from here. Follow me, babe!"

Kristin followed him as he put one arm around her and guided her to the boat's starboard side. Her head was down and she grimaced as her wounds throbbed with pain. She sobbed after she realized what was going on. Someone else was dragging the unconscious Scottie to safety as well. A raft appeared behind Robie and other people on board began helping to inflate it. Just then, the captain ran over to assist.

"Grab the other end, son," he said. "It inflates from my end!"

"Yes, sir!" was the reply.

Calmly, they inflated and launched the ten-person raft over the starboard side. As a few people climbed in, other vessels were working their way in for the rescue.

"We'll be OK. Everyone in," the captain said firmly.

After filling one raft the captain remained to help others disembark. Pamela, the first mate, was assisting other people about fifteen feet away. A canister of compressed air made a whooshing sound as the second raft inflated. Passengers, wearing their orange life vests, cheered at the sight. Somehow calm prevailed. Many of the people who had abandoned ship earlier were being dragged out of the water by rescuers. They were blue from the cold harbor water, but they were alive.

Cries for help could be heard around the perimeter of the boat. Some passengers near the *Queen* dog-paddled to the waiting rafts. Passengers in the rafts assisted them over the side, each dragging the cold water into the bottom of the rafts. No one cared. They were being saved. The birthday girl, Mary Ellen Sawyer, climbed in and said nothing. She was stunned and unable to speak. She came close to dying on her fortieth birthday; she would have this memory forever. She did not know where her friends were. She was concerned for Terri, but was unable to call out her name.

Slowly the *Queen* took on water from the severe gash in her side. She listed even more to the left and now a portion of the side where the plane was attached began to go under. The angle of the starboard side was approaching 30–35 degrees off the surface of the harbor. The captain yelled to the remaining passengers to get off immediately.

"Everyone, abandon ship! Everyone! With or without vests—everyone off!" he ordered. "We have no time! Get off! You'll be OK. Abandon ship!"

No one hesitated. Even the most timid of passengers jumped into the harbor. With a loud frightening noise of metal grinding, the remains of the Dressler 205 ripped itself from the side of the *Queen*. The water she had taken on took her tail first. There was a loud rush of water as she entered the swell like the footprint of a whale that had just breached. Where she went under, there was a circle of calm water that radiated with fire away from the descending fuselage. She disappeared so fast that even the fireboat's crew and the crew of other craft couldn't believe their eyes. The *Queen* began to right herself toward the starboard side after the plane vanished.

Everyone had been removed from the airplane before it sank. The anterior portion of the cabin with twisted wires and hydraulics was the last thing to be seen. In the middle of the area where she disappeared, some carry-on luggage popped out of the water. On her descent, everything that was loose on the floor or in the overheads quickly emerged from the center of her "footprint." If it was loose and could float, it appeared on the surface of the harbor. Some rescue boats moved in to retrieve the luggage. The hovercraft and some USCG boats had grabbed many people from the water. Captain Pete had helped as well. He had inflated his raft and people were aboard his dinghy and in his raft.

The *Ellie May* had one person on board besides Pete—Mary Hutton had been placed there after being assisted by the scuba diver from the hovercraft. Pete had tossed a rope ladder and now she sat safely in the back of the boat. Mary had never gotten the diver's name, but she would remember that partially covered face forever. A light from Pete's boat had guided her to the ladder. Captain Pete had focused on the port side of the *Queen*. Among the fire and debris, he was able to spot Mary and the diver. The other rescue craft had wisely been deployed to the starboard side where the majority of the cruise boat's passengers were stranded. On her way to Pete's boat, Mary had bumped into a body floating nearby.

"Ohhh!" she screamed. "Help me! A body! Ohhh! Someone help!"

"Never mind," someone replied. "Never mind."

"Get to the boat, please," the diver said, referring to the *Ellie May*.

Deciding to focus on helping those who were calling for help, Captain Pete decided not to spend time retrieving the body—the decapitated body of Captain Bullock. That task would be left to divers, after Mary was safely aboard the *Ellie May*. First Officer Bell was still missing. No one had seen Bell from the moment of the crash. A pious woman, as Mary sat shivering in the night, she bowed her head in prayer. *Whose body is it? Some family had just lost a loved one and didn't know it*, she thought. *They were going to be very sad.* It was obvious that she was thanking God for sparing her life.

Captain Pete spotted another passenger and tossed a life ring to the man. He grabbed it as Mary and Pete assisted him into the boat. Mary recognized him as another passenger, but she had no idea who he was.

Robie and Kristin were safe in a raft that was picked up by the USCG. A seaman medic was attending to Kristin's wounds but her face and eyes were buried in Robie's chest and arms as she clung tightly to him. She did not want to see what the Coast Guard officer was doing. A new bandage and gauze replaced the paper towels and would hold her over until she could get to the hospital. A doctor would need to anesthetize the wounds and then look for pieces of shattered glass. She would then have to have sutures. For now the bleeding had been stopped by the pressure of the bandage.

Scottie, still unconscious, would be immediately airlifted to the hospital. Overhead the helicopters from ALERT and the state police cast their searchlights on the scene below. Most of the passengers from the boat and plane had been retrieved from the cold water. A few remained in lifeboats and other rescue craft would pick them up. The TV news helicopters broadcast much of the rescue live although from a distance. However, the telephoto lenses on the TV cameras gave the appearance of being at the scene.

A TV news cameraman videotaped a body bag being hauled into the hovercraft, figuring it would make a dramatic lead-in to the 11 P.M.

The diver, who placed the body in the bag, knew from the name badge on the pocket and bars on the sleeve that this was the pilot who had tried to save his plane and passengers. *That will be his legacy*, thought the diver, *to be pictured with the body bag on TV news*. Perhaps in the future, the mayor of Boston would give the pilot's widow an award, a United States flag, a pin or some other trinket. How trite was the thought, to the diver. No doubt TV Channel 3 would cover that ceremony too. A trinket for a hero's life lost. He wondered if the camera crew had zoomed in on the uniform's identifying marks before the body was placed in the bag. He knew that the pilot's wife, not aware of the crash, would soon get a call from the state police saying that her husband was dead.

Still, another flight uniform was missing. Officer Bell had not been seen or retrieved. His dark blue uniform would not be easy to spot in the harbor waters. Rescuers wondered if he was alive. They hoped to find him tonight, before the tide changed.

34

Fire Captain Jerry Daley and trooper Smith had coordinated the rescue and were exhausted from the trauma of the unexpected crash on Boston Harbor. They had done a marvelous job of pulling the rescue units together from the airport and combining the efforts with the USCG.

"I think we're ahead of this mess," Daley commented.

"This has been one hell of a night," Smith replied. "Who would have expected this?"

"We still have a long night ahead. Will they open Logan now?"

"Don't know. I just don't know!" replied Daley.

"The controllers have not advised us of any changes yet," Smith said. "We'll wait and see, I guess."

Both Daley and Smith continued to monitor the rescue mission from their consoles. They were pleased with the initial results of the rescue although it would be a while before passenger casualties could be assessed due to the murky waters of the harbor. Daley had already ordered the land-based fire rescue teams back to their fire stations. There would be no runway emergency, and the two runways with foam would be cleaned. The fire crews would return after that and wait for further orders from the command posts of ALERT. No one knew if any more flights would depart that evening. More people in the terminal had become aware of the disaster and that Flight 2158 was not returning to Logan. The mood at Gate 23A was sedate—even prayerful. NEAir personnel tried to be informative and comforting. Some relatives and friends of passengers had not left the terminal prior to the disaster.

The LifeLine helicopter had shuttled some of the injured to the local hospitals. They also had transported three or four bodies that had been retrieved by the hovercraft to the morgue, one of them Bullock's.

From the hovercraft, Bullock's body bag was raised slowly by a winch to the hovering helicopter. Distant television cameras focused on the body bag on a gurney, then on the metal basket attached to the cable from above. The basket was lifted to the waiting helicopter crew at the door. There would be no rush to the hospital; there was no patient to save on this flight. With all their training, knowledge and equipment aboard, there was nothing the doctor and nurses could do but accompany the corpse. The helicopter pilot knew he was carrying a fellow pilot in the back of his aircraft —that a heroic colleague was dead.

An autopsy would be performed by coroners and forensic pathologists summoned by authorities. The cause of death—decapitation—was already known, but Massachusetts law required autopsies for violent deaths or when the cause of death was unknown. Blood and tissue samples would be taken to negate or prove recreational drug use, alcohol abuse or natural anomalies of the major organs.

"He almost saved it," a nurse said, somberly.

"All pilots are skilled," someone else said. "They take their lives in their hands each day and are responsible for the lives on board their flight."

"What the hell happened here?" the doctor asked remorsefully.

"Yeh. Why was the boat there?" someone asked.

"He had it made," a nurse said. "Without the boat—he had it made! People injured or dead for no reason," she continued. "Why here? Why in Boston Harbor?"

They sat in silence for the remainder of the short flight. After this run, they would be returning to the harbor, to assist the rescue crew again.

Spectators near Commercial Street stared at the helicopter above them. The sound of its engine reverberated off the buildings of Boston's North End. It made a throbbing "WAH-WAH-WAH" sound as if it were compacting the air around its fuselage. Sirens on the harbor rescue craft continued to ring out as the craft headed for ports with waiting ambulances. Ambulances were everywhere, on both sides of Commercial Street.

Somewhere between seventy and one hundred people would need medical attention. No one knew how many people were dead or were alive. It would be hours before those statistics would be available.

35

Word of North East Air Flight 2158's peril was announced at 8:00 P.M. at Manchester New Hampshire Airport, but with no detail. The officials knew the flight's fate but would not elaborate on the crash or the fate of passengers. No manifest of passengers' names on the plane or boat could be provided until the next of kin were notified of confirmed deaths. Since rescue was still in progress, there were limited updates from the NEAir staff. People awaiting that flight were summoned over the intercom by NEAir personnel for an "important message." Many of the waiting friends and relatives circled the airline desk for word of the latest updates from Boston. Although they had much information from their supervisors, the NEAir officials were reluctant to release details. They merely stated that the plane had made an emergency landing in the waters near the airport and that the rescue of passengers was ongoing.

People awaiting news of their loved ones cried out for more information. They sobbed and tried to console each other. Some people awaiting the passengers ran to phones to call North East Air's corporate phone number in hopes of gathering additional information. All the telephone lines rang busy. No one could get through. Others, on cell phones, attempted to call as well. There would be no updates for quite a while.

Martin Palmer's girlfriend, Monica, sat staring out of the lounge window at Manchester Airport. Tears ran down her cheeks as she sat silently in the dim lights. As other people in need of a drink entered the bar area, she sat alone sipping a glass of wine. No one went near her. The pain was obvious. The TV was tuned to a Boston TV news station. She could not watch the progress of the rescue. She just knew that Martin was dead. She felt it deep inside her soul. He was scheduled to be on 2158 and would have arrived in Manchester by now.

At that very moment she heard her name paged in the ceiling speakers nearby. All she heard was her name, followed by "white courtesy phone, please." The pager repeated the message twice. Monica ran to an airport white house-phone. She remembered that one was near the ladies' rest room. Picking it up, it slipped and fell from her hands. She grabbed it and an operator asked her name.

"This is Monica, was I just paged?"

"Yes," replied the operator. "We have a call for you. Please stand by."

Monica just knew that it was some official from the police or airline about to tell her the sad news of Flight 2158. She had one hand flat across her face, the phone in the other hand.

"Monica, Monica, honey, it's me! Martin. I'm OK."

"Honey!" she cried out.

He wept. "I missed that flight. Can you believe it? I missed the damn flight that just crashed! Is that fate or what?" he added.

"Oh, honey, it is so great to hear your voice," she responded.

"I know, baby, I know," he said. "I didn't want you to worry. I'm glad I could reach you. You OK?" Martin asked.

"I am now, honey," she sobbed. "I am now!"

She sank to the floor in a yoga position and continued to weep. He was silent for a moment, because he, all of a sudden, realized that she was experiencing pain and joy at the same time. She really thought he was gone. The news was not encouraging on TV and no one seemed to know anything. He was silent at the other end and was crying himself. He finally realized just how much she really loved him. The feelings were mutual.

Once composed, she whispered, "Thank God you're OK. Thank God you are safe!"

"I know. I feel like the luckiest guy on . . . ," Martin said.

". . . the planet?" She added, "You are, honey. You are!"

He wept also, and finally regained his composure.

"I'm OK! Are you OK?" he asked.

"I am now, honey. My prayers were answered," she whispered.

"I know. He must not have wanted me now. There must have been a reason why I was spared," Martin responded.

"Maybe, I'm the reason," she said.

"I'm sure of *that!*" he agreed. *"You're* the reason!"

"Hope so," she said.

He tenderly told her to relax for a while and then go home. He would not fly home tonight and might not get out of there for many hours. He would get some rest and grab a limousine in the morning. *No plane for me, for a while,* he thought. If he was quick he could get into an airport hotel for the night. There were two or three nearby. If he had to, he could walk to at least one nearby hotel. In a worst case scenario, he would stay in Terminal E and sleep with the other people awaiting news of the fate of friends and family. They seemed in shock and their eyes were glued to the TV monitors. He would decide what to do in a while.

"I love you!" Monica said, with sincerity. "Please call me later, after you find a place to stay."

He paused, then said, "OK, hon, I'll be in touch—soon. I'll keep you posted on what's happening."

"Give me a little while," she said. "I'll be home shortly."

"Drive safely," Martin said affectionately. "I love you."

"Me, too. Bye, hon!"

Shaking, she hung up and tried to stand. Her knees were weak, but she would be OK. A slight smile came across her face. She was one of the few people who knew their loved one's fate. Few other people waiting had heard from the airline in Boston.

As she settled her bar bill, the bartender asked, "Everything OK, ma'am?"

"Thank you. Yes! I'm OK now," she said.

"Drinks were on me!" he said.

"You are so kind. Thank you. Everything is much better now, much better now."

"You're welcome. Safe travel!" he responded.

"Thanks. Bye. Thanks again—you're sweet to pick up the tab," she added.

" 'Night," he replied. He watched her leave. She was still shaking from the telephone call as she left for home. She would not be able to sleep, waiting for Martin's next call.

To the west of Terminal E, where Martin remained for a while, was where the *Queen* was disabled. The Coast Guard had done its best to save the passengers and crew. Everyone aboard had either jumped over the rails, or had been rescued. The captain and first mate were the last to leave. The Coast Guard hoped to deploy supplementary flotation to aid the *Queen*. They contemplated attaching buoyancy gear to elevate the left side. With that, they might be able to get her closer to shore and in shallower water, but time would not allow for that. Additional absorbent floats were placed around her to curtail the spread of diesel fuel. The harbor now smelled of Jet A from the plane and oil from the boat, but fortunately, the fire on the water's surface as well as on the deck had been contained or extinguished.

The chop in the harbor had mixed some of the oil and fuel into a mix-ture known as "mousse." The oil-water emulsion would be a brown, coffee-colored combination by morning. Most spills, according to the marine chem-ists, disappear by evaporation. At least 75 percent of spills vaporize into the atmosphere. The remainder of the residue in the water migrates with the currents, and could affect area beaches and harbor wharves. The sticky, smelly residue would get trapped in floating garbage, soil boats moored nearby, and generally make the harbor unsightly for months. A massive cleanup by professional environmentalists would be needed.

Waterfowl and some sea life could be affected and die. An EPA envi-ronmental impact statement would be needed to assess the damage to the harbor area. Sea traffic by other ships and smaller boats would be restricted for many weeks. Shoreline soil evaluations would be needed to assess con-tamination of the harbor banks, land and subterranean water quality. To do this, the EPA would need to bring in marine chemistry consulting firms to assess site cleanup and remediation. Local consultants of this nature ex-isted in the Cambridge area at Acorn Park, west of the city. Bids would be needed from two or three environmental consulting firms. Few were quali-fied to handle marine chemistry analytical services. The process would take weeks, and, in the short term, the Coast Guard would begin early mop up of the most seriously affected sites. Containment of the drifting mousse was critical. Steam-spraying of shoreline rocks and beaches would be imple-mented as soon as possible. Specialized watercraft would be brought in with absorbent flotation gear and special pumps to suck in surface water for oil-water reverse osmosis separation. Technology for this type of oil spill correction existed in the Boston area. In Wilmington, Massachusetts, one company had perfected this method of oil cleanup. In the wee hours of the morning, some of the early cleanup approaches would already be in place. The USCG would fly in a special cargo of absorbent containment floats. They would be deployed and stretched out some fifteen miles—the present location of the oil slick drift.

The *Queen of Shoals* made groaning noises as she took on more water. Her cabin and deck lights were faded or out as the incoming water short-circuited the electrical system. She was dead in the water. The left side of the aft portion was now submerged up to the deck. Water had reached Kristin's bar, and bottles, cups and other paper products were floating about. A beer keg had disconnected from its compressor and floated off like a buoy into the harbor. The buoyancy of the *Queen* was decreased by the water that had entered her hull. The USCG was losing the battle and her. With no relief from dead bilge pumps, there was no way to stop the water from entering the large gash in her hull. A piece of the plane's propeller was still stuck in the left side of the boat. It had pierced a side wall on the deck like a knife—a testimony to the severity of the crash. As the hull softly rolled in the night, the captain and first mate watched from a Coast Guard vessel positioned on her port side. Both harbor pilots were safe but their ship was dying in front of them. Her United States' flag and the logo cruise flag of the *Queen* still flew.

Pamela was sad as she saw her pride and joy in peril. The captain had his arm around her. He was holding back his own tears and trying to console his dedicated first mate.

"There was nothing we could do," he whispered to Pamela. "Nothing. It's not our fault, yours or mine."

"I know," she sobbed. "I wish we could have seen it coming—just for a moment. I could have . . . "

"Easy on yourself," the captain stopped her conversation. "We could never have known. Thank God we got off. You, me, the passengers. We got off!"

"I know, but it doesn't ease the pain, sir. Just look at her! She's sinking!"

"I know," he said compassionately, and with tears of his own. "She can't hold that much water—she'll never stay afloat."

"She's sinking," she said quietly.

"Yes, Pamela. I'm afraid so," he said.

"My God, why?" she cried. "Why does this have to happen to the *Queen*?"

"I don't know Pam. I don't have an answer. They can't hold her up with floats. It's too late!"

"Oh, God," she whispered, bowing her head in prayer.

Rescue craft circled her bow and stern sections. A crane barge was being towed from the commercial wharf area, one that was used for construction and maintenance of the Mystic Tobin Bridge. It would be too late. In a matter of minutes the *Queen* would go under, right there in front of the captain, the crew, the rescue craft and hundreds of bystanders on the shore. Searchlights illuminated her wheelhouse, bridge and the flags above her. Her name, *Queen of Shoals,* shone brightly in the night.

First the stern and then the wheelhouse slipped rapidly below the waterline. There was a gasp from the crowd. The United States' flag and mast was now horizontal, almost parallel to the water's surface, then the flag hit the water. Next, the bow became submerged. As the *Queen* slipped below the frothy mixture of fuel, water and oil, a giant plume of water surged upward and the last flickers of flame on the water's surface were quickly extinguished.

It was devastating for her crew watching the beautiful boat disappear. Searchlights scanned the surface but the boat was gone. The *Queen* was settling quickly to the bottom. Small bits of debris surfaced after she disappeared; the water's surface was littered with chairs, vests, paper products, bottles, food, wooden objects and passenger jackets and other garments that popped to the surface like popcorn. It was the *Queen*'s last gasp. The harbor was silent for the moment, except for a breeze that stirred the debris. There was an eery scene of rescue boats and rafts convening at an empty place in the dark harbor. But, the nightmare was not over.

36

The Sumner and Callahan tunnels were a major accomplishment in their time, but were now constantly in need of maintenance and repair. The lighting in the Sumner, completed in 1934, was often dim, the walls dirty from vehicle exhaust and the art deco-style wall and ceiling tiles, obsolete. In dire need of repair, sections of the tunnel's cosmetic interior were often replaced at night when there was less traffic. The Callahan was finished in 1961.

A third tunnel, the new Ted Williams, was a vast improvement in tunnel construction and decor. It was long needed as an alternate for traffic flow to the airport. It was built south of the Callahan and Sumner—modern and brightly illuminated. Ted Williams was present for the opening ceremonies and had "christened" it himself at its dedication. He and many of his dedicated Red Sox fans shed tears that day. The name was a tribute that was well deserved by Ted and was overdue by the city of Boston. The opening of the third tunnel was just the beginning of a massive plan to alleviate traffic congestion in downtown Boston. The lowering of the southeast expressway and Route 93 would be Phase II. Bostonians called it the "Big Dig."

The tunnels were encased inside a huge conduit twenty feet under the harbor bottom. The Sumner, a combination of cement and metal, was submerged over a half-century earlier at a depth sufficient for large ships to pass over it. The segmented tunnel casing was fabricated from 3/8-inch pressed steel and eighteen inches of reinforced cement. Forty-five pound tee-rails were added to strengthen the steel shell. Acidic water, pollutants and other debris in the harbor contributed to their eventual need for serious structural renovation. A cutaway view of the length of the tunnels resembled a shallow V-shape. The middle of the tunnel was lower than the entrances and the exits. The grade/slope was designed at 4.2 percent on the Boston side and 3.4 percent on the airport side. The horizontal lighting of the tunnel was accomplished by long fluorescent light tubes. Many flickered due to older bulbs and worn-out ballasts. The wattage always seemed too low for passing motorists because it did not illuminate the surface area of both travel lanes very well. The output of the bulbs was probably less than the footcandles necessary to properly illuminate the tunnel. People often complained to the toll takers about the dimness and supplemented the lighting with their headlights. Toll takers weren't interested in their complaints; their primary job was to collect tolls.

Within the Sumner and Callahan tunnels were massive fresh-air ducts and vents positioned at the level of the vehicles. Exhaust fumes were continuously withdrawn from the ceiling vents in each tunnel. Electrical and other services traveled the entire one-mile length behind the walls.

The earth sometimes can shift along the New England coastline. There are a few faults in that area and occasionally they shift in a manner similar in nature to California's fault lines. Although not as geologically active as the West Coast faults, they are present in New England. Fault lines along the New England coast were mapped in the 1940s. One fault was discovered running from the Boston area to Nashua, New Hampshire. Due to the type of geology and subterranean stability, scientists thought it unlikely that earthquakes would do extensive damage to Boston and the tunnel system. Over the years, though, minor tremors in the low range of the Richter scale had shaken and shifted New England's coast. Most construction in Boston, including the tunnels, allowed for these occasional tremors. Engineers, years ago, had taken the possibility of tremors into account when they designed the underwater passageways.

South of the Commercial Wharf area, were the pieces of NEAir Flight 2158. Her wings, with the engines still attached, appeared to be still flying southward but underwater. Much of the cockpit and control panel had been ripped off during impact with the *Queen of Shoals*, and they sank separately. Her horizontal stabilizers were slightly elevated and the rudder stuck at twenty degrees left. The air trapped in some compartments and the cabin caused the plane to descend slowly. She traversed the water like a glider, impact-ing nose first into the silt at the bottom of Boston Harbor, forty-five feet below the surface.

USCG sonar had located the cabin's final position almost immediately, enabling a Coast Guard cutter to begin to cordon off the wide portion of the harbor that would be needed for the plane's retrieval. They had yet to find the cockpit and nose of the ill-fated flight. All parts of 2158 would be needed for the FAA to reconstruct the plane. If needed, the USCG would solicit the assistance of the Woods Hole Oceanographic Institute on the south side of Cape Cod. Their deepwater, unmanned, mini-sub, *Nemo,* was utilized to retrieve portions of a space shuttle disaster in Florida and had assisted other FAA searches in a recent plane crash off Long Island. *Nemo* would locate missing segments and critical parts that sonar might not find easily. There was need for rapid retrieval of the airplane since tides and currents might disperse some pieces, making them more difficult to locate.

Local barge cranes and dive teams would quickly secure cables to the fuselage. She was to be loaded with inflatable flotation devices or possibly oil-filled balloon-like buoys that would help raise the plane slowly to the surface. Once elevated, she would be placed on a waiting barge and taken to a hangar for examination.

The FAA and NTSB reports would combine toxicology results from the pilot and structural evaluations from the recovered fuselage to deter-mine what factors, mechanical or human, contributed to the plane's de-mise. Of extreme importance to the inspectors was the retrieval and evalu-ation of the fuel tanks, the fuel controllers or pumps, cockpit instrumenta-tion and tape recordings of engine and avionics function. Did a malfunc-tion in the pumps or fuel lines cause the engines to quit? Was there con-tamination in the fuel before takeoff? Was it the right fuel? Because 2158 had remained relatively intact when she went down in the harbor, there would be good data on the structural integrity of major systems and critical components. If the left wing stayed intact upon descent, the fuel in the critical left wing tank would not be contaminated by seawater. The right wing was damaged and partially shredded upon hitting the cruise boat. Therefore it was surmised that most of the fuel on fire on the water's sur-face was from the right wing tank. The investigators desperately needed to retrieve the intact left wing for full examination. It would most probably have the answers that they needed relevant to the crash.

37

The popular party cruise boat was rapidly descending to the harbor floor just above the Sumner Tunnel. As the *Queen of Shoals* slammed into the brown-gray silt on the murky bottom, the weight of her hull caused her to embed herself deep in the mud. Hitting the harbor bottom sent out shock waves that were picked up on the seismographs at Massachusetts Institute of Technology's earthquake detection laboratory five miles away. Researchers at the Cambridge lab thought that the seismograph had detected a shift in the continental shelf off the coast of Boston. The detection of the movement was deceptive since the event happened closer to the harbor. Scientists were puzzled by the readings on the chart. There had been no prior tremors and, there were no aftershocks.

The impact of the *Queen* on the bottom was similar to a small earthquake in the 1.0 range on the Richter scale. The impact sent underwater waves around the wreck. Her length and immense tonnage of metal sent a plume of silt upward like a mushroom cloud from a nuclear explosion. The chocolate brown mixture would dissipate and drift for days in the underwater currents. Tidal flow would take the silt out to the outer banks and eventually out to meet the warmer waters of the Gulf Stream. Entering the murky harbor bottom at a slight angle and stern first, the *Queen* slowly leaned a few degrees from vertical and came to rest on her bridge and center flag mast. She was nearly forty feet down, and almost upside down. Air bubbled out of her internal chambers and shattered windows.

Glass from the partially crushed bridge windows was strewn about her. The teakwood console in the bridge was destroyed and its splinters would rise to the surface and float away. They would end up on shore as souvenirs for beachcombers.

Directly below the *Queen* was the midsection of the Sumner Tunnel. Encased like a tomb, the tunnel ran perpendicular to the boat's length. Deep in the Sumner Tunnel, a mass of stranded vehicles occupied both lanes of traffic going west. Passengers who had remained in their cars felt the jolt when the boat hit bottom above them, but they had no idea what had happened. The impact was enough to jar fluorescent bulbs free of their sockets and damage electrical lines and lighting fixtures. Many bulbs came down, smashing as they hit vehicles or the road. A few lights flickered in the Callahan Tunnel adjacent to the Sumner, but the jolt did not produce any damage of consequence.

Shortly after 8:20 P.M., passengers remaining in their cars in the Sumner noticed that the fresh-air intake vents in the center of the tunnel had a brown, water-like effluent emerging from various rectangular louvers.

"That's odd," one motorist said to another. "Should that be?"

"I don't think so," said the second man. "I've never seen that."

"Me either!"

"Wonder if they know 'bout that?"

"Doubt it. . . . It just started to leak!"

"The jolt! Did you feel that?"

"Yeh! What the hell was that? That's not normal!"

"Jesus! Is this place leaking? I think it's leaking!"

"We better tell somebody. Someone! Phone? There has to be one close by!"

Guided only by dim tunnel lighting and headlights, the two stranded motorists raced in the dark for a phone on the tunnel wall. Pretty soon two, then four, then more intake vents had brown water emerging from them. It smelled like salt water, they thought.

"Jesus! Do you smell that?"

"What? Smell what?"

"It's seawater! Shouldn't be any seawater here!"

"I know! Those air vents aren't for water! The friggin' Sumner is leaking!"

"Let's go. . . . Come on! . . . Hurry! . . . We'll tell people, as we leave."

Fast and furious the water kept spilling onto the roadway. It was now pouring into the midsection at an increasing rate. When other people began to notice, pandemonium broke out. People began running toward each end of the tunnel.

The Sumner Tunnel was now flooding at a steady rate. The people knew that it wasn't the fire pipelines that had burst. It wasn't the pipes for fire hose connections for car fires. That would have been clean, clear, fresh water. This was harbor water, dirty, smelly, salty harbor water. It could be from anywhere. People could not see any wall damage, and the walls obscured the source of the problem.

"Move it! Move it! The tunnel is flooded!" someone yelled. "Move one way or the other! Just go! The tunnel is flooding . . . go! Hurry!"

Families helped one another to escape by helping their own first. But as fear overtook them, other people bypassed assisting the older folks. They just wanted to escape.

By now the toll takers and passengers nearby knew that there was a crisis in the darkened tunnel. They could see people emerging, soaked up to their ankles. Included in the group by the tollbooth was Jack Danton. Local stations on car radios outside the tunnel reported that the *Queen of Shoals* had sunk in the harbor, but announcers were unaware that the boat had gone down directly above the Sumner Tunnel. They had no clue that the tunnel had been damaged. Traffic had begun to move slowly through the Callahan Tunnel, and the state police on the Boston side were busy evacuating exiting tunnel vehicles. Hearing of the leak in the Sumner, some police returned to the Callahan entrance and rerouted the traffic from the major interstates and ramps that were bound for the Callahan. Reduced traffic was needed for safety reasons and to prevent more congestion than already existed at both tunnel openings. Even the spectators standing on the harbor roadways near the Italian North End were asked to move. The traffic jam in the harbor area of the North End and by the tunnels was increasing, due to the Big Dig construction. With some exits closed and new overpasses under construction, there was no easy way for state and local police to divert the traffic, especially during rush hour. In Boston, some of the streets still followed the routes of cow paths that existed in the 1800s. There is no rhyme or reason for the layout. Some roads were designated for one-way traffic so it was not easy for the police to divert congestion away from the tunnels, Faneuil Hall or Quincy Market.

Forty-five minutes after the boat sank or the initial leaks in the tunnel were detected, the first engineers arrived at the Sumner midsection. They were aghast at the enormity of the problem. They had little knowledge and no fail-safe plan of what to do, although the engineers had copies of the older tunnel design schematics. The water, though shallow, was spreading rapidly through the tunnel. The engineers recognized that they would not be able to fix the problem easily within the Sumner. They might know more if they could get behind the tile-covered walls. The limited access behind the wall and failure of adequate lighting added more complexity to their analysis, and they risked injury or drowning.

The engineers for the MTA and MASSPORT worked closely with their management. They had initiated oversight of the crisis and were now huddled together to assess the safety of the remaining people stranded there, and developing a strategy for their safe removal. They also had to find the point where there was the influx of seawater and stop it if they could. They had limited time to perform these tasks. Police had provided small aluminum boats and inflatable rafts as rescue craft for those who had been too frightened to leave their cars as the water deepened. As trapped passengers were extricated, police disseminated orange vests, which the passengers donned before leaving the tunnel.

Complacent engineers and officials were caught off guard by the disaster. The tunnel leaking? The thought had not seriously entered their minds. The tunnel was more than six decades old. So what did they know back then about the lifetime of tunnel construction? What was the life expectancy of the materials? Could the tunnel erode with time? What about stress fractures? Tunnels don't last forever.

On the eastern end of the Sumner, Jack Danton had removed his suit jacket and rolled up his sleeves before entered the tunnel to assist people in any way that he could. He followed police officers and toll takers who had entering the tunnel on foot to try to help rescue motorists. Kevin O'Malley and Tom Harper joined Jack Danton. Tom's recent EMT training might become useful.

Jack was an excellent manager at work. He knew how to delegate and make decisions—skills that would be valuable tonight. In the distance Danton could see lights that flickered back and forth from hand-held flashlights carried by some of the rescuers and engineers. Some cars, not yet under water, were vacated but the people had left their headlights on to assist those who were trying to escape the rising water. Jack, Kevin and Tom passed two abandoned four-wheel vehicles and turned their headlights on high beam. The batteries would last for a while and the Broncos and Blazers had higher headlights than cars. It would take much longer for the rising water to short-circuit the power supply from their batteries. *The accuracy of TV commercials for longer-life batteries would be tested tonight,* Jack thought. By now most of the car engines either had been turned off or had stalled. The air quality was poor but not as bad as earlier when most vehicles were still running. He could hear people crying out in fear, deep in the tunnel.

The Boston end of the Sumner Tunnel had been cleared of traffic by the state police. Tow trucks were working to remove vehicles. They would back in and remove cars one by one, dropping them off outside the end of the Sumner. Tow operators Fred and Dave worked feverishly to vacate the two lanes. Other local commercial tow trucks arrived to take the cars from the tunnel exit to a temporary parking lot nearby, under the elevated Route 93. They would be stored there until their owners could claim them. Some motorists who had emerged from the flooding tunnel waited for their cars to be hauled out. Some even volunteered to go back in to get them, but the police and tow truck operators prevented them from entering. It was far too dangerous.

"Tow and drop, tow and drop" was the motto for Dave and Fred. They rushed to remove the cars closest to the Sumner exit. The rising water had a long way to go before it would reach the tunnel's end. However, the longer it took to remove the stranded vehicles, the worse the tow operator's chores would be. Aside from the cars, at least two buses were caught in the middle section. They probably could not be removed before the water would saturate their interiors.

About one-third of the way into the eastern end of the Sumner, Kevin and Tom could hear someone yelling for help. The words were not clear as they echoed off the tile walls. It was a man whose wife was almost eight months pregnant. His wife was in the back seat of their car; she had gone into premature labor due to the stress of the event and the fumes. A state police officer arrived about the same time Kevin and Tom reached the car. The water was halfway up the wheel covers on the car. The officer radioed the request for an ambulance. Before they evacuated the woman from the tunnel, an ambulance would already be waiting at the end. The three men decided that she needed to be removed from the car in order to best assist her. They were afraid that she was already in full labor. Her water had burst and she was already experiencing contractions. Tom checked his watch. He knew the labor signs from class. These were not Braxton-Hicks contractions; she was most likely in full-blown labor. She was breathing deeply and crying out in pain. She feared for her life and for that of their baby.

"One and a half minutes apart," Tom said. "How far along is she?" he asked the husband.

Her husband responded with a Spanish accent, "Seven half ta ate."

"Is this her first child?" the cop asked.

"No . . . no . . . du more," was the response.

"She'll go fast then. . . . Let's get her out! We'll take her where we can evaluate the situation. If she's had other kids, she'll go fast!"

Kevin, Tom, the husband and the state police officer managed together to carry the terrified woman closer to the tunnel's end. It was not deep enough for a rescue boat so they carried her across outstretched arms. The contractions were now becoming more frequent and with greater intensity. A quick look revealed the head of the baby had crowned. There was no time to evacuate her.

Jack heard the commotion and headed toward the others attending to the mother. He found an unlocked minivan and the officer quickly opened the back hatch. Someone flipped the back seats forward and they eased her into the back of the van. It was wide and somewhat comfortable. There would be no time to get her to the ambulance. The cop radioed that she would need to remain in the tunnel and that the baby was rapidly emerging. The crew of the ambulance outside the tunnel rushed into the tunnel with a gurney and portable incubator. The woman was now in full progressive labor.

Contractions were now thirty to forty-five seconds apart and increasing in strength. With the aid of a flashlight, the officer saw the head emerging and knew they would have to deliver the baby. The husband knelt at the woman's head and whispered encouraging words in Spanish to his wife. An occasional scream of pain resonated throughout the tunnel. Myriad flashlights surrounded the van. Tom had EMT training and Jack's background as a reproductive biologist would help them with the birth.

"Shoot!" said Jack.

"What's wrong?" said Tom.

"Nothin', 'cept she's well on her way! Multiparous women go fast!"

"Mul . . . what?" Tom asked.

"Multiparous! Means she's had other kids before. Sorry for the 'tech' term," Jack said.

"Here? She'll give birth here?" asked Tom.

"Yup. A-OK. Right here! Gimme some light!" ordered Jack.

"AOK. The head is almost out. I'll have to rotate the baby's head!"

The water was well above the boots and shoes of the group as Jack leaned into the van with the woman spread-eagled in front of him, her husband comforting her.

Jack gently turned the head of the baby to the side. Some amniotic fluid emerged from the mouth of the baby. That was OK, he knew—throat and lungs were clear. With one shoulder out, a gush of blood, amniotic fluid and meconium followed.

Over the shoulders of Jack and Tom was another head and voice—an ambulance attendant. Everyone moved aside to give him room. The ambulance attendant suctioned the child's mouth and applied some gentle pressure on the side of the child's head with both hands. His hands would help the baby's shoulder emerge. Then, the torso would deliver rapidly. The EMT had sterile gloves on, which he had donned as he ran through the tunnel to reach the van. Another ambulance attendant arrived and placed a prepackaged sterile drape under the mother's legs. The baby would fall gently onto the drape instead of on the newspapers that they had found in the car. Kevin had heard that in an emergency an opened paper would be cleaner than most other options. He thought that might be a temporary solution until help arrived.

Fifteen seconds later, the baby emerged completely. The mother gasped in relief. The baby had not taken a breath yet. The attendants wiped off the protective white vernix coating on the baby's skin. Once the film was removed with sterile towels and gauze, it was obvious that the child was a beautiful, perfectly formed boy.

"He's beautiful," someone said. "You have a son! A little boy!"

The mother nodded nervously, looking for additional reassurance.

"Yes!" the attendant responded positively. "Everything's OK!"

"You sure? No cry?" worried the father.

Just then there was a wail from the child that resounded out of the van and into the Sumner. His flesh tone went from blue to pink in five seconds. At that moment in the Sumner, Master Felix Mendosa was born. He wiggled on the surgical drape and was rapidly covered by the ambulance attendant.

He was still attached to the placenta which had not yet been delivered. The umbilical cord was tied and then cut by the attendant, and the baby placed in a warm portable incubator.

"You OK ma'am? Feel OK?" asked the attendant.

"She doesn't speak much English," Jack told him.

One attendant checked her blood pressure while the other called the hospital. All vital signs seemed normal.

"Help us get her on the gurney, please," he requested of the others.

"Sure. What else can we do to help?" Kevin asked.

"Nothin', thanks. Let's get her and the baby outta this cave!"

Tom Harper stood in awe of the sight of the mother and child, realizing that this was what his future occupation might be. An EMT with lots of rescues and deliveries, he daydreamed. He couldn't wait to call his wife to tell her of the event. He was amazed by Jack's knowledge and direction, and was pleased at how well they had worked together.

The mother hardly saw her baby since it was crucial to get them safely out of the tunnel. The father thanked them and whispered prayers as they hurried for the exit. The van door would remain open as they departed the tunnel—its owners maybe never knowing of the miracle that had occurred in their vehicle.

The cries of the newborn overshadowed the sounds of the tunnel confusion. His cries could be heard emanating from the incubator. Other people smiled at the miracle that had just happened. Out of the depths of the disaster of the day, a shining, positive moment had occurred. A child was born to replace at least one of the lives that had been lost in the harbor above.

Jack Danton was pumped now and had made his way further into the tunnel. He assisted an older woman out of her car. By the time he had opened her door the gas pedal was under water. She sat there frozen from fear. He helped her through the water to the walkway in the tunnel and showed her that she could hold the handrail on the way out. Jack would accompany her and she would be safe. The water was now rising to the level of the walkway. This was the same catwalk that Kevin O'Malley routinely patrolled during his "beat."

As Jack helped the woman along the catwalk, they came upon a stranded bus and checked the inside for passengers but everyone had already evacuated. Their driver had left before the passengers did; he had gone for help, but never returned.

"How are you doing?" he asked the elderly woman.

"Better, now that I know I can see lights up there at the end," she said.

A volunteer rescuer passing by in a raft shined his flashlight on Jack and the woman as they made their way along the catwalk.

"You ride with me," he called.

"No thanks. We're almost there," said Jack.

"OK, but you're on your own. You don't have a lotta time," the man in the raft said.

"Thanks. We're outta here!"

Jack urged the woman to pick up her pace. They would make it out OK without assistance. He realized it had been an hour or so since he had talked with Fawn, and hoped she wasn't worried.

It was now almost 10:00 P.M. Outside the tunnel, engineering experts with hard hats discussed measures to stop the influx of water. If that could be achieved, they could then begin to pump the tunnel. The capabilities to accomplish task number two now existed. Massive pumps were being set up everywhere. The experts were wondering how the hell they would stop the water. Once the central portion of the tunnel was flooded to ceiling height, water pressure might equalize a bit and reduce the flow of the harbor water and mud. But that approach did not seem to be practical.

Experts decided that the best immediate solution to closing the fracture would be to drop gravel by the ton directly adjacent to the *Queen*'s location at the bottom of the harbor. Barges of gravel or even coal from the nearby Boston Power Works plant could be brought in to the site rapidly. Large barge cranes could cover the tunnel fracture and strengthen surrounding weakened earth with gravel or coal until repairs could be made from the inside. The massive amounts of stone and coal would plug most of the leaking fissure. The sheer weight of the loads would probably be a temporary solution. If it could hold, the Sumner would be pumped out and construction personnel could be sent in to remove the cement lining and weld huge plates of steel to the existing superstructure. Time was of the essence. They had no time to install an exterior positive pressure caisson used for the pouring of underwater foundations. It could not be in place in rapid fashion but would be a long-term option for major repair at a later date.

If the gravel or coal dumping option was feasible, the massive amounts of temporary fill could be dredged out after tunnel repairs were made internally. The coal option appeared to be the best and fastest method to use to stop the flooding of the Sumner. Preliminary contact by phone with the Boston Power plant personnel had shown them to be extremely cooperative with the crisis at hand and they had agreed to do whatever they could to help.

The engineers decided to go with that option. They would seal off the flow of water by dumping coal obtained from huge coal piles stockpiled beside the power station. It was being stored for the forthcoming winter. Brought in by barge and by rail, there was plenty in stock that could be spared. A barge, still full in the harbor, had arrived the day before and had yet to be unloaded. It could be utilized to dump massive quantities of coal in a short period. The shovel could handle twenty cubic feet at a time, and when strategically placed over the *Queen*, it could surround her and the fracture to the tunnel casing in less than an hour. Underwater video cameras would help the shovel operator in the placement of coal to strategic areas. The crane operator would focus on the circumference of the vessel to ensure sealing off the fissure in the tunnel jacket.

The hovercraft and rescue craft continued to search the harbor as the night wore on. A tally of the rescued at 8:45 P.M. showed that most of the plane passengers and boat passengers were accounted for. There were seven deaths and forty-seven persons with varying degrees of injuries that required medical attention. Hypothermia was also an issue for some of the rescued. Even in late summer, the harbor waters are cool. Currents from the two daily tidal changes bring some cold Atlantic Ocean water into the inner harbor. But the primary loss of life was due to drowning or severe injury during the impact of the plane with the cruise boat. Two passengers on the port side had been killed instantly. Others were killed before they had a chance to put on life vests. First Officer Bell was still missing and presumed dead. There was virtually no way that he could have survived the impact of the cockpit and boat. As the search continued, only his hat was found.

A medical examiner had been called to begin the autopsies at a Boston hospital. Dr. Wayne Bonner was the pathologist responsible for examining Captain Bullock's remains. He would have two other bodies to autopsy after Bullock. The completed FAA and NTSB reports would contain Bullock's toxicology data, and Bell's later if it became available. All information was needed. Did the blood contain any substances of abuse? What was the cause of death? Obviously, once they opened Bullock's body bag, they knew the cause of death for Bullock—he had been decapitated.

Once Bell was officially declared missing, the state police dispatched two troopers to his home north of the city. They wanted to tell Marisa Bell in person—standard protocol for NEAir and the police. They were concerned that she may have already heard speculation about his death on the television.

When the police arrived at 9:50 P.M. the house was dark and the shades were drawn and Marisa Bell did not answer the door. Perhaps she was asleep, had gone for a walk or to see relatives. Surely she had seen the news and may have heard that the crew was missing or dead. Was she distraught? What toll would the loss of her husband take on her? Was she suicidal? Every scenario crossed the troopers' minds.

They checked the garage and found it closed and the car was not there. They would try again later.

"Let's go," a trooper said.

"Yeh. Don't think she's around. I hope she's back soon."

"Hope someone has told her by now."

"Probably not—they just told us—she can't know."

Returning to their patrol car, they called to explain their situation at the Bell residence. The officer in charge requested that they return to headquarters.

38

After he was told the news of the harbor plane crash, Bob Connolly told his supervisor that he felt ill and was going home to rest. He looked pale from being told of the plane and boat's demise. It was well after 9:00 P.M. and he had already stayed well beyond his shift. Connolly didn't look ill to Tony Tomasi, but Tony would not question him. Tony remained at Gate 23A to assist the FAA and NTSB officials who were expected to review the parking and refueling area. He could provide them with the routine maintenance procedures for the Dressler 205 in Connolly's absence. The FAA would need to know every detail of the last minutes before 2158 departed for Manchester, and Tony was scared. Only Bob would have some answers that the experts would need. And he was gone.

Connolly headed up Route 1 toward Route 1A , hoping to bypass some of the traffic. He chose not to go home; he needed a drink. In a few minutes he arrived at Big Irish Jim's where he ordered a shot and two beers. He remained quiet at the bar and didn't want to be disturbed. A few patrons were sipping beers, but by and large the lounge was empty. The lights were low and the one over the pool table was lit, but no one was playing. The place reeked of hops and yeast—years of spills and beer-soaked wood floors. The TV was on overhead and Channel 3 had coverage of the crash site. The news was focused on the recovery of the wreckage. Occasional interviews of local spectators filled the void for real updates. The bartender observed Bob was in a pensive mood and said very little to him.

As Bob drank his first brew, Tony Tomasi, at the airport, greeted investigators who had just arrived in official FAA four-wheeled vehicles. They

188

had floodlights on the roof rack, which supplemented the halogen yellow lights of Gate 23A and the adjacent parking area. They would want to inspect all areas where the plane had been parked before departure. They would evaluate the gate area, the refueling area and the route that the plane took when it was towed from one to the other. The FAA would interview the fuel truck driver as well as all ground personnel and mechanics involved in the loading and refueling operations.

The manifest, the maintenance log and copies of the evening's fuel slips would be reviewed in detail. All procedures were normally signed off after completion of each task. The FAA and NTSB inspectors would verify who had performed what task, when it was done and where. A series of cross-checks existed during refueling. The "fueler" records would show the number of fuel truck gallons before and after refueling. That was the actual fuel load delivered to the wings. It was recorded by the "fueler" in "pounds" on a written slip and handed to the captain. Another cross-check involved the gate agent who would verbally ask the captain if he had fuel, prior to departure. The cross-check procedures had been mandated by the FAA years earlier following a Canadian airline crash. There had been confusion over the recording of liters versus gallons. That plane crashed when the pilot thought he had more fuel than was on board. The safeguards had helped prevent confusion since then.

The main fuel storage tank for the refueling trucks would be inspected as well. Any possible connection between the fuel's original source and the plane would be researched thoroughly. That fuel storage tank would be shut off and guarded until they could sample the stock fuel for contaminants. It was clear from the cockpit conversations with controllers that the fuel, fuel pumps, fuel lines or complete engine failure, either alone or in combination, were the reason for the aircraft emergency.

The fuel truck had not been used since the 2158 flight. Samples of the Jet A in the truck would be taken by investigators. The truck would be impounded until it was no longer suspected as contributing to the crash. Questions remained for the FAA and NTSB. What caused the engines to quit? Was 2158 refueled with the proper fuel? Was the fuel contaminated with water or a noncombustible solvent? They would examine every possibility. Fuel samples would be sent to an analytical chemistry laboratory in Cambridge, which was equipped with gas chromatography (GC) and high-pressure liquid chromatography (HPLC) analytical equipment. If there was suspect fuel on Flight 2158, the analytical results would surely show up as extraneous "peaks" on the printouts of the analytical data. The "detectors" in the GC or HPLC could determine the most minuscule amounts of contaminants, if any were present. When the analytical results of the samples were compared to control samples of pure Jet A, there would be additional spikes on the printout if contaminants existed. The volatility and combustion of the samples would also be evaluated.

A confusing factor in the crash was that the plane's engines performed normally for a portion of the takeoff. It had also idled for some time on the taxiway. Preflight check and general engine function appeared normal during the taxi. They also appeared normal at takeoff.

Was there a mechanical failure? Were parts of the fuel assembly, pumps or fuel lines defective? The plane had flown earlier without any reports of "mechanicals." Once it was retrieved from the harbor, the FAA and NTSB could reconstruct the aircraft and then pull the engines, check the fuel lines, fuel pumps and other critical functions of the electrical power supply relevant to the proper operations of the plane. Hopefully, the engines were still intact. The inspectors would know a lot more in the hours and days to come.

"Seen the news?" the bartender asked Connolly just to make conversation. He was hand-drying drink glasses.

Connolly replied yes and snapped, "'Course I've seen it! I was working tonight. Just got off! The plane was ours. I mean *ours!*" he added. "She was a North East Air flight."

"Really? Your plane? NEAir's?" asked the concerned bartender.

"Yes," Bob replied, "She ran fine when she left. I helped load her. She was fine."

"What happened?" asked the bartender. "Do they know? Hell, I don't understand."

"Don't know. Engines stopped dead in the air!" said Connolly. "Fuel problem, they surmised!"

"Sorry man. Sorry to hear of the tragedy. You OK?" said the bartender.

Bob replied quietly, "Yeh. I'll have another shot, if you don't mind. It really shook me up. I felt ill when they told me she went down. I'm on my way home. But needed some 'courage'—know what I mean?"

"Don't blame ya for bein' down. Drinks are on me tonight!" the bartender said sympathetically.

"Thanks," replied Bob as he thrust his head back tossing the shot of whiskey. He chased it with a beer.

"Nice of ya to comp me," he said to the man behind the bar. "Kind of ya!"

"My pleasure. You're one of my best 'regulars'!" he laughed back, as if he had a drinking club at Big Jim's.

Connolly didn't respond and sat staring off into space, deep in thought. The bartender moved to the other end of the bar and took an order from someone who had just walked in. He knew Bob was despondent but also had seen him depressed in the past. *He'll be OK,* he thought. The situation and his mood were understandable. The only time that Connolly left the bar was to make a call at the pay phone by the men's room. He was only gone briefly and the bartender assumed that he was calling home and going to the rest room. Connolly often called home if he planned to stay awhile with the boys. But tonight none of his buddies were around; this wasn't even a night when he normally would be at Big Irish Jim's.

About twenty-five minutes later, a young woman arrived at the bar. She sat some three or four stools away from Bob. It was unusual to see someone of her class and beauty at Big Jim's. She really turned the heads of the patrons. Well-dressed, attractive and very sexy, she ordered a dry red wine. The bartender was courteous and poured her his best—a Chianti from a gallon jug. He poured it below bar level so that she would not see the bottle or the label. He was embarrassed by the quality himself. *She deserves a far better product,* he thought.

She sat there quietly sipping her wine. Connolly glanced over at her a couple of times and then clasped his hands around his mug of beer. His head was low and he stared at the mirror behind the bar. She caught his eyes in the mirror in front of them. She appeared shaken. In all the years that the bar had been in operation, no one ever came in like this lady. Usually they were local "slugs" who had a personal problem and came in to drown their sorrows. This woman was quality and probably more used to cocktail parties and elite social functions with well-known people from Boston. *She is probably a doctor or lawyer's wife. She could be a model,* the bartender thought. *She's that attractive.*

The bartender, sensing her distress, asked, "Ma'am? You OK?

There was no immediate response. Then she said, "Yes, thanks. I'm fine."

He nodded and went back to cleaning glasses.

The woman looked over at Connolly. The bartender figured that look indicated that she knew him or they knew each other.

She whispered to Connolly out of the side of her mouth, "You probably heard, right? They haven't found him."

"I know. Probably won't," he responded abruptly.

"How do you know that?"

"Shhh! Not so loud . . . I don't . . . but News 3 . . . "

She interrupted, "What do they know? That's hearsay!"

"If he's alive somewhere, everyone will find out. There will be complications," he retorted abruptly and uncaring.

"Why?"

"Because!" Connolly retorted.

"Because why?" she said.

"There's FAA and NTSB all over the gate area right now. They . . . they will retrieve the plane and go over it with a fine-toothed comb! They needed to hit land," he continued. "They needed to end up in . . ."

"In what? Pieces?" she asked. "Are you telling me, this was no accident?" she asked him. "Tell me!" she demanded, "Are you implying something other than a mechanical happened? Tell me!" her voice raised abruptly. The bartender, hearing her outburst, and thinking there was trouble, headed towards them. Connolly waved him off.

They sat quietly for a moment. He then continued, "The plane is intact . . . they'll find the problem! I could be fucked!"

"You know what happened? You know? You planned it? You *made* it happen?" she sobbed. "You bastard!"

He cut her off, "Shhhh! Listen . . . not now . . . go home! I'll call you later. We can talk then—not here, not now," Connolly said, looking straight ahead into the mirror behind the bar.

She began sobbing, then realized that the other customers might be hearing some of the conversation.

"They'll put two and two together . . . the NTSB. . . . It'll take some time, but they'll do it!" he mumbled.

"You! Me! Him! They'll know," she said quietly.

"We need to leave . . . need to get outta here. You go first!" he ordered.

She quietly stood up, red wine half gone and started to leave. Her purse strap got caught on the stool. She unsnarled it and looked at him with venomous eyes, "Don't call me later! You hear me? You planned this! Didn't you? You planned . . ."

Frantically he piped in, "I'll call you . . . later . . . I'll call you . . . tonight."

"Don't. Don't you dare . . . call me! Oh, my God!" she mumbled, as a wave of nausea overcame her at the thought of what he had said. She stepped quickly toward the door. Her heels made a clicking noise from her rapid steps. The door at the bar closed and she was gone. Connolly sat there alone, twisting a stir rod from the bar accessories. He said nothing.

The bartender came over and quipped, "Jesus, Connolly! Wad ya say, Romeo? You scared her off!"

"Nothin'. Nothin' at all. Couldn't afford her! She wanted more than I had," Connolly said.

"Hooker? Are you sayin' she was lookin' for a John?" the bartender asked.

"Yep!" Connolly continued.

"Damn fool. I would have spotted you some money! She was Fiii... ne!"

"Dime a dozen," he said. "There's plenty more up Route 1."

Connolly got up unsteadily after he finished his beer. His hands had a tremor. He left the bar without saying good-bye to anyone. It was clear to see that his mind was elsewhere. As the door closed, a patron asked the bartender, "Where'd he go?"

"Don't know . . . just up and left. Home probably," the bartender said. "I guess he had worked the airport tonight and he was depressed. That was a NEAir flight that went down. He knew the plane. It was one of his gates. On a brighter note, did you see that chick?" the bartender continued.

"Yeh. She was awesome. Fuckin' guy scared her off!"

"Claimed she was a hooker!" replied the bartender.

"She was no hooker. They don't look like that. They don't buy their own booze!" said the patron.

"Don't know. I'm only tellin' ya what the 'stud' said. You know him? He's a stud, right?"

"Stud my ass!" said the patron. "He's about as much a stud as that bar stool."

"Probably right. Talks it up pretty good when he's looped," the bartender said.

They would talk about the beautiful lady all evening. When other patrons came in for a nightcap, they would bring it up again. She was a lasting memory for that bar. The TV continued to broadcast the events of the evening. It was late but the newscasters would cover the crash for many more hours. Newspapers would be going to press with the first editions for the next morning.

✈ ✈ ✈

Marisa, wife of First Officer John Bell, pulled into her driveway. She found the note from the police attached to the door. She sat in the kitchen for a while, alone and in the dark. Some of her neighbors saw her headlights as she returned, but none called. They did not want to intrude on her grief. She lit a candle, poured some wine and stared at their wedding picture. She began to cry. She wished she had never met Connolly when she had been out jogging. She wished she hadn't been so lonely that she had sought him in bed or that she had flirted with him until he desperately wanted her to break up with John. It was then she saw his jealous side. She never thought he would kill to be with her, even though he had said, she thought jokingly in the heat of passion, that he wanted them to be together forever—someday. For Christ's sake, he was just someone who satisfied her desires in lonely times. A neighbor. Would he really have killed? Dear God, no! She repeated softly to herself, "Oh, John, I'm sorry. I'm so sorry. I loved you. I really loved you. Please be alive. Please let them find you—alive."

The affair was not worth his loss, not even close to what she had, in total, with John. *What if I indirectly caused his death,* she wondered. This was not supposed to happen. None of this was supposed to happen. We were to go away together sometime and rejuvenate our life, our love . . . our marriage.

The phone rang as she sat there. The caller ID listed it as "MA State Police." Fearful of what Connolly had told her in the bar, she did not answer the call and quickly turned off the answering machine. She would not sleep tonight. *This is the worst night of my life,* she thought. She would call them in the morning.

She cried herself to sleep in the chair.

39

With the Sumner flooded, the engineers decided to convert the Callahan to a two-way conduit in and out of the city. Often when repairs were performed on one tunnel, they would use the other tunnel for both directions of traffic. It worked fine late at night when traffic was slow or sparse. Tonight it would be needed to alleviate traffic on both sides of the harbor. They had critical backup everywhere.

By midnight, the officials hoped to reopen the Callahan, but it would be quite a feat. By then the cement "Jersey barriers" would be in place and traffic could be safely separated. Tolls would be eliminated until further notice. But getting people and vehicles moving was the second priority. Solving the crisis in the Sumner had to come first.

Above the tunnel, harbor boat traffic was all but eliminated. Rescue and crash retrieval crews remained and were setting up equipment to recover Flight 2158. Sealing off the "open wound" above the tunnel was a priority. The water was coming in at a rate beyond the engineers' belief. Only one shipping lane was open and all recreational boating was banned. USCG and local harbor marine patrol boats and officers cited anyone near the area. Only official rescue or retrieval craft were allowed in the area of the disaster.

At 11:30 P.M., the coal barge was towed from the Boston Power plant. Two tugboats hauled the coal barge to the site. Working as a team, the harbor pilots maneuvered the barge as if she was a tiny rowboat. Normally the coal was used for steam generation to run the massive electric power-producing turbines at the power station. Soon the barge would be anchored just to the side of the spot where the *Queen* had disappeared under the chop. Workers from the power plant, experts at their trade, had been called in from all over the surrounding communities. They were volunteering their services to aid in counteracting the disaster at hand.

The USCG vessel that had found the *Queen* and confirmed her location by sonar was moored near the barge. The fact that the *Queen* was the largest sunken object on the harbor floor facilitated her quick discovery. She was large enough that even a pleasure craft with a fish-finder could have spotted her hull. The crane operator on the barge was ferried out to the site. He would work the massive shovel with a "grid" that had been charted by marine officials. Placement of the coal was critical since he did not want to bury the boat while sealing the fracture.

The *Queen*'s stern, which was jammed in the mud, would be surrounded with coal. It was at the base of the stern that water was channeling an entry into the "shocked" tunnel casing. If properly placed, tons of coal would be sucked toward the open wound beneath the boat and eventually clog the open fissure.

The airport was partially reopened at 11:00 P.M. and was allowing planes to land on two active runways. Runway 33L, however, from which 2158 had departed, was still closed and it would remain closed until the tarmac had been inspected for evidence of engine parts, which may have fallen off upon takeoff. Historically, critical engine parts had been lost on other flights and this inspection was routine. From the terminals facing Runway 33L, some pickup trucks with yellow lights could be seen moving slowly along the entire length of the asphalt. Inspectors on foot were shadows in the night. Residual foam made the task more difficult.

Planes began to descend into Logan. Twelve or fifteen had been stacked up for more than an hour. Earlier flights that had critical fuel levels had been diverted to other airports. Passengers, whose travel was supposed to end in Boston, were bused that evening to Boston or would be flown to Logan the next morning. Other passengers, using Logan as a stopover the night of the crash, would be rebooked and would make other connections in the morning.

Although planes were now allowed to land at Logan, as yet none were permitted to take off. By now the air traffic controllers at Tower Central who had assisted Flight 2158 were exhausted. They were relieved by a new staff, but many of them remained in the tower. They were depressed by the events since they had done their best to get 2158 back home. They would drink coffee and console one another. A psychiatrist and a minister were available if they needed mental or spiritual support.

The controllers thought they might have done better, such as putting 2158 somewhere other than the harbor. The crash was not their fault, but they took it personally. People were dead and that was hard for them to accept. Their job was to keep people safe and alive and they were proud of their long track record of safety.

The area around North East's Gate 23A was still bustling with inspectors and NEAir officials. Inside the terminal, they were on phones just adjacent to the check-in desk. All NEAir flights were posted as cancelled.

Outside the building, the area where Flight 2158 was refueled and the area of passenger boarding was cordoned off. Yellow bands of plastic with the words POLICE LINE—DO NOT CROSS were strung around the periphery. Designated gate areas under investigation were now well lit by special emergency trucks with portable generators. It was like daylight and the white lights contrasted with the pink and yellow high-intensity vapor lights near the terminals and surrounding NEAir gates.

Investigators wanted to talk with Bob Connolly, the Gate 23A maintenance man and baggage handler. But they hadn't been able to reach him. They been informed that, perhaps distressed by the crash, he had gone home sick. They needed his input on the final minutes of 2158. He might have noticed something that would provide a clue toward the fate of the NEAir flight. Repeated phone calls to his home had failed to reach him. He was paged by his supervisor as well. There was no response from Connolly. His wife, tired of waiting up for him, had put the children to bed. Then, fed up with numerous phone calls from airport officials, she had taken the phone off the hook and turned off the answering machine. The constant "beep . . . beep" sound of her phone off the hook was silenced with a pillow that she placed over the receiver. She attempted to get some sleep. She knew that Bob would eventually come home. *He can deal with the calls*, she thought.

Jack Danton arrived home in Cambridge at 1:30 A.M. As a volunteer rescuer in the Sumner Tunnel, the state police and toll takers allowed him to be one of the first cars to traverse the now two-way Callahan from the east Boston side. That was the least they could do in appreciation for his help with the evacuation of stranded passengers in the Sumner.

Once inside their condominium/apartment, he saw Fawn asleep in the chair. He leaned over and kissed her on the forehead. An infomercial for exercise equipment was on the TV. He gently picked her up and carried her to the bedroom. The romantic dinner and lovemaking would wait; he was still psyched-up from the evening's events and she was out like a light from waiting for him. He could see what she had prepared—the dinner table, the wine, the flowers, the sheer nightgown that she was wearing, the candles and the card on the dinner plate—evidence that he had been missed. He had a gift for her as well and it would wait until the morning. He had found her a natural emerald ring on his trip west. She would love it.

He took off his business suit, ruined from the mud and water and from brushing against the cars in the tunnel. He coughed repeatedly from the intake of the residual air that he had been subjected to during the ordeal. Changing into his Red Sox sweatshirt and pants, he plopped himself down in the large chair that Fawn had been sleeping in. The beer in his right hand tasted good as his outstretched arm hung over the armrest. He stared out the window at the Boston skyline across the Charles River. He would have hours of stories to tell her in the morning. For tonight though, he did not want to think any more. His brain was saturated with the experiences. He had helped a woman give birth—a moment that he would remember the rest of his life. It would be a story to tell his children and grandchildren someday. For a brief moment he pictured them having children. *What will it be like?* he wondered. They were young. Those kinds of responsibilities could wait.

As much as he had helped that evening, the disaster was still ongoing as he sat there. It would continue for days. He felt bad that people were working while he was resting with a beer. He got another one. He would have three that night.

Jack would not be traveling this week. He had much follow-up and paperwork to do from the West Coast trip. He would be back at Logan the following week since he had a trip to Chicago already planned—another damn trade show, another exhibit booth. *By then,* he thought, *I might be ready to travel again.* For now he just wanted to be home. He never appreciated the life that he had until now. At least he was alive and he had Fawn in the next room. Some other people tonight were mourning the loss of loved ones. He could not comprehend not having Fawn in his life. He fell asleep with half a beer wedged between his hand and the chair.

40

After midnight, divers specialized in underwater recovery were in the water assessing the plane's wreckage at the bottom of the harbor. Underwater lighting was lowered to assist the divers in their surveillance of the wreck.

Swimming methodically around the fuselage they radioed the state and condition of the aircraft up to investigators on the numerous vessels above. Flight 2158 was intact except for the missing forward compartment, cockpit and a portion of the right wing. Both engines remained attached to the wings. Her front section was in the muck. The divers felt that they could bring her up in one piece. The wing-tip segment was not near the wreckage but probably was not far away.

Oil and residual fuel from the severed right wing bubbled up to the surface. Lighter than water, the fuel and hydraulic fluid streamed upward reminiscent of the constant "bleeding" of the USS *Arizona* at Pearl Harbor.

Divers moved toward the front section of the plane. Much of the forward cabin and galley was buried in the mud. The passenger door on the left side was open and beckoned the divers to enter the passenger cabin. The scene was surreal. The luggage compartment door in the aft section remained closed throughout the landing, crash and sinking. It would not be opened until she was brought up to the surface. Only after a thorough investigation would the luggage and personal belongings be returned to the passengers. NEAir would work as quickly as possible to return belongings to their rightful owners.

When North East Air's top management arrived, they were ferried to a construction barge by the Coast Guard. The barge would be used for the retrieval of the airplane's parts. The CEO of North East Air, Roland C. Bradford, lived in Andover, Massachusetts. He was an ex-pilot who had worked his way up the management ladder. Usually immaculately dressed for business, he stood on the barge dressed in jeans, an L.L. Bean work shirt and a baseball cap. He had donned a NEAir life vest; this was no time for formal dress.

After midnight, a team of expert managers from Dressler USA arrived at Logan. Another flight of technicians and engineers from Dressler Europe would arrive the next day.

The Dressler USA technical staff knew airplane's specs and would advise the recovery team on the best way to salvage the wreck from the water. They would also be invaluable to the FAA and NTSB investigators in pinpointing engine failure, fuel pump/fuel line problems or structural anomalies as they related to the crash. To date, there had never been an engine failure in a D-205. The European technicians were as concerned and interested in the investigation as was North East Air's top management.

A report came in that the USCG had located the cockpit nose and console instrument panel about one hundred yards south of the fuselage. A black box of tape-recorded aircraft data was located in the rear of the plane. There was no pilot voice recorder but engine function and other avionics data would have been monitored and stored during the short flight. If intact, a taped accounting of the malfunctioning engine parameters would be invaluable to the investigators.

The emergency locator transmitter, which normally aids rescuers in finding a missing aircraft, appeared to be nonfunctional. It never activated after the crash. It might have helped locate the cockpit portion of the plane much faster. The recovery team now had most of the critical portions of the airplane located. They would rush to bring those parts to the surface where the plane could be reconstructed in a designated hangar at Logan Airport.

A second dive team entered the area where the cockpit was located. Due to its smaller size, it probably could be retrieved sooner than the fuselage. Divers confirmed that no crew or passengers were contained in the cockpit wreckage. First Officer Bell was still missing; they had hoped his body would be in the cockpit area. The shredded seat belts were noted by the divers. The pilots must have been ripped out of the forward cabin.

Other boats scoured the harbor for Bell. Even Captain Pete Thompson and some lobster company workers joined in the search. Pete had never gone home after transferring his rescued passengers to other craft. A friend of Mary Hutton's drove to Boston to pick her up and take her to New Hampshire. Pete had taken a liking to Mary after he rescued her from the water. She reminded him of his deceased wife, Ellie May. Before Mary departed for shore, they exchanged phone numbers. He promised to call her soon to make sure she was OK. *Perhaps I could see her again sometime*, he thought.

Pete caught a three-hour nap in an anteroom of the lobster company building. This was not the first time he needed to stay over. Foul weather had stranded him before. The owner of the company, Ted Price, was happy to oblige the ol' captain. Pete had originally planned to head home to look at his temperamental engines but decided to stick around and assist in the next morning's search. The *Ellie May*'s engine-tuning could wait. He decided to help with the search even if it meant that he wouldn't get out to his traps.

✈   ✈   ✈

In the middle of the night, both the barge and crane were temporarily relocated to the area of the cockpit's discovery. Although highly unusual, the search and salvage crews decided to work through the night to retrieve what they could before spectators might arrive by boat or plane in daylight.

It was decided that the cockpit would be retrieved first and then the plane's fuselage. The frame below the pilot's seats contained a structural crossbar to which the divers could attach a cable. It became exposed during the crash. The metal crossbar was in the location where the schematic drawing of the plane had shown. In addition to attaching a cable, two large flotation balls were attached to the cockpit and inflated on each side of the forward cabin. The divers released canisters of compressed air, which inflated the two spheres. Flotation would assist the crane in lifting that section of the nose to the surface. They also prevented the cockpit from sinking if the cable snapped or became disconnected during the ascent.

With cable and flotation gear in place, the crane's winch began to lift the nose section to the surface. It would not take long for the cable to be retrieved on the enormous metal spool of the crane. When the orange flotation spheres appeared near the surface, the operator gently lifted the cockpit and forward cabin structure into the air. The crane slowly swung around ninety degrees as water and mud poured from the forward section of Flight 2158. Much of the pilot's seat area was missing. Mud was impacted in the console and instrument panel, but it appeared to be mostly intact. "Dress," a portion of the manufacturer's name, could be seen painted red on a white background on the outer shell of the cockpit. It was a sad sight for the staffs of Dressler and North East Air. It was their plane—a Dressler 205 had gone down; one pilot was dead and the other still missing. The CEO of North East Air grimaced as the crane's operator gently lowered the cockpit section onto the barge. It sat there almost level, as if in position for flight, but cocked slightly to the left. It was quickly draped in a blue tarpaulin and secured to the barge with chains for transportation to the wharf.

The recovery crew still needed to raise the fuselage and wing section. Three hundred feet away, working underwater using supplemental lighting, the submerged divers were deploying and inflating additional flotation gear directly into the cabin of the fuselage. The orange inflatable units were two by ten feet and oblong in shape and resembled the pontoons of a seaplane or the inflated side of a raft. Once inflated, they would fill a good portion of the passenger cabin. Strategically placed at the point where the wing attached to the fuselage, they would aid in maintaining the buoyancy of the midsection, where the weight was the greatest. That section near Row 3 contained the weight of the center portion of the wings, the two engines and the point where the fuselage joined to the wings. The cables for retrieval of the plane would be crossed like an **X** incorporating the wing and fuselage. The divers would focus on harnessing the focal or pivotal point of the heaviest section of the plane. Once dislodged from the harbor bed, the fuselage and wing assembly would rise flat and level to the water's surface, aided by the buoyancy of the flotation gear.

The construction barge, with the cockpit on deck, was now repositioned over the site of the fuselage. Four forty-foot cables were attached to a loop at the end of the main cable. The segments would be wrapped around the fuselage and wing, like the ribbon on a Christmas present. The center cable would join the four shorter cables at midsection and on the top of the wing. The recovery crew had decided against bringing 2158 up tail first, like a fish hanging head down. The engineers from Dressler thought that the tail would likely break away from the body of the plane once it was in the air. It was critical for the salvage operation to maintain the integrity of the wings and engines.

During the rigging of the submerged plane, officials could see the enormous shovel loads of coal being dumped in the area where the *Queen* and plane had gone down. TV news crews had not relented. They continued to broadcast the events going on in the harbor. TV stations knew that coverage of sensational tragedy increased viewership. Each TV station tried to outdo its competition with the most up-to-date live reporting. Their live news coverage went from the night of the crash directly into the morning hours of the salvage operation.

Once the cables were rigged to retrieve the large portion of the plane, the divers returned to their support craft in the harbor. They would remain suited up, but it was clear from the color of their faces that the water at that depth was cold. All exposed areas of their skin were beet-red. One diver remained in a raft near the cable. He sat holding it loosely as it entered the water. He would check the connections once the plane reached the surface. Only after that evaluation would she be raised onto the barge.

With the cable taut, the recovery process began and the aircraft was pulled gently out of the mud. The plane emerged with a jolt and then leveled off as planned.

The main cable was marked in white every five feet. At twenty feet, the diver in the raft first saw the wings and fuselage beneath him. He cautioned the crane operator to slow down. Gently, 2158 rose to the surface. The crane operator, guided by the diver's instructions from the water's surface, handled the cable with precision. The crane operator and the diver were in total synchrony.

The diver entered the water and swam under and then around the aircraft. It was a precarious maneuver should the cables slip while he was beneath the plane. He checked all connections from the main cable. Everything was perfect and he emerged from the water and returned to the raft. He signaled a "two thumbs up" and the crane operator inched 2158 slowly into the air as if she were in flight again. First to appear, as she left the harbor, were the propeller tips and the top of the wing. The remainder of the fuselage followed and the extensive damage to her body became evident to the workers. She rotated freely from the single strand. A rush of water descended out of the passenger door and from the front of the plane. The diver added two guide ropes to the undercarriage of the fuselage. One was attached to the front of the plane and one to the aft section. The ropes would be utilized by two workmen on the recovery barge to orient her into proper position on the deck.

Like a jeweler setting a diamond, the crane operator positioned the Dressler over the center platform and began lowering 2158 onto the widest section of the barge. Two Dressler technicians grabbed the guide ropes and turned her lengthwise on the deck of the barge. They held her steady in position as the crane operator lowered her onto the barge surface.

Before they covered it with a tarpaulin, the investigators and Dressler staff walked around the aircraft for a preview of the damage. The plane rested on her left wing tip, supported by temporary wooden braces. The left strut below the wing was still intact. The right strut had been severed from the crash. Once the braces were secure, the main cable was slackened and the other cross-cables released, making a deafening rattle and screech as they hit the deck. The crane operator retracted the main cable and turned some ninety degrees away from the airplane. The limp central cable swung lightly in the breeze above the harbor. The recovery crew had done their jobs perfectly and in record time. The two largest pieces of the aircraft were now on the deck of the barge and the recovery crew was pleased with their success. It was now 4:00 A.M.

Dressler technicians surrounded the charred right side and the remnants of the forward cabin area, looking for superficial clues to the fate of 2158. The engines were intact and showed little damage except for the initial fire during takeoff. The engine fire on the left side had been extinguished in the air before it could do serious damage to the cowling and exhaust manifold. The propellers were intact on both engines but their fluorescent-painted reflective tips were bent back from the impact with the water. Less than two-thirds of the right wing remained. It had broken off just outside the right-engine housing. Some hydraulic lines for the flaps were severed and dangled like spaghetti. The right-side fuel tank in the wing was ripped open and a large portion had disappeared when the right wing-tip was sheared off. The passenger door to the plane hung open as it did underwater. The plane was covered in a blue tarp similar to the one placed over the cockpit portion.

The barge was guided to a wharf on the same side of the harbor as Logan Airport. Waiting at dockside were large flatbed trucks that would take the two pieces of the fuselage to Hangar 10. There 2158's remains would be reconstructed as best as NTSB officials could. They would reassemble the forward and aft sections. Other pieces still missing would be added as they were recovered. Dressler employees' help would be invaluable to the reconstruction of the D-205.

At noon, the second day, the oceanographic research ship from Cape Cod would arrive in the south end of the harbor. It would make the route to Boston in record time. Firmly suspended on her aft section was the re-nowned mini-submarine *Nemo*. The *Nemo* would help locate the remaining aircraft parts. A map-like grid of the harbor was devised by the USCG. They would deploy the *Nemo* to 300 designated portions of the grid. The exploration would be meticulous and if parts from the aircraft were down there, chances of finding them were good. The team from Woods Hole also had a new device with side-scan sonar that could be dragged behind the boat. It could draw a topographical underwater landscape of the debris field. It was experimental, but had been used to find portions of the *Titanic* off the Atlantic coast. It was recently utilized for finding portions of a jumbo jet crash off the south coastline of Long Island, New York. Within a few days, the missing smaller portions of Flight 2158 would most likely be retrieved and reassembled in Hangar 10.

41

Robie Brooks accompanied Kristin to the hospital. She needed stitches on both hands. The emergency room physician, Dr. Shapiro, removed additional glass embedded in her wounds. She was administered a local anesthetic, Xylocaine, by injection into the open surfaces of each wound. He used a syringe filled with sterile saline to flush out all foreign matter and the glass fragments. The smaller wounds were closed with "butterflies." Once the local anesthetic took effect, the larger wounds became numb and she felt much better. One laceration was very close to the tendons that controlled her thumb. A few millimeters closer and she would have lost the use of it. The doctor took his time in closing the wounds with silk sutures. He wanted to reduce the incidence of scarring on her hands. She had beautiful hands and nimble long fingers.

Robie waited patiently for her in the waiting area. He was concerned that Kristin had lost substantial amounts of blood. She had felt weak and he was afraid that she might show signs of shock. The medical personnel had given her fluids with electrolytes to drink on the ride to the hospital and her light-headedness had gone away. She did not need an IV. The secondary effects of the injuries were probably from the trauma of the night. Robie was genuinely concerned for her. He knew that the cuts were painful and that it would take weeks for her to heal. They had become very close on the way to the hospital. Robie actually felt as if he had known her for a long time. It was that level of comfort for both of them.

As he perused an outdated issue of *People* magazine, he mourned the fact that his "Strat" and Martin guitars had gone overboard. He was accustomed to the playability of these instruments and enjoyed the wonderful history behind them. *It won't be the same with a new "axe,"* he thought. Both instruments had floated away in the dark and probably washed up on the shoreline of the harbor. He envisioned the "Strat's" candy-apple red finish repeatedly kissing some rocks until the guitar neck was unrecognizable. Someone walking along the beach would find it a month from now. He surmised that the person who would find it probably would wonder what fool would toss a guitar like that away. He figured that the more fragile Martin was shattered or burned.

Robie knew that the band members had been rescued and that they were OK. He would call them sometime the next day. They had lost their equipment, too. Drums, cymbals, mikes, speakers, amps and extraneous speaker cords had floated off or were already at the bottom. The band had insurance so all the equipment would eventually be replaced. *We may need to cancel some scheduled gigs in Cambridge*, he thought, *since we have no equipment to set up or play.* He was bummed. The bass player, Joey, had managed to save his own guitar. That instrument would be the only historical memory of the original band equipment. Some of the guitar's electronics would need to be replaced since it made some contact with the salt water during Joey's rescue. The USCG didn't consider the bass a priority in all the confusion of the night but allowed him to bring it along anyway. He held it cross-armed against his chest on the rescue boat; it was like a baby to him.

Robie's train of thought was broken by the emergence of Kristin from one of the examining rooms. She had both hands pretty well covered in bandages. Dr. Shapiro cautioned her, "Now, don't peek, ya hear!"

"I won't," Kristin assured him.

"If you do, they won't heal properly," Dr. Shapiro warned her. "You need the pressure on the wounds so they heal properly and to reduce scarring."

"OK, thank you again, doctor," she said.

She hugged the intern as best she could without using her hands. The doctor winked at Robie. Looking away from the physician she saw Robie sitting there. He had been waiting for least three hours.

"You still here?" she asked coyly.

"Yep. You OK?" Robie asked.

"Better now, hon, they ran out of sutures," she joked.

"Really? How many ja get?" he asked.

"I figure a good thirty-five to forty stitches total," Kristin replied with a bashful gaze. She was looking for sympathy. "Hurt like hell when I went in. They poked and prodded to get all the shrapnel out!"

"What's the note?" he asked her.

"Just a prescription for some painkiller. I'll get it tomorrow—he gave me some samples to hold me over until then."

"Man, I could use some painkillers," Robie joked.

"I share," she replied with a smile.

They both laughed as he kissed her forehead.

"Can I get a hug, like the doc got?" he asked.

"Sure! Can we go home now?"

"Sure," he said, "Where's home?"

"Beacon Hill—just down the road from the State House," Kristin bragged. It was an affluent part of Boston. Famous people reside there.

Fortunately, there were cabs waiting outside the ER entrance. Robie whistled for the closest one. He assisted her in. She was helpless with her hands bandaged, and her pain was obvious as she attempted to slide over the back seat. He helped her get comfortable as she leaned on his shoulder. He could smell the antiseptic, but he could smell her perfume as well. He was definitely falling for the woman. The chemistry was there.

Robie and Kristin's cars were both still at the harbor parking area for cruise boat employees. They would get them in the next few days. They were still dressed in the clothes that the Red Cross had provided after they were rescued. Though not attractive, the outfits were dry and warm. They kidded each other about their fashion.

"Revere Place, please," she told the cabbie, "151 Revere."

There was no response. He just drove there. En route, she commented on her outfit, "Sexy outfit, eh? A bit baggy but oh so chic!"

"Oh, yah. Matches beautifully with mine," Robie laughed.

"Told the doctor it was a new 'designer' from Italy. Very expensive," she continued. "The doc joked with me and said, 'What designer might that be?' 'Roto Crossi,' I told him. The doc never stopped laughing," she chuckled. "You see, Robie, dear, 'roto' means red. I made up the Crossi, you know, for Red Cross!"

"I get it. Very creative you are, you are!" he retorted. "How're the hands?"

"Been better—they throb—there's some pain."

"Anesthetic may be wearin' off," Robie said. "You can take another pill when you get home. That should help."

"Sounds like a deal," she said softly. "You'll be my nurse. OK?"

"OK!" he replied.

Kristin was playing up to him big time and he was loving it. She had been through hell and even still was in a decent mood and laughing. A woman in a good mood after that kind of a night was not expected. He told her that she looked especially cute in her "Roto Crossi-es." Her building was halfway up the cobblestone road, in one of the oldest sections of Boston. Street lamps were authentic gas lamps from the olden days and their footsteps on the brick sidewalk echoed from the narrowness of the street. It was designed originally for horse and carriage. It was only one way because only one car could fit on the narrow path. Wall-to-wall apartment buildings of old brick lined both sides of the road.

He took her keys out of her pocketbook. There was no way she could grab anything with both hands bandaged. One finger was free on each hand. The rest were extensively wrapped in gauze. Dr. Shapiro had suggested that she see her own physician to remove the stitches in fourteen days and evaluate any complications. Infection would be the most likely side effect.

Robie helped Kristin to her couch in the living room. She had decorated the apartment very well for her income level, he observed. After tonight though, she would be out of work for two weeks anyway. Maybe she could get paid time off or disability payments for a while. She would be checking with her boss in a couple of days. They were excellent employers and were very concerned about their employees' livelihood, as well as the cruise boat.

Robie noted the family photographs on the walls and on the end tables. He commented that she and her mother looked very much alike. Kristin gestured as best she could at a picture of a younger sibling of hers—her sister who lived in Hartford. She would call her tomorrow to tell her of the disaster in Boston. They remained close-knit even though Hartford was some ninety miles from Boston. As she and Bobby talked, they purposely avoided the TV and the news stations. They had enough for that evening. It was now very late.

He leaned over and asked, "Can I get you anything? Perhaps some soda or a drink?"

"Hey," she said smiling, "that's supposed to be my line—'get you a drink'—I'm the bartender!"

"Some bartender you are! No hands!" he laughed. "Not tonight," he said as he went to the fridge. "I'm waitin' on you!"

"OK, but can you make me some tea? The bags are right above the stove."

"Tea? Sure. I can make tea!" he said, confidently.

"You, my friend, are a sweet man!" she retorted.

"Yes, I am!" Robie boasted. "Be right back."

"Modest, too!" Kristin joked.

"Totally!" he laughed.

Robie placed the teapot on the back burner and helped himself to a beer. He then went back and sat down next to her. He felt very comfortable around her. They relived part of the day through conversation. It was easy for them to console one another.

He jumped up when he heard the teapot whistle. She liked chamomile tea—sort of calming after a very intense day. He brought her tray with a bowl of sugar and a little pitcher of milk. He didn't know that she took her tea without cream and sugar, but she was gracious and thanked him for the thought. There was no way she could hold it with all the gauze on her hands. She leaned on his shoulder as he picked up the mug and helped her drink the tea. As she sat there quietly by him, she asked, "Is Scottie OK? Did you see him?"

"Don't know. I think they admitted him," Robie said.

"Hope he's OK. He's my bud, ya know," she continued.

"Yes, I know. I'm sure he's OK. He was conscious when we left. He was out cold for a while. I'm sure he's all right. They probably just want to keep him for observation."

"Hope so," she added. "Robie?"

"Yes?"

"Hold me please?"

"Sure, babe. I'm right here," Robie said, lovingly.

She could not return the hug—her hands throbbed. She had taken a pill with the tea, hoping it would help. She felt comfortable in his arms.

Robie took a book of matches from a small bowl on the coffee table and lit a scented candle. The matches were from a place that he had often played in Cambridge.

"I've seen you play there," she whispered to him. "That place—there! I've been there."

"You have? When?" he asked.

"Oh, a couple of weeks ago," she said.

"Really?"

"Yes," she said, coyly, "I've seen you guys play before. You were pretty cute that night!"

"Cute?" he said. "Why cute?"

"Don't know. You just were! Like tonight!" She perked up. "You're cute! And thoughtful. I like your style. I like you!"

He thought for a moment without responding. Had she been checking him out previously? He never knew of her interest in him, and certainly hadn't seen her elsewhere. She didn't reveal any more secrets.

They both sat quietly on the couch and stared at the candle flame. A tear rolled down her cheek and he noticed the wetness as it rolled onto his skin. He looked at her and said nothing.

She whispered, "Can you believe today? Can you believe that we are alive?" She continued softly, "Some people are gone, and we're alive. Robie? Do you believe in fate?"

"Yes, I think so," he said. "Why?"

"Me, too, I believe. You! Me!" she said, bashfully. "This *may* be fate."

"Could be—just could be," he whispered.

He leaned over and blew out the candle. The digital clock on the bedside table said 2:30. They fell asleep together on the couch for a while. In the middle of the night, he carried her to the bedroom. He covered her and lay next to her. He was on top of the covers; she was tucked under them. In the brief moment of knowing him tonight, she saw a sensitivity unmatched by other men she had known. She was comfortable with him being here. She was not afraid. They had been through hell together and were very attracted to one another. The cars at the wharf could wait a couple of days.

The next morning they would become even closer. He would make love to her five times in the course of the day. Injured or not, there was no way she would not enjoy him or the moment. He was soft and gentle all day—careful not to hurt her hands. He focused on pleasing her, not himself. In the end they would both be totally gratified. She had ways to satisfy him without using her hands. They devoured one another, and it was apparent to both that they were falling in love.

42

Bob Connolly finally arrived home after driving around aimlessly for hours. The back light was on by the garage. The rest of the house lights were out except for the kitchen light over the stove. It was always on to greet him. He noticed the note on the refrigerator.

It said: "Honey, please call your boss—he called 3X. See Caller ID list. I did not answer his call. Love, Me."

The phone was off the hook and under the pillow. The answering machine was off as well. He put the receiver back on the wall phone base and turned the answering machine back on. There were no other messages stored—just the ones from his boss.

He entered the bedroom. *She's sound asleep*, he thought. He checked on the kids down the hall of the ranch-style home. All the bedrooms were on the same floor, the first floor, separated by a bathroom. The kids were fine. He went into the bathroom, then lay down on the bed still clothed; his wife lay next to him but under the covers. She was not really asleep; in fact, she hadn't been able to sleep all night. She could smell beer from his breath in the air; from his pores perhaps. His clothes smelled like smoke. He was at the bar again. The damned bar!

Connolly lay back on his pillow with his hand behind his head, pondering the earlier conversation at the bar. He had jeopardized his job, his family, his children and his life over a beautiful woman, his neighbor. And now she was angry with him.

He had no idea how to continue to cover up the mess of the crash and the affair. The plane was supposed to end up in pieces on land, somewhere between Boston and the New Hampshire border. If it had gone down on land, it would have shattered in a million pieces, he thought. Most of the fuselage and wings would have been burned in the fire that would have ensued. What would he say to the officials tomorrow? What did they know already? If the plane was recovered intact, they would realize what had happened. He needed to anticipate what questions they might have tomorrow. He practiced those questions in his mind and what the answers would be. The TV news at the bar had indicated that the plane was mostly intact. This scared him since the NTSB and FAA were always thorough in investigating crashes. He knew that the cockpit and galley area had separated upon impact with the boat. This was to his advantage, but he was also aware that they had found most of the larger pieces. If the wings and instrument panel were in good condition, they would put two and two together and figure out what happened. His wife heard him sigh deeply and very often. He alone had the answer to the fate of Flight 2158.

He didn't return the phone calls from his boss at Logan. He would need to stay awake to think of their questions. They would have lots of questions—lots of probing questions. He blinked his eyes first very slowly as he stared at the textured ceiling. The more he thought, the more he blinked. His eyes were dried out from the alcohol in his system. He blinked again. His eyes felt better when they were closed. They did not reopen.

Before she went to bed, Connolly's wife had figured out that Bob was in some kind of trouble—big trouble. The phone calls from airline officials had been frequent that evening. He had been unusually distant lately and she had been blaming herself for his restlessness and boredom. He was spending more time at Big Irish Jim's than usual, even missing the kids' soccer games. Sometimes when he stumbled into bed she thought she detected the fragrance of perfume on his clothing. Tonight, though, she only smelled beer and cigarettes. He was snoring and mumbling in his sleep. She thought she heard him say a woman's name—it wasn't her name—was he dreaming? But she feared him when he was drinking and wasn't about to ask any questions—even the next day. Why make things worse or go looking for trouble? She turned her body toward the wall and closed her eyes.

Across the street from the Connolly's residence, a state police car pulled up and stopped. The trooper noted on paper: Time, "3:30 A.M. Connolly's

213

vehicle in driveway." The license plate was confirmed as Bob's. The trooper then radioed the information into his evening supervisor.

A few minutes later, the Connolly telephone rang again. His wife heard it. She let it ring.

43

The investigators, who had gone directly to the gate to begin their investigation immediately after the crash had observed that the baggage handler, Tony Tomasi, seemed nervous around the NTSB and FAA officials. In fact, he had pretty much stayed in the background until they had a specific question.

The main fuel storage tank had been sampled. So had the fuel truck. Field tests showed that the samples did not indicate any contaminants were in the bulk fuel supply.

Because Connolly could not be reached, the investigators focused on questioning Tomasi that night. They hoped that Tomasi could answer their questions. They were wrong. He only assisted Connolly on occasion and didn't talk with his co-worker that evening until NEAir 2158 had long left the boarding area. Then Connolly had asked him for help cleaning up the traces of fuel on the asphalt. But, Tomasi had purposely avoided asking Connolly about that situation. Besides, spills were not that uncommon. Engine oil drippings were common as well. *There wasn't much fuel on the ground,* he had thought.

After noticing an odor of jet fuel concentrated in a trash can, an investigator called Tomasi over to the waste container near the maintenance shop.

"Mr. Tomasi," the investigator began.

"Yes, sir?" Tomasi replied.

"Are you aware that the waste barrel has a Jet A smell to it. There are some paper towels here with fuel on them. Why might they be in this trash can?" he asked sternly.

"Ah . . . ah yes, sir," he stammered. "Someone had a minor spill earlier in the night and we cleaned it up."

"Do you normally throw combustible materials in the trash? Is that common procedure?" the inspector drilled him.

"No, sir, we normally don't," Tomasi replied. "We were in a hurry and must have forgotten to dispose of them to the volatile chemical storage cabinet. We normally place them in special containers that have vented, nonexplosive caps."

"You know, Mr. Tomasi, this is a serious hazard and an FAA violation in the maintenance area," the inspector told him.

"I know, sir," Tomasi said. "We were in a rush before another plane arrived."

"Where was the spill? Can you show me?" the inspector said with wide open hands. His interest was now piqued. Where was the spill?

Tomasi nodded yes. He pointed to the area where the 2158 flight had sat during boarding.

"You mean here . . . right here?" the investigator asked.

"Yes," he nodded again, "there."

The inspector knew that 2158 had parked there. He took his flashlight and surveyed the area. He could not see much that did not look like normal patches of oil or fluids that often are seen in plane parking areas.

"What happened?"

"Don't know, sir," Tomasi responded, "I was just told to clean it up."

"By who?" asked the inspector. "Who asked you to clean up the spill?"

"Bob Connolly, my associate."

"Did he spill fuel?"

"Don't know, sir, I was just asked to clean it up. That's all I know, sir."

"One more thing. Tony?"

"Yes?" Tomasi responded, shaking from the barrage of questions.

"Do you know who fueled the flight? Flight 2158. Did you help with that?"

"No, sir. I'm not sure who did that. I was not assigned to that flight."

"Would it have been Connolly? Is that his job?"

"Yes, sir. Probably, I mean—not sure. That would have been his job, that night."

"Thanks, Tony. You've been a great help," said the inspector.

"Yes, sir. You're welcome."

Tomasi was sweating under the arms and on his forehead. It felt like the "Spanish Inquisition" to him. All those questions, one right after the other. He was shaking.

The inspector flashed his light back and forth over the area. A faint trail of a fuel stain on the tarmac could be noted when the flashlight was held at an angle. His light caught a flash of metal on the ground. It was an Allen wrench—a small Allen wrench. He had almost passed it over, while walking and following the fuel spill track. The inspector took out a piece of tissue paper and picked it up. He folded the tissue and placed the tool in his breast pocket. He did not know if it meant anything, but it would be added to the overall report. His main concern tonight was that it could puncture the tire of a future flight that might park there. He did not want another potential accident from a blown tire on takeoff.

Tomasi was allowed to go home. He was tired from the entire night and tragedy. It was an aircraft that he was just learning about since the Dressler 205 was new to the fleet. He was young, just twenty-three, and could not handle the fact that one had crashed or the intensity of the investigation. Once he got home he would swipe a couple of his mom's Valiums to relax. Two 10 mg tablets might help him sleep tonight. There would likely be more questions tomorrow and he needed to be alert. In bed, he thought, *Why did Connolly leave me with the inspectors? Dammit, Connolly was responsible for the flight. He knew the most about it and wasn't even there to help in the investigation.* Feeling betrayed, Tomasi finally curled up in a fetal position and went to sleep.

The investigation intensified the day after the crash. The fuselage of the Dressler 205 sat on the floor of Hangar 10 at Logan International Airport. Dan Baldini, an experienced NEAir fuel technician arrived early at the request of company officials. The first order of business was to remove any residual fuel from the left wing. Some fuel samples had already been taken by the FAA investigators while the craft was on the barge and were sent immediately to the analytical laboratory in Cambridge. The remainder of the left-wing contents would now be removed. The remaining Jet A would be pumped into a waiting, empty fuel truck. The investigator had anticipated that she was still nearly full—7,000 pounds—from the original refueling before takeoff. That translated into 800 U.S. gallons of Jet A. After taxi and takeoff, she probably had 6,800 pounds, or 775 gallons, remain-

217

ing. Half the fuel—3,500 pounds—would have been the maximum in the left wing. With the short flight, investigators estimated that 350–400 U.S. gallons, or 3,000–3,500 pounds still remained in the left-wing tank.

Baldini secured a fuel hose to the underside of the left wing. With a twist, the male end of the hose locked with the female receptacle on the wing. A gasket prevented leaking during the withdrawal of the fuel. To prevent static electricity and potential sparks that might ignite the fuel during unloading, he attached a wire from the plane and truck to a special grounding pin in the hangar floor. He thought that it would take seven to ten minutes to pump the fuel from the left wing.

After a minute and a half, the fuel meter stopped spinning. The pump began to whine at a high pitch and Dan ran over to check the hose and pump connections. It had lost prime or suction. He shut down the pump motor and removed the hose. Everything looked OK to him and he reconnected the hose and resumed pumping. The pump immediately began to whine again. Baldini was baffled. The meter indicated that forty gallons had been withdrawn so the pump had worked for a while. He tapped the top of the wing in two spots. It sounded hollow like kicking an oil drum. He looked at the wing. There were no obvious punctures, tears or breaks in the outer sheeting or skin, of the left-side wing cover. It was completely intact. He checked the connect/disconnect valve to see if the valve had been jammed open during retrieval of the fuselage. It was in the normal position, closed. He tapped the wing in five different places including two locations on the bottom of the wing. Everywhere that he hit the metal with his fist, there was the sound of an empty fifty-five gallon drum. *The damn wing had no fuel in it*, he thought. *How could that be?* Just then, a technician from Dressler, one of the group that had arrived earlier from Europe, and an NTSB investigator came over to where he was standing by the wing.

"You withdrawin' fuel or playin' the drums?" someone cracked.

He snapped back, "Drums? I ain't playin' no drums!"

"Pump trouble?" the inspector asked.

"Nah. Pump's OK," Baldini replied. "There's no fuel!"

"What?" the inspector asked, looking surprised.

"No fuel. There is N-O fuel. Only forty gallons came out!" Baldini reiterated.

"Are you sure?" a Dressler mechanic asked, tapping the wing with his knuckles.

"Yeh, she's bone dry! I tell you—there's no fuel!" Baldini repeated.

"Where'd it go? There's no damage!" the inspector quizzed him.

"Beats the shit outta me," Baldini answered. "Never seen this before! Never!"

Everyone scoured the wing for a pinhole, a break somewhere. Nothing was seen. They ran back and forth, looking at previously inspected areas—once, twice, sometimes three times.

"She must have lost fuel in the crash," someone concluded.

"I don't think so," Baldini replied.

He disengaged the hose and checked all the flanges. Then he reconnected and tried the pump again.

"There's no damage for a leak. Nothin'! I tell you . . . there is nothin' in there!"

"Jesus!" the FAA inspector cried out. "She should have almost half left in there. This is totally baffling!"

"I know, I would guess 300 or more gallons," said a Dressler technician.

Baldini said, "My guess? Do you want to hear my guess?"

"Sure!" they said, almost in unison.

"She never got loaded," he said. "They NEVER refueled her! Perhaps they forgot to!"

"Can't be," the inspector added, "The log said she was 'tanked up' before departure."

"'Cording to the records, she supposedly got topped off to 6,875 pounds."

Someone piped up, "Hey . . . maybe they 'dumped it' on the way in to lighten the load. Ya know, to increase the lift and extend the glide! Possible?"

"Not possible," the technician from Europe piped up. "The '205' can't 'dump' fuel! She's not like a jet, ya know, like the big birds. This plane can't dump fuel on command! Not possible."

"Shit, if she never got refueled—that explains why the engine cut out. No fuel! No engines!" Baldini added confidently. He continued, "The residual I just pumped out was probably from the area of the tank below the fuel pump intake. That's where the dirt and water settles, if it's contaminated," he thought out loud. "What we got out, probably couldn't be sucked up while she was airborne."

"Bottom of the barrel, you mean?" asked the FAA official.

"'Xactly. Bottom of the friggin' barrel!" Baldini replied. "She probably had enough for taxi and takeoff, but not enough to get to Manchester."

"But . . . why the flame out? Why the fire?" asked the investigator.

"Don't know!" responded a Dressler technician. "They can backfire! Perhaps that's what happened. Could have been the result of a jet backfire. Sort of like your car when it's runnin' bad. Blew a fuel hose in the process, maybe."

They shook their heads in disbelief. They would need to pull the fuel controllers and open the left-wing tank. A visual inspection was needed. No one could believe she was empty or that she might not have been refueled.

All of a sudden the inspector, who was deep in thought, yelled, "Hey! The gauges! The fuel gauges! What do *they* show?"

They all moved to the cockpit assembly positioned in front of the fuselage.

Earlier the cockpit had been gently sprayed with water to remove the mud and silt from the console. The left and right fuel gauges, one per engine, were not damaged in the crash and, in fact, looked almost new. The cockpit console has similar gauges in most planes. The two fuel gauges sit in a panel to the left of the airspeed and altitude indicators, altimeter, rate of climb indicator and compass. In the cluster of gauges above the fuel indicators are the other avionics for engine function and communication. Each pilot can see the fuel levels in the center of the console.

"Are they intact?" he asked. "Can you see?"

"Don't know," a Dressler technician replied, peering in to see the console.

"Yep! They look good," he continued. "Intact! Both of them!"

"Wadda they read? . . . Dammit! . . . What do they say?"

"Full! They read full!" the mechanic said in amazement.

"No shit!" someone piped in, peering over his shoulder. "They're reading almost full."

"Are you shittin' me, you guys? What do you mean full?" snapped the inspector.

"Look for yourself!" the technician offered.

"Jesus! Can they be removed easily?" asked the inspector. "Can we look at 'em?"

"Sure. The only thing that holds them are four Allen screws!" was the technician's response. "Get me the Allen wrench set! Please!"

"Pull 'em! Both of 'em. Let's have a look," the inspector said.

"Careful!" said the inspector to the mechanic. "We need those intact."

The technician stopped for a moment and looked slowly over his shoulder at the inspector. His eyes widened as he took a deep breath.

"I know!" was the response in defiance, "I've done this before!"

"Sorry," said the inspector apologetically. "Sorry . . . just nervous!"

"So'kay . . . me, too. Just give me a minute, sir," said the technician. He was as anxious as the others to take a look at the gauges.

The inspector knew that the Dressler technician was competent. After all, he thought, he built the damn planes. In less than five minutes all fuel gauges were removed and lying on a makeshift table in the hangar. The needles on each gauge matched almost perfectly. They were positioned at the equivalent of nine-tenths full.

"Can't be!" said the FAA inspector. "Nine-tenths full? Can't be," he reiterated. "The right-side tank was destroyed and the left side is empty. How can they read full? The damn right tank was destroyed. It's partially missing!"

There was no response to his question. Baldini took off his baseball cap and scratched his head. They looked at each other for a second.

An astute Dressler technician turned both gauges over and examined the mechanisms behind the needles. He could see a foreign object, not normally present, in the mechanism of the gauges. It was like wax, a "waxy" rod of sorts holding the needles in place—in the "full" position. Each gauge had the foreign material strategically placed behind the mechanism controlling the position of the needle.

"What's this?" he said, as he took a magnifier to the wax rod and mechanism. "This isn't normal—it's definitely not part of the original gauge."

"Looks like a waxy substance—soft and malleable," the inspector commented.

"Yeh, looks sort'a like beeswax. Feels like it, too!" added the technician.

Other Dressler mechanics and the NTSB representative took a closer look. The needles indicating the fuel level had been jammed meticulously into one position with the waxy substance: full, or nearly full. The substance was soft but rigid enough to hold the needles in place.

"Holy shit!" someone cried out. "They've been rigged! They've been rigged to read full!"

"Are you sayin' this was sabotage? That the crash was planned?"

"Possibly," the technician said, looking at the inspector. "Sure hints of it."

"This is horrible!" Baldini piped in. "The pilots were faked out! They thought that they had fuel. They probably had none. Or not enough to go ten miles!"

"But . . . but why?" the inspector asked. "Who would do this? Why?"

Baldini mumbled to himself, "Who the hell worked that night? Who was on duty?"

The records would show who signed off on maintenance and refueling procedures. The FAA and NTSB had the records and log on the table. Baldini peered at the initials and gasped! The records had his initials beside the refueling. It even looked like his signature. He stood there shocked and puzzled. He didn't even work that night. *What the hell is going on?* he wondered. He called the FAA inspector over to show him the log. He had nothing to hide.

"Inspector? Look at this! The records show my name—my initials for the refueling of 2158. I wasn't even on duty that night. I was off. I didn't even work that shift."

"You sayin' someone put your initials there?" the inspector asked suspiciously.

"Yes sir! Whoever did this was trying to frame me and steer everyone away from themselves," Baldini added. "I never worked that shift—honest!"

The records showed a "DB" beside the refueling slip, and another one beside a cockpit voucher. The voucher showed that a light bulb had been replaced on the console. It was a "DR 3116" bulb for a gauge on the instrument display. The comment beside the "DB" initials was: "routine check. VOR bulb out . . . replaced with new DR 3116–JB 6:00 PM."

Dan Baldini was mortified—speechless—by what he saw. The color left his face. Someone had used his name on a cockpit service call and for the refueling of 2158. He was being implicated in something for which he had no involvement. The NTSB investigator, seeing the shock on Baldini's face, sensed that he was telling the truth. The inspector didn't believe for a minute that he could be involved.

Held at an angle, it was clear to see that the gauges were altered. The needle wouldn't move if the tanks were empty. Everyone in Hangar 10 wondered if this suspected sabotage and murder was the work of a disgruntled employee. But who? It would be easy to verify Baldini's work schedule. Obviously, his schedule would show him not there and the time clock needed his ID card to clock in and out.

A NTSB inspector was on the phone calling the FBI unit at Logan. They would dispatch a team immediately to Hangar 10. The crash was no longer suspected as an accident and the initial inspection team had already uncovered a potential problem other than the earlier speculation of a "mechanical."

Many questions remained. Who had worked last night? The NTSB and FAA inspectors pondered the wax rods. A small sample of the material would be sent immediately to the analytical laboratory in Cambridge. They would know its composition in just hours.

The NTSB inspector theorized that the waxy substance could melt. But why? If the plane were to have a fire, or if it crashed, or if the cockpit heated up at some point during the flight, the wax might melt. *Sure!* He thought. *The pilots thought they had a full load of fuel. Somewhere in the flight, the wax would melt and might go undetected. The fuel gauges and needles would operate freely and accurately show that there was no fuel. If the plane crashed and burned, there would be little evidence of the wax, even if the gauges were intact.* He concluded to himself that the person or persons who perpetrated this crime were experts in avionics and were devious beyond comprehension. They also wanted someone dead. *But why? There were no dignitaries on the flight. This wasn't a terrorist attack. An international terrorist wouldn't blow up a commuter. A jet maybe, but a commuter to New Hampshire? Nah!* he thought.

The inspector kept his theory to himself. In the meantime a sample of the waxy substance left the building in a small vial. It would be sent to Cambridge in a state police patrol car and under guard. Both its chemical composition and physical properties would be determined. Additionally, he would have them do a melting point determination and volatility analysis. In the end, the Cambridge lab would provide data on everything about this compound. All the inspector knew was that it looked like beeswax but it wasn't yellow in color. He was now on a "mission from hell" so to speak. He would be talking to the investigators at the scene of Gate 23A. Together they would try to solve this accident—or murder. Their data in the hangar would be combined with the evidence from the gate and fueling area. All records for that evening would be scrutinized thoroughly. If Baldini had nothing to do with it, who did?

44

When the FAA finally roused Bob Connolly the morning after the crash he was asked to report as quickly as possible to the office at Logan Airport. The FAA investigator said that they and other investigative agencies needed to talk with him about the maintenance and baggage loading of Flight 2158. Investigators said they hoped that he "felt better" after such a traumatic evening—an emotional time for anyone who worked for North East Air.

He prepared himself for some of the questions that might be asked of him. He carefully thought out all scenarios that they might allude to. He had not had time to catch the morning TV news and did not know what updates the FAA and NTSB might have on the crash. As he dressed hurriedly and grabbed a traveler's mug of coffee, he was not aware that much of the plane had been retrieved during the night.

As he drove south, he wondered what could be left of it anyway. She had hit the boat at a high rate of speed, and sank to the harbor bottom. Surely the instrument console had been severely damaged in the fire and crash. Nothing to worry about, unless Tomasi talked about the spill.

Because of the traffic problems in and around Logan Airport, he was told that an unmarked state police car would meet him at a designated spot on Route 1 and escort him. Once at Logan, Connolly would be interviewed by NEAir, FAA and NTSB officials. He was considered to be the missing link to much of what they had found in the last twelve hours.

Bob's wife was suspicious of her husband when he left to meet with the board. The morning paper had mentioned a Marisa Bell as the name of the missing pilot's wife. She knew that the Bells lived in the neighborhood and that Bob had spoken to her occasionally. Suspecting Bob's past infidelity, she wondered if there was any truth to the rumor in the neighborhood that someone at NEAir had been involved with Marisa. She decided that it was time to muster her courage and confront him when he came home. Yet, she was scared of the truth. What would it mean to their lives?

Knowing that the neighborhood was crawling with media, she stayed inside all day and kept the children home from school with her. She doubted that Bob had read the paper—he wasn't much of a reader, so he probably wasn't aware of the media's speculation about the love triangle. But the more she thought of the article, the more infuriated she became. She suspected everything and ruled out nothing. And as the day wore on, she had imagined him in every possible scenario. As she began to cry, her children left her alone and went to their rooms to play.

Sabotage was a real concern for the investigative teams. All data indicated that the plane was not refueled, the fuel gauges had been altered and records had been changed or fudged. The speculation reeked of a planned plot to bring down Flight 2158.

While the FAA, NTSB and other officials were waiting for Connolly, a pleasure boat located the leather zippered log of Officer John Bell, floating near Governors Island. It was Bell's day-to-day calendar containing preflight notes that he recorded while awaiting Bullock's arrival and the departure of 2158 from the parking area of Gate 23A.

When the investigative committee heard of the recovery, they decided to postpone the remainder of the meeting until the log and its contents could be reviewed.

Bell's log book and calendar was soaked from seawater. It would be difficult to turn pages without ripping or destroying the potential evidence, so officials decided that the log would undergo a new process designed to restore wet paper to its original condition. The process involved freeze-drying. The water-saturated log would be frozen with dry ice. This was rapid freezing at -79 degrees Celsius. The log would be placed in a frozen chamber, or lyophilization unit, which would then have air pumped out, producing a vacuum. Under freezing conditions and in a vacuum, the ice would be removed by sublimation, vaporized and removed in a gaseous form. With this process, ice goes from a solid state to a gaseous state without first becoming liquid.

In a few hours after the water was removed and the log's pages were dry, they looked as if they had never been wet, except for a residue of sea salt. The writing was readable and the pages were intact.

What they would find were the preflight notations that Bell had written while waiting for Bullock to arrive. The notes were written in cursive: "console light replaced—burned out."

A second line listed the mechanic by name: "B. Connolly."

There was now hard evidence from Bell's notations that Bob Connolly had been in the cockpit before the plane left for its flight to Manchester. Bullock had only seen Connolly loading baggage, but Bell had obviously conversed with him briefly and then recorded the data for his own records. Although a specialized light bulb had supposedly been replaced in the instrument panel, there were no written records in the NEAir Service Area of a DR 3116 light bulb being issued to a mechanic for a Dressler 205. The parts department manager had no record of such a request. No paperwork existed and no part had been logged out of the service area by the manager. Investigators now had additional questions for Connolly.

✈ ✈ ✈

Bob Connolly was grilled behind closed doors. The interviews focused on the fuel spot on the tarmac and his handling of the Tony Tomasi incident. Connolly began to realize that Tomasi had already been questioned and there was a possible discrepancy in their stories. However, Connolly denied any knowledge of the fuel spill on the pavement.

"I know of no problems with the 2158," he claimed confidently. "She was running fine when she left the gate."

"Mr. Connolly, we have notations that you may have serviced the console of 2158 and replaced a light on the VOR panel. Did you do that?"

Connolly shook his head in the affirmative, but did not elaborate. The interrogation continued and many questions were asked in the next few hours. The preliminary data from the plane's retrieval and reconstruction of its parts left many discrepancies to be addressed. Investigators did not want the initial interviews to be confrontational and accusatory—merely informative.

After the first session was over, Connolly's boss took him aside. His supervisor was aware of the newest rumors in the media, but he also wanted to give his employee the benefit of the doubt and to shield him from tabloids and reporters.

Connolly's boss suggested that he stay overnight in a nearby motel where he would be easily available to investigators, but also avoid the press in the meantime.

"We've arranged for you to stay in a motel near the airport," said the supervisor.

"Why's that?" barked Connolly, defensively.

"Bob, the investigators are just beginning to collate the data from the crash. Your input will be needed as the information is submitted from all agencies involved. Having you close by will enable us to reach you more easily. It will help us resolve what happened during the final hours before the plane departed. You are an important witness to the overall flight prep and we value your input as a qualified airline technician. There have been rumors that the flight might have been sabotaged and we will need to know about baggage loading and other factors, which you may have witnessed, as causative factors to the demise of the flight. Can you help us?"

Connolly felt empowered by his boss's statement.

Important? His input was important? he thought.

His supervisor would not elaborate further, but he obviously had information that he could not share with Connolly. The boss sensed that Connolly was not aware of the rumors circulating in the news.

Connolly agreed to stay at the motel, with his expenses covered by NEAir. He would call his wife after he checked in to his room.

The thirty-room motel was on Route 1, north of the airport. It was near an area he frequented for its topless bars. He figured he would buy a six-pack from a convenience store, have some beers in his room, then hit a club to see some young flesh. He decided to call home first.

When his wife answered, he sensed she was depressed and full of questions. He rambled on about the day's activities, and she lost her courage to confront him about Marisa Bell.

"I'll be in touch," he said. "They need me nearby for tomorrow's investigation. I hope to be home after that. OK?"

She hesitated, then said, "OK. I'll tell the kids you have to stay in town."

Connolly hung up the phone and headed for the door. The neon lights from the club flashed in his face. Relaxed by the beer, he felt unfazed by the day's interview, and was ready for some T&A.

He would return to his room at 2:30 A.M., ready to sleep. He would be awakened at 7:00 A.M. by a call from his boss. He was needed to review new evidence in the airport conference room by 8:00 A.M. A car would pick him up.

45

Tons of coal from the barge had been dumped over the area near where the *Queen* was resting. Some coal had moved with the water flow into the fracture below the *Queen*'s stern, ending up in some of the vents in the tunnel. The process had worked; the water level in the Sumner had peaked and was no longer rising. The midway point of the tunnel was half full and the amount of water leaking into the fractured casing had been reduced.

Tunnel officials needed to immediately evaluate the situation and could not wait for the leak to be completely sealed off. They couldn't wait for the tunnel to be totally pumped out either. They could take a boat into the mid-section and open an upper panel behind the wall or ceiling. It would then be possible to view the damage. With the service bay areas to the exhaust fans elevated above the water line, the divers and engineers could enter the maintenance panel doors to the ventilation and electrical areas.

Once they had the opportunity evaluate the damage, welders would be brought in to seal off the fracture with plates of steel. Although a temporary solution, it would solve the problem until major repairs could be completed outside the tunnel. The welded panels would be layered for strength and would be thicker and stronger than the surrounding structure.

Simultaneously, other tunnel engineers focused on how they could rapidly remove the water that had accumulated in the middle of the Sumner. They would combine the pumps from area fire trucks as well as auxiliary pumps from a local construction company. The pumps were massive and were often utilized to maintain dry construction holes for the placement of cement footings during road construction. The effluent from the various pumps would be directed with temporary conduits into the storm drainage systems of the east Boston area. The large size of the storm-drain piping would not be taxed greatly since the pipe diameters under the streets were five to six feet. Large generator trucks were rented to run the pumps and flexible intake pipes and fire hoses were introduced into the tunnel. They would be moved inward as the water level decreased.

It would take a day or more to get all the water and mud out. Then they would deal with the disabled cars in the midsection where water was the deepest. They would have to be retrieved as well. One car—an older model Volkswagen beetle—was bobbing like a small boat due to its virtually airtight "uni-body" construction.

Tunnel engineers who would access the damage in the midsection were directed to the central service bay. It was almost halfway into the Sumner. A scouting party of engineers had just converged at the site. A second group of civil and mechanical engineers were ferried to the area where an access panel had been opened.

Once the engineers were behind the wall, they scanned the ceiling of the tunnel housing with a series of powerful flashlights. The damage was readily apparent. Flashes of light in the previously darkened casing showed a fracture of almost six feet in length. That small slit, where the sections of tunnel were joined in the 1930s, was responsible for the massive amounts of water in the tunnel. The *Queen* was directly above them and they could hear the rumble of coal being dumped from above. It was a frightening sound that was magnified by the hollowness of the tunnel casing.

Confident that the water flow had been halted, construction welders were summoned. The massive pumps had already reduced the water level to below the catwalk allowing others to approach the site of the damage more easily. Welding equipment and steel plates were brought in by flat-bottom water craft, which rode low in the water from the weight of the steel panels.

It was clear to the engineers that once the fracture had been sealed, they would need to move the *Queen*. The tonnage of the vessel could encourage further damage. Removal of its weight from the general area of the fracture would reduce the stress on the submerged casing in the harbor.

✈   ✈   ✈

The *Queen* leaned at a ten-degree angle off vertical. Her position would facilitate the ability to move her off the top of the tunnel casing. Cables could be attached to her forward section and then to two tugboats; she would be literally dragged to the side, bow first. The *Queen of Shoals* would not be moved until the metal plates had been welded in place. That process of welding was estimated to take between one and two hours. Two to three workmen began to work feverishly on the critical project.

They knew that the pressure of the harbor water on the coal piles at a depth of forty to fifty feet had caused the pieces of black rock to interlock as an aggregate. It had formed a "Band-Aid" of tightly connected coal pieces around the boat's hull. As the silt that was stirred up as the coal fell settled back between the black rock it had formed a mortar-like putty between the lumps. Once the *Queen* was moved, the piles of coal would settle further into place above the fracture. The metal plates would be in place before she was moved.

By four in the morning, the toll takers at the eastern end of the Sumner had ended their shifts and gone home. There would be no tolls collected for many days. The area around the tollbooths was now a parking lot for fire trucks, pumps, generators, and service vehicles. Yellow and red flashing lights were everywhere. Enormous floodlights on tripods were erected at the end of the Sumner so that halogen lights could shine deeply into the abyss. Generator motors were humming everywhere.

Electrical engineers and technicians were already repairing the power outages in the tunnel. Internal water pumps, exhaust fans and motors, and the lighting that had been short-circuited were now being restored. It would take a day to replace electrical panels and substation units. Transformers had blown and electrical lines would need to be replaced. Temporary electrical conduits were run into the tunnel to restore power.

As the water receded, tow trucks backed in and removed the vehicles as they could be safely reached. They would have forty or more cars, cabs, buses and trucks to remove. It would take an additional forty-eight to seventy-two hours to rid the tunnel of water and debris. The Sumner would be closed for two or three weeks pending initial repairs. It would take longer if there were complications along the way. The governor of Massachusetts and the mayor of Boston had both held press conferences to assure residents that everything that needed to be done would in fact be done.

In concert with the tunnel repairs would be the movement of the *Queen*. The placement of coal had been completed, but officials had decided to leave the barge on site until the *Queen* had been relocated. Additional coal might be needed once she was moved by the tugboats.

Rescue and recovery vessels in the harbor continued their search the next day for First Officer Bell and additional pieces of wreckage. Sonar had found other pieces of the right wing. The grid was being followed segment by segment. From time to time, a piece of baggage was found on the bottom. Cruise boat chairs and deck gear also littered the harbor bottom.

Captain Bullock's flight bag had also been found. It was open and on its side not more than fifty feet from the hull of the boat. It would take just a week to retrieve 95 percent of Flight 2158's wreckage. Normal boat and ship traffic in the harbor would be opened again, although some lanes would remain restricted. The Harbor Marine Patrol made sure that critical areas were not violated by small craft. Fishing boats had priority and commercial freight vessels were guided in and out of port by tugs.

As the days passed, TV news crews no longer emphasized the harbor activity in their sound bites. They tended to cover the tunnel repair and interviewed critical MTA and MASSPORT engineers. The engineers didn't mind the notoriety exposure. When else would the public recognize their efforts?

The TV news helicopters appeared overhead only sporadically. Usually, the aerial "skycam" shots were focused on pumping water from the tunnel. News reporters were not allowed inside the tunnel due to the liability and the possibility of injury. MASSPORT and the MDC had done what it could to insure safety, but they were not allowing unauthorized personnel into the hazardous area.

Human-interest stories dominated the newspapers, and interviews with boat and plane passengers went on for days. Even Kristin and Robie were interviewed. A headline read: Couple on fatal cruise boat fall in love!

They would get extensive coverage on local TV evening magazines. One late-night TV talk show had even indicated interest in their story, and they were shown sympathy for being temporarily out of work. The best that could happen was that Robie's band EXZILLERATION would get great exposure from the interviews. The publicity led to top-quality gigs and fame for the band. Several musical instrument companies and local music stores donated equipment to the band, just for the publicity.

Another headline had focused on the birth of the baby in the tunnel. The baby, Felix Mendosa, would be remembered in many stories about the tragedy. Hispanic TV stations followed the baby's life for weeks. The media also featured pictures of toll takers, medics, troopers and even Jack Danton, for their role in rescuing the mother and child.

Hollywood-style tabloid newspapers were into the emotion of the events as well. They increased their circulation by surmising that John Bell was alive and well and stranded on an undeveloped island. The local Boston tabloid called *Undercover,* was a "rag" of sorts and had released a shocking picture of Captain Bullock's body before it was placed in the body bag. It was a fuzzy photograph from a telephoto lens, but one could see many details of his decapitation. It was shameful that the tabloid had no sensitivity for his wife's grief.

A smaller, but significant story on page two of the most recent edition of *Undercover* hinted at the possibility of sabotage and further alluded to the "Boston Triangle." It did not refer to the disaster as mimicking the haunting missing vessels of the famed Bermuda Triangle, but rather insinuated a love tryst in Boston. The hypothetical triangle hinted of fact. It alluded to two men and a woman, closely linked to the airline business. The article, although subtle, caused enormous attention after its initial publication. Confidential data from the Hangar 10 ongoing investigation was highlighted in a portion of the text. The FAA and NTSB inspectors who were shown the article were shocked to learn that confidentiality had been breached. They needed to issue a statement dispelling the rumors before the possible motives for a crash were released from the Board of Investigators. Data to date was only supposition and speculative. The observations were too investigative for release to the general public.

Attempts to force the *Undercover's* editors to retract the article were in vain. They stood by their source and the content, citing their First Amendment rights. They did not care what the FAA and NTSB had to say. They knew that they were "on to something big" and the small unauthorized, anonymous article was only the beginning of what the tabloid magazine suspected.

National tabloids immediately jumped into the action. Every grocery store nationwide had the Boston plane/boat tragedy on the cover by the second day. Reporters hounded Logan officials, MTA personnel and the relatives and friends of Bullock and Bell. The officers' homes became targets for watching the day-to-day activities of the wives and were saturated with reporters and "rubber-neckers" in their cars. Reporters at the more ethical newspapers, such as the *Boston Gazette*, wondered if the tabloids were on to something.

The FAA investigators had already gathered substantial data on the crash of 2158 and the *Queen of Shoals*. The day after the accident, they were able to reassemble many of the larger pieces of the plane in Hangar 10. Those parts which needed identification were laid out around the fuselage awaiting the Dressler technicians' input. They would know where each belonged.

Because of questions raised by the newspapers and tabloids, investigators decided to have a preliminary meeting to compare their findings to date and then another press conference during late afternoon of the third day. They would share with one another their basic findings on the harbor retrieval effort, the Gate 23A area, the analytical findings, Hangar 10 data and the results of Bullock's autopsy. The reason for the preliminary meeting was in part due to the fact that the tabloids had some information, which was not fabricated. If the inspectors were to quell the rumors, they needed to have a joint press conference with officials from Dressler, NTSB, FAA and NEAIR. While the tabloids had focused on the Bell situation, there were other lives lost besides the pilot's.

Relatives of the people who had died needed to hear and see something official, not the trash that had been printed in the newspapers and publications. Getting to the bottom of the rumors that the flight was sabotaged, and that their loved ones died unnecessarily, was of paramount importance. An official press or news release was needed by the FAA and the NTSB. The FBI would be present at any potential news conferences, but would not comment on the fate of 2158.

It would take months for the final report to be issued, but initial findings could be discussed behind closed doors between the various teams of investigators. They would all have information that would eventually summate to a probable cause conclusion. They were professionals and had a natural intuition and knack for finding the less obvious causes of tragedies such as 2158.

✈   ✈   ✈

After the paparazzi descended on her neighborhood, keeping a twenty-four-hour vigil, Marisa Bell had become a captive in her own home. She was trapped—a victim of innuendo and supposition by the ever-present media vultures. From the first morning after news of the crash, she kept her window shades drawn and refused to go outside for any purpose. Belinda, her closest friend, a woman that she trusted, offered to bring her groceries and the mail and newspapers. Marisa gave her a pattern of knocks to use so that she would know who was at the back door.

To a lesser extent, the media also staked out Bob Connolly's home. The real focus, however, was on the Bell residence and Marisa. The reporters wanted to interview her, and to get her picture on the cover. After all, beauty and sex appeal sold tabloids and magazines.

By the third day, headlines in the *Undercover* implied that Marisa was a member of a "Lonely Wives Club" or LWC. The tabloid fabricated a club of lonely pilots' wives and claimed that she was just one of many "club members" who were having affairs. There were pictures of Marisa when she was eighteen, twenty-one and twenty-five; when she was a cheerleader; during her college years, and more recently at a NEAir social event. The papers were calling her the "mistress of the Boston triangle," and she felt that her life, as portrayed, was being ruined by the daily exposure of this story.

Then a front-page article in *Undercover* stated that there was new evidence from an unnamed source that Marisa Bell's husband, John, was murdered by her jealous lover. The tabloid implied that there was sabotage and coercion and that the 2158 flight was brought down to kill Marisa's husband. That way the two lovers could be together, the article insinuated. However, there still was no evidence of collaboration between anyone and no concrete evidence that Bell was dead. Attorneys who specialized in libel and character defamation suits began to hound her. Marisa stopped listening to messages on her answering machine.

46

It didn't take long for a reporter from *Undercover* to find a neighbor of Connolly and the Bells who was willing to talk. Thelma Hopkins was a spinster and not much into the neighborhood chitchat. Most of the time she stayed inside her semi-darkened home, a small Cape with bushes that had overgrown her property. She was approached by an *Undercover* reporter on false pretenses. The man who knocked on her door said that he was a private investigator gathering information about a potential divorce case. She was asked if she knew Marisa Bell who lived around the corner. Did she actually know her? If so, what was she like? Was she friendly? Did she have friends? These were the leading questions he brought up before getting more specific. Thelma rarely had visitors and this visit from a fine young man broke up the monotony of her day. The mailman was about the only person who recognized her. Her windows were kept shut, causing the air to feel stale in the living room. The atmosphere in the home was that of a dingy, old home of an era gone by. Lace-covered end tables and Victorian furniture dominated the decor. She had brought much of it with her from the United Kingdom, where she had lived for many years. *Both she and her house appear to be old and stark*, the reporter thought.

She offered him tea and he accepted. Thelma didn't know much about the neighbors or Marisa Bell. She had noticed Marisa jogging around the block on occasion but had never met her. Thelma indicated that most neighbors appeared friendly; some were more friendly than others. And she casually mentioned that another of her neighbors, Bob Connolly, had impeccable timing—he rarely missed Marisa's jaunts.

Thelma sometimes volunteered more information than the man wanted to know, but he never stopped her. A chatterbox once she got started, she rambled about the neighbors. He listened intently for clues, occasionally taking notes. Thelma said she thought Bob worked at Logan Airport, sometimes at night. Thelma regarded Marisa as a fine young lady but thought that Bob was a sleaze—those were her exact words. She had noticed that Bob was often in his front yard pretending to do yard work when Marisa jogged by. As Thelma sat on her porch or fussed with her yard, she would listen to them talk. Bob would joke with Marisa about the fact that she didn't *need* to work out. It was obvious that she was in fine shape, so why bother. She would joke back that she always wanted to look nice and that she was getting older. She did not share her age with Connolly. The odd thing, she said, was that Marisa seemed to be attracted to his humorous comments. Sometimes in a neighborly fashion, she would rest and chat for a while. Connolly knew that she had a husband named John and that he was a pilot. Bob was a mechanic for the same airline. It was obvious to Thelma that they, Bob and Marisa, had something in common.

When Marisa would continue her jog, Bob often watched her until she was out of sight. Thelma found it odd that he would then put down his tools and go back inside his home. Thelma had surmised that Bob "fancied Marisa" because he was a sleaze, to start with. Work was probably not what he had in mind when he was out in his yard.

Mrs. Connolly was the one who often mowed the lawn or raked the leaves in the fall. Bob did little and often sat on the front steps drinking beer while his wife planted the flowers.

Thelma Hopkins didn't think that the Connollys had much of a marriage. Mrs. Connolly was the one who took the kids to their sports events, did the laundry, hung out the clothes and did the grocery shopping. Bob was seen doing little. As she talked, Thelma occasionally paused, saying, "Oh, you don't want to hear about that."

Her visitor's face would light up and he would say, "Sure I would. Tell me more."

He was jotting notes wildly. Encouraged, she continued, "Young man, he did nothing," speaking of Connolly. "He's a voyeur of sorts!"

"Really? How so?"

"Yes—always lookin' at ladies' behinds and stuff. Did it with Marisa," she continued. "He thinks he's a ladies' man, I guess," Thelma added.

"Really, you don't say."

"Yes," she smirked. "Seen him whistle at lots of women—including her."

The visitor suddenly seemed pressed for time and indicated that he must move along. He had to file a report and needed a couple of hours to pull it together for his boss. Thelma understood.

Before the man left, he thanked her profusely for her time. He handed her an envelope and a piece of paper. He said, "Please initial this document. It proves that I was here. My management requires that I get the initials so that they don't think that I'm ridin' all day doin' nothin'," he told her.

"Sure. Enjoyed talking to you," Thelma said, feeling comfortable with the conversation.

She never read the document that she signed. He told her that the envelope was a "token" of their appreciation at the investigative agency, and that some of her insight might help with some legal issues.

"If need be, may I contact you in the future?" the man asked.

She nodded yes and he walked toward the front door.

"I hope I've been of some help. Nice talkin' with you, Mr. . . . By the way, what's your name?" she asked him as he walked down the steps.

"Jones. Mr. Jones."

After "Mr. Jones" drove off in the Cadillac, she opened the envelope. Inside she found five crisp, new, one hundred dollar bills! She was flabbergasted. She had not seen that kind of money in years. The serial numbers were sequential and the bills stuck together. She fanned out the five Ben Franklins. *Why did he give me these?* she wondered. She hadn't told him anything. She was dumbfounded. *Do private investigators give money away?* She sat down and wondered what she had initialed. It had looked like a receipt. *Did I sign a receipt for the money?* she wondered. She had no copy for herself.

Thelma Hopkins placed the envelope in a dresser drawer. She sat back in her chair in the quiet of the house. She thought about what he had asked her. The original questions were about Marisa Bell but he seemed very interested in her comments about Bob Connolly. *Why? Were the Bells getting a divorce?* she thought. Not that she had heard or was aware of. He never asked about Marisa's husband. Why so many questions about Marisa?

Thelma went back and starred at the open mahogany drawer. The envelope was directly in front of her. She counted the money again. It looked real enough, but why did he give it to her? What did all this mean? His name was Jones. Yeh, sure. Mr. Jones. What was his real name? The more she thought about it, the more she worried. Was the man a charlatan? He was not a private investigator. Who was he? Why her? She placed the tea-cups in the sink, but then took his back out and did not wash it. *Finger-prints*, she thought. Save his fingerprints! Never know. Might be needed.

Thelma looked outside. The Cadillac was gone, and along with it, her opportunity to write down the numbers on his license plate. But she vaguely remembered that there was a U and a 1 on the plate. In between she didn't have a clue what numbers or letters were there. He would never be back and would not call. There was no business card for her to refer to.

The very next day the newspapers had articles referring to the latest issue of the weekly *Undercover*. The new edition was out and Thelma's house was pictured within a series of other shots, on the cover. The head-lines on the cover included the statement:

MURDER OF 2158 PILOT BELL—NEIGHBOR SUSPECTS NEIGHBOR

A second byline inside featured the line:

2158 —FATE—MISSING PILOT'S WIFE LINKED TO NEIGHBOR

WAS PILOT MURDERED BY WIFE'S LOVER?

The article began: "Bob Connolly, NEAir flight mechanic and neigh-bor of First Officer Bell and his wife, Marisa, has been linked to the demise of NEAir 2158. Connolly and Marisa Bell suspected as lovers! Connolly caught in front of his home having intimate chatter with Marisa Bell. She was dressed in a skimpy jogging outfit. They were laughing and frolicking. Did Connolly sabotage 2158 as a jealous act—to be with her? An elderly neighbor thinks so. . . ." and it continued with speculation based on the conversation with Thelma.

In addition to the new articles hot off the presses, artists' sketches of Marisa and Bob Connolly illustrated the article. It showed them talking in front of Connolly's house. Marisa's likeness was not flattering; she looked more like a hooker than a beautiful woman.

The day after "Mr. Jones" had been at Thelma Hopkins' home, she went to the local supermarket for a few items. Thelma made her way to the checkout line and scanned the candy displays and the nearby newsstand. Although she was not one to buy trashy magazines, she noticed the head-lines on *Undercover*, and was shocked. They focused on her neighborhood and the Flight 2158 crash. The reference in the article to an elderly woman being interviewed about a tryst in the neighborhood was reminiscent of her conversations with "Mr. Jones." Trying not to be obvious she stared at the cover while still looking straight ahead. She could not see the details but saw the Connolly name. She needed to take home a copy to review. When she got closer to the rack, she grabbed a copy and quickly rolled it up. As she was about to buy it with her groceries, the young cashier behind the register said, "Did you notice, ma'am?"

"Notice? Notice what, dear?" Thelma asked of the girl.

"The tabloid! The *Undercover* magazine! The one in your hands!"

"Yes, what about it?" Thelma responded, with a puzzled look.

"Why they've solved the plane crash! . . . 2158! . . . The pilot was murdered—sabotage by some jealous man! Awesome article! You'll love it! Don't you just love that stuff?"

The young girl continued, "Right here, an 'affair' happened right here—in our town!"

Thelma stood confused and taken aback by the cashier's comments. She fumbled for her money and some coins fell on the floor beneath her. She didn't bother to pick up the loose change but grabbed her bag and quickly left the store.

"Your change, ma'am—it fell!" the cashier yelled.

"Never mind. It's only a penny or two," Thelma responded.

"Have a nice day," the cashier said, chewing her gum.

"Ah, yes, dear. You, too."

After Thelma left the cashier looked down at the floor. There was some 75 cents, not pennies, on the tiles. *Odd*, she thought. *That was something worth picking up. But why didn't the nice old lady pick up the coins?* she wondered.

Thelma rushed out of the store scanning the paper as she carried her groceries to the car. Fumbling for her keys, she dropped something from the bag. She didn't care. She saw her name in print in the text as she scanned it. She was "the neighbor" who had been interviewed in the article.

Thelma sat in her car, not believing what she was reading. The article talked of an affair between Marisa Bell and Bob Connolly and their plot to kill her husband by sabotaging the flight. The fatal flight was not an accident, but murder. The details of the article specifically said how they would get together in front of one or the other's house. Exercise, jogging and yard work were the guise for getting together. The neighbors were really lovers.

The article got worse. Statements by Thelma had been taken out of context and expanded upon. Most of what was printed was sensationalism and nonfactual. Any mention of womanizing had been inflated to sexual encounters, something she had not even suggested in her conversation with "Mr. Jones."

What have I done? she wondered. She had been duped and hoodwinked by "Mr. Jones." The document she had initialed was probably a disclaimer, not a receipt or document for his boss. He had lied to her. *He took advantage of me,* she thought. She had chest pains and reached into her handbag to pop a "nitro," which she had for her angina. She placed the tablet under her tongue and leaned back. The pain immediately subsided. She drove home distracted and came close to having three accidents. She even passed Marisa's house on the way to her own. The Bell house seemed quiet. The Bells' mailbox flap was open and nothing was inside it or in the newspaper tube.

Thelma didn't even bother to put the groceries away. She sat down in her chair, and stared at the older model telephone—black with a rotary dial. After her heart stopped pounding quite so much, she would make two calls—one to the police and the other to a dear friend, a lawyer. She needed to report this "sham" to someone.

The police knew that she was elderly and responded immediately. She told the officer every detail of the conversation that she had with "Mr. Jones." She showed the policeman the money. He raised his eyebrows when he saw five Ben Franklins and the tabloid headlines. He knew that she had been taken advantage of and suggested that she speak to her attorney. At her insistence, he took the tea cup as "evidence." The teacup was from a set that her mother had given her. She did not want them to break it or lose it. The officer assured her that it would be returned to her, unbroken. The officer had seen her pop another tablet. She noticed his concern and told him it was an arthritis pill. He would not know the difference.

After the officer left, she scanned the tabloid again. She was no longer named as Mrs. Thelma Hopkins, but the "elderly nosy neighbor" on Maple Street. What would the other neighbors think of her? She was the only elderly person around. She sat shaking in her favorite chair, waiting for her lawyer to call. The minutes were like hours.

The possible scandal had now captured the interest of the *Boston Gazette*, the largest paper in the Boston area. The *Gazette* had assigned investigative reporters to check out the allegations printed in the tabloids and bandied about on talk shows. The tabloids were "reporting" front-page stories with headlines that read: "Flight mechanic neighbor of 2158 pilot linked romantically to pilot's wife." "Neighbor, overly neighborly!" Added to that was the implication of Thelma Hopkins' purported interview with the tabloid.

By the time legitimate press tried to reach Hopkins, she would not open her door.

47

Marisa Bell's friend, Belinda, was well aware of the newspaper and TV reports of the crash. With John Bell missing, she knew her friend was in pain. On the day after the crash, Marisa, in her despair, had confided her most intimate secret—that in her loneliness, she had been unfaithful to John. She had slept with Belinda's brother, Bob, on occasion. Although Belinda had already suspected as much, she felt that this was just a time to listen to her friend without criticism. Belinda just wanted to be there for her friend, offering love and compassion as needed. She said she would visit Marisa each day to try to assure her that things would be OK. Belinda knew in her heart that John was dead, but would not share that gut feeling with Marisa. There was always hope, but it diminished by the day.

Belinda stopped by Marisa's house as she had been doing for several days following the crash to bring groceries and consolation. Marisa just wanted to be left alone, so she refused to answer the door or phone, or even to listen to the numerous messages on her answering machine. Belinda had, by her presence alone, offered welcome and silent comfort. When she realized how distraught Marisa became with every new news bulletin, Belinda told her that she should not read the paper or watch television. "Let's just listen to music and try to forget things for awhile," she suggested. So Belinda would place Marisa's mail and newspapers on the kitchen table, turn the TV off and turn on restful music. And she was willing to just sit with Marisa, without asking or saying anything. When Belinda left, Marisa would return to the television news and force herself to read the papers that her friend had brought in.

Belinda again used the tapping code, which Marisa had suggested on the day after the crash. The street was filled with cars and television vans hoping for a glimpse of Marisa or a first interview. Brenda was tired of having to dodge the camera crews and news hounds as she made her way to the house.

When Marisa failed to come to the door after the specified pattern of knocks, Belinda was worried. She went into the garage, found the spare key, which was hidden in a little seed bag hanging from a nail, then entered the back door to the kitchen and called to Marisa. There was no answer. She knew that Marisa often sat in the den near the TV or in the bedroom.

"Marisa, are you there? Marisa? It's Belinda! Brought you some supplies, hon."

"Marisa?" Her voice got louder. "Marisa?"

There was no response. Belinda walked down the hallway of the ranch-style home to the bedroom. The door was ajar. Belinda slowly opened it.

Off the side of the bed was a leg—a pale, lifeless leg exposed from the knee down.

Belinda screamed, then rushed in as she cried, "Oh, no! Oh! No! Please, no! Marisa? Marisa? Oh, my God, Marisa?" Belinda put her hands over her mouth as she rushed to the bed. Marisa's angelic face was on the pillow. There was a bullet hole in her chest and the mattress was saturated with blood. She apparently had been dead a while.

Belinda stood there in horror and disbelief, trying to remain calm. *Perhaps she is still alive*, she thought. She held her hand over Marisa's mouth, then nose. No breath. Her chest did not rise and fall. Marisa was dead.

A pistol lay on the floor near her hand. A crucifix on a gold chain was in her other hand, entwined in her fingers, her nails impeccably painted. She looked like a china doll. Her nightgown was a gorgeous flowing garment accented with red lace that wrapped about her and followed her beautiful lifeless body. Except for the darkened blood stains about her, she was almost peaceful in sleep. She was as sensual in death, as she was in life.

Belinda stepped back in silence. She mumbled to herself, "Police. Got to call . . . police." Then Belinda's voice got louder as she paced, "Fuckin' press! The fuckin' press! Bastards. You bastards!"

"Marisa. Oh, Marisa," she cried out still pacing back and forth. She couldn't think. "You said you wouldn't let them get to you! You promised me! They wouldn't get to you! Marisa," her voice faded. "You said."

There was complete silence in the room. The silence was deafening. Belinda was now terrified.

Belinda grabbed the phone. There was no dial tone. She checked the cord. Disconnected! She found the phone jack and plugged it in. Dial tone!

Belinda dialed 911.

"Emergency 911!" was the immediate response at the other end.

"23 Maple! Send help! 23 Maple Street. Please hurry! Ambulance— police—anything please—please hurry—there's been a shooting. Please come quick!"

The 911 fire-rescue unit was only a short distance from the neighborhood. As the dispatcher tried to calm her down and garner additional information, Belinda stopped speaking. She could hear sirens in the distance.

"Ma'am, are you there?" the dispatcher asked "This is 911 dispatch. Are you there? Help is on the way. Ma'am?"

Belinda quietly responded, "Yes. Yes, I'm here. I'm sorry. She's dead. My friend is dead. Please hurry!"

"Ma'am. Stay calm. They're on the way. Stay calm. I need you to give me more info. Please tell me. Are you sure that she's dead? Your friend. Are you sure?"

"Yes," was Belinda's reply. "She's dead. No breathing. No pulse. She's gone—a gun—suicide. My God! My friend, Marisa. Dead!" Brenda rushed out of the room and collapsed, the phone to her ear.

The dispatcher would remain on the phone with Belinda until the ambulance and police arrived. She would keep her calm and ask her additional nonthreatening, noninvasive questions. She heard sirens and then a police car pulled up in the driveway. When no one answered the door, the officers kicked it open and ran inside, and found Belinda, still sitting with the phone on the floor and apparently suffering from shock.

"Ma'am, where?" the policeman asked.

"The bedroom. The far bedroom . . . . she's . . . she's in the bedroom on the left," she whispered, then sobbed and put the phone on the floor.

One of the two officers cautiously went back to the bedroom. The other policeman picked up the phone and told the dispatcher, "Officers on site. We've got it under control. Thanks."

He hung up the phone and addressed Belinda.

"Ma'am, are you OK? Ma'am, your name?" he asked.

"Belinda. My name is Belinda."

"Belinda. You OK? Can I get you some water or help you up?" the policeman said, in a reassuring manner.

"She said she wouldn't let them get to her," Belinda mumbled.

"Belinda?" he said softly. "Who get to her?"

"Them!" she pointed. "Those fucking bastards. Them!" She pointed to the tabloid on the table, which had been left on Marisa's back doorstep by a reporter. It was the latest one. The daily newspaper was there as well. Both had front-page articles on the alleged affair.

Opened to page A2 of the *Undercover* was the headline "BOSTON TRIANGLE REVEALED—2158 PILOT'S WIFE AND LOVER SUSPECTED."

The article continued, mentioning Marisa's name in it fifteen times. Bob Connolly's name was mentioned just as many.

✈ ✈ ✈

The policeman in the back room called for his partner. He whispered to him in the hallway. "Signal 7. No rush for Unit 2. She's dead. Appears self-inflicted," he said to his partner.

"It's a 9mm Italian-style pistol," he continued. His pen was in the trigger loop. It swung upside down and unbalanced from the uneven weight distribution of the chamber and barrel.

Immediately after the police arrived, an ambulance drove up. Thelma watched from the window as it passed her house. She was careful to stay hidden behind her curtains. She was puzzled by the need for both a police car and ambulance in the neighborhood.

The police radioed ahead for the coroner. It would take a while for him to get back to the morgue because he was on the other side of town playing golf. He would get the page on the eleventh hole and was pissed that he had just hit a lousy three-iron shot and had to leave the course. He had been playing well to that point, and had a forty-one on the first nine holes. His buddies laughed as he left.

"There goes your potential seventy-nine. You might have broken eighty today," one playing partner said.

"Next time, I'll get you next time! Emergency! Gotta go," the coroner said.

A member of the ambulance crew tried to console Belinda. A policeman guarded the bedroom door. A bed sheet had been placed over the body, except for the one pale leg that draped over the side. The gun had been packed in an evidence bag, marked with the name Marisa Bell, the date and time. It would end up as Exhibit 1. A police photographer arrived to photograph the grisly scene from all angles—standard procedure. Belinda sat at the end of the hallway staring at the bedroom. She could see the periodic flashes of the camera. They briefly illuminated the framed pictures of John and Marisa together in happier times.

A handwritten note was found beside her body. It would become Exhibit 2. The note read:

"My Beloved Husband John—If you are alive, I just want you to know that I loved you, and you alone completely—

I loved you with all my heart and soul—

I never meant to hurt you—I would have never left you—he meant nothing to me—you were the only one! I did not know that he would do this, I swear—I will always love you, darling—even in death—as in Life!

I LOVE YOU—with all my heart!

Love, Missy

P.S. Please tell Belinda that I'm sorry and I love her, as well. She was the best friend anyone could have.

When the policeman read it out loud, Belinda sobbed loudly. He consoled Belinda by telling her that Marisa was distraught and probably died very quickly from the wound. She did not suffer, he assured Belinda. "Hey, the note says you were her best friend," the policeman said. "This has got to be tough on you, finding her here like this."

Belinda nodded. Through clenched teeth she whispered to herself, "Those tabloid bastards. They killed her."

The coroner, wearing his golf shirt with a score card tucked in his back pocket, arrived in his black Buick station wagon. The blackened rear windows were a testimony to the task at hand. He spent twenty minutes taking samples of blood and examining the body before it was removed. He was meticulous in his note-taking and showed no emotion. He knew an autopsy would be needed; all violent deaths required an autopsy. He rolled the body over to examine the back. The bullet had gone through her body and was lodged somewhere in the bedding. He anticipated that the woman's death would be ruled a suicide and the cause of death would be a single gunshot that had pierced her heart, a lung and her spine.

Before she was placed in the black body bag and placed on a gurney for transport to the morgue, Marisa's face was briefly exposed. She was stunning, even in death. Police guessed that she had shot herself in the chest to avoid disfiguring her face. She was not vain, but would have avoided the alternative in case John Bell was found alive and saw her body in a casket at her funeral.

Belinda went over to the gurney as they passed by and gently kissed her friend's cool forehead.

With John missing, and presumed dead, many of the mourners would end up being complete strangers, as well as friends such as Belinda. Belinda would end up helping Marisa's parents with the funeral arrangements. Marisa would be buried in a family plot, overlooking a pasture and river, just outside of Boston.

Neighbors watched as the gurney covered with a tight white sheet was removed from the home. The frame and wheels of the gurney were collapsed and slid into the back of the coroner's station wagon. The only identification on the car was printed on the side doors. It said:

CORONER

MERRIMAC COUNTY

The black door slammed shut and the car slowly pulled away and turned the corner by Thelma's house. She was afraid to ask anyone what had happened, deciding instead to wait for the 6:00 P.M. news. The TV would surely cover what had happened that morning on Maple Street.

The police remained for another hour. There were details to record and the home needed to be secured before they could leave. The back porch light would be left on. Police would routinely patrol the home site for days. Orange ribbon streamers with the words POLICE LINE-DO NOT CROSS would surround the outside of the house and property. It would remain until the autopsy was completed and foul play had been ruled out.

While the police attended to their reports, Belinda continued sitting in the den, weeping. The police offered to give her a ride home. The officer, who had been very comforting to her, said they had a few more questions. And would she mind telling them one more time what had occurred. She repeated her story, about coming to the house and finding Marisa, but begged the cops to protect her from the media "vultures," who were now waiting for both her and the police to come outside.

The police shielded her from the reporters and cameramen as they took her quickly to a squad car. A Cadillac pulled up with the plates "UNDRCVR-1." The elusive "Mr. Jones" had returned—this time with a photographer. He would join the parade of vultures on the front lawn of the Bells' home,

249

staying behind the orange lines and questioning anyone that they could. A recent stack of *Undercover*'s lay in the back seat of the Cadillac. It was "Mr. Jones" who had placed the complimentary copy of the new edition in Marisa's mailbox a day earlier, which the well-meaning Belinda had taken in to her.

The officer drove off with Belinda and looked in his rearview mirror.

"Ma'am, I know your name is Belinda, but I'm sorry that I never got your last name. We will need your last name for the report," he said kindly.

Belinda looked up gently, and said, "My name? Oh sure, my name . . . my last name is Connolly. C-O-N-N-O-L-L-Y. Belinda Connolly."

"Thank you, Ms. Connolly," he replied slowly. He was puzzled.

The policeman made a mental note of her name and spelling; he looked perplexed. He knew the name Connolly from the news, but could not believe the coincidence. The man Marisa Bell was supposedly having an affair with was of the same name. Connolly—spelled the same way.

As the police car left the neighborhood, the police crime unit arrived in a large van. Their work had just begun. The police already had pictures of the bedroom death scene but the crime unit would need to find the bullet and any other relevant information.

The officer driving Belinda home thought for a minute and hesitated. He then commented, "Ms. Connolly, would you mind a few more minutes of your time? I know you are distraught but I would like you to answer some additional questions . . . if you don't mind. May we stop at the police station for a minute or so. Do you mind?"

"If I can help, I'd be glad to," she replied. "I'd be *very glad* to help in any way possible."

Bob Connolly was questioned again, for two more hours on day three, while some of the other investigators met in another room reviewing the investigative reports to date. Daily analysis of the aircraft and lab reports filtered in slowly. Representatives included the FAA, NTSB, local and state police, plus the U.S. Coast Guard, Harbor Marine Patrol, NEAir officials, ALERT, Logan fire department and Tower Central. The large conference table had hastily been set up in a room inaccessible to the press—on the seventeenth floor of the control tower. State police allowed only authorized personnel with credentials into the meeting; that list of names had been provided in advance to the guards. Once the preliminary data was reviewed, the officials would have a unified announcement or press release for the reporters waiting outside.

The reporters had assumed that there would be another general announcement to refute or confirm the suspicion of sabotage with respect to the flight of NEAir 2158, but they had no idea where and what time that announcement would happen. To date the daily briefings had been with one FAA and one NTSB spokesperson. No briefing had occurred the day before because data collected from the various agencies was being collated.

Although they still lacked Bob Connolly's day three testimony, the investigators had enough information to begin to evaluate the fate of NEAir Flight 2158. Photocopies of the lyophilized notes of Officer Bell's diary had just arrived.

Four hours into the private meeting, the investigators would conclude:
- that Flight 2158 was sabotaged.
- that fuel was not loaded.
- a light bulb was not changed in the cockpit. The engines failed due to no fuel to the pumps.
- the pumps were deemed functional. The records for fuel loading were altered, and a fuel spill during simulated refueling was covered up by mechanics and support staff.
- console fuel gauges were altered to deceive the pilots into thinking that they had a full load of 800 gallons.

Additional observations suggested that:
- the sabotage was probably caused by a jealous lover involved in a love triangle.
- one man was an NEAir employee.
- the second person was John Bell.
- the third person, a female in the love triangle, was Marisa Bell, the pilot's wife.

These observations still needed substantiation. A call from the state police, north of Boston, would provide the necessary details.

Connolly sat in the room awaiting the investigator's return from a coffee break. Before the break, he had been questioned for more than two hours. His ass was sore and he was fidgeting with a pencil and pad in front of him.

When the FAA investigator returned to continue the questioning, he was accompanied by two state police officers.

The FAA investigator did not sit down but stood directly beside Bob.

"Mr. Connolly?" the investigator asked.

"Yes, sir?" he responded.

"Mr. Connolly," he repeated, catching Connolly off guard, "Are you having an 'affair' with anyone?" The question was asked boldly.

As Connolly jumped up, the officers stepped forward.

"What the hell kind of question is that?" Connolly asked angrily. He was dumbfounded.

"What's with the police?" he demanded.

A trooper sat him down with the touch of his hand on his shoulder. The trooper was gentle, but stern. He said nothing to Bob Connolly but guarded him carefully.

"I thought that you wanted my input on 2158! What the hell was *that* question?"

At that point, a trooper asked, "This, Mr. Connolly, is a formal interview. Do you wish a lawyer present?"

Bob was silent for a second. He turned white. "Lawyer? Why would I need a lawyer?" he asked.

That was one question he had not anticipated in his drive from home to the airport.

"Mr. Connolly? Do you wish to have a lawyer present? Yes or no?"

"No," he replied quietly, "I don't know why I would need a lawyer."

"Mr. Connolly, we just received a call from the local police in your hometown. They wish to talk to you immediately. They have asked us to take you there."

The trooper continued, "Mr. Connolly, a neighbor of yours, Marisa Bell, is dead! She committed suicide today."

"What? Marisa? What do you mean . . . dead?" he said, stunned.

"Mr. Connolly, Mrs. Bell is dead and you have been implicated in the circumstances surrounding her death, and that is not all," the trooper continued.

"You have been implicated in the sabotage and fatal demise of Flight 2158, as well as the attempted murder of First Officer John Bell," he said. "Do you know Mrs. Bell?"

There was no immediate answer. Bob Connolly slumped into his chair. He was now a whitish-gray, like the blood was sucked out of him. He mumbled, "Dead? Marisa Bell dead? John Bell? Attempted murder?"

"Yes, Marisa Bell died today and her husband, John Bell, is still missing, and presumed dead, somewhere in Boston Harbor," the investigator added.

Bob Connolly was in shock. He stumbled for words. Then he said, "Me? Why me? What's the relationship to me?"

"Mr. Connolly. Your sister, Belinda! She found Marisa. They were close friends, right?"

He nodded yes.

"Belinda found her in the Bell home, dead! She died from a single, self-inflicted gunshot wound," the trooper said.

Bob Connolly looked sullenly at the investigator, then to the troopers and then back at the investigator. His face was drawn and pale as he took a deep breath and slumped into the chair.

The trooper continued, "Bob Connolly, we will be placing you under arrest for the sabotage of Flight 2158. You have also been implicated in the death of Captain Bullock and the probable death of John Bell."

The investigator stared intently at Connolly. One of the troopers stepped forward, stood in front of Bob, and pulled a pocket-sized card from his shirt pocket and read:

"Mr. Connolly—you have the right to remain silent. . . . "

Epilogue

NEAir flight mechanic Bob Connolly would be indicted and found guilty of the sabotage of NEAir Flight 2158, which caused the death of seven people. His sister, Belinda, would end up testifying against him.

Captain William Bullock and First Officer John Bell would be posthumously honored by North East Air and the Airline Pilots Association for their heroic efforts to save the flight.

Marisa Bell would be buried alone. Her name would be cleared of any direct involvement in causing the disaster.

Jack Danton and Fawn DiNardi became engaged one month after the disaster. The celebratory dinner in the Italian North End included lobster, cannoli and an emerald ring.

About the Author:

Jack Polidoro, Ph.D., known to many as J. P. Polidoro or "Dr. Jack," grew up in Pittsfield, Massachusetts. He received his master's of science degree (1968) and doctorate in animal science/reproductive physiology (1972) from the University of Massachusetts at Amherst, Massachusetts. He received his bachelor of arts degree in biology from C. W. Post College on Long Island in 1965.

He has been in the pharmaceutical/biotechnology research area for thirty-four years, eighteen of which have been in the marketing and sales arena for companies in pharmaceutical contract research. He currently markets the services of a biomedical company in northern Nevada.

Dr. Jack has also been a prolific songwriter/acoustic music performer for more than thirty years and has written some 120 songs in the folk/adult contemporary style. Since 1984, he has produced six albums/cassettes/CDs.